The Cadillac Man

John Wayne Comunale

MW00623990

DEATH'S HEAD PRESS

Houston, Texas
www.DeathsHeadPress.com

Cover Art: Paul Harrison

Book Layout: Lori Michelle
www.TheAuthorsAlley.com

Part I
The Truck Stop

These things happen when you travel the same stretch of highway for hundreds of miles. You can sometimes sync up with other drivers you're within a mile or so of either behind or in front, so it made sense to see the same car at two different filling stations. He noticed the man the first time he'd stopped and thought it was just a coincidence when they ran into each other the second time.

Rick didn't become concerned until the truck stop.

He pulled up next to one of the many pumps and immediately noticed the man across from him pumping gas into an old, black Cadillac. The year of the model was hard to pin down, but the emblem on the grill was unmistakable.

The car blended flourishes of classic flair in the exaggerated fins running alongside the trunk as well as the design on the front end, but those features bled into a body-style too modern looking to be vintage. The Cadillac was obviously some kind of custom job, because they didn't come off the assembly line looking like that regardless of the decade.

Rick took his foot off the brake and cruised forward to a pump further down the row. The brief half-second glance he took out the window confirmed what he already knew, it was him. The man was pale and thin but not sickly-looking and wore his complexion and stature like a man twice the size with three times the confidence.

He wasn't particularly tall, but the black suit he wore elongated his limbs creating the illusion he stretched well beyond his six-foot frame. His face was pallid and framed by shockingly blond, shoulder length hair. The color wasn't artificial but looked out of place on a full-grown man and therefore jarring. His eyes were dark, but Rick couldn't tell their exact color through the shadow his hair cast across the top half of his face.

Rick tried to keep an eye on him while pumping his gas, but as far as he could tell the man wasn't paying any attention to him. The dial on the pump began to crawl as Rick's tank reached its capacity, and when he withdrew the nozzle from his car the Cadillac Man did the same. Rick took his time fiddling with the pump and pretended to have a problem putting his gas cap back on hoping the man would get in his car and drive off.

His heart sank when from the corner of his eye he saw the man walking from his car toward the smudge-covered glass doors of the truck stop. Rick had to go inside to pay for his gas, something he'd hoped the Cadillac man had done *before* he pumped, but the two appeared to be on the same route in more ways than one.

He contemplated getting back in his car and sitting there until the man and his Cadillac were back on the road, but decided he was being silly. So, what if this man was at the same gas station as Rick *again*? They were just two travelers on the same road who just so happen to follow the same pit-stop schedule. It didn't mean anything, did it?

Rick pushed his suspicion down into the same place he put the other things he didn't want to think about and strode across the parking lot up to the truck stop. He was trying to consciously come off cool like he didn't care about anything, but it was hard to imitate the effortless swagger of the man who walked in before him.

The aisles of brightly colored junk food and abrupt transition from sunlight to artificial fluorescence disoriented Rick, as he struggled to adjust unable to locate the Cadillac Man. He told himself he was being paranoid again, but unable to lower his guard.

His first scan of the space warranted no results. He couldn't readily locate the man and stepped slowly toward the counter while his eyes further scrutinized the store.

The smell of burnt grease and stale cigarette smoke was thick enough to taste and would more than likely require strong drink to wash from his palate. A belt or two from the bottle of bourbon in his console would do the trick, and he smiled to himself happy to have come prepared.

Rick stood at the register fishing cash from his front pocket when he heard a door open then abruptly shut from somewhere behind him. He didn't have to turn around to know the man had come out of the restroom at the back of the store.

Every muscle in his body tightened and he clenched his teeth in anticipation of what he did not know. A confrontation perhaps, but one in which Rick was unaware of his part? Footsteps against the scratched and dirty tile grew closer, and the unique sound told him the man was wearing boots. The footsteps got within three feet of Rick before he heard them moving in the direction of the door.

His muscles loosened some as he turned to watch the Cadillac Man walk out without so much as a glance in his direction. When he looked back the cashier looked confused and mildly concerned.

"Are you okay mister?" The clerk was young, and scruffy, and seemed genuinely concerned. "You looked like you were going to faint or shit your pants, or something."

"Oh . . . sorry about that," Rick felt instantly stupid. "I'm fine, but I could use some water. I'll be right back."

Rick retrieved a bottle of water from one of the store's coolers, and then shopped around for items he didn't want or need. He just wanted to give the Cadillac Man a head start in order to put a good amount of distance between them. He returned to the counter with the water, a bag of pretzels, and some candy he chose randomly from one of the aisle's end caps.

He forced himself not to look out through the glass doors as he brought his purchases to the counter and paid for them with the gas. Rick didn't want to see the black Cadillac. He didn't want it to be there, and if he didn't look outside, he could let himself believe the car and its driver were long gone.

He couldn't kill anymore time shopping the sparse selection the truck stop had to offer, and once he stepped outside, he was going to have to deal with what, if anything, was waiting for him.

"Be careful out there mister," the cashier said stuffing Rick's purchases into a greasy-looking plastic bag. "I've heard tons of horror stories about people falling asleep or getting sick behind the wheel."

The clerk paused and turned toward the doors, his eyes daring Rick's to follow, but he refused to let them. The clerk blinked and held the pause while gazing out at the pumps in the parking lot. It was as if he were a battle-scarred war veteran staring into nothingness while scenes of the atrocities he'd witnessed played across the screen in his mind.

The silence reached the point of uncomfortability and took several steps past it, but Rick would not look outside. Looking meant seeing and seeing made it real whether the man was still outside or not.

"You could lose control or roll your car." The clerk snapped his head back to face Rick and finished bagging the last of the candy that would never be eaten. "Better safe than sorry. If you need to pull over and rest, you should."

"Yeah, thanks," Rick said taking the bag from the clerk's filthy fingers. "I'll try and keep that in mind."

Rick pocketed his change, took the bag, and tried to

make it seem like he wasn't stalling as he tied the handles of the plastic bag together. The look the clerk gave him as he fumbled with the bag was now pure annoyance, and Rick suddenly wanted to put distance between the two of them almost as badly as he wanted distance between him and the Cadillac Man.

Satisfied with the half-assed knot he'd tied Rick turned from the counter toward the door. He didn't realize he was shaking until the plastic started to rustle, so he took it in both hands holding the bag in front of him. The glare of the setting sun against the glass kept Rick from being able to see if the Cadillac was still parked at the pump outside, and his mouth became impossibly drier with each step like the moisture was being sucked from his body through the bottoms of his feet.

"Sir?"

The clerk's voice sounded like it was a hundred miles behind him, but he was startled, nonetheless. Rick was within a few steps of the door when he stopped and turned back to the register. His eyebrows unconsciously moved halfway up his forehead in an expression of impatient expectation for what the clerk had to say.

"Have a nice day."

Rick scowled and mumbled a response as he turned back around, pushed open the door, and stepped outside. The Cadillac was gone, and he heaved a deep breath as the weight from the stress he'd put on himself suddenly lifted from his chest.

He smiled as he strolled to his car and even giggled at how foolish he was for being paranoid. If this man in the black Cadillac had ill intentions toward Rick and meant to do him harm he could've, and more than likely *would* have already tried something. There were no other cars in the lot or parked at the pumps, so the man could have easily waited for Rick to come out if he wanted to jump him.

So, what if they'd made eye contact when he drove by the man minutes earlier? That was what happened when

9

people sensed they were being stared at, and Rick had to admit he was the one doing the staring. The man in the Cadillac had just as much reason to be paranoid of Rick since he too was sharing the experience. What if the man in the Cadillac had the same suspicion that he was the one being followed? Rick decided if he happened to be at the next place he stopped he'd say something to him about the strange coincidence. It was possible the man hadn't even noticed.

He got in his road-dirty, red sedan and tossed the greasy plastic bag onto the passenger seat before fastening his seatbelt. Rick started the engine and absently looked up into the rearview mirror as he put the car in gear but left his foot on the brake when he noticed what was in the reflection.

The clerk was standing at the door staring out at him. His face was an inch from the glass, and Rick could clearly see the kid's eyes were fixed on him. The feeling he was being watched from all sides scratched its way up his back like an electrified wool sweater.

His eyes snapped forward when headlights passed across his windshield, but they were from a moving truck pulling into the truck stop.

Rick rotated his neck slowly scanning the parking lot for any additional pairs of eyes, but as far as he could tell there were none. He lifted his foot from the brake and took one more look into the rearview mirror before pressing down on the accelerator much harder than was necessary.

The car bucked forward a few feet but sputtered out and stopped short as the engine died. Rick twisted the key in the ignition again, but it refused to turn over. The motor screeched and coughed approaching the point of flooding out before he finally relented. Rick sighed, smacked the steering wheel in frustration, and reached up to adjust the rearview mirror.

What he saw chilled him, and while he didn't understand exactly why, he felt the overwhelming urge to get as far away from the truck stop as possible. He immediately tried to start the car again to no avail.

The clerk still standing at the door staring only now he was smiling.

————————◆————————

Thomas didn't want to move, but as much as he hated the idea, he had to acknowledge feeling better the further down the road he got. The emotional vise began to loosen, and with it his muscles relaxed. He could breathe. He could actually breathe like he was able to do back before everything started to go wrong.

Thomas took in huge gulps of air that filled his lungs and pushed his chest out forcing him to correct the bad posture he'd fallen into. He was suddenly smiling but couldn't decide if it was euphoria from the rush of oxygen, or genuine happiness from finally being away from everything.

It was all over now, and he was already finding himself comfortable with letting the entire portion of his life fade into a distant memory He had no plan, or any idea where he was going. Thomas used to have a friend in Detroit, but he couldn't remember his name, or how to go about locating him if he did. Still, he pointed the truck in the direction of the Motor City, and if he settled on somewhere else along the way so be it. It wasn't a real plan, but it was all he had.

For a while Thomas thought about what his life would be like if he didn't find a new place to start over? How long could he wander from place to place living out of a moving truck? He'd have to move around constantly parking in mall lots and campgrounds throughout the country. The moving company would miss their truck after a day or so past the return date, but as long as he didn't get pulled over Thomas figured they wouldn't be able to find him.

The credit card he used to rent the thing was the last card still in both his and Erica's name that still worked. The information he'd left with the rental service was hers since he didn't have a phone let alone a residence for them to come look for him. The company would end up calling Erica when the truck wasn't returned making it her headache, which was of no consequence to him.

Thomas glanced absently at the gas gauge on the dashboard to see he still had a quarter of a tank. He didn't need to stop at the moment but thinking about the credit card made him paranoid. He had some cash, but not much and planned on getting as far as he could on the card until it didn't work anymore.

He decided to fill up now and grab some food just in case the rug was pulled out from under him sooner rather than later. Thomas signaled and maneuvered the mid-size moving truck over to the far right lane and saw a sign a sign promising gas and food at the next exit.

He slowed as he approached the entrance of the lonely, desolate-looking truck stop, but was forced to bring it to a complete stop before turning in. A black Cadillac was exiting at the same time and made such a wide turn Thomas would have t-boned the strange-looking car if he hadn't been paying attention.

The Cadillac sped away kicking up a cloud of dust, and Thomas watched it quickly disappear up the entrance ramp to the freeway. He wasn't angry with the driver surprisingly, but he was left with a feeling of uncertainty. For a moment he considered continuing without stopping, but his stomach had been growling since the minute he'd thought about food a few miles back.

Thomas pulled the truck up to one of the many pumps of which only one other car was parked next to, but the owner was inside with the engine running about to leave. He climbed down from the cab, stretched, and looked around to get a lay of the land. The place was completely empty or at least appeared that way, and if it weren't for the Cadillac and the nondescript sedan at the pump Thomas would've guessed the place was closed.

The Cadillac Man

He shook off his paranoia, slid the card in the slot on the gas pump, and hoped against hope it still worked. When the screen finally announced the card was approved, he pumped the truck full of gas, and then headed into the store to see what they had to offer in the way of food. A glare prevented him from seeing the young clerk standing at the glass door looking out and smiling.

———•◆———

Janine sat in one of the well-worn, leather chairs in the waiting room of the dealership's service department. She'd been there an hour and a half and was on her fourth cup of stale coffee, one of the few amenities offered to waiting customers. Another was popcorn made to look fun and festive as it popped within the glass casing of the old-style popcorn stand made to look like it came from a carnival forty years ago.

She decided to stick with coffee and forgo the popcorn due to the amount of people, both children *and* adults, using their hands to scoop popped kernels into red and white striped bags. Janine didn't even use public water fountains anymore and didn't understand how people could be so careless when it came to hygiene particularly when indulging in something meant to be communal. She hadn't been truly sick, except for allergies, in the last three years, she aimed to keep the streak going by avoiding things like the popcorn petri dish where germs were left to incubate in the butter-flavored lukewarm moistness.

She couldn't help but blame the black Cadillac at least partially for her current situation. The car had come up behind her so fast she'd barely time to react. Janine was going five miles per hour over the speed limit herself, but the Cadillac was going significantly faster and had to have been approaching speeds in the triple digits.

Janine quickly switched lanes to let the black streak of a car fly past her and it was a few seconds later when she heard a pop. The significant pull on the steering wheel confirmed her tire had blown. If it weren't for the Cadillac, she wouldn't have had to change lanes, and most likely would not have run over whatever punctured her tire.

Janine wasn't even at the halfway point of her trip and had already been sidelined by a flat tire. Luckily, she was an exit away from a Honda dealership when it happened, so she was able to slowly navigate her way to the service department. She could change the tire by herself and had done so several times in the past both with this vehicle and the one she owned before it. She'd even helped change the tire of an ex-boyfriend who proved to be inept not only in bed, but also when it came to any kind of mechanical work.

She'd paid for the maintenance package when she bought the car, so she figured she'd take advantage of it and just let the dealership patch the tire. It wasn't a good idea to drive very far on a donut spare anyway, plus she'd been putting off getting her oil changed as well. She took the flat as a sign and asked the oil to be changed along with fixing the tire.

Janine was starting to get antsy as she realized how much the stop was throwing off her timing and was starting to regret asking for the extra service when her name was finally called.

"Janine? Your car is ready."

The service agent approached her with a clipboard containing the paperwork she needed to sign.

"Thank you," she said standing to accept the clipboard.

"Sorry for the wait," added the ginger-headed service agent. "It's been a pretty busy day."

"Not a problem at all," she said scribbling her name next to the spaces he'd marked with a highlighter. "What was it that popped my tire anyway? Was there a nail or something stuck in it?"

"Well," the agent paused and looked out the window before turning back to Janine. "It was the strangest thing. There wasn't a puncture in the tire at all, and to tell you the truth we couldn't find any reason for it to have gone flat."

"What?" Janine was concerned now. "What does that mean?"

"It means the tire just went flat. It's odd but one of the older guys said it happens from time to time. It could have been an issue with the pressure that caused the tire to slip off the rim, or something along those lines."

Janine paused not realizing she had scrunched her facial features together in a way that must have looked angry rather than confused.

"I'm very sorry about that and assure you everything is completely fine now ma'am. You shouldn't have any more problems."

The service agent shifted his tone to one slightly more professional than the casualness with which he'd approached her. She softened her expression into a smile when she realized what he was reacting to.

"Oh, that's fine," she said. "I'm not upset about it, and I'm certainly not blaming anyone. It just struck me as odd for a second. I had no idea something like that could happen?"

The agent smiled, lifted his hat, and ran his greasy fingers through his hair before placing it back. Janine could tell by the black fingerprints on the bill it was a nervous habit the man performed a few dozen times a day.

"I'd never heard of it either, but according to Zeke I guess it happens. Anyway, I got it parked right out front for you with the keys inside."

"Thank you," Janine said still smiling.

She handed him back the clipboard, and the agent smiled while lifting his hat again this time nodding to her.

"You're welcome and thank you again for waiting. Be careful out there now."

Janine sat in her car and readjusted her seat and steering wheel, which had been moved by the much taller service agent who brought it around. The thought of what happened to her tire being such a random thing didn't sit right, but she was trying to convince herself not to worry.

It was fixed now, and it could have been much worse. She was glad she didn't lose control and injure herself, or worse someone else. Janine shrugged it off like she was able to do with things she knew she had no control over, and by the time she sped up the entrance ramp and re-entered the highway she'd forgotten all about it.

When she was close to being twenty miles from the dealership Janine noticed she would need gas soon. She'd been too hung up on the time already lost to double check the necessities and was about to lose more time because of it.

Under any other circumstances Janine would never stop so soon after just doing so unless it was an emergency, and while she thought she might be able to push it a little bit further she ultimately decided against it. If she miscalculated and ran out gas before having another opportunity to stop, she'd lose far more than the six or seven minutes it would take her to fill up now.

It wasn't worth the risk and Janine checked her blind spot before signaling, changing lanes, and exiting the freeway. A sign before the exit told her there was a truck stop up the road, and as she came down the ramp, she could see the sign about a half-mile away. It was only just approaching dusk, but the yellow sign with large, black lettering was already lit up, and it popped against the purple sky commanding Janine's attention.

She signaled again as she slowed to turn into the entrance despite no one else being around to benefit from her courteousness. It was a habit her father had ingrained in her during their driving lessons together. She even used her signal when backing out of a parking spot, and her friends would ridicule her mercilessly for the useless gesture.

It bothered Janine to be made fun of, but she didn't dare break the habit even temporarily for their benefit. She didn't want to risk accidentally slipping up when her father was in the car with her. He would revoke her driving privileges without a thought at the slightest infraction and had done so enough times Janine wouldn't dare test him.

Once she'd taken a few seconds too long to pull the parking brake after putting the car in park and she didn't see the keys again for a week. She knew he meant well and was being overprotective, but it came from a good place. Even so knowing that didn't keep her from still harboring a slight resentment.

Janine was a grown woman now beholden to no one, and she had her own car to operate how she saw fit, but even so she couldn't shake the habit. She wasn't sure she wanted to.

She turned into the truck stop and pulled the small, black Honda up to a pump across the lane from a mid-sized moving truck. The only other car she saw was a dust-covered, red sedan at the pumps two lanes over on the other side of her. It sounded like the driver was having an issue starting the engine but kept cranking away despite it.

Janine knew the sound of a flooded engine when she heard it and this one was very close to hitting that note. If the driver didn't give it a rest, they'd find themselves stuck here a lot longer than they'd like by making whatever's wrong worse.

Finally, the person behind the wheel stopped turning the key and the engine fell silent. Janine stood at the pump looking for her credit card when she heard something else coming from the red car, but it wasn't the engine this time. It sounded like the person in the car was screaming.

———————•◆•———————

When Thomas entered the truck stop, he didn't see anyone else inside immediately. The register at the counter was unmanned now, but he didn't think much of it figuring the clerk was elsewhere in the small store stocking or taking care of one of the many mundane duties a job like that came with.

He wasn't currently feeling any of the telltale pressure

on his bladder typically associated with stops on long road trips, but while he was here, he would try to squeeze something out. He didn't want to get back on the road only to have to stop thirty minutes later just to take a leak.

He'd tried to piss in bottles on road trips when he was younger but could never bring himself to do it even when driving alone. His friends could do it with no problem and would dump the piss out of the window to fill it up again. Thomas could never shake the mental hang up even as an adult, and still opted for the toilet over a bottle to this day.

He turned down an aisle on the way to the men's room and was flanked by a variety of chips from plain potato to spicy jalapeno on one side, and enough candy to give half the state diabetes on the other. He slowed to study some of the odd-looking wrappers realizing he'd never heard of most of these candies.

"Star Sprinkles? Sugar Blast? Gummy Babies?" Thomas randomly read some of the names out loud as he passed by. "Whatever happened to just plain Skittles?"

He realized how strange 'Gummy Babies' sounded and did a double take to get a better look at the package thinking he must have seen it wrong. When he looked closer the cellophane bag appeared indeed full of baby parts made from the gummy confection. There was a multi-colored rainbow of baby heads, limbs, torsos, and some that resembled tiny organs, but that couldn't be right.

"We got Skittles too," came a voice from behind him. "They're just a little bit further down the aisle toward the end."

Thomas, somewhat startled, whirled around to see the voice belonged to a young, sandy-haired clerk who was now behind the counter. He hadn't been there a second ago and seemed to have appeared from nowhere. Thomas figured the young man must have been kneeling to stock cigarettes on the lower shelf, which was why he hadn't seen him when entering the store.

"Oh, thanks," Thomas answered. "You've got quite a . . . selection here. There's almost too many choices, right?"

Thomas laughed mostly out of nervousness in hopes to break the awkward embarrassment he felt over being caught talking to himself, but the clerk didn't reciprocate the false levity. He just stood and stared, and while it was subtle and almost imperceptible Thomas swore the clerk was shaking his head.

"Well, thanks again," Thomas said turning back toward the bathroom. "I'll pick some up on my way out."

He chuckled again as he walked into the bathroom where he felt instantly better to be out the clerk's line of sight. He was just a kid working at the truck stop probably to save money for a car of his own, or to run around chasing tail with his buddies, but something about his demeanor gave Thomas the creeps.

Still, he could relate and remembered being around the same age having to work shitty jobs to put money in his pocket and keep his parents off his back. Thomas never worked in a gas station, but he did work a year and a half in a garage doing oil changes and changing out spark plugs. He hated every second of it, but it was how he was able to buy his first car.

Thomas knew exactly how the clerk felt and dismissed the reservations he'd had about him being creepy. He was just trying to get through his shift and his attitude certainly wasn't aimed at anyone in particular, so Thomas knew not to take it personally. He'd just misinterpreted the boy's apathy for being standoffish and that was that.

He stepped up to one of the two urinals hanging on the wall, unzipped, and began relieving himself. The flow was strong and steady despite feeling like he didn't have to go at all five minutes prior, but maybe the clerk startled the rest of it out of him. Thomas laughed to himself over being freaked out by the clerk especially after what he'd been through in the past few weeks. Having to deal with a possible punk-ass kid who may or may not have a chip on his shoulder was nothing.

A synthetic fruit smell came wafting up from the urinal

suddenly, and Thomas guessed his piss finally activated the scented soap cake he'd been concentrating the bulk of his stream on. It was sweet but phony like the way fruit-shaped candy might smell with the taste being nothing more than a weak impersonation of something resembling flavor.

He looked up at the ceiling and twisted his neck from side to side trying to ward off stiffness from setting in as he zipped his pants and stepped back. When Thomas reached out to flush, he looked down and froze. He didn't stay that way for long though and jumped as he pulled his hand back stumbling over himself to get away from what he couldn't believe he was seeing.

Overflowing from the shallow bowl of the urinal were life-sized versions of the candy he'd seen in the package of 'Gummy Babies'. There were the limbs, torso, and what were now unmistakably entrails, and something resembling a liver or kidney all made of different colored gummy candy.

The head sat atop the piss-soaked pieces, but there was something different about it as it was made up of translucent yellow candy except for the eyes. They were real. They were actual human eyes, and when Thomas stumbled back, they cut upward in his direction.

A scream caught in his throat, and he fell back against the sink covering his face with his hands when the small gummy mouth opened and emitted a high-pitched squeal. Thomas uncovered his face, a scream now cocked and ready to fire from his throat but the launch was aborted suddenly. The gummy baby parts were gone, and there was nothing in the urinal save for the mostly disintegrated pink soap cake, and a couple of soggy cigarette butts.

Thomas blinked and looked all around the small bathroom for any sign of dead babies, candied or otherwise, but there were none. He was alone. He stood still for several seconds trying to shake the very real image of a dismembered gummy-baby from his mind. The eyes made more of an indelible mark though and would require time and distance to scrub from his memory.

He couldn't do anything about time, but he could sure put distance between him and whatever the hell he saw, or thought he saw, in this godforsaken truck stop bathroom.

He grabbed for the door but stopped to look back before yanking it open. The urinal was still empty, but the sight did little to ease his mind. He pulled open the door and set out down the aisle taking purposely elongated steps to quicken his pace. He paused momentarily at the section he'd seen the Gummy Babies in but couldn't seem to find them again.

Thomas turned to look back down the aisle but found his view blocked by the clerk who was now standing very close to him.

"Jesus Christ!" Thomas flinched at the sudden appearance of the kid. He hadn't even heard him approach. "Do you always sneak up on customers like that?"

"I have what you're looking for."

The clerk was half-smiling completely unaffected by the outburst. His hands were behind his back. Thomas took another step away from the clerk and lifted his hands slowly not knowing what to expect.

"I told you they were a little further down the aisle."

Dangling from the clerk's greasy fingers was a bag of Skittles.

———————◆———————

Janine removed her credit card from the pump and the words *Please Pay Cashier Inside* flashed across the screen for the second time.

"Damn it!" She cursed under her breath and jammed the card back into her wallet.

It always happened when she was in a hurry without fail. Her card would work one hundred percent of the time if she had no place to be and all day to get there. She opened the driver side door to retrieve her purse from atop the center console and shoved her wallet inside before slinging it over her shoulder. She was starting to feel pressure on her bladder from the dealership coffee anyway, and decided she'd use the bathroom. She could also grab a snack and stay on the road as long as possible before having to stop again for a late supper.

She made her way past the pumps toward the door of the truck stop trying not to look in the direction of the red sedan but couldn't help sneaking a glance. She only let herself look for a moment but saw a man in the driver's seat with his head down against the steering wheel.

Janine didn't hear the wailing she'd heard coming from the car when she pulled up anymore, but the man's shoulders rocked in a way that could only accompany sobbing. She was too empathetic to just brush it off and genuinely felt a pang of sadness for the man despite not knowing him, or his plight. She selfishly hoped the car would be gone when she came back out, but only so she wouldn't be tempted to intervene. Janine didn't need any more delays.

The first thing she noticed when she walked through the door was the bright shine glancing off various products lined up down the aisles. They looked like they were coated with something to purposefully reflect the light from the buzzing fluorescent tubes above, but there was no uniformity to it. It was spread haphazardly across products with no consistency of placement or amount used.

It was like someone took a paintbrush soaked in grease and walked down each aisle randomly wiping it across various items. The closer she got the more it looked like the mystery reflective substance actually *was* grease, and the smell of fried food and cigarette smoke hanging in the air suddenly made sense.

Janine thought maybe she wouldn't get anything to eat from the truck stop after all, or more importantly she shouldn't. Regardless of the food items being wrapped and sealed the thought of grease tainting everything within the building turned her stomach.

There was another man in the store standing in the candy aisle, and Janine figured it was the driver of the moving truck since she observed the cab was empty when she walked up. The clerk was there as well as signified by the pale-blue button-up shirt with 'truck stop' written across the back exactly as it was on the sign out front.

The two faced each other like they were having a conversation, but neither were saying anything. The clerk wore a sarcastic-looking grin, and the expression seemed to be the only form of communication passing back and forth between the men. The young clerk broke eye contact for a moment to look over and acknowledge Janine. She smiled nervously and nodded before turning toward the register as she stepped up to the counter.

A moment later she heard the clerk's footsteps coming up the aisle behind her on the way to back to his designated post, and Janine tried unsuccessfully to repress the spasms of a shiver from shaking her back and shoulders. She crossed her arms against her body to protect against the draft from the vent she'd just noticed above her head.

The clerk made his way around to the other side of the counter and stood in front of Janine; the same wry smile cut a crooked path across his face. She waited for him to speak, but he just stood and stared waiting for her to make the first move.

"Uh, h-hi," she stammered. "The screen said to pay inside, so can I get twenty-five dollars on pump—"

She craned her neck to try and see the number of the pump she was parked next to, but her view was obscured.

"It looks like you're on pump six."

The clerk said this without looking outside, or down at his register, which was both odd and creepy. Janine wanted to pay, get gas, and get the hell out of there, so she overlooked his strange demeanor. He probably knew which pump she was on because he'd seen her drive up, and there were only two other cars so that helped him narrow it down.

"Oh, okay," Janine answered trying to look past the clerk rather than directly at his face. She waited for him to start pushing buttons, or flipping switches, or whatever he had to do to move their interaction along, but he just stood there smiling. A strange fear grabbed at where her belly was connected to her throat and twisted slowly with a steadily increasing intensity.

She was struck with the urge to run. Not run to her car and drive away, but to just run. Janine could picture herself bolting from the counter, pushing through the door, sprinting out across the lot, and disappearing down the street. She felt the muscles in her legs burn with anticipation the longer she stood there. A scream was starting to build around her diaphragm only she had no idea why?

"That'll be twenty-five bucks." The clerk's words snapped Janine from the strange fear holding her hostage.

"I'm sorry?" She altered her tone hoping to mask that she'd flinched.

"You said you wanted twenty-five bucks on pump six, right? So, I need twenty-five bucks."

"Oh yes, I'm sorry."

Janine's face burned from the flush of embarrassment as she dug her wallet out of her purse to retrieve the credit card that wouldn't go through at the pump. The clerk accepted it between a greasy-looking thumb and forefinger, his grin unwavering. He swiped the card through the reader next to the register, and both of them stared at the small machine as it beeped waiting for a receipt to be spit out the top.

When it didn't come, and the young clerk began shaking his head Janine felt the twist of fear again.

"It doesn't look like this card is going through ma'am. Do you have another one?"

"No, that can't be right," she said even toned this time. "I mean, there must be a mistake. Would you mind running it again?"

Janine forced a wan smile while the clerk spun the card between his fingers. He was still grinning, still shaking his head, and her calves ached fiercely with the urge to run again.

"No problem," he said finally swiping the card through the reader again, and again it was declined.

"I-I just don't see how that can be possible? There's no reason why it shouldn't be working. Is there something wrong with your machine, maybe? Excuse me sir, are you having trouble using your credit card here?"

Janine called over her shoulder to the man in the candy aisle, but he was staring down at the bag of Skittles he was holding apparently lost in the depiction of a rainbow of flavor.

"Well, I could always call it in," the clerk said. "We don't have to rely on the machine working or not then."

Janine turned back to face him again and nodded. "Yes please, that is if you don't mind?"

"Of course not," the clerk said, though his expression indicated the opposite.

Janine wasn't in the mood to argue about his shitty attitude, and instead smiled through his cynicism as if it had no effect. The clerk picked up the receiver of a phone from behind the counter smudged with greasy black fingerprints. He punched what seemed like way too many numbers into the keypad, paused to listening before punching more numbers, and then repeated the entire process. He paused yet again before taking the receiver from his ear to relay the verdict to Janine.

"They say it's no good too," he said with a shrug.

"That's not possible. May I speak with them please? I'm sure there's some kind of misunderstanding I can help clear up."

The clerk shrugged again and handed the receiver across the counter to Janine. She held it to her ear but didn't have a chance to say anything.

"There's no misunderstanding ma'am," came a familiar

voice through the receiver. "And just so you know it won't help any if you run . . . "

Janine froze as the fear twisted unbearably tighter making it impossible for her to run now even if she wanted to. The voice on the phone belonged to the clerk standing in front of her whose smile burst suddenly apart into the jagged shrapnel of uproarious laughter.

————————•◆•————————

Rick didn't want to go back into the truck stop, but he'd been given no other choice. Even if he jumped out of his car and ran down the road until he collapsed it wouldn't be enough distance to make a difference. He knew it the second he walked into the truck stop and could admit that to himself now.

He wasn't ready to believe how much he knew, or that he'd navigated to this place on purpose by way of some kind of subconscious takeover. He clutched the steering wheel despite knowing he wouldn't be going anywhere anytime soon, or ever for that matter.

Through the windshield he could see the gash carved by the Cadillac's rear driver side tire from the hasty exit, but *he'd* be back.

And now as Rick sat behind the wheel of his car at the truck stop it was impossible to pretend, he didn't know he wasn't going to be able to leave this place. No matter what he did he couldn't change it, and he sure as hell couldn't stop it. He was going to have to get out of his car, go back inside the truck stop, and face what he knew was going to play out. A momentary pang of guilt pressed into the area where his neck and chest met when he thought about the others who would be involved.

They had no idea everything they'd ever done in life played a crucial part in bringing them here to this place at this moment. Not that having the information would've helped change anything. It never helped Rick to know, which was why he wished he didn't, but wishing was for kids throwing pennies in a fountain. No amount of wet loose change would help him or the others.

Rick relaxed his fingers and allowed his hands to drop from the steering wheel to his lap. His breathing had normalized after the erratic gasps and sobs, and he focused on his breaths drawing in slowly then releasing with a similarly steady flow.

He reached over across the passenger seat and opened the glove box. It was completely empty save for the thirty-eight-caliber snub-nose revolver. The type of weapon was often referred to as a 'police special' since they were standard issue for a lot of police officers in the mid to late fifties.

It had belonged to Rick's grandfather who worked on the police force for the small Pennsylvania town he'd grown up in. The gun was passed to Rick's father who in turn passed it down to him. He didn't recall when he first put the weapon in the glove box, but it remained untouched since. It only had five bullets in it, the lawyer made sure to tell him that twice before he took possession of the gun, but Rick wouldn't need a sixth.

Hell, he wouldn't need the five for as much good as they'd do. A gun would be as effective in this situation as a child's blanket would be if used to deter an actual nightmare-creature from a dark pit of evil.

Rick swung open the door, stepped out, and let it close gently behind him unconcerned with whether it shut all the way or not. He left the keys in the car dangling uselessly from the ignition, and after taking a few steps wished he would have left the gun behind as well. The thing was heavy, and awkward, and pushed uncomfortably into his gut.

He moved it a few inches to the right of his belt buckle and adjusted his gait to help redistribute the weight as he walked, which put a small hitch in his step. It made him wonder if cowboys walked the way they did because the guns hanging from their hips were throwing off the natural rhythm of their step.

Rick was halfway to the truck stop door when he heard the engine of an approaching car coming from up the road behind him. The Cadillac Man was back.

———————◆———————

Thomas held the bag of Skittles with both hands and stared down studying it intently as the clerk walked away to help a woman waiting at the counter. He knew what he was supposed to be looking at. He knew the letters on the bag were supposed to spell the name of the chewy, fruit-flavored candies it held only what he was seeing didn't make sense.

The bag was red with big white letters across the front with a rainbow twisted across the background while pictures of the small roundish candy randomly dotted the remaining space of the field. But that's not what he was seeing at all. The bag was red because it was sticky with blood, and the letters across the front weren't in any language he recognized.

The pictures of the multi-colored candy pieces were actually tiny, severed heads. Baby heads. The same pair of eyes that had been staring at him from the gummy head in the urinal was staring up at him from each face on the package. He looked to the counter and while the clerk was helping the woman at the register, he stared past her at Thomas. He was still smiling.

When he looked back down the bag was even bloodier and nearly slipped from his fingers. The packaging was coming apart disintegrating in his hands, as the candy within appeared to be bleeding to death. But that couldn't be right because there was far more blood than the bag would have been able to hold.

From somewhere behind him Thomas heard the wail of a baby crying and dropped the bag to clamp his hands down over his ears. The bag hit the greasy tiled floor at his feet and colorful candy pieces exploded from either side upon impact sending them bouncing and sliding across the aisle. He thought he heard the woman standing at the counter call something out to him, but when he looked up, she was facing the clerk who was now holding the phone to his ear.

Did the clerk recognize him? Did he know what Thomas had done? Was he calling the cops?

Thomas looked back down at the mess on the floor and knew he was fucked.

———————◆———————

Janine pulled the receiver from her ear and looked from it to the laughing clerk. He wasn't looking at her, but past her like he'd been when she walked up. Chemicals for producing fear and confusion shot from her brain and through her system keeping her legs locked in place. The flight half of her fight or flight response mechanism had been compromised, and she'd never developed the fight aspect.

The clerk continued to chuckle, turned around, and stepped back toward the corner behind him. Janine thought for sure he was going for a weapon of some kind only she didn't know what? Different scenarios of items she could be bludgeoned to death with flashed across her mind in the split second before he turned back around. He was holding a broom in one hand, and the handle of a large dustpan in the other.

Janine remained frozen holding the phone out from her ear as strategies on how to defend herself from a broom attack began to form. The clerk wasn't looking at her as he shuffled down the length of the counter and came out from behind. She watched him from the corner of her eye and held her breath as he approached, but the clerk continued past her. She craned her neck around and saw the man in the aisle was looking down at the floor where a bounty of loose colorful candy was scattered around the aisle from a broken package lying at his feet.

The clerk wasn't planning a surprise broom-attack on

her. He was simply going to clean up the mess of candy and was laughing because he apparently found it very funny. A tinny squeaking voice came from the earpiece of the receiver Janine forgot she was holding. It didn't sound like laughter anymore, and she slowly brought the phone back to her ear.

"Hello? Hello? Ms. Beringer are you there?"

The voice on the other end belonged to a woman and not the truck stop clerk.

"Uh, Hello?" Janine finally managed.

"Hello Ms. Beringer, this is Anna with Master Charge."

"Yes. Hello, were you able to correct the problem with my card? It should be working fine because I just used it at th—"

"I'm sorry ma'am, but we won't be able to reinstate your account at this time."

"What? Wait, what does that mean? I've never had any problems with it before."

There was a brief pause on the other end before Anna the operator answered Janine's question.

"I'm showing your card was flagged as being compromised, and for your protection we've deactivated it. Don't worry though, we already have a new card being processed that will be sent out first thing in the morning by two-day mail."

Janine felt the blood rush to her face though she wasn't flush with anger this time, but despair with a solid underlying base of fear.

"I —I can't wait that long for a new card. I won't even be home in two days! I'm on a road trip right now, and I need my card to get gas not to mention everything else. It's the only credit card I have."

"Thank you for calling Master Charge," said the voice on the other end. "It's been my pleasure to help you tonight. Are there any other questions I can answer?"

"What? Yes, there is another question. What am I supposed to do without a credit card so far away from home? How am I sup—"

"Once again, we at Master Charge thank you for your patronage, and are here to assist with any needs you may have twenty-four hours a day, seven days a week. Thank you and goodbye."

"Wait! Don't hang up! I asked what am I supposed to do now?"

Janine's question was answered by a dial tone, and she pulled the receiver from her ear once again this time holding it out in front of her staring in disbelief. The woman had completely ignored her, and the sudden realization of what that meant sat heavy in her stomach like a lead softball. Without a credit card or cash Janine was stranded at the truck stop in the middle of nowhere.

She heard the clerk start laughing again, but this time he was right behind her.

———◆———

Thomas turned his hands overlooking for blood while the clerk swept up the mess. He'd felt the warm stickiness of the substance covering them, seeping behind his fingernails, and filling the deep cracks in the web of his palm. Now, they were perfectly clean without even the least hint of being stained red.

Maybe the blood was a hallucination, but Thomas was not imagining the severed hand he saw in the clerk's dustpan as he swept candy into it. Some of the small colorful pieces stuck to the partially congealed blood around the exposed bone like sprinkles on a strawberry sundae.

Thomas looked from the hand to the clerk who smiled and winked before turning to head back toward the counter. Now that the clerk wasn't standing over him, he could feel the sensation return to his legs. Thomas wanted to get as far away from this place as possible, and he was going to need them to do it.

While able to move again Thomas knew he wouldn't because he couldn't. Just because he'd regained control of his extremities it didn't mean he could just waltz right on out of the truck stop, get in his moving truck, and keep heading on down the highway. No, leaving wasn't going to be so easy only he didn't know *exactly* why.

This, whatever this was, had to be his payback. Whether orchestrated by Erica, or fate, or somehow both, the score would inevitably be settled. Thomas took a step back, and then another trying to work out the uncomfortable pins and needles sensation in his feet. He shifted his weight back and forth as he slowly scanned the store until the uncomfortable feeling dissipated completely.

He was looking for another way out besides the front door, but from where he was standing, he couldn't see one. There was usually a secondary entrance to most truck stops located on the opposite end of the building, so he walked back toward the bathroom and past it in order to see if the same held true for this unfortunate location.

Thomas cursed under his breath when he rounded the corner to see not only was there no second door, but the store itself ended in a solid wall just ten feet past the bathrooms. The place was already on the small side, and from his new vantage point it felt smaller. Against the wall was a large freezer, the kind that laid flat with the door that opened from the top. It spanned the entire width of space from wall to wall with the words 'Ize Creem' crudely spray-painted across the front of it.

It was the kind of freezer his father had as a child, and Thomas remembered it was where they stored the meat he brought home from hunting. Every fall his father and uncle would embark on a weeklong hunting trip of which Thomas's mother was not fond. She'd get over it when they showed back up with three or four deer strapped to the roof of the old, pale-yellow Scout.

The men would process the deer themselves in the shed out back they'd set up specifically for such work. They also processed the kills of several other hunters in the neighborhood earning what his father referred to as 'running around money'.

Thomas's favorite part of their coming home was getting to wash the dried drips of blood off the old hunting truck. The bucket of soapy water would go from pink to red fairly quickly depending on the number of deer. He wasn't sure why he'd become so fascinated with the red water in the bucket. He was even more confused with why he felt compelled to taste it. The result was not pleasing, but he didn't think it would be. Still, the urge was strong and easy to give in to, so he let it have its way.

When his father and uncle were preoccupied with their deer carcasses Thomas crouched in front of the bucket and removed the sponge, but not without thoroughly wringing it out first. He skimmed the surface with his fingers before plunging his entire hand in to give it a thorough stirring.

He watched the crimson whirlpool he'd created spin for several seconds until it slowed enough for the froth to have been pushed to the sides of the bucket. Thomas gave one more quick glance toward the shed before cupping his hands together, dipping them into the bucket, and bringing the liquid to his lips.

The filthy, red water was gritty, and Thomas ground his teeth against the unpleasant texture. The liquid itself was thin and lacked the body of what he guessed a mouthful of actual blood would have. The taste was awful having been completely dominated by soap and grime, but underneath it all was the tiniest note of copper he recognized.

The flavor did trigger a memory in Thomas of a time he'd bit his tongue while his mother was washing his mouth out with soap. He was testing the limits of the language his parents would let him get away with, and he'd clearly blown well beyond them based on the severity of his punishment. The wound occurred during his initial resistance, and while minor it bled just enough to mix with the soap to make for a sour sting. He involuntarily swallowed enough of the combination to feel its creeping burn crawl its way down his esophagus.

The water in the bucket, while somewhat similar in flavor, was much worse than what he'd tasted during his punishment, and yet he found himself salivating for a second handful. He'd just dipped his cupped hands in again when the bucket was suddenly kicked away followed directly by a hard smack to the side of his head courtesy of his father's giant, leathery hand.

"What the hell you doin' boy!"

Thomas's father's voice was angry, but it was hard for him to keep his lips from turning up into a smile. The old man was upset but couldn't help being amused by his son's odd behavior. Thomas could hear his uncle laughing from the shed but couldn't see past his father's looming frame.

"Somethin' ain't right with that boy," his uncle called out still chuckling before addressing Thomas directly. "What the damn hell's wrong with you boy!"

Thomas had fallen back on his ass and was now propped on his elbows staring silently up at his father anticipating another smack that didn't come.

"Well, come on and get up son."

He held out his hand and Thomas grabbed the giant paw wondering if his hands would be that big one day, as he was pulled to his feet. He couldn't tell from his father's expression whether or not he was in trouble, but even as he stood there hovering on the brink of tears Thomas felt deep inside what he'd done was not wrong, or at least not entirely.

The strange and sudden craving to drink the bloody water felt like the right thing to do, it felt like what he was *supposed* to do only he hadn't done it exactly right. He didn't know what the 'right' way was, but felt he was on the right track. Thomas felt a confidence birth in him giving the assurance he'd know what to do when the time was right.

"Son," his father began crouching down to be at eye-level with Thomas. "Do you have any idea how sick you could get from drinking that water? There's dirt, and germs, and worst of all blood."

Thomas felt a sudden quickening of his pulse when his father said the word, and his salivary glands kicked into high gear.

"If you're thirsty go in the house and ask your mother for something to drink, or at least drink clean water from the hose. Use your head son!" His father stood back up now; the familiar stern aggression having returned to his voice.

"I—I'm sorry pa." Thomas finally managed to eke out a soft apology that for the first time in his life didn't think was owed.

"Now, I want you to go inside and brush your teeth right away. You hear me? Then, ask your mother for a big glass of water, and after you finish it bring two beers out to the shed for your uncle and me."

Thomas nodded, and his father turned to head back to the shed. He watched the man shake his head and hold his arms out in an exaggerated shrug as an expression of exacerbated aggravation. Thomas heard his uncle laughing again from the shed. His father looked back across the yard at him still standing in the driveway, pointed at the house, and gestured with a wave for the boy to get in there and do what he said.

Thomas trudged into the house and went to the bathroom, but he didn't brush his teeth as was demanded of him. Instead, he stared at his pale sickly form in the mirror, and for the first time in his short life felt like everything was going to be all right. He felt like he was in control of something for once, and he very much enjoyed the feeling.

He emerged from the bathroom several minutes later and went to find his mother in the kitchen. He asked her for the beer his father requested, but not for the glass of water he was told to drink. His mouth tasted foul and there was still grit between his teeth, but it didn't bother him anymore.

There was just barely a touch of what drew him to drink from the bucket in the first place lingering amongst the overpowering disgust, and Thomas wasn't ready to wash it away just yet.

His mother had been busying prepping for the dinner she would cook in a couple hours and was obviously oblivious to what happened outside. Thomas was worried she might have heard the bucket clatter across the driveway and look out the window over the sink to investigate as she often did, but it was not the case this time.

She retrieved two cloudy brown bottles from the fridge, used the opener attached to the wall beside it to pop the caps off, and handed them to Thomas. He dutifully walked them out to the shed and delivered them to his father and uncle as instructed where he was then told to put away the sponge and the bucket and roll up the hose.

Strangely enough it was the last time Thomas would wash his father's old yellow Scout. Apparently, the small side business of processing deer had outgrown the shed, so his father and uncle rented a space close to the center of town to work out of. This became the first stop after a hunt, and his father started running the Scout through the carwash before bringing it back to the house.

Thomas didn't know if his father was concerned with his son drinking from the filthy bucket, or he just decided he wanted his truck to *actually* be clean. He never brought it up, and neither did his father, but whenever Thomas asked if he could go to the new space, it was always met with a resounding no.

When he was fourteen, he snuck out one night, rode his bike to the where his father and uncle now processed the deer, and used a spare key he'd liberated to let himself in. There was a large freezer there too just like the one in their basement, but when Thomas opened it, he found it quite different from the one they had at home.

———————◆———————

The Cadillac Man didn't have to leave the truck stop when he did. It was his last stop after all, but he decided to give everyone a little extra time to situate themselves. They were all there, and by now must have realized they couldn't leave.

The reasons they *can't* leave are separate from the reasons they don't, but the distinction is never quite clear until they arrive. By then it's too late, but it already was well before they'd made it to the truck stop. The one who'd been most aware of this fact was the hardest to rein in despite his extensive knowledge of the situation.

The man in the filthy, road-worn, red sedan, Rick, reacted instantly to the Cadillac Man's presence the first time he'd stopped along his trip. They were both still a ways off from the truck stop, and the Cadillac Man knew he didn't have to start turning the screws just yet. He wanted Rick to know he was close so there would be no misunderstanding as to where this was going, or where it would end.

There would be no glimmer of false hope, no faint possibility of escape, no flash of courage or strength to fight back. There would only be the end, and the Cadillac Man wanted Rick to remember this. There was plenty of time for his mind to wander down the path of reason and rationale before arriving at the truck stop, but the Cadillac Man would not grant him this indulgence.

He would be at every stop along the way, his presence a constant indicator of what was to come. This way Rick could only try to forget between stops rather than entertain notions of changing the inevitable. He would kill any fight still existing in the man one mile at a time until he arrived at the truck stop ready to accept his fate.

The black Cadillac slowed as the lit-up, yellow and black sign came into view above the tree line. The harsh light cleaved into the night sky like a knife through a blackout curtain creating a contrast so aggressive it looked superimposed. The car turned smoothly into the lot with a quiet sleekness not unlike that of a stalking predator; by the time you know he's there it's already too late.

The Cadillac pulled up to where the old, red sedan had stalled out close enough to barely kiss the front bumper. Across the row he saw the moving truck and the Honda parked aside their respective pumps right where they were supposed to be.

The man stepped from the shiny darkness of his automobile in time to see the door of the truck stop close behind Rick.

———————◆———————

"What'd they say?" tthe clerk asked through a smarmy chuckle as he replaced the broom and resumed his position behind the register.

Janine handed the phone back across the counter to him shaking her head unsure of how to even reply.

"They . . . they said my card had been compromised," she finally managed. "They had to cut it off."

"So that means it doesn't work presently? Is that right?"

Janine would normally never allow anyone to speak to her the way the clerk was without giving them quite a large piece of her mind in return. She was always extra-patient with people in the service and retail industry, because she understood how awful people could be for no reason.

This exchange had gone too far though. The clerk clearly crossed a line when it came to the etiquette of exchanging dialogue with a customer, but more than that; the expression on his face plainly said he knew it, *and* he didn't care.

Janine took a moment to breathe and attempted to keep her anger at bay for the time being at least. She was quickly becoming alert to the drawbacks of her situation, and the options immediately presented to her were few and unattractive. To get back on the road Janine would need the help of the clerk in some capacity, and she couldn't run the risk of jeopardizing their relationship by hurling insults until he cried while begging to be put out his misery.

She was going to have to play nice, for now.

"Well, that's too bad," the clerk said. "You can't trust anyone these days, right? Of course, it might be a bit of our own fault for trusting technology so much too."

Janine nodded while thinking about the words she wanted to say, and how to arrange them in a way that would evoke a desirable response. This was the first thing the clerk said to her without using an obnoxiously sarcastic tone, which she took as a good sign. If the clerk was indeed softening to her, then getting his help may not turn out to be as difficult as she first thought.

She wasn't above using her feminine wiles to help things along as well, and while it wasn't a tactic Janine liked to employ her current predicament called for it. The clerk was a young man after all, and while Janine was in her early thirties, she looked much younger than her actual age. She took good care of herself, worked out, ate right, and did a myriad of other things most people resort to when it's too late to slow the looks of aging anyway.

Janine didn't have any kids, which she also credited for her youthful glow and tight, but soft skin. The way she understood it having children heaped a completely new kind of stress on a person that must be managed constantly as it never fully dissipates. She didn't have to worry about that kind of stress or of any kind really.

Her father paid for her schooling, so she wasn't saddled with the crippling amount of student debt her peers faced upon graduation. Her post-college job came easy as well facilitated by a call from her father while her friends were forced to take shitty part-time jobs while trying to jumpstart their careers. They battled it out with dozens of other potential employees all vying for the same entry-level position that's just as shitty, if not shittier, than whatever temporary gig they'd been able to land out of school.

Janine was attractive and led an easy enough life, but she wasn't ignorant to her privilege. She wasn't one to manipulate people's feelings for her own gain, but desperate times tended to curb one's morality in exchange for survival. Janine had friends she watched do this to every boyfriend they'd had from high school all the way to the poor bastard they tricked into marrying them.

She'd also unfortunately witnessed a revolving cast of women who did the same thing to her father, which made her more sad than angry. Janine thought the world of her father, and in her young eyes he was without flaw or fault. She hated to think *he* could be susceptible to the basest of ploys, but more so she hated how happy he was to let it happen again and again.

Janine pushed aside the memories and the attached emotion to focus on her present task. The rough plan she'd been cobbling in her head over the last few seconds didn't consist of much, and she hoped she'd be able to roll with the punches while filling in the gaps along the way.

She relaxed her face first to let the aggravation lines across her forehead go slack and smooth, which allowed her to be more expressive with her eyes. She took a slow and silent deep breath next to help loosen the muscles in her back. Janine struck a confident yet relaxed posture, which was another part of the package designed to disarm the young clerk.

She placed her hands down on the counter and leaned forward slightly letting her lips curl into a subtle, coy smile before his eyes. The clerk was either completely unfazed or totally oblivious, and his expression did not waver. His eyes refused to dip below her neck to catch a glimpse down her shirt, which was the whole purpose of her bending over in the first place. The clerk was unresponsive to her opening moves, and she didn't have much left past that.

It occurred to Janine she'd just assumed the teenage

clerk was attracted to females without considering for even a moment he could be gay. The thought she wasn't as attractive as she believed came as a glancing yet unexpected blow to her self-esteem. Maybe in the eyes of the clerk she *did* look old?

Maybe he was used to balling women much younger and dumber with bodies Janine was unable to compete with anymore no matter how much she went to the gym? It would be easy for him to ignore her flirting if that was the case, which made her feel even worse.

A mixture of embarrassment and shame met at the back of her throat, but there was no time to deal with the emotions. She'd have to chastise herself over the misstep later preferably while in her car speeding away from the truck stop and its creepy clerk, but to make that happen Janine was going to have to think on her feet.

She noticed the clerk was only halfway paying attention, and his gaze drifted past her again. Janine was in a losing battle for the clerk's attention, but still had to try so she cleared her throat loudly before speaking.

"I was wondering," Janine's voice was noticeably softer, "if there was maybe another way to take care of paying for my gas?"

"We take cash too," snapped the clerk, her subtle implication going once again unnoticed.

His tone implied he was annoyed by the question altogether, and it wouldn't have mattered even if she'd have flat out said she'd blow him for gas money. What Janine was selling the clerk wasn't buying, and now she was reeling against the ropes struggling to somehow change course.

He looked past her again, and Janine turned to see the man who'd spilled the Skittles was still there only now he was standing in front of a large freezer at the back of the store. She sighed and stepped back from the counter before attempting to start over.

"That's kind of the thing, see," Janine said, her voice

now void of the overt flirtation she'd slathered it in just moments ago. "I don't *have* any cash. All I had was that card to use the enti—"

"There's an ATM on the side of the building outside," the clerk cut her off.

Janine's jaw clenched as she bit down on hot waves of anger to prevent them from creeping into her face betraying the character she'd decided to play. She took another slow breath and went to start again.

"Well, I can see how you would think that would be helpful, but like I was saying I only have the one card. It's not going to work in an ATM machine either."

A nearly imperceptible wave of anticipation rolled across the clerk's face, and Janine picked up on the subtle change in expression. It was one shared by both children and grown men, but for entirely different reasons. The clerk was anticipating something.

"Probably just as well." The telling quiver retreated behind the clerk's eyes as he turned his full attention on Janine. "The ATM machine is out of order anyway."

He grinned, winked, and went back to looking at whatever he found so interesting behind her. In that moment all pretense was dropped, and Janine no longer cared about currying the favor of some greasy-faced geek just to get a couple bucks in gas.

"What the fuck?!?"

Janine stepped back widening her stance as her body language morphed into a physical interpretation of the anger and frustration she'd been holding back, keeping inside. There was no mistaking her intent this time. The clerk didn't reply verbally responding instead by narrowing his eyes in quizzical curiosity further inciting Janine's fury.

"Why the hell would you suggest I use the ATM machine when you know damn well it doesn't work?

"I figured it still might be worth a try."

The clerk's grin broke out into a full blown, toothy smile dripping with the kind of smugness that triggers mothers to slap the shit out of their children. Janine didn't have kids but was not immune to the reaction the expression evoked.

"Worth a try? What is with you, and what the hell is so funny? Is there a manager here I can talk to, or *anyone* else who isn't a dickless smartass with half a brain?"

Janine was getting loud but wasn't concerned with reining in her volume. Normally, she didn't need to shout when engaged in confrontation, because the weight of her words did not rely on volume. She could deliver a devastating dressing-down and appear as if engaged in a normal and pleasant conversation. Janine wasn't concerned with attracting attention in a place like this, at least not anymore, but the clerk remained unfazed maintaining his smirk.

"Hello? Are you going to pretend you all of a sudden don't hear me now, because I can get a lot louder?"

She glanced behind her expecting to see the man at the back of the store approaching the counter to investigate, or at the very least watch the show, but he was still standing in front of the freezer with his back to her. The only difference being his hand now rested on the handle, but he hadn't opened it yet.

Janine didn't need anyone to fight her battles for her but thought if the man was on her side the two together may have an easier time 'convincing' the clerk to help her out. She thought it was possible the man was deaf, or mute, or maybe a little of both as she recalled how he'd just stared at the candy on the ground without saying a word while the clerk cleaned it up.

Janine was zero for two so far today but being down in the count never stopped her before. She opened her mouth to launch another venomous assault when the clerk spoke up before she could begin.

"Manager?" He said the word like it was foreign to him, like it was something Janine made up. "Ain't no manager here today. Just me."

Janine had half expected him to say *he* was the manager, but this was just as equally unhelpful.

"Today?" She fired back. "What's that mean, *today*? And the answer better not be that he's not here today or any day, because there is no manager!"

The clerk's eyes widened for the first time in their exchange, and his smile followed suit becoming somehow toothier, and more offensive than seemed possible.

"Ah man," he said with a laugh. "You ruined my joke!"

If the counter weren't between them Janine would have taken a swing at him right there, but as it stood, she would have to continue her verbal assault.

"FUCK YO—"

Janine was cut off by a gunshot this time, and the sound pulled both their attention to its origin. Standing just inside the door was a disheveled man holding the smoking revolver he'd just fired into the ceiling. A smattering of dust and debris from the tile above lay in clumps across his left shoulder.

His face was red and puffy like he'd been crying. It was the man from the car outside, the one Janine heard screaming and bawling. The one she'd tried to ignore.

———————◆———————

He didn't remember walking up to the freezer, but he was standing right in front of it. He ran his hand along the cold, smooth surface of the lid, and brought it to rest beside the handle. The tactile sensation was like that of rubbing polished stone, but the memory it triggered was not as pleasant as the touch.

The misspelled message on the front of the freezer had the best intentions of conveying to customers its contents were that of sweet, frozen treats, but Thomas didn't see it that way. He couldn't. In his mind he was back in the small, dark room where his father and uncle processed deer looking down on the lid of their freezer, only this time he already knew what was inside.

44

Thomas's mouth filled with saliva, and he swallowed twice to keep it from escaping the corners of his mouth. His mind flashed to the image of gummy baby parts in the toilet, what he hoped had been a hallucination, and he stared down at the freezer salivating even more at the thought.

It made sense for him to have seen body parts as candy during his short 'spell', because that's what they were to him; sweet, delicious candy through and through. It wasn't babies, not until recently at least, but he could see how they'd be on his mind now.

It was hard for Thomas to consider nature verses nurture when it came to him mostly because he couldn't imagine himself not being the way he was. It wasn't what his father did, and it wasn't what he found in that freezer. While it may have jumpstarted him down the path it wasn't responsible for birthing what was inside him. It was already there.

When it all came out Thomas's dad and uncle said it was an accident, but what else were they going to say? There was a body in the freezer of their shared business after all, but it probably would have gone undiscovered for some time if Thomas hadn't found it.

It looked like they'd tried to cover the body with large cuts of venison, but the effort was sloppy and hurried, and ultimately served no purpose. The face was the first thing Thomas saw. It peered up through clouded, unseeing eyes from between two hearty deer flanks punctuating the frozen rictus of terror looking back at him.

Thomas moved the vacuum-sealed meat to uncover the rest of the body and found the man naked and curled into a twisted unnatural position. The body was obviously taller than the freezer was wide, so some modifications were made to fit it in.

The dead man's left arm was twisted up behind his head so far it looked like his hand was peeking out the other side to wave. His right shoulder had been snapped and the arm folded behind the man's back, but the fit was still tight. The man had not only been tall, his shoulders were broader than the average person. They were broader than his father and uncle's shoulders, he knew that much at least.

Both legs were bent back at the knees with the right one maneuvered in a way so the man's foot was sticking out from between his legs just below the groin. There was a hole in the center of the man's chest, the kind of hole a bullet from a rifle makes. The skin around the wound was jagged like paper torn around the edges, and the only blood left was a shiny, crimson circle around the hole. It was frozen but thick like strawberry preserves and dotted with tiny, white patches of frost.

Thomas stared down into the freezer at the body for what felt like hours, and it might have been for all he knew. He'd had a complete disconnect from the passage of time forgetting its rules and their linear bias. Misty cold waves of translucent fog rolled over the rim and fell to the floor where it hovered like a roving phantom searching for a crack back to hell to disappear through.

Thomas knew he couldn't lift the body out of the freezer by himself, but his desperation to do so grew feverishly by the second. For the first time since opening the lid he broke his gaze from the contorted body and stepped back to take a look around the room. He didn't know what he was looking for but hoped something in the small space would inspire him. Thomas saw the two-by-fours first, but the idea didn't click until he spied the cinder blocks stacked in the corner.

The back of the freezer was butted up against the wall, but the body and the meat made it far too heavy to move even the least bit. He was going to have to try his plan from another angle, but still confident it would work. Thomas picked up a cinder block in each hand, moved them about two feet from the side of the freezer, and stacked them on each other lengthwise.

He selected a two-by-four hoping it would be long enough, and found it was when he placed one end beneath the back corner of the freezer while laying the board across the stacked bricks. Thomas grabbed hold of the other end of the two-by-four with both hands and pushed down with every bit of strength his fourteen-year-old body had to give, which turned out to be just enough.

He was worried the board would snap before lifting the back edge of the freezer, and while it did hold up, he could only raise it an inch off the ground. Thomas went back to the front of the freezer, started grabbing the vacuum-sealed cuts of meat, and scattered them across the floor behind him until the man's body was the sole occupant of his icy coffin. The positioning of the body looked even more ridiculous without the meat obscuring certain details and reminded Thomas of a Stretch Armstrong doll.

He could now see the deep black and purple bruising around where the legs and shoulders had been broken. The frost over those areas added a sparkling gloss to the deeply damaged tissue as if meant to distract from and downplay the severity.

Thomas kicked packages of meat out of his way as he headed back to his crude lever and fulcrum system. This time there was much less resistance, and he was able to lift the back end enough to topple the freezer forward on to its side. The body spilled out onto the venison-littered floor as he'd hoped it would, and now the thing deep inside of Thomas took over.

His father and uncle found him several hours later when they entered their workspace the next morning with a client in tow who was picking up the meat they'd processed from his kill. Thomas used to wonder, back when he still thought on the scenario regularly, if things would have turned out differently if his father and uncle had been alone when they discovered him.

Would they have attempted to cover the incident up to protect themselves, and if so, what would that look like?

Thomas couldn't imagine a single scenario that didn't end with him in the freezer as well, and the beating he'd receive would most likely be what put him there. But, as it were they did not discover Thomas alone, and there was no amount of covering up able to alter the fact.

The newspapers said Thomas had eaten the man's arm and half his torso when he'd been discovered, but the stories weren't entirely true. He didn't eat the whole arm, nor was he anywhere near being half done with the torso. Thomas only ate the sweet insides while reporters made him sound like a cannibalistic glutton.

To devour an entire arm would be challenging to complete within the amount of time he'd had with the body, let alone eating something else along with it. Thomas peeled the skin back and down like a wrapper frozen to the popsicle within and attacked the chewy filling beneath. He sucked blood from muscle and swallowed the small chunks whole when they broke off into his mouth.

It was slow going at first until the body had a chance to thaw some, but it gave him the opportunity to take his time. Thomas was able to familiarize himself with the process at a pace that allowed him to learn without making a huge mess.

He barely remembered anything about his father and uncle walking in with their client to find him at the center of the grisly tableau.

Sometimes Thomas would see their faces in his dreams twisted and ruined in eternal and agonizing disgust now permanently etched into the fabric of his subconscious.

Things moved quickly after the incident including the arrest of his father and uncle whose 'accident' story didn't hold too well. They explained the wound in the man's chest as a hunting mishap, and they panicked and hid the body until they had more of their wits about them to go to the police. What they couldn't explain were the two slugs in the man's head, which each blamed the other for putting there.

The man in the freezer's name was Walter Capenelli

and after a bit of investigating it was discovered he'd never been hunting a day in his life. He lived upstate and was reported missing two and half weeks ago by a wife who seemed less than thrilled upon hearing the news he'd been found. She was equally nonplussed when they told her he was dead.

Whatever issues there seemed to be between Walt and his wife she was never considered a suspect, and their marital woes were in no way connected to his death. Walter's wife might have been relieved to be rid of him despite the reason being he had died, but she didn't have anything to do with it.

The stories Thomas's father and uncle gave were vague and conflicting. One of them said it was a robbery gone wrong while the other told a long, drawn out story of murder for hire. Some days they would implicate or outright blame certain sects of organized crime for strong-arming the two of them into doing the 'hit', and some days they denied the mafia was involved in any way.

Thomas was immediately hospitalized following the event to test for bacteria or other blood borne pathogens he might have ingested and was free of both. When the doctors cleared his physical health, he'd been sent to a children's psychiatric ward on a different floor of the same hospital. There were tests, and evaluations, and questions, but Thomas didn't remember much about his time in the hospital.

He was cognizant of being there, but what he'd done with Walter's body made the thing inside him stronger. Thomas remained mostly in the background of his own existence while that other part of him manned the controls for a while. He didn't get to hear much about anything going on outside the hospital especially not the trial, but from what he understood the chaotic event it became took the spotlight off him, at least for a while.

When the shouting matches, fistfights, and parade of questionable character witnesses finally came to a close the trial ended in life sentences for both men. No real charges had been levied against Thomas mostly since he was a minor and had nothing to do with the actual killing of Walter.

Having him remanded to the psychiatric hospital to receive what they called 'vital and constant' treatment sated the state as far as punishment was concerned. He would be re-evaluated when he turned eighteen, and if all was well in the eyes of his doctors, they'd allow him to leave. Thomas's mother never came to visit him at the hospital, and he never saw her again.

Much later when he'd been out of the hospital for quite a while he learned about his uncle dying in prison. It had happened years earlier only two weeks into the life sentence he'd been given. Apparently, he made a huge scene when being moved to his cell one day and was screaming about Thomas's father being evil. He'd screamed, and gnashed, and spit until the guards subdued him with help from their clubs.

They said his uncle was hollering the whole time about Thomas's father being the devil, or in line with the devil, and that someone should kill the man before it was too late. The next morning the guards found his uncle hanging by a bed sheet from the bars of the small window at the top of the wall in his cell. When Thomas tried to find out what happened to his dad no one seemed to know. He'd been transferred from this prison to that prison, then to another, and somehow the paper trail ended with a question mark.

Thomas was told things like this weren't uncommon, and what most likely happened was his father died somewhere along the line and his file simply was never updated. It didn't bother him that they couldn't tell him what happened, but he could see how that might upset other people. Thomas didn't care either way, and when he got out just wanted to start his life.

He moved to a new town where it didn't take long for him to meet Erica. Thomas began to move forward leaving his past far behind and mostly forgotten.

Now, here he was at a truck stop standing in front of a freezer identical to the one his father and uncle had, and it felt like the time between instances was separated by only seconds. It was time. It was time to open the freezer again. Thomas closed his fingers around the handle, but before he could pull it open a gunshot sounded from behind.

The black Cadillac had yet to pull into the truck stop, but Rick knew it was about to and quickened his pace. Having the gun shoved into his pants was heavy and awkward and didn't seem to be at all like it was in the movies. Maybe it was possible to get used to having it there, and with practice he could figure out the nuances of walking with a weapon in his waistband?

More than likely though, this would be the first and last time he would do such a thing. The cold metal dug into the soft skin of the fledgling beer gut he'd been steadily growing, and tiny bits of extra skin were getting pinched as the gun shifted with each step.

When he was a few feet from the door he gave up on trying to situate the thing opting to carry it the remaining short distance. Rick still wasn't sure what he was going to do once he was inside, or how to best handle the situation? It was that goddamn 'clerk', Jacobi was his name, which would cause the most trouble, and be the biggest problem until the Cadillac Man made his entrance.

Rick thought back to seeing the Cadillac Man at all the stops he'd made before this one, and how he'd actually convinced himself it was nothing. He forbade his subconscious from leaking the truth but could only hold it back so long before it broke free flooding his head with memories he badly wanted to forget.

He reached the glass door and paused to look back over his shoulder at the other two vehicles parked at the pumps. Rick watched the man in the moving truck walk into the store, and he'd seen the woman arrive just after his car refused to move any farther. He knew she heard him wailing. She saw him crying. She would cry too if she knew what he did, but there would be plenty of time to cry for all of them soon enough.

Rick reached out and put his free hand on the door handle but didn't pull right away. He could see the clerk and the woman inside at the counter through the glass but was distracted by what started playing in his head.

He was back there again.

He saw the shop and the meeting happening all over again. He saw the blood, and he saw the woods, and then he saw only black until he saw the face. It cut into the darkness like a glass etching and left an impression just as permanent in his mind. It was the face that freed Rick, but cursed him at the same time, and he couldn't have it one way without the other.

It was the face of the Cadillac Man. Not the way he presented himself, but what he actually looked like. Rick didn't know why the Cadillac Man changed his appearance and figured he wouldn't understand the answer if given to him, so he didn't put much thought into wondering. It didn't matter anyway.

For just a moment he let himself remember the blood and the woods again, and involuntarily smacked his gums against the sudden salivary assault. His mouth went dry in the instant he heard the unmistakable rumble of the black Cadillac as it slowly turned into the truck stop.

Rick snapped out of his daydream, pulled open the door, and stepped inside. He fired the pistol into the ceiling before realizing he'd done it, and the report made the gun sound much more threatening in the small space of the store. Suddenly, there were six eyes on him attached to faces bearing expressions ranging from confused to terrified.

"Okay, listen up," Rick yelled louder than he needed to, but his ears were ringing. "We're almost out of time."

---◆---

"FUCK YO—"

The expletive caught in Janine's throat as the sound of a gunshot ricocheted off the walls of the small store like a pinball stuck between bumpers.

She'd seen the door open from the corner of her eye, but her focus was being furiously directed toward the clerk. There was a time when Janine would have sensed something was wrong regardless of her being engaged otherwise, but she'd let herself get soft and weak since she'd been running. That was what she was really doing, running. Trying to forget.

She'd reflexively gone to cover her head, and as she watched white dust from the ceiling fall in slow motion was sucked into a memory triggered by the noise. Suddenly, she was back where it was dark, when she had to start running. Everything Janine did was to help him, but her father didn't see it that way.

That's why he tried to get rid of her himself. Daddy's little girl had overstepped her bounds and in turn left a huge mess she had no intention of cleaning up. Janine told him how he was being used and taken advantage of, but it turned out she couldn't have been more wrong. The droves of women throwing themselves at her father weren't the blood-sucking mosquitoes she took them for, but her father was a spider luring them to his web with gifts and money where he quite literally grew fat on their blood.

By the time Janine found all this out it was too late, and instead of having a commonality between father and daughter over which to bond, the two were irrevocably turned against each other. Both Janine and her father had been so deep within their own darkness they couldn't see how close they were to one another, or how similar.

Rosy was the first one Janine acted her thoughts out upon, although she'd planned it in her head dozens of times with other girls. There was nothing particularly special about Rosy that set her apart enough from the others. She was just the one who was there.

Her father liked Rosy quite a bit and had in fact insisted she go by 'Rosy' instead of her given name, 'Rose'. Janine could tell the woman didn't like the nickname by the way she subtly flinched each time it was used. Rosy was young, too young for Janine's father as far as she was concerned, but she felt this way about all the women he brought home.

Once it was done Janine's sole regret was she hadn't started earlier. She didn't intend on getting so carried away in the moment, but when she'd started tearing hunks of flesh from the woman's midsection, she found herself wanting to shove them into her mouth, so she did.

She had a taste for it now.

Her father hadn't been suspicious when Rosy vanished as was the case with most participants in his revolving door love life, but when Layla disappeared his demeanor toward Janine began to change. Two days later when he couldn't find Corrie after leaving her in the living room for five minutes to retrieve his glasses from the study he went directly to his daughter.

Janine was sitting in the dark when he came for her. She'd disabled the lights of the panic room weeks ago after the first time and continued using it out of convenience. Janine hid and pounced on Rosy when she'd come down to the basement for a bottle of bourbon from her father's collection. They were stored in an ornate cabinet he'd built for the specific purpose of housing his rare and expensive spirits.

The bottle Rosy took from the cabinet was twice her age with rich and nuanced qualities her palate was far from refined enough to perceive or appreciate. She could be drinking a sixty-year-old bottle of Louis VIII brought over on a private jet, or a fifth of Old Crowe from the drug store down the street and wouldn't know the difference.

Maintaining a stupefying buzz throughout the day while lying by the pool was all she was concerned with aside from exploiting Janine's father's weakness for pretty young women.

Janine took Rosy by surprise leaping from the darkness of the panic room and pulling her in. With the door closed it didn't matter how much noise the woman made since the place was completely soundproof, but Janine didn't give her a chance to scream. She went into shock when the ripping and eating started, but despite the horrifying brutality of the attack Rosy slipped into death with the ease of passing through a beaded curtain.

By the time her father came for her the panic room was rife with the co-mingled stink of death, and the sweet bouquet of fresh blood. He entered the code to open the door and found Janine on the floor gnawing a deep gash in Corrie's left shoulder. Remnants of other women lay scattered around her like something from a nightmare, and not a single surface had been spared the touch of blood.

Corrie desperately clung to the life being forcibly drawn out of her in the slowest, most painful way. Janine snapped the woman's neck, although begrudgingly, when her father opened the door prematurely ending the administration of suffering.

Janine looked up at her father and felt the change between them. She was different now having awakened something inside that could never be put back to bed, but something had changed about her father too. Or had it? Whatever happened to Janine allowed her to see for the first time what her father was, and what she had become.

He slammed the door behind him as he stepped inside sounding a sharp crack, which was silenced immediately being sucked into the soundproofing without a hint of lingering decay.

The white, plaster dust resumed falling from the ceiling at a normal pace as Janine was thrust back into reality ripped from the memory she'd involuntarily slipped into.

She watched the man with the gun moving his lips but had no idea what he was saying.

She was hungry now.

———— ♦ ————

The Cadillac Man had just stepped from his car when he heard the shot. A group of black birds nesting on the roof exploded into hysterical squawking as they scattered in different directions away from the truck stop. He knew it was Rick who fired the pistol, and the Cadillac Man could only smile in reaction to the man's futile attempt.

Of course, Rick would be the one to resist the most, but he'd anticipated as much, and didn't blame the man for trying. Rick had gotten away once already after all, but it was no easy feat and more costly than imagined. Still, there's something about a human being's instinct for self-preservation that deludes them into promising the impossible or unthinkable in order to save their own skin.

This was Rick's problem, or one of them at least. He wasn't a pleaser as much as he was an attention junkie willing to do what it took to appear likable in the eyes of anyone and everyone. When he was in school he would do anything to get kids to be his friends like steal from the teacher's desk, or even run behind an unsuspecting girl during recess to flip her dress up giving the boys waiting across the playground a free peek.

He was hooked on manufactured adoration, and like any good junkie, Rick felt the need to up the ante when it came to his attention seeking antics. Stealing from the teacher's desk was one thing but setting it on fire was far beyond the scale of mischief. Rick had graduated to cold and calculated destructive violence.

He stayed after school one day and waited outside until his teacher, Ms. Blankenship, left half an hour later. He'd been carrying the bottle of lighter fluid in his backpack all day and was happy to be getting rid of the constant sloshing of the added weight.

He cleared her desk of some folders, a cup of pencils, and the chalkboard eraser before spraying the desktop with a light misting of the accelerant. He did the same to the armrests and back of the accompanying chair careful not to use too much since it needed to dry out before class resumed in the morning.

He opened the top drawer of the desk and filled it with a quarter inch layer of lighter fluid without removing any of the contents and closed it slowly hoping it wouldn't leak through the binding overnight. He returned the empty bottle to his backpack and walked across the room to open the three windows lining the wall.

Next, Rick carefully returned the items he'd removed from the desk earlier to their original places. It wasn't a perfect plan, but he intended to act quickly enough to garner the desired result, and then bask in the subsequent attention to follow.

The next morning his classmates took their seats while Rick lingered at the front of the room, his hands buried deep in the front pockets of his jeans. The teacher entered, nodded to the class before approaching her desk, but paused as a scent she would never associate with her classroom confused her olfactory senses.

Rick quickly stepped in front of the desk already striking the match he'd retrieved from the box in his pocket. The desk ignited in a quick flash that sent Ms. Blankenship stumbling back into her chair. Embers clinging to the sleeves of her sweater lit the armrests, and she found herself wrapped in a ring of flames.

She panicked reaching for the drawers hoping to find a book or folder with which to beat back the flames, but her hands came back coated in lighter fluid. The fire leapt to her hands starting the process of burning them down to useless black stumps. Now the teacher erupted from behind the desk flailing while making noises like tiny screams that were actually desperate gasps for air.

Ms. Blankenship stumbled toward the door and

collapsed face first in the hall with her feet still inside the classroom twitching madly. Rick stood close to the desk frozen in place as he took in the triumphant result of his plan. The flames danced from the desk behind him creating an eerie hellish tableau for the captive audience. He smiled and turned to face his classmates expecting the expression to be reciprocated but was instead met with horrified looks of anticipated terror. They thought he aimed to go after them next.

Before Rick could assure his classmates he intended them no harm the fire alarm sounded, and water exploded from the sprinklers in the ceiling. The rest of the children screamed and ran from the room doing their best not to trip over the smoldering and convulsive body of their teacher. Rick was stunned. He didn't understand how his latest performance had backfired when it all went according to plan?

He stood in the classroom lost within his own reasoning oblivious to the water raining down until a fire fighter threw Rick over his shoulder and carried him outside. He didn't notice at the time but had he looked behind him after being dried off and given a blanket would've seen a black Cadillac parked on the street in front of the school.

———◆———

For just a moment Thomas was back home, but not with his family; he was with Erica.

The gunshot decayed, and he pushed the memory aside as the knife in his boot rubbed gently against his calf to remind him of its presence. He clutched and unclutched his fingers around the handle of the freezer again before pulling his hand away. Thomas turned slowly on the ball of his foot until he was facing the front of the store where a man with a gun stood just inside the door.

A halo of white dust danced in the light around the man's head like he was a saint delivering the new gospel, and the gun was a gentle reminder you didn't have a choice but listen. The only exit Thomas could see or was even aware of was the door the man with the gun was standing directly in front of, and it didn't look like he was going to relinquish that position voluntarily.

Through the glass behind the man, he saw the headlights of a car pull into the truck stop and park next to one of the pumps. Another person walking into the store could distract the man long enough for Thomas to grab his knife and make a move, but that was *if* the person came inside. They could pay at the pump and be on their merry way without a clue as to what was happening inside the greasy truck stop walls. Or the man could just shoot the person when they walked in and eliminate any chance of a distraction altogether.

The man caught Thomas staring from the back of the store, and he slowly raised his hands in front of him palms out to show the gunman he wasn't up to anything or trying to be sneaky.

"You back there," the man said addressing Thomas while waving the smoking barrel in his direction. "Come over to the counter and join the rest of the party pretty-boy."

Thomas nodded his head while taking slow deliberate steps to the front of the store with his arms held up to chest level, hands open in a sign of surrender.

"Okay sir, okay," Thomas said while taking snail-paced steps. "No one here wants any trouble, so why don't you tell us what you want. The three of us will surely help you get exactly that so you can be on your way."

"Trouble?" The man with the gun made a face like he'd never heard the word before. "Oh, it's way too late for that."

The man gestured toward the glass door behind him but didn't turn around to look.

"Trouble is the reason we're all here, and I have a feeling you know what I'm talking about. The three of us have been in *trouble* for some time I imagine, and now our own personal reckonings are coming. I know you saw him pull up."

The man addressed the last sentence to Thomas who was still slowly making his way to the counter without taking his eyes off the gun. He *did* know what the man was talking about.

"Three of us?" asked the woman standing in front of the counter pointing across to the clerk. "What about him?"

The clerk hadn't stopped grinning since the gun was fired and was now unsuccessfully trying to suppress his giggling. He looked from the woman in front of him to the man with the gun and shrugged.

"He's a part of all this," answered the gunman. "He's not one of us though, he's with . . . him."

This time when the gunman gestured to the door behind him, he allowed himself to steal a quick glance outside. His expression went slack before twisting in to one of terror as a reaction to what he saw through the glass. He stepped away from the door and backed up to the counter keeping his eyes on whatever was approaching.

"Hurry!" The man with the gun was yelling at Thomas now. "Get your ass over here. I told you we don't have much ti—"

The door flung open, and the man who'd pulled into the truck stop moments ago was now standing in the small store with them. He was tall, and pale with shockingly blond hair, which stood in hard contrast against the stunningly sharp black suit.

"No Rick, I'm afraid you're wrong." The Cadillac Man's voice was deep and smooth without even the slightest touch of gravelly distortion. "There is *no* time left."

———◆———

Rick burned his teacher to death before the Cadillac Man came into his life, but the incident did make him aware of the boy's potential. He remained in the periphery of Rick's life for years watching and waiting for what was only inevitable. The Cadillac Man wouldn't have to get this one through an intermediary like the others, because Rick would come willingly. He would have no choice.

He wasn't like the others, Rick. He hadn't been used to barter with the Cadillac Man like so many before. He'd made his own declaration of allegiance long ago, and yet now chose to stand in defiance at the end.

As for the man, Thomas, and the woman, Janine, they had no control. Their parents were responsible for sealing their fate with the Cadillac Man without their knowledge or consent. The Cadillac Man's steady influence worked like a slow poison to change the two of them in all the right ways until it was time to be collected.

Rick didn't have to be changed and drank greedily from the Cadillac Man's cup to feed the darkness inside of him. But something happened to Rick along the way.

His parents' lives fell apart, and they abandoned him to the state after what he'd done to his teacher. Rick's father started having an affair, and up and left his mother without any notice. She went on to move back to Wyoming where she lived with her sister until she died disavowing all knowledge of ever being married or having a son. To her nothing of the past existed anymore.

The teacher survived the incident, but barely and not in a way she could take solace in. Her hands were rendered useless, as the fingers had fused together making them into blackened, oversized, lobster claws. She was blind, completely deaf in one ear and mostly in the other, and her nose was flat and melted against her face. She was burned on over eighty percent of her body, which turned her skin to a mess of deep red scars no amount of plastic surgery could correct.

She jumped from her hospital room window hours after she awoke and learned the extent of her injuries. No one could figure out how she'd been able to do it in her condition, and so quickly. The attending nurse wasn't two steps from the room when she heard the crashing of equipment behind her.

She rushed back in to see the window open with monitors and I.V.s scattered across the floor below the sill. The teacher jumped without bothering to disconnect the tubes and needles inserted into her, and they'd followed along before being forcibly detached.

The nurse rushed to the window as a group of doctors, nurses, and orderlies raced toward the commotion. She looked the twenty-three stories down and saw the grotesque, crumpled body. One of her legs was bent back behind her, and a widening ring of red began to slowly spread out from under her.

Ms. Blankenship's head burst open on impact, and the pressure forced her brain out onto the sidewalk in a lumpy red pulp. The nurse saw the black Cadillac pulling out onto the main road from the hospital exit, but it didn't register with her as anything important to note. She no longer wanted to see the horror show on the ground and raised her gaze to see anything but.

Rick had no idea his actions would invoke the Cadillac Man, or that the two would eventually be inseparable.

———————◆———————

The hunger left as quickly as it came on having been shoved to the bottom of Janine's priority list after the gunshot, albeit temporarily. Her ears were ringing, and she didn't realize the man at the back of the store was attempting to start a dialogue with the gunman until she saw him approaching from the corner of her eye.

There was something said about 'three' and 'trouble', but Janine was too rattled to fill in the gaps despite the desperate, wide-eyed expression on the gunman's face. An expression that shifted to fear as the man suddenly rushed toward the counter to escape whoever or whatever he saw approaching the door.

She sensed the man from the back of the store was now

just off to her side, but she didn't dare take her eyes away from the door. When the Cadillac Man walked in, she realized she *couldn't* look away. His presence was jarring and familiar at the same time, but not in a way that brought Janine any comfort. A rush of anxiety squeezed her lungs empty as her blood pressure spiked, and she leaned forward to grab the edge of the counter for balance.

Janine squeezed her eyes against the swelling pain between her temples while unintentionally grinding already clenched teeth. In her mind she saw herself kneeling on the floor of the panic room with decaying bodies of half-eaten women all around her just as she'd seen it reflected in her father's eyes. Something was different, though. There was a man standing behind her now, the man who'd just walked into the truck stop. His thin, elongated frame, black suit, and startlingly blond hair were unmistakably identical.

There was something else about the man dressed in black before her that went beyond the twisted vision playing in her head. Janine knew him. He was one of her father's associates, or partners, or possibly even a client. She couldn't recall the exact relationship that tied this man to her father, but she'd seen the two of them together on many occasions.

Janine recalled entering her father's office one afternoon as a young girl to ask him to play a game with her, but as usual he didn't have time. When she turned to leave the man in the black suit was sitting in a leatherback chair her father kept close to the wall of bookshelves, book in hand, and nose buried within. He glanced up, acknowledged Janine with a smile, and went back to reading.

She remembered another time as a teenager strolling into her father's office to ask for money, something Janine did with regularity. He pressed some folded bills into her outstretched hand without pausing from his phone call, then waved her away like he was signaling for a waiter to take back the soup.

She didn't notice the man in the black suit was standing on the left side of the room until she'd turned to leave, and while mildly startled she didn't let herself flinch. He was standing beside her father's very well stocked bar pouring brown liquid from a crystal decanter into a matching glass with a single, large cube of ice at the bottom. His eyes hid in the shadow of his long-ish, blond hair, but she knew he was looking at her because he nodded a greeting same as before. Janine left the office without returning the gesture.

She ran through several other scenarios where she remembered seeing the same man in her father's office but hadn't placed any significance on the occasions until this very moment. People came and went so often he'd joked about putting in a revolving door, but if her life depended on it Janine wouldn't be able to pick anyone else her father worked with out of a lineup.

She made it a point to remember the daily string of women flowing in and out of the office, but never had a reason to pay attention to the men. Yet, she could easily recall seeing *this* man in the office reading a book, or fixing a drink, or sifting through files in the cabinet.

Janine felt a sharp tug on her elbow, and she snapped from her memories back to the present situation. The tug came again, and she looked to her left to see it was the man who'd moved from the back of the store.

"Uh . . . Hey," he said to Janine without removing his eyes from the Cadillac Man. "Do you two know each other or something?"

"What?"

She looked back in the direction of the door to see the strange man in black was staring at her.

———◆———

Thomas didn't know where he remembered the Cadillac Man from until he got within a few feet of the counter, and it hit him. The memory was fuzzy and abstract like he was trying to remember a dream he'd had about the man, only couldn't recall the details or context for him being there. As he slowly walked up the candy aisle toward the counter as instructed the memory came into sharp focus, and with each step details dropped in like puzzle pieces until the picture was complete.

The Cadillac Man had worked at the psychiatric hospital where Thomas was held, or at least he thought the man worked there. He certainly remembered seeing him around enough now that he was thinking about it. The man's strikingly angled posture and abstract thinness was too unsettling for him to forget, and he'd know it if he saw it again, which happened to be now.

Thomas remembered the man being around the hospital doing things like checking charts, filing stacks upon stacks of folders, or he might have been pulling the folders out. It was possible the man was responsible for making the stacks, but he couldn't be certain. Anytime Thomas saw the strange man look in his direction he'd immediately look at the floor and walk away.

The Cadillac Man's appearance wasn't the only thing about him that gave Thomas the creeps. He moved about the hospital with sleek anonymity avoiding contact and conversation with supposed co-workers while forever occupying his time with what amounted to busy-work.

The man was never on a set schedule like doctors or orderlies, so there was no telling when or where Thomas would see him. Sometimes he saw the Cadillac Man early in the morning on the way to breakfast. Thomas would pass the nurses station down the hall from the cafeteria, and the man would be by the file cabinets stacking or un-stacking folders. The nurses working around him seemed indifferent to the constant smack of folder against folder ignoring what had long since become background noise.

There was nights Thomas would lie in bed and see the unmistakable, bright, blond hair in the window on the door of his room, but when he looked again it would be gone.

There would be stretches of days where Thomas didn't see the man at all, and even longer stretches where he seemed to never leave.

Thomas remembered when he had to tell a group of doctors about what he did to the man in his father's freezer. They furiously took notes as he recounted how the hunger took over, how he'd given himself over to it. They were in one of the bigger rooms typically used for daily group sessions, but that day Thomas was the only patient present.

There were several nurses hovering around the perimeter of the seated doctors. They weren't taking notes but listening intently in order to better understand how to care for their newest charge. Among the nurses lurking a step behind their shoulders Thomas saw the Cadillac Man's head appear, disappear, and appear again through the gaps as he paced in the back.

When they were through asking questions, he was escorted back to his room, but the Cadillac Man had left long before then. Thomas couldn't remember exactly when, only that he'd stopped seeing the blond hair pass between nurse's heads long before he'd finished telling the story.

It didn't matter though, because the Cadillac Man knew how it ended. He was there when it happened.

———— ◆ ————

The Cadillac Man leveled his gaze at Janine before shifting it to Thomas allowing for the prolonged eye contact to spark their individual memories of him. He didn't have to bother with reminding Rick.

The Cadillac Man took a step toward the counter, and Rick swung his gun pressing the barrel against the side of the clerk's head.

"Just hold it right there," said Rick cocking the hammer of the .38 back with his thumb. "I think you should do some talking before coming any closer."

The Cadillac Man

The clerk let loose a laugh he could hold no longer, which further unnerved Rick while ratcheting up the tension for them all. Jacobi was a faithful imp to the Cadillac Man, but his intelligence was limited, and he couldn't help but laugh at everything. A bullet in the creature's head wouldn't do anything other than poke a hole in it, and if Rick turned the gun on the Cadillac Man, well; it certainly wouldn't be the smartest thing for him to do.

"Rick," The Cadillac Man's voice was like a bow gliding over strings in the hands of a master violinist. "I think you know better than this."

"What the hell is going on?!"

Janine's scream ruptured the tension between Rick and the Cadillac Man but only for a moment, and her outburst made the clerk laugh even harder.

"Shut the fuck up, man!"

Rick shouted and jammed the gun harder against the clerk's head. He couldn't be sure, but it felt like the barrel sunk into his skull, and he pulled it back quickly to see it wasn't the case.

"Janine," the Cadillac Man turned his attention back to her. "I'd be more than happy to explain *what the hell is going on*, but I need for Rick to stop trying to deny the inevitable."

"What? How do you know my name? Is this some kind of joke?" Janine's stern exterior faltered for the first time since her frustration with the clerk spiked.

The Cadillac Man smiled with and gave a tsk while shaking his head. He didn't expect she would act so blatantly oblivious, but he wasn't surprised either. Janine had always been smart, and never needed more than a gentle nudge from time to time to send her off in the right direction.

Besides, of the three of them she'd most recently spent time with the Cadillac Man, but he was used to them trying to forget. She'd remember soon enough.

"Look man," Thomas was doing his best to keep his voice calm and even while forcing his memories of the Cadillac Man back beneath the mental boulder he kept them buried under. "I don't know how you know these people, but I'm not involved with them, okay. Why don't you just tell me what I need to do to get out of this situation, and then you can settle up whatever business you have with them after I've gone on my way."

The clerk burst into hysterical, hyena-like laughter at Thomas's remark prompting Rick to pull back and bring the butt of the gun down on the side of the young man's head. The clerk turned suddenly back to Rick with a snarl brandishing a mouthful of newly pointed teeth, and his eyes had turned unnaturally yellow rimmed in red.

Rick flinched, stepped back and used both hands to point the gun at the chest of the transformed clerk. He showed no fear of the weapon and gnashed his teeth while white and yellow foam pushed from the corners of his mouth and ran down his chin creating a small beard of rabid death slime.

"Enough Jacobi!'

The Cadillac Man's voice resonated with an authoritative quality reserved for issuing instruction as well as warning. The clerk's face returned to its original pimpled pubescent visage in an instant eliciting a double take from Rick.

The change was so quick it may as well not even have happened, but it did, and he saw it. The clerk went back to giggling, but not before winking and blowing a kiss to the man pointing a gun at his chest. Rick was trying to maintain his composure, but it was clear the incident rattled him.

"Thomas, I must say I'm ashamed." The Cadillac Man turned his attention back to the man standing next to Janine. "First, the fact you would negotiate for your own safety while leaving your friends here for me to do what I will, well; that's just bad manners."

"I . . . I don't know them." Thomas's voice was just above a whisper now. "They aren't my friends."

"Selfishness has always been an awful character trait in you Thomas," the Cadillac Man continued, "but I've come to expect nothing less. While you may not recognize them, I assure you there is a connection between you all, and while you may not be friends directly, you're closer to each other than you realize."

"I don't know what you're talking about?" Thomas's voice had returned to full strength. "I don't know any of these people, and I sure as shit don't know yo—"

The memories he had of the Cadillac Man burst from where he'd tried to bury them and flooded his mind with begrudging recognition before he could finish his sentence.

"There it is," the Cadillac Man said with a smile. "Just because you refuse to let yourself believe something doesn't mean it didn't happen. Just like with Erica."

His left eye began to twitch at the mention of her name. Thomas was not ready to let those memories out from the mountain of delusion he'd buried them under. He saw Janine turn slightly to look at him from the corner of her eye. She was remembering how the Cadillac Man came to be involved in her life and could only imagine what these two men had done bind themselves to him as well.

"Okay," said Janine to the man in black standing across the store from her. "I think I know why you're here."

———————•◆•———————

The time in the panic room, the last time, wasn't Janine's first encounter with the Cadillac Man. Not by far. She saw his thinly sharpened body standing behind her reflected in her father's eyes, but already knew he was back there. While she'd seen the Cadillac Man from time to time in her father's office during many of her regular stops to request money, the first time he spoke to her was in the lobby as she was leaving one afternoon.

Her father's office was on the fourteenth floor of the

building it resided in, which was actually the thirteenth floor, but old superstitions die hard. According to the building directory and the buttons on the elevator the cursed floor not only didn't exist, was never to be spoken of.

Janine stepped from the elevator looking down into her open purse where she was busy situating the wad of bills she'd freshly procured from the ATM machine she called 'daddy'. The Cadillac Man was sitting in one of the expensive, designer, leather chairs in the lobby. They were arranged in a way that only made sense to the over-priced designer who was never asked to explain themself.

He waited to speak until she passed directly in front of him.

"Janine, a word if you please?"

She gasped and jumped back with a start clutching her chest as her purse fell to the polished stone floor. Her keys, makeup, wallet, and the cash from her father spilled out around the man's feet.

"What the . . . heck!" Janine exclaimed clamoring to scoop the loose items back into her purse. The man sitting in the chair did not move to help. "What's the big deal scaring me like that, huh? What's your problem anyway?"

The Cadillac Man waited to answer until she'd collected the items and stood back up.

"It's not me who has the problem, it's your father," he said. "I was hoping to speak with you about it if you would be so kind?"

Anger turned to fear at the mention of there being a problem with her father, and she was suddenly interested in what the man had to say.

"My fa—" She struggled to find her voice and swallowed back the sudden knot in her throat. "My father? What do mean he has the problem?"

A thought occurred to Janine, and she clutched her purse tight against her chest while slowly turning her right foot toward the front door. She was prepared to run and hoped to get a surprise head start in what she thought might possibly be a race for her life. Janine had heard about things like this happening, the abduction of wealthy and powerful people's children; she never thought it would happen to her though.

"Please, relax," the Cadillac Man said. "I'm not here to hurt you. I'm here to help. I just need you to listen to me."

Janine used to lie awake during the hours it was considered too late to go to sleep, but too early to get up, and wonder what would have happened had she turned and run before he could say another word? Would anything have been different had she not stayed to listen?

Janine believed she dictated her own path in life and wasn't beholden to anyone or anything especially not an invisible boogey man called 'fate'. Or at least she liked to believe so until that day at that moment. Janine knew she was bound to the Cadillac Man long before encountering him but only realized it right then.

He stood up and Janine noticed how the thin frame and long appendages worked to exaggerate his height. She also thought it was odd for a grown, adult man to have such startlingly blond hair, especially one who worked in a professional setting. Outside of self-proclaimed 'artists', and those with perpetual Peter Pan Syndrome it just seemed out of place.

On the other hand, she didn't know anything about the man standing in front of her, so he very well could have been one or both of those things. There was no darkness at the roots that she could see, and Janine guessed it was either a naturally occurring pigment issue, or he spent a lot of time and money to make it appear so. Either way she'd already decided after a few seconds that it suited him, and intentional or not it created a curious contradiction to the rest of the Cadillac Man's look.

"Well?" Some of the original anger was returning now, and Janine felt her patience thinning. "Are you going to tell me what this is all about or what?"

"Would you mind taking a walk with me?" The Cadillac Man gestured to the door. "I'd rather not discuss this inside the building."

"Fine," said Janine after an exaggerated, dramatic sigh.

When they approached the door the Cadillac Man reached out and held it open. Janine stepped outside and thought she heard the man stifle a laugh as she walked past.

———————◆———————

"Wait! Stop! Shut up!" Rick was shouting back at Janine while keeping one eye, and the gun trained on the clerk. "Don't talk to him. Nothing good comes out of talking to him."

"Why?" Janine fired back. "Do you know this blond-headed fuck too?"

"I thought it was quite clear by now that I was the common denominator here," the Cadillac Man said with an intensity that snapped the attention back on him.

"Don't answer him," Rick yelled. "This is all another one of his games, and I'm not playing anymore!"

Mention of the word *games* triggered another memory for Janine transporting her back to that first conversation with the strange man from the lobby that simply went by Cadillac Man. He'd used the word to describe what this supposed harem of women were doing with her father, playing games. These were very expensive games though, and the Cadillac Man told her if somebody didn't step in and do something soon Janine's father would be bankrupt in less than two years.

She didn't like hearing it, but not because she felt empathy for her father, or pity for his lustful weakness. It was because it would mean the end of her free ride, a free ride she'd intended to last well into the future. This couldn't happen if what the Cadillac Man said was true. Janine didn't want just *somebody* to step in and do something either; she wanted that somebody to be her.

He liked Janine for this reason. She was already motivated by a kind of greed that had its roots buried deep into her bones. It was the kind of greed you couldn't remove from a person without it killing them.

The Cadillac Man thought of Janine as a shark forever hunting with no motivation in life other than satisfying its never-ending hunger. Anything attempting to keep a shark from eating was eliminated without a thought, which included other sharks. There's no love lost amongst hungry hunters where eating and death are concerned.

For a shark not eating means death, and whether it comes now from another shark, or later from starvation it still comes. Despite the delivery method death always ended the same way. Dead is dead no matter how early or late you come to the party.

Janine was so completely primed by the time they'd had their first conversation the Cadillac Man needed barely touch her to put the hunger inside. It may as well have leapt across the space between them like electricity between Tesla coils. A light touch on her back was all it took as he gently guided her through the door. It was so subtle Janine wasn't aware it happened. The Cadillac Man had to stifle his laughter from how easy it was to push this domino over.

Now here she was in the truck stop trying to beat back the parts she didn't want to remember.

"Games?" The Cadillac Man posited the word as a question aimed back at Rick. "The games are over I'm afraid, Rick, but you're right about not playing anymore. You've already played, and you lost. All of you did, which is why I brought you here together. It's time for me to collect my winnings."

———————◆———————

The Cadillac Man wasn't being completely honest with the three of them. Thomas and Janine had been locked into playing and were destined to lose before taking their first steps by way of those who *did* have a choice. They just so happened to choose wrong. Rick was different though. He came willingly.

Janine's father was a man named Marshal Beringer who'd made his fortune starting as part of a hedge fund and transitioned to running the largest investment firm in the city within the span of two years. He was an attorney with a master's degree in finance who risked everything to luckily come out on top. His intimate knowledge of law and money played a large part in the success of his firm, as Mr. Beringer knew how to operate a scrupulous business without technically breaking any laws.

On the surface Mr. Beringer was an intelligent businessman who set himself up to succeed across every platform of his life, but it was only that, surface. In reality Marshal Beringer was a two-bit conman with an eighth-grade education. Marshal Beringer couldn't run a dishwasher let alone a successful investment firm. The Cadillac Man was responsible for all his good fortune, and all he wanted in exchange was to be fed. Forever.

Thomas's father and uncle didn't lead the same kind of life as Mr. Beringer, but they owed the Cadillac Man as well. The two of them didn't want riches or career success, but instead invoked the Cadillac Man's touch to get away with things they'd already done, were planning to do, and things they'd yet to think of but would do in the future.

The man Thomas found in the freezer wasn't the first person his father and uncle killed. It seemed their hunting trips weren't strictly limited to deer, but included more than a few other hunters, hikers, and campers. The two of them didn't kill for money, or even sport, but because they were compelled to. The brothers were bona-fide sociopaths who got their jollies from snuffing out life.

The trouble was they knew they couldn't get away with it forever and were already considered suspects in several of the killings they had done. The net was closing around them when they made their deal with the Cadillac Man. He made it all go away like it never happened, and quite literally it never did.

When Thomas's father and uncle killed anyone from then on out it was like the person had never existed. There was no mention of it in the papers or on the news, and no one ever came around asking about their daddies, or husbands, or brothers. The person was simply erased and any knowledge of them having existed was erased along with them. The two were granted an eternal immunity, which allowed them to remove a person completely from existence anytime they pleased, and all they had to do was feed the Cadillac Man.

The men were greedy and arrogant though and didn't take their deal as seriously as they should have, which was why the Cadillac Man sent Thomas to their workspace that night. The charm had been lifted, and they realized it when they found Thomas eating a body that should have been blinked out of existence.

The brothers learned the hard way the Cadillac Man's hunger was not to be ignored, and for that he took Thomas far earlier than the agreed upon time.

Rick was a different story from the other two. He wasn't ushered to the Cadillac Man unknowingly through a conduit of greed by way of someone else's choices but came to him as a child knowingly *and* willingly. His parents were selfish messy failures who couldn't care less about their son, or how dangerous his craving for attention had become.

He lacked the ability to think beyond his actions when it came down to it and drew no barriers between positive and negative. It was all the same to Rick, and he craved it regardless. This abhorrent quality alone was enough to put him on the Cadillac Man's radar, and it brought the dark-suited man to town just in time for Rick's fiery premeditated delight of an attention grabber.

The boy bound himself to the Cadillac Man the day he set his teacher on fire creating the perfect storm of nonchalant chaos needed to bring them together. Like he'd done with Thomas, the Cadillac Man stayed in the hospital Rick was sent to. He was visible to only the boy, and only when he wanted to be seen.

He kept a leash on Rick after his eventual release from the hospital. It was a long leash, but a leash, nonetheless. He put his hunger into Rick, which was a perfect catalyst to re-activate the unique hunger already within. There was no middleman brokering a deal to put the two of them together, so their bond was especially rare.

It wasn't supposed to come to this for Rick, because he was different. The Cadillac Man was grooming him to be the closest thing to a protégé he would ever have. The Cadillac Man's position was one of permanence, so Rick could never really take over for him, but their relationship was still mutually beneficial. They each had their hunger sated with no repercussions for Rick, and no extra work for the Cadillac Man.

The arrangement worked fine for quite some time, but something changed when the Cadillac Man eventually started spending less, and less time with Rick leaving him to run on a sort-of autopilot. There were deals to be brokered, collections to be made, and other business to take care of. Rick didn't require much guidance, and he certainly didn't need persuasion when it came to feeding his hunger.

He woke up one morning after having not seen the Cadillac Man for several weeks and felt different. He wasn't hungry anymore, and when he tried to remember what it was like when he had been he couldn't. The memory became harder to grasp with each passing day until Rick couldn't recall his relationship to the Cadillac Man at all.

He could remember other things about his life, but only parts when the Cadillac Man was absent from it. This made for several gaps, which his memory simply filled in with colorful experiences. Most of what filled in the missing pieces came from situations Rick saw on television or movies, or even from conversations he overheard between other people. Sections of make-believe scenes were inserted into his memory's timeline where they would make the most sense.

Eventually enough time passed for the false memories to cement themselves in place forming a mostly false narrative. The life Rick now remembered having was nothing like the one he'd actually been living. According to his warped and doctored recall he had been briefly married to his high school sweetheart who was tragically killed in a boating accident off the Florida Keys on their third honeymoon.

The parents *he* remembered were retired and living in Maine, and Rick often thought he should call or visit more often. It was just so hard to get away from work what with him being on the road all the time, not to mention this was their busy season. Plus, with his wife gone and no kids to attend to Rick liked to stay busy to keep his mind off the grief he felt from her loss.

The Cadillac Man had been away from Rick for too long and didn't anticipate the effect it would have on the influence he held over him. Rick found he wasn't sure who he really was, or what he was supposed to be doing, and his subconscious fabricated a life to keep him from blowing a fuse.

This change was still relatively new for Rick, so it wasn't hard for the Cadillac Man to coax forward his *actual* memories right there in the truck stop. The shock of the truth was confusing, which accounted for his defiant behavior as well as the gun despite its uselessness.

False memories attempted to contradict what was real, but their flimsy construction folded quickly beneath the crushing weight of reality. Rick was still fighting to reject the conflicting memories even now despite the Cadillac Man standing ten feet in front of him, but he would fold completely soon enough. He'd only been driving for three weeks after all.

His job didn't really keep him on the road all the time, because he didn't have a job. The day Rick woke up not hungry with everything mixed up in his head he'd gotten into his beat-up, old, red sedan and started driving. The more miles he drove the more his life story changed and distorted in his head until it became what he believed was his actual life.

It wasn't long before the Cadillac Man started showing up at all the places he stopped including this one. Rick didn't have any customers to call on, or meetings to be at, or conferences to attend, but as far as he knew he did. He'd been perpetually on the road in route to a destination he'd never reach because it didn't exist.

Now, Rick was in a very real place being made to remember the very real life he'd lived that brought him here. He didn't know who the other two people in the truck stop with him were, but he pitied them.

———— ♦ ————

Thomas remained the quietest of the three. He didn't need reminding of the disdain he felt for the Cadillac Man, and his blood boiled at the mention of Erica.

His jaw clamped down, and his teeth set to working at a slow and steady grind. It was a bad habit he thought he'd kicked a while back after nearly smoothing down the grooves of his molars, but here he was at it again like he'd never taken a break. He flashed to the candy baby parts in the urinal again, and thought he heard the clerk giggle.

One child was the price. One child in exchange for help from the Cadillac Man was the standard deal, or one of them at least, and not just any child either. You couldn't kidnap some random kid or purchase one from a black-market auction. There had to be a connection between the child and the person wishing to consort with *him*. There had to be a bond, because that was what he was most hungry for.

With Thomas and Janine, the bond between parent

and child was what sweetened the tender morsels, and even better; Rick's attachment to the Cadillac Man was like being tapped into a constant feeding tube. Thomas was troubled from having the hunger put into him at such a young age, but he had his father and uncle's selfishness to blame. He resented them for it. He resented the Cadillac Man as well.

Thomas wanted to start over, tried to start over. When he got out of the hospital he couldn't exactly stay in his hometown after what happened. His father and uncle were serial killers, and though they were dead or thousands of miles away, people didn't tend to forget about horrendous crimes committed in their own backyard.

It wouldn't have mattered if Thomas walked around wearing a sandwich board declaring he wasn't going to be like his father and uncle while handing out copies of his hospital release papers. The people in his hometown would always pre-judge him for what they did halfway hoping Thomas would go into the 'family business' just so they could say *I told you so*.

Once there are pictures in the newspaper of you as a child eating chunks of a mutilated dead body there's no way to come back from it. No matter where he went or what he did people would always know and alter their behavior accordingly so as to not become his next meal.

The Cadillac Man wanted him to stay, tried to convince Thomas everything would be fine while knowing full well it wouldn't. He left as soon as he was discharged and drove out of town in the old yellow Scout that had belonged to his father. It felt good to have that part of his life in the rearview mirror, but he had no idea what to do next.

Thomas drifted around for a while living out of motels or sleeping in the Scout never staying in one place for long. The situation was ideal because once he gave in to his hunger he just left and moved on to the next place. There was minimal effort on the Cadillac Man's part to keep Thomas from getting caught since he moved around so much, but things became complicated when Erica came into the picture.

Something about the woman made Thomas believe he could rid himself of the hunger and the Cadillac Man for good and start a real life of his own. He hadn't yet accepted there could be no such thing.

His eternal obligation took a backseat to love and ignorance where it remained for a while. The Cadillac Man allowed Thomas to believe, albeit temporarily, that he was strong enough to break the bond between them only to harshly remind him later just how weak he was.

The Cadillac Man removed the sensation of his attachment to further lull Thomas into a false sense of security. When he told her he was staying in town Erica helped to get him on doing shiftwork at the local sawmill. Thomas lived out of a motel for a while to save enough money for an apartment of his own, but by then he and Erica's relationship was at the point they felt ready to move in together. Of course, the decision made even more sense when Erica announced they were going to be parents.

He was experiencing a high level of happiness wherein memories of his youth and the Cadillac Man had all but vanished. Thomas got a raise at the sawmill, and everything with the pregnancy was moving along nicely without any issues, or even the slightest discomfort. He was living a better life than he thought he had any business doing, and each day was better than the last.

The Cadillac Man rolled into town just as Thomas reached the height of his happiness, and he felt the sticky presence instantly. He refused to acknowledge the feeling and pretended not to notice when the troublesome black car came around the bend snaking past the sawmill with a silent slickness. Thomas told himself it was just a shadow and went about his work without looking up at the road for the rest of the day.

When his shift was over, he kept his eyes down on his way through the parking lot to the old Scout. On his drive home Thomas looked straight ahead through the windshield and nowhere else even when changing lanes. He was almost up to the door of the apartment he and Erica shared when it hit so hard he stumbled and reached for the wall to steady himself.

The hunger was back, and so was the Cadillac Man.

————————◆————————

"Do you need more? If that's the case I can do that, *we* can do that."

Janine was speaking like she believed there was something she could do to get out of the present situation.

"I said don't fucking talk to him!" Rick was yelling, but his tone carried a childish lilt betraying to his authoritative intent. "And *we* are not doing anything for him."

"Look man," Janine fired off at Rick, "I'm trying to get us out of this, but you're not helping improve our situation by waving around a gun and yelling orders!"

"Rick is right, you know," the Cadillac Man said bringing the attention back to him. "I'm sorry how rude of me to assume you were all already on a first name basis. Janine, the fellow with the gun is Rick, and Rick the woman attempting to reason with you is Janine."

"Don't try to distract us with yo—"

"And the quiet fellow next to her is Thomas," the Cadillac Man cut him off. "Now, as I was saying Rick is right in that you are not doing anything for me, but Janine I do appreciate your initiative. There isn't anything left any of you can do, because it's already been done, and while I will always require more it won't come from the three of you anymore."

"So, what's this all about then?" Thomas's voice was a soft contrast to the yelling of his newly introduced friends. "If you say we already did what you wanted, then why are we all here? What's the point of this?"

The Cadillac Man turned to Thomas, a practiced smile on his face.

"Oh Thomas," he began. "You of all people should know what the *point* of this is. It's only been a few days since I last reminded you, so surely you haven't forgotten again already?"

Thomas opened his mouth but balked, the response lost somewhere in the connection between his brain and tongue. Had it only been a few days ago since the Cadillac Man delivered his harsh reminder? Thomas struggled, and now he couldn't seem to remember just how long he'd been driving the moving truck.

His recall played out in his mind like the brief flashes of a grade school filmstrip. Thomas didn't know if it was because he was only allowed to remember it that way, or if it was how he'd experienced it?

There was blood, and a lot of it. It happened fast like there were a few scenes missing between frames. One second everything was fine and normal, and a blink later the apartment was bathed in a wet, candy-apple, crimson lacquer.

Thomas saw Erica when he entered the apartment, terror reflected in her face. He saw her run to the bedroom; he saw her on the bed. He saw hands ripping her clothes off, and those same hands ripping open her skin. They were his hands. He saw Erica's mouth open and assumed she was screaming, but couldn't hear anything save for a low, droning buzz in his ear.

He watched *his* hands, pull the flesh apart and dig deep into Erica's torso. He felt it before he saw it, the baby. It was small, and still had three months to cook, but all the parts and pieces were there. He took the slick red infant in his gore-caked hands, the umbilical cord still connected to the ruined insides of its mother.

In the next slide Thomas saw his teeth biting through the fleshy tether while slurping up the fresh flow of fluids. The last glimmer of life left Erica's eyes as he brought the baby to his mouth, an image reflective of depravity from the lowest depths of hell.

He watched chunks of the child disappear in a time-lapse video until mushy pink and yellow pulp slid through his fingers back into the dead woman's womb. The texture was like chewing silly-putty with bits of peanut shells crushed within, and a tart sweetness rolled across his tongue urging him on demanding more. He remembered he wanted to stop, but the Cadillac Man wouldn't let him.

In the final images he saw a flipbook-style presentation of his face getting closer and closer to the hole he'd dug in Erica until his head was buried inside, and his mouth was full again.

------------◆------------

Before temporarily lifting his influence, the Cadillac Man and Rick were thick as thieves. Much like Thomas, Rick moved around as well roaming from place to place with only one goal anytime he stopped, which was to feed. The difference between them being Thomas knew where he was going, and what he was going to have to do when he got there.

Rick's connection to the thin blond man in black made him oblivious to the influence over him. He believed he was fully in control of his life and decisions, as he drove aimlessly back and forth across the country perpetually on his way to a meeting he'd never reach. The cold darkness inside of Rick was what made it so easy to manipulate him into a relationship beneficial to them both.

On one level he craved the kill yearning to create death in order to sate his natural desire, only he was unaware the Cadillac Man had taken over the reins for that aspect of his life. Rick didn't inherit his sociopathic tendencies from his relatives like Thomas. Violent behavior didn't run in his family, and there was no chance a distant half-cousin serial killer would pop up.

Rick was born with a hole inside of him that needed to be filled with a certain specific desire, which he first confused for attention, but then came to realize it could only be filled by administrating death with his own hands.

Rick's need to throw as much death as possible into the bottomless hole inside of him was like the Cadillac Man's hunger. The need was ever-present with the relief being joyless and short-lived. He would have fallen into this lifestyle regardless of the Cadillac Man's touch and would've eventually acted on his urges but wouldn't have been as successful without help. Sure, he may have been able to get away with a few random murders, but Rick would in no way have been as prolific with his body count had it not been for his silent, symbiotic partner in crime.

Rick's current behavior would have sent a small pang of sadness through the Cadillac Man had he been capable of feeling the emotion. The temporary loss of an important connection might inspire despondency in some, but his stoicism dominated all other emotion. The two of them were here now in the truck stop together, and it didn't matter what Rick thought he could make happen, because the Cadillac Man *knew* what was going to happen.

This was the end for all three of them. He was through toying with Rick, Thomas and Janine, and was bored by their defiance. The Cadillac Man was ready to leave.

———————◆———————

"He doesn't speak for me, okay." Janine gestured at Rick. "I don't give a shit what he says. I'm not with that guy!"

"You're right he doesn't," the Cadillac Man said, "but in a roundabout way you are with him."

"No, I'm not okay! I'm not with this asshole either." She shot her thumb in Thomas's direction. "I'm not with anybody but myself, and I want to know what *I* can do to get out of this place, and away from all of you?"

The Cadillac Man cracked a genuine smile unable to decide if he was tickled more by her strength or ignorance? Janine's voice went low, and her tone was cold and even as she spoke.

"It's the girls, right? You want some more girls? I can

do that for you. I can drive back into town, and I'll find them. I'll find a lot of them."

The clerk started to laugh, and a long, black tongue hung from his open mouth down past his chin. He'd started to look different again, but not like the drastic change he'd momentarily shifted in and out of a few minutes earlier. The differences were subtle enough not to be jarring, but overt enough to make a difference, and suddenly the clerk didn't look so young *or* human anymore.

His brow was more pronounced, and the skin beneath his eyes turned black and purple. There was the tongue of course, but the mouth of crowded teeth gone pointy was far more troubling. The clerk's skin turned a greenish-yellow like earwax spread over jaundice before it went stark white, and the softer characteristics of his face had gone hard and jagged. The man holding the gun who she'd just come to know as Rick was looking at the Cadillac Man and didn't notice the difference in his quasi-hostage.

Something about the change in the clerk's face looked familiar to Janine, and she realized she'd seen him before. He was at her father's building the day she met the Cadillac Man in the lobby. Janine probably wouldn't have noticed him at all if she hadn't spotted him following along behind them.

There had been no one else in the lobby when she'd been confronted with the news of her father and his trouble, but as they approached the door to leave Janine heard the chime of the elevator from behind them. For moment she saw the reflection of the person who got off the elevator in the front door before it was opened. It was the clerk only he looked like the version of him she was seeing presently.

She saw him again as the Cadillac Man lead her down a short path connecting the building to a small courtyard area off to the side offering a sparse splash of green in an otherwise paved landscape. The clerk was wearing a suit then similar to what the Cadillac Man wore only it somehow wasn't as dark. It was black, but the one the Cadillac Man wore was deeper and richer with implied despair. It was the kind of black you couldn't stare at for too long for fear you'd be sucked inside and lost forever.

The clerk was trying to be inconspicuous then, but he wasn't trying too hard, and Janine caught the Cadillac Man glimpse behind as they talked re-alerting Janine of the creepy tagalong's presence. Suddenly, Janine remembered where else she knew the clerk from.

"It was you!" Janine pointed as she approached the giggling clerk. "You were the one who helped me. You drove them to me!"

For Janine to add to her collection of death in the panic room she needed her father's harem of gold diggers brought to her one at a time. At first, she didn't realize the women were being delivered. She was under the impression they were among the daily parade of leeches looking to suck more blood from her personal reserve.

Janine only saw the Towne Car drop the women off a few times, but she usually knew they were there from hearing them clomp around the house like uncoordinated sows. She remembered seeing the driver through the window assuming it was one of her father's many employees he had drive his floozy-of-the-day around town until it was time for his 'appointment' with her. That driver was the clerk.

He didn't work for Janine's father, but the women as well as Janine were under the impression he did. The ladies would receive a message saying a car was being sent to take them to Beringer estate, which wasn't something out of the ordinary. The trip meant a payday for them, so they were always right on time, and ready to go when the car showed up.

It was no different than cattle being ushered up the death-chute for their turn at the 'take a hydraulic nail gun to the head' game, and Janine was more than happy to be the one pulling the trigger over and over again. The women who threatened her inheritance and lifestyle were the lambs. Janine was the slaughter.

"It was him," Janine said tugging on the clerk's sleeve. "He brought them to me, he can help me bring them again."

Rick grabbed the clerk by the other sleeve and pulled him away from Janine's grasp, which coaxed another round of cackling from the inhuman servant of the Cadillac Man.

"Look, lady," Rick started. "I'm trying to help you here. I don't know how deep you're already in, but you don't want to get any deeper. I can promise you that."

"Fuck you asshole!" Janine was pissed now and desperation was fanning the flames of her fury. "I don't need your help or your advice. I know what I'm doing!"

She yanked the clerk back hard enough to pull his shirt from Rick's grasp, and he let her keep hold of him this time. Janine pulled him along with her in the direction of the Cadillac Man, and he started laughing so hard she had to shout in order to be heard over him.

"Send him with me!" Janine declared as she approached the Cadillac Man. "He can help me find more of the girls for you, and you know I'll come back since he's with me."

She was within three feet of him when the Cadillac Man raised his palm halting them in their tracks. Janine tried to keep walking but couldn't manage to get any closer than she was. It was like she'd stepped on a conveyor belt keeping her from advancing despite how hard she tried. She still struggled against the power of the Cadillac Man refusing to be deterred so easily, and the clerk mocked her efforts while continuing to ramp up the intensity of his laughter.

The obnoxious guffawing was suddenly silenced by a loud pop coming from somewhere behind the two of them. Janine realized her face was suddenly wet, warm, and sticky. She was covered in the blood and brains of the clerk who now had no head, and literally became deadweight in her clutches.

She let the clerk's body fall and looked up to see the Cadillac Man also covered in crimson spatter. When she turned around Rick was lowering the smoking barrel of the pistol.

———————◆———————

The puddle of blood-like fluid spread quickly out from beneath the fallen, headless clerk, and stood out strikingly against the floor despite its dingy greasiness. Thomas's first thought was it couldn't be blood on account of a purple tint hiding behind the already bright and rich red.

It moved differently as well.

Real blood, or at least the *human* blood Thomas was familiar with was watery whereas what was leaking from the clerk had a much higher viscosity. The liquid appeared to be rolling rather than flowing and crept along slowly most likely because of its weight. Thomas was hypnotized by the blood's steady approach as it appeared drawn to him. It wouldn't let him look away.

Thomas suddenly *wanted* the puddle to get to him; he needed it to. The hunger came quick and hit hard. If he could have doubled over he would have, but invisible bonds kept him locked in position forcing him to suffer the twisting cramps while standing upright.

Thomas heard pounding coming from the back of the store, and even if he could move, he didn't have to look to know what it was. It started loud and steady but was becoming heavy and erratic with each second. Someone, or something was in the *ize creem* freezer, and desperately wanted out.

Thomas saw the freezer where his father and uncle kept their victims in his mind thinking how similar it looked to the one at the back of the store. He watched a much younger version of himself walk up to that freezer the night he snuck out unsure of what he'd find, or why he'd come? The pounding reached an aggressive desperation from blows powerful enough to lift the entire freezer an inch off the ground.

Thomas remained trapped in his memory, and the pounding came from the freezer he was seeing in his mind. He watched the young Thomas reach out and grab the handle on top of the freezer where it rested for only a moment before yanking it up and open.

Thomas was ripped from the memory to find himself mid-air having leapt to the headless body of the clerk driven by a maddening hunger, which refused to let him think of anything but. Time had resumed its normal pace around him, but Thomas didn't notice the sudden swiveling of heads in his direction. His only concern was the hunger. He was now at its command.

He landed hard coming down on his knees a moment before his elbows cracked against the linoleum covered concrete floor. Thomas expected the clerk's body would cushion his landing, but he'd somehow missed it altogether. Figuring he'd overshot his target Thomas rolled over expecting it to be just behind him, but it wasn't. He also realized he should be wet and sticky with the clerk's strange blood, but he was dry and clean.

Thomas jumped quickly to his feet, the hunger's demands muting any sensation of pain he should have been experiencing. He turned in a circle searching for a body that was no longer there, and as quickly as he'd leapt up Thomas dropped to his knees. This time he could feel every bit of the pain as his already injured knees met the floor for the second time in the last thirty seconds.

The body and the blood were gone, but the pounding from the large freezer continued. Thomas lifted his head from his chest to see Janine, Rick, and the Cadillac Man were all looking toward the back of the store. Whatever was inside the freezer had gotten stronger, because now the power behind each blow lifted the appliance off the ground a full six inches.

Each bang coming from the inside of the freezer was now immediately followed by a louder, more aggressive crash from the unit smacking back down against the floor. It was moving as well inching slowly away from the wall with every tiny leap. Still, the lid held tight refusing to budge against the barrage of attacks from within, and regardless of intensity the padded seal held tight.

Thomas couldn't help but smile as he realized what was happening. He saw himself in his father and uncle's workspace standing in front of their freezer again for a moment, but the hunger wouldn't let him linger in the memory now demanding one hundred percent of his conscious attention. The hunger wanted what was inside the freezer, and Thomas aimed to get to it.

He stood, turned, and took deliberate steps toward the freezer. His footfalls matched up with each hop of the appliance making it seem like they were the cause until Thomas found himself standing in front of it. The pounding stopped and the sudden silence was jolting. He lifted his hand to the handle when he heard Rick cry out from behind him.

"What are you doing? Don't open it! He wants you to open it!"

"No!" Janine cried. "Don't listen to him. Open it! Open it! He wants you to open it, so give him what he wants so we can get out of here!"

Thomas glanced over his shoulder and saw Rick still next to the counter, but the gun was trained on him now. Janine remained by the Cadillac Man, the two of them looking in Thomas's direction. Janine looked frazzled and desperate, and for some reason the blood and brains hadn't disappeared from her face or clothing. The Cadillac Man was clean again and wore no expression.

Thomas looked back down at the freezer and gripped the handle on the lid. Rick would have screamed out again in protest if he'd had time, but Thomas's movements were fast and smooth. As he turned and tugged the handle in a

90

single, flawless motion, he saw the face of the man he'd found in his father's cooler flash across his mind.

The lid shot open with a force that ripped it from the hinges. It shot up into the ceiling with a smack and clattered to the floor in the newly created space between the freezer and the wall. Thomas didn't realize anything had escaped until it pounced and rode him to the floor where he suddenly found himself lying on his back looking into the mutated face of the clerk.

Icy, clawed hands held his arms to his side while the creature-faced clerk waited the moment Thomas needed for it all to sink in. When the recognition flashed in his eyes the clerk opened his mouth wide and reared his head back. Thomas watched the rust colored, bayonet-like teeth push further out from black gums reaching lengths the size of the clerk's mouth could no longer accommodate yet they continued to grow.

Thomas struggled but he was pinned in place beneath a body much heavier than it should be. He refused to close his eyes as the clerk's mouth came down against his neck, only instead of his flesh being pierced and ripped away it felt like a cold, dead, fish mouth pressed against his skin. A beat later the mouth started to laugh.

———◆———

"I'll take that."

Rick felt the weight of the pistol disappear and looked up from the scene on the floor to his empty hand. The Cadillac Man was now holding the weapon examining the barrel before tucking it away somewhere within his jacket.

The clerk, who had been about to maul Thomas on the floor in front of the freezer, was now standing next to the Cadillac Man. His head was fully intact, and his clothes were just as they'd been when Rick couldn't take the laughing anymore and pulled the trigger to make it stop. He waved at him before kicking the giggle-box back into full gear.

It felt like the clerk's body evaporated around him in an instant, but the moist ring of slobber on Thomas's neck remained. He lingered for a moment in confusion before rolling onto his stomach, pushing himself up quickly to his feet. He wasn't sure what happened, but he wanted to be ready if it happened again. The hunger was gone from him, but the fog it left behind was difficult for Thomas to fight through.

He thought he remembered blood, and lots of it, but the floor and ceiling were clean. Thomas was having a hard time putting together what happened between the clerk being a headless, blood-soaked corpse on the floor to now standing next to the Cadillac Man with his head reattached no worse for the wear. He suddenly remembered the freezer and whirled around to see it lidless and empty behind him. Then, he remembered who'd been in it, and turned back to face the clerk-creature and the Cadillac Man.

Janine was a wreck, and despite the clerk's miraculous recovery she remained spattered in his gore. She saw the whole sequence completely from where she was standing including the gun disappearing from Rick's hand and reappearing in the Cadillac Man's like it had momentarily popped in and out of existence.

She saw the clerk on top of Thomas, she watched the already exaggerated teeth grow longer and sharper in the beast's mouth before he vanished nearly too fast to perceive. Now, he was standing next to the Cadillac Man blocking the only door, and he was laughing again.

Janine wanted to scream out her frustrations, and while she still had her voice, she lacked the ability to articulate her feelings and opted to remain silent. She'd never been one for talking anyway. She much preferred actions over words, and once the time was right, she was going to act. For now, she would stew on her emotions, and channel them into the formulation of her plan.

Rick didn't try to go for his gun, and frankly was glad

to be rid of the thing. He knew it was wrong to pull the trigger, knew it wouldn't work, or help, or contribute positively to the situation in any way. All he succeeded in doing was prolonging the inevitable.

Rick was ready to accept there was no way out of this, no way to escape the Cadillac Man and the dirty dealings he'd wrapped them up in. He looked over at Thomas who still seemed mildly unsure of what just occurred, but hopefully it was enough to shock him out of any hope for escape.

The woman, Janine; she wasn't ready to accept she'd been licked at all. Rick could practically hear the gears turning in her head behind eyes shifting back and forth between the clerk and the Cadillac Man. He admired her spirit but pitied her for the foolishness that would be her undoing. She wouldn't be going down without a fight.

"Are you satisfied?" The Cadillac Man asked the three of them. "Was the result of Rick's 'attempt' to . . . alter the current situation enough to tamp down any remaining embers of hope you may have smoldering in your tiny minds?"

None of them answered, and the clerk continued to laugh attempting to modulate between a giggle and a chuckle, which eventually became full-blown, knee-slapping laughter. The Cadillac Man held his palm up, and the clerk went silent mid-guffaw.

Rick felt Thomas's eyes on him and looked back over to meet them. Thomas's hands were at his sides, and he was clenching and un-clenching fingers into fists while rocking his weight back and forth between the balls of each foot. His eyes shot from Rick's to the clerk and the Cadillac Man, and then back to Rick's hoping the man understood his non-verbal communication. Rick picked up on the intent the man was trying to get across and was very much against it.

He knew Thomas was trying to signal that he was about to rush the two of them and wanted Rick to help him do it. Rick widened his eyes, tightened his jaw, and shook his head as subtly as possible, although he didn't know why he was being surreptitious about it? Quite frankly, he was having a hard time trying to understand why Thomas wanted to attempt something so foolish?

He thought maybe the man was still in a fog from the surprise freezer attack, but even so Rick thought he would have had some sense knocked into him at least. You couldn't surprise the Cadillac Man because he already knew before you tried. He knew everything.

Thomas grimaced to show his dislike of Rick's response to his call to action and nodded to say he would go it alone then. Rick flinched as something bumped up against his arm, and he looked to see Janine had backed away from the men at the door for the imagined safety of the counter. He looked past her to see the Cadillac Man staring at Thomas who was glaring back practically telegraphing his impending attack.

Rick saw Thomas was on the verge of an attempted strike and stepped past Janine intending to tackle him before he reached the Cadillac Man, but that was as far as he got.

"No, wait!" Rick cried.

It happened fast like a gunfight in the old west where the motion is so concise and smooth, you're already shot by the time you realize your opponent had fired. The heel of Thomas's right foot came away from the floor a fraction of an inch when the Cadillac Man had nodded at him halting his forward momentum.

Thomas was suddenly yanked backwards into the air with his head down, and arms and legs out in front of him like he'd been socked in the stomach by an oversized, invisible, boxing glove. He flew all the way to the back of the store and smacked against the freezer.

The lid shot up on its own and landed atop the freezer with a semi-silent hiss as the seal locked into place before the machine slid back up against the wall. Thomas was semi-conscious and groaned from the floor, his back still up against the appliance.

Afraid he knew what was coming next Rick turned quickly to grab Janine but was too late. She was already lunging for the Cadillac Man's neck.

————◆————

When he finally had a grip on himself and realized what he was doing Thomas pulled his face from the sloppy red pile he'd made of Erica and stepped away instantly revolted. He rubbed the back of his hand across his eyes smearing blood across his vision adding a morbidly red tint to the scene.

He took another step away from the bed, but his foot came down on something slick and meaty, and he slipped falling onto his back. The floor around him was wet with blood and flecked with discarded bits of gnawed gristle. Thomas sat up quickly and pushed himself back across the floor until he was out in the hallway. There, he was able to find enough purchase to get to his feet without slipping, but he dared not raise his head until he'd stepped past the open doorway. He couldn't bear to take in the entirety of what he'd done again, and instead made his way to the living room.

He started to run by the time he'd reached the end of the hall and made a beeline for the front door. A few of the ladies in the apartment complex had thrown Erica a small shower over the weekend and presents for the baby were in a stack next to the couch. Thomas stumbled into the pile sending several packs of diapers, some second-hand onesies, and a bag of loose pacifiers, bottle nipples, and three different sized rattles sprawling across the floor in front of him.

His forward momentum wouldn't allow him to correct his course, so Thomas continued through the pile. He stepped on one of the rattles and stumbled, and then slid on a diaper that had come loose of its package, but he maintained his balance this time. When he made it to the front door, he grabbed the knob but didn't turn it right away.

He turned to look one last time at the apartment he'd never get to see again. Thomas wanted the image burned into his brain, so he'd be able to remember what being happy was like, because he knew he'd never feel it again especially not after what he'd done in the bedroom.

Satisfied with the still image of a life he couldn't return to, Thomas yanked open the door and ran into the Cadillac Man. It startled him more than anything else, and he jumped back stepping again on a rattle, but was unable to catch himself this time. Thomas fell back into the pile of baby shower presents he'd kicked over, and immediately started to push himself across the floor away from the Cadillac Man.

When he smacked against the couch he cried out, but not in pain. He didn't want to go back to the Cadillac Man. He didn't want to feel the awful hunger again. He'd sooner die, but even his own mortality was out of his control.

The Cadillac Man stepped inside, and the door closed behind him on its own. He took slow, deliberate steps across the living room toward Thomas. He crushed a rattle and snapped the backs from pacifiers beneath the heel of his black boots. Thomas's wail turned to a whimper but fell completely silent when the Cadillac Man stood over him.

He looked up into eyes partially hiding behind long strands of blond hair as they narrowed in scrutiny of his pathetic state. If this were anybody else, if any regular person had him in such a vulnerable state Thomas would try to reason with them. He might try to barter for his freedom, or even his life.

He would beg and plead if it would help his situation, but Thomas wasn't dealing with a 'regular person' by any means, and already knew there was nothing he could do or offer now.

A smile slowly eked its way across the Cadillac Man's face as he shook his head and sighed.

"Get up Thomas," he said. "You know what to do."

He did too. Thomas knew exactly what to do.

The moving truck was out in the parking lot where the Cadillac Man said it would be, and the keys were dangling from the ignition. Thomas backed it against the short sidewalk leading up to the front door of his apartment and hopped out leaving the truck running. He walked around and unlatched the backdoor, but only slid it open about two inches rather than all the way up.

Thomas paused midway to his door and looked around. He hoped not to see any of the few familiar faces he knew in the complex even though it didn't matter if they saw him or not. Once he rolled out of town the Cadillac Man would make sure no one remembered seeing him load the truck, because no one would remember he existed.

It was more for him since he couldn't bear the added guilt of having to look any of them in the face while pretending everything was okay, which would be a hard sell regardless since he was covered in blood. Once the Cadillac Man worked his magic Thomas would be erased from their minds completely.

The door swung open on its own as he approached, and he walked through the living room, down the hall, and back into the bedroom where the Cadillac Man waited. Without speaking Thomas un-tucked the sheets from between the mattress and box spring and pulled the four corners up together keeping the remains of Erica contained in the makeshift sack.

She was mostly bones and mush now, so it was easy for him to carry the bedding with her in it back out through the apartment and throw in the back of the moving truck. When he latched the door and turned around, he saw the shiny red trail he'd left behind. It cut the sidewalk down the center lengthwise like the jagged incision of an untrained hand.

Thomas started for the apartment but stopped short when he saw the Cadillac Man standing just inside the open door shaking his head. There was nothing else he needed to take with him. Thomas lowered his head, made his way back to the truck, and climbed up into the driver's seat. He buckled his seatbelt, adjusted the side mirror, and looked up just in time to see a black Cadillac exit the parking lot.

It moved up the road away from the apartment complex with a sleek fluidity of gliding on a street paved in black ice. Thomas watched the car make the bend and disappear before slipping the truck into gear. The sun was beginning to set, and despite the lingering warmth, Thomas caught a sudden chill. He rolled up the window as he maneuvered the box truck through the parking lot, and had the heat turned on by the time he reached the exit.

He looked down the road the Cadillac Man had driven and turned out of the lot in the opposite direction. He couldn't get rid of the chill despite increasing the temperature of the cab, but after a few more miles he got used to it. He merged onto the freeway and did his best to maneuver using only the side mirrors.

He didn't realize he'd just cut off the big black Cadillac.

———— ♦ ————

Janine planned to sink her fingernails into the Cadillac Man's soft, pink neck like she had done to so many of the women he'd brought to her. She could practically feel the skin being pierced and broken, and once she had a grip she'd pull until handfuls of wet flesh came back. She would bring it to her mouth while continuing to rip with the other hand and spit the mouthfuls back in his face. That would show the Cadillac Man what she thought of his 'hunger'.

Janine thought she heard someone call out from behind her to stop, but she wouldn't have been able to if she wanted, and she did *not* want to stop. Something unexpected happened when she made contact though. The give she'd expected to feel was absent and replaced by something hard and solid like the stone of a statue.

The tips of Janine's fingers bent back on contact snapping the bones at the first knuckle of all eight fingers. The sound was loud, and while it reminded Rick of a string of firecrackers going off the successive crack of breaking bone made him flinch.

Janine heard her fingers break before she felt any pain as her brain tried to make sense of what went wrong in her attack. Reeling she stepped back thinking at first, she'd missed her intended target and hit the glass door behind him, but that couldn't be right because the Cadillac Man was still standing right in front of her. She looked from his smirking face down to her ruined fingers unwilling to process what she was seeing.

With the broken digits her hands looked foreign like they belonged to some kind of animal with double-jointed fingers for climbing mobility, and it was confusing to see such appendages attached to the end of *her* arms. She felt warm wetness meandering down the lines of her palms and looked closer to see the skin was broken on several of her fingers. The jagged edges of red-rimmed bone peeked out from holes they tore through Janine's skin at the breaking points.

The pain hit fast and sharp like all eight wounds were competing for intensity. They all sent their excruciating signal through nerve receptors to her brain with each arriving a fraction of a second later than the last. In the moment she inhaled before unleashing a tortured wail the brief silence was polluted by the clerk's laughter. The pitch of his voice had changed now having shifted into a deep atonal resonance, the very sound of which conjured images of wickedness.

The mixture of Janine's screams and the clerk's evil upsetting laughter morphed into a sharp dissonance that physically hurt Rick to hear, so he slapped his hands against his ears. The sound turned Rick's stomach sour, and he leaned back hard against the counter now grabbing at his gut.

99

It didn't take long for the sour feeling to turn into hunger, and he attempted to fight the oncoming sensation from overtaking him unsuccessfully. He didn't even know why he was still trying. Rick opened his eyes and looked past the free-flowing gout of blood from Janine's broken fingers to the Cadillac Man just as he raised his hand again to silence the clerk's laughter.

The combined sound of laughter and screaming was so disruptive Rick didn't notice it stopped, because he had to adjust to hearing silence again. The Cadillac Man had quieted both the clerk *and* Janine this time with the motion of his hand. Rick understood why the clerk reacted as such since he was simply an imp named Jacobi conjured and controlled by the Cadillac Man, but Janine was clearly in agony, and it would take more than a *shushin'* to shut her up.

Rick saw the reason she'd quieted down so quickly when the woman turned around. She didn't have a mouth anymore.

Her lips weren't sealed shut by adhesive or sewn together with tightly spaced sutures. There was just nothing. Not even a trace of something having ever existed in the space on her face, and Rick inadvertently moved his hands up to his own mouth relieved to find it was still there.

Janine brought the bleeding, broken ends of fingers to the empty spot on her face, and the panic in her eyes reflected a new heightened level of fear as what happened sank in. She raked her busted open fingertips across the lower half of her face trying to pierce it with the exposed bone, but all she did was smear the area with blood, as the flesh would not be penetrated.

Rick felt another hunger pang lurch through his gut and looked over at Janine still uselessly pawing at a mouth-less face succeeding at nothing but using her mangled fingers to push blood around.

———— ◆ ————

Janine was in a full panic, and any form of commonsense or logic was completely overridden by the emotion. Even the pain in her fingers had been pushed aside, for the moment at least, with all effort and available mindshare being used to open a mouth that was no longer there.

She desperately tried to tear into the lip-less patch of flesh but couldn't manage to break the skin. Janine smeared so much blood across her face she could no longer find purchase against the slimy red skin. She wanted to scream, tried to scream, but couldn't get her vocal cords to work either.

Janine couldn't even muster a grunt, a groan, or any sound whatsoever, but she stopped trying as soon as she realized something else was changing. With the absence of a mouth Janine had been ferociously breathing through her nose pulling in air and blood with each inhale while blowing out blood and snot on the exhale. It was suddenly becoming harder for her to pull those breaths in and force them back out, because her nostrils had started to close.

Janine's nasal passages weren't being restricted by the congregation of fluids, or because her sinus cavities were beginning to swell. Something else was working to steadily narrow the holes in her face, and the sensation she felt as it happened was so unnatural, so different that under other circumstances she might have found it was pleasurable or even erotic. Right now, though, there was nothing enjoyable about the experience.

The flesh within her nostrils was fusing together, and slowly constricted her breathing as it filled the remaining empty space. Just as her airways were nearly choked off Janine felt the skin between her nose and where her upper lip had once been begin to move like tiny hands were inside kneading it into dough. A moment later the square-inch of writhing flesh leapt up covering her nostrils and flattening the cartilage in her nose down against her face.

Janine couldn't speak, and she couldn't breathe, but she could still feel. Her broken fingers had swollen into plump, purple sausages, and the skin around them was tight and thin like a water balloon filled to the point of exploding. She could feel her heartbeat through the broken exposed bones like the pulsing shock from touching a fork stuck in the wall socket repeatedly.

She dropped to her knees defeated, shoulders slumped, arms at her sides. Her lungs were starting to burn from lack of oxygen, and they pushed into her ribs and back still full of the last breath she'd managed to seize. Janine didn't realize her ears had closed up because there was nothing to hear. Silence hung in the truck stop like ugly drapes nobody wanted to talk about, thick and uncomfortable.

Through watery eyes Janine looked up at the Cadillac Man, but could only think of her father, because she knew he was the reason she was here. Janine was nothing more than something to barter to him. She was like a pig he sold at the market without a second thought, and now she was off to the slaughter as he went about his day.

The Cadillac Man offered a smile that harbored no sympathy, but she hadn't expected any from him. The flow of Janine's tears stopped, and she felt the odd sensation of flesh rearranging itself on her face again. There was a slight pressure at her temples and her vision was obscured by sentient dermis as it crawled across each eye to meet in the middle.

Janine was dead only a moment before her eyes were completely covered with the last thing she saw being the Cadillac Man's face, then his boots, and that was that.

The lack of oxygen hadn't been what killed her, though. Thomas got to her before she had a chance to suffocate. She didn't hear him coming because she couldn't, and she was almost blind just before it happened, so she was unable to detect motion in her peripheral. The pain in her lungs and hands was so intense she didn't feel him ripping her throat out, which was the last her heart could take before rupturing a valve.

———————◆———————

Rick hadn't seen the skin close up around Janine's mouth, and after watching what happened to the rest of her, he was glad he didn't. She couldn't make any noise, but she didn't need to for him to know she was suffering. He could see it all in her eyes, and since those were the last to go the excruciation of her final moments played out for Rick through them.

It looked like the lower portion of her face folded itself up over her nose completely covering her nostrils obliterating its shape leaving the area flat and formless. When she fell to her knees Rick saw her left ear was now a pink mound, and he assumed the same had happened on the right, but her hair covered that side of her head.

An inhuman, primal, scream pushed its way from deep in Thomas's belly where the hunger lived bringing with it foamy saliva flecked with bile. Rick didn't notice the man had roused from being thrown against the freezer, but now Thomas stood within feet of him. He was on Janine in an instant diving for her neck as she'd attempted with the Cadillac Man only he was able to achieve the desired result.

With an impossibly strong grip his fingers dug in easily and pulled the left side of Janine's neck away bringing her torn jugular with it. The spray was amazing as the dangerously high blood pressure she was experiencing shot blood from her neck like a wide-open fire hydrant. It didn't last long though since the extreme rush exploded her heart. Rick could tell the moment it happened too.

The blood-spray he'd been hit with dripped into his eye casting a murky, crimson, haze across his vision. He wiped it away with his fingers, and watched Thomas take the girl quite literally apart. He'd completely separated the head from her body and lapped at the flow from her neck until it dwindled to a trickle.

He ripped her open next grabbing the inside of her

neck and pulling apart the flesh along her throat until he reached the ribcage. Thomas repositioned himself, adjusted his grip, and cracked open her chest with a satisfying snap. Then, he thrust his face into the opening he'd created before the echo of the sound could decay. The furiousness of Thomas's mastication was punctuated by the feverish frenzy of his attack.

The viciousness with which he tore and devoured hunks of organs was like that of a wild animal gone mad with hunger, and he couldn't seem to eat Janine's inside meat fast enough. Rick looked up from the disaster to see the Cadillac Man smirking while he watched, but oddly enough for the first time the clerk was not smiling.

He hadn't made a sound since being silenced by a wave of the Cadillac Man's hand but had continued wearing the sarcastic shit-eating grin on his face until now. The clerk scowled now like something between a sneer and a sulk, which added a more disturbing touch to his already abstract features.

Without his permanent smile the clerk looked downright evil.

Rick noticed the clerk rocking ever so slightly back and forth on the balls of his feet and glanced down to see the Cadillac Man had a tight hold on his forearm.

He was holding him back.

———————— ♦ ————————

While it felt like forever the whole thing was over as fast as it started. Thomas withdrew from Janine's now semi-hollow torso and sat back on the floor with one leg out in front of him, and the other pulled up to his chest. He leaned his blood painted face against his bent knee and looked off at nothing like he was trying to give the thousand-yard stare a run for its money. The rage his face so recently displayed now changed to show the pitiful sorrow that comes with being broken.

Rick heard something and looked up from Thomas's

mess to the now very agitated clerk who was grinding his teeth. There was an underlying growl woven into the unsettling sound adding a shrill harmony to the invasiveness of its tone. The clerk was rocking much faster now, and the cold white skin on his arm turned a dark purple color around the Cadillac Man's grip as he held the imp at bay.

Rick's stomach turned again, but from nausea this time while the hunger still nagged regardless of his revulsion. He looked back down at Thomas. His eyes told him the man had retreated deep into himself, and Rick envied his mental escape despite the wretched triggers required to bring it on.

The clerk started panting, and while the grinding stopped the growling intensified. The skin on his arm was broken around the Cadillac Man's grasp, and the purplish/red blood oozed out from between the thin white fingers. The clerk's frenzy had clearly reached its apex, and now he would need satisfaction.

He suddenly barked like an auto-tuned Doberman, and the uncomfortably pitched sound snapped Thomas from his trance. Wide-eyed he jerked his head back and looked up at the clerk. He then looked back down at what was left of Janine on the floor in front of him, and immediately managed to scramble to his feet without slipping in the blood he'd been sitting in.

Thomas looked from the clerk to the Cadillac Man, and back to the clerk who opened his mouth wide. He released a multi-pitched, inhuman shriek like the miserable lamenting of a children's choir being boiled alive. Without hesitation Thomas leapt over the pile of Janine and ran past the clerk and the Cadillac Man toward the freezer. The clerk snapped at him as he rushed by, but the Cadillac Man held the monster in place.

Thomas came to a sliding stop, threw open the newly attached lid of the freezer, and hopped inside letting it fall closed behind him. The Cadillac Man let go of his arm, and the clerk leapt to the freezer with a remarkably unnatural quickness. He grabbed the lid just before the seal touched down, threw it back open, and jumped in on the heels of Thomas.

The door fell closed with a thud and seemed to suck the air out of the truck stop leaving it momentarily caught in a vacuum silence. Rick glanced over at the Cadillac Man who'd not taken his eyes off the freezer. When Rick looked back the freezer door burst open, and a geyser of blood exploded from within.

———————•◆•———————

There was such a tremendous amount of blood it would have been almost comical any other time, but now it was only truly terrifying. It rocketed out from the freezer with enough force to hit the ceiling, which shot spatter across the room all the way to the counter. The tops of Rick's shoes were dotted in red, and he felt the warm, wet sprinkles hit his forehead but made no effort to wipe them away.

As the geyser slowed a crimson wave rolled over the side of the freezer in a steady gush as if the tide was coming in. It suddenly didn't matter that blood had gotten on Rick's shoes, because he now found himself standing in the stuff up to his ankles. The blood leaked beneath the shelves and covered the entire center aisle of the small store in an inch of opaque red liquid before the flow finally tapered off.

Rick looked around and realized there wasn't a single object or surface in the entire store that hadn't been touched by blood, until he saw the Cadillac Man who'd somehow been spared the mess. His blond hair was clean and effortlessly in place as usual, and his suit remained in pristine condition.

Even the Cadillac Man's boots were clean and stayed that way as if somehow repelling the blood. Rick wasn't surprised, though. He knew the Cadillac Man didn't like getting his *own* hands dirty, which was why he bartered his magic for vessels.

He needed them to do the work, to consume the flesh, and by being bound to these vessels he was able to live. The Cadillac Man absorbed the energy he required through the death they produced, and when they'd been all used up, he collected the living receptacles absorbing them completely and finally into himself.

The twisted, parasitic relationships between the Cadillac Man and those he did business with had been going on since before time as we know it existed, and no one ever refused his gifts. This allowed him to thrive for millennia without ever going hungry. There was always someone more than willing to trade on the lives of their loved ones for their wish to be granted, and there always would be.

This was why Janine's moist and hollowed husk lay before Rick, or at least what the tidal wave of blood hadn't washed up against the far wall, and he knew Thomas wasn't coming back out of that freezer.

But he was supposed to be different, right?

Rick figured the only reason he knew the things he did about the Cadillac Man was because of a unique connection the two of them shared. He wracked his brain trying to remember what the Cadillac Man had said about it, tried to recall what exactly it was, but he couldn't until he looked up from the floor and met his eyes.

Because I chose this.

Rick heard himself say it in his head before he said it out loud.

"Because I chose this."

The Cadillac Man smiled and pointed back to the freezer. The blood was starting to bubble over again.

———————◆———————

Rick was right. It wasn't Thomas's head that breached the surface of the blood-filled freezer a moment behind the bubbles, and while it was the clerk his appearance had been altered again. His face had become more monstrous, and despite being covered in blood Rick could tell scales had replaced his skin. Jacobi wasn't playing 'dress up' anymore. This was his actual visage.

His nose was flattened back against his face like a bat, and pointy, bone tips protruded from the tops of his razor-sharp cheekbones. His hair was gone and replaced by spiky, bone protrusions of varying length that jutted from his head like dozens of sharpened finger bones. The pale-blue, truck stop, uniform shirt was gone as well, and while Rick couldn't yet see the clerk's lower half, figured the pants were gone too.

Blood ran off his shoulders and chest and rolled in thin rivulets between the scales serving to highlight their separation. He grabbed the lip of the freezer to pull himself up and over sloshing more blood and sending another small waterfall pouring down the sides. His long, white fingers were punctuated by sharp, black tips extending exaggeratingly long from each one.

As soon as he was out of the freezer the lid slammed down shut behind him. Rick was more than sure that if he were to re-open it right now the blood would be gone, and so would Thomas. The clerk's pants were missing, just as Rick had guessed, and his lower half was equally as white and scaly. In place of genitalia was a flat smooth bump like that of a genderless doll, and thick blue veins crisscrossed through the area before plunging down the inside of his legs.

The clerk, now in his natural form as Jacobi, stood and stared across the store at Rick. His yellow, red-rimmed eyes were bigger now, rounder. Rick could feel the heat of their glare piercing into his head and hoped the creature would turn away before his brain cooked inside his skull.

The blood continued to run down the white, scaly, muscled body of the creature, which made for a terrifying presentation of crimson-soaked horror. The blood caught beneath the scales gave them the strikingly sinister look of a thousand closed eyelids weeping red tears.

The blood was starting to find its way through cracks and under doors leaving shallow, red puddles lingering in the low spots of the floor. Jacobi took heavy, deliberate steps toward Rick splashing through the remnants of the flood like an obnoxious child after a rainstorm. Rick looked to the Cadillac Man who was still looking at the creature striding across the store with a confident stomp.

Rick had no idea what he was supposed to do? He thought the Cadillac Man would do something, say something, but it was becoming increasingly obvious there would be no intervention as Jacobi was now within six feet. His stomach suddenly cramped hard again, and Rick's mouth filled with a liquid he thought was bile at first but was saliva instead.

The hunger fell sudden and heavy reflexively sending his salivary glands into overdrive. Drool ran from the corners of his mouth to his chin where it hung in long slimy strands before falling to mix with the blood at his feet. Out of the corner of his eye Rick saw the Cadillac Man looking at him now, and he was smiling.

Jacobi opened a mouth overcrowded with pointed teeth sprouting from his gums at all angles with chunks of partially masticated flesh stuck in the spaces between, Thomas's flesh. Jacobi lunged for Rick's throat and was on in him an instant, but the creature didn't realize he was far from in control of the situation.

When Jacobi made his move Rick did as well leaping into the beast while maneuvering his soft neck flesh away from the impending bite. He didn't realize he'd sunk his own teeth into Jacobi's scale-covered shoulder until his mouth filled with blood.

The beast shrieked and thrashed trying to shake Rick off, and he pushed uselessly against the chest of the man whose mouth was attached to his shoulder. The struggle was useless, and Rick clamped down harder provoking desperation in the creature's frantic scream.

Jacobi stumbled backwards and Rick rode him to the ground while ripping away the hunk of shoulder he'd filled his mouth with. He quickly spit it out and wasted no time going back in for another bite, this time further up around the neck. The blood came hard and fast overfilling Rick's mouth before he could swallow, and he pulled away to let the spray flow freely.

The creature writhed and bucked beneath him, but despite the great power Jacobi possessed he could not get out from under his attacker. It was like Rick had suddenly been filled with lead or was able to manipulate gravity making his pull against the Earth much stronger than anyone else's. Whatever he was doing kept the Cadillac Man's imp pinned against the floor unable to escape.

Rick's face was coated in the red and purple tint of Jacobi's blood, and as he went in for another bite it flowed down his chin past the collar of his shirt soaking it while covering the upper half of his torso in the stuff. The imp was still screaming in agony begging for the help of his master until his voice softened from cries to a whisper. Rick expected at any second the Cadillac Man would pull him off Jacobi and toss him effortlessly across the truck stop, but the help Jacobi pleaded for did not come.

Still, Rick worked with the fevered intensity of a death row inmate gorging himself on his final meal before taking the long walk to the gas chamber. He fit as much flesh into his mouth as he could before tearing another hunk away spitting it off to the side. He wanted Jacobi's head and worked fast and efficiently to gnaw away at what was left of the flesh attaching it to the body.

Rick went back in for another bite, and his teeth closed around something hard. He'd hit the spinal column and would have to work around it for now. He pulled away and bit into to the other side of Jacobi's neck, but the creature barely reacted when the first chunk was ripped away. He wasn't dead yet but getting close, and Rick could feel Jacobi's body shudder beneath him as he continued to rip through connective tissue with his teeth.

Jacobi wasn't screaming or talking anymore and could only manage a soft grunt from what little was left of his throat. A few bites later Rick found himself on the other side of the spinal column, and he pulled back to see the thin, cylindrical bones were the only thing keeping Jacobi's body attached to his head. It was an odd sight, cartoonish.

Rick grabbed the exposed spinal column with both hands and repositioned himself with one foot was on Jacobi's chest, and the other on the floor next to him. Then, he pulled with all his might, which had somehow been magnified since the attack began. Rick wasn't tough or strong, and he didn't work out or do anything really when it came to exercise.

He was just an average sized guy with no visible muscle tone, and a small, soft paunch big enough to just hang over the front of his pants. Rick shouldn't have been able to overpower and subdue Jacobi, and he shouldn't have been able to do what he was about to, but he remained undeterred.

He adjusted his feet for leverage and was about to pull when he saw the creature's eyes grow wide, and its mouth open and close soundlessly like a fish out of water. There was no reason it should still be alive but based on what had happened in the truck stop so far it wasn't surprising.

Rick tightened his grip around the spinal cord and pulled up with all his might. There was a muffled pop followed by a wet slurp as the head slid free. With the resistance broken Rick slowly lifted the head with a little more than half of the spinal cord dangling. The separation occurred at one of the lower vertebrae, and what was left hung from the base of the detached head like a grotesque tail.

Rick held the head up and looked it in the eyes satisfied with the absence of life in them, but then he heard the laughter. He was looking right at the clerk's severed head and could clearly see the mouth was not moving. The lower half of his jaw fell slack leaving his mouth partially open with the tip of his tongue barely breaching the lips and hanging to the left.

Rick was confused and examined the head again trying to pinpoint the laughter before he realized it was coming from behind him. He took his foot off Jacobi's chest and turned around to see it was coming from the Cadillac Man. Rick held the head up high above his own and started to laugh as well.

———————◆———————

When Rick was a much younger boy, well before he set his teacher on fire, he learned about evil the way most children his age did from Sunday school classes in a stuffy church basement. The lessons were cryptic and distorted through the lens of religion, and served mostly to confuse and instill fear, which would make the children easily controllable when they reached adulthood.

While their message was based on fabrications and fairy tales the church was right about one thing. There was good reason to fear, but not because it scared people into falling in line. The reality of evil was far beyond the grasp of any scholar religious or otherwise, and what made it so scary was the lack of rhyme or reason.

True evil, the very real kind of evil adheres to no rules or boundaries. It is a force existing solely to perpetuate its existence by any means necessary. There are no prayers to dissuade it, no magical items able to repel it, and no deity to stand in its way. There is no great conqueror of evil from the past with plans to come back and stop it once and for all, and there is not one prophesied to come.

Evil is chaos controlled only for evil's sake and is distributed in many forms. Its solitary goal is to absorb as much energy as possible by way of extraction from its victims. It chooses indiscriminately from hordes of human cattle without concern for innocence or purity, nor does it yield for any amount of karma. This is the answer to the question of why bad things happen to good people.

The truth is it doesn't matter how good or bad you are, how you treat your fellow man, or how much you believe in anything. Any god that's ever been conceived, taught on, or followed has always only been another extension of evil. To say their intent is thinly veiled would be an understatement in that they've all killed, lied, and misled while continuing to feed off the energy of their followers. The ones who loved them the most always find a way to justify their god's action, or rationalize it away as being part of something bigger, something more important not meant to be understood by human beings.

No matter what form evil manifests itself in it figures out a way to keep the cycle going. The Cadillac Man does it by granting small, surface wishes in exchange for feasts made up of entire families, or even entire tribes of people. He sated his appetite for misery on countless *Thomases* and *Janines,* and while Rick was more of an anomaly it didn't make a difference. The Cadillac Man's ruse was simple, but so were human beings, and it had yet to prove ineffective.

He'd spent millennia perfecting his methods of misfortune and knew how to pull suffering out of his victims from a mostly mental perspective. Physical suffering was more instantly gratifying, but mental suffering could be made to drag on for a lifetime and thereby more sustaining by far. The Cadillac Man knew all the right carrots to dangle, and all the right fancies to tickle to ensure evil never went hungry.

It didn't make a difference how a person came to grasp the concept of 'evil', because few ever came to have a true understanding, and even fewer would admit to it. Rick was born with the understanding. It was inherent, which made him an excellent tool for the Cadillac Man to wield easily especially since he was able to get to him at such a young age.

Now, it was time for Rick to be put out to pasture, but not before using him one last time

————•————

His boots were surprisingly clean when he slid behind the wheel of the slick, black, behemoth of a car. The Cadillac Man pulled the door shut and adjusted the rearview mirror catching the reflection of flames forcing themselves through the narrow space around the front door of the truck stop. The fire worked its way up the front of the building, as he turned the key in the ignition bringing the massive engine beneath the hood of the Cadillac to life.

The glass door exploded open, and the sudden rush of additional oxygen stoked the flames into a giant fiery frenzy. They shot through the new opening with an intensity that made the building look like a fire-breathing beast. The Cadillac Man chuckled as he shifted the car into gear and eased past the pumps on his way to exiting the parking lot.

He brought the car to a full stop at the edge of the ramp and clicked the lever next to the steering wheel down to activate the left-hand turn signal despite there being no traffic for miles in either direction. A second, smaller explosion came from inside the burning truck stop, this one launching unrecognizable, charred projectiles all the way to the gas pumps.

A smoldering chunk of debris nearly made it as far as the back of the big, black Cadillac, but rolled to a stop four feet short of its bumper. The thing was blackened and had taken a lot of damage from bouncing off the cement drive, but it was still recognizable as Jacobi's skull. The teeth were a dead giveaway, and the sharp, high cheekbones gave added confirmation.

The Cadillac Man put the car in reverse and backed up until he heard the burned-up skull crunch beneath the fat, rear tire of the driver side. He stopped, shifted back into drive, and stomped on the gas kicking a mixture of skull and gravel up as the Cadillac peeled out of the parking lot, and made a wide, sweeping, left turn in the direction of the highway.

The imp's head had been a trophy for Rick, a symbol of his understanding. He understood in that moment the true unbridled chaos in which evil existed, as well as the ends it would go to in order to ensure its survival. Rick also knew he wasn't going to make it out of the truck stop alive, but more importantly he knew why. Evil was indiscriminate, and because of that The Cadillac Man spared no one. Not even those who came to him willingly.

As the menacing, classic, black car roared up the service ramp and entered the expressway another larger and louder explosion came from behind. The Cadillac Man couldn't see anything of the truck stop in his rearview mirror anymore save for the yellow sign with black letters standing out against the purple curtain of dusk.

The sun was already below the horizon throwing the final rays of the day like a hail Mary offered up to whomever was in the right place at the right time to witness. The last of the light played off the dark clouds rolling in outlining them in pink and orange. In the distance thunder was announcing its intentions for the rest of the evening while flashes of lightning signaled their approval.

The clouds blotted out any light the moon could muster, and as the last remnants of the sun's illumination were pulled behind the Earth darkness arrived in its entirety. A raindrop hit the Cadillac's windshield before an even fatter one spread wide on impact and followed immediately by a slew of larger drops working to distort the road in front of him.

The windshield wipers kept the kaleidoscopic rain from obscuring his vision, and the powerful headlights slashed a clear path through the wet darkness. The Cadillac Man gently pressed the accelerator to the floor, and the engine responded accordingly roaring through the night at top speed unaffected by the weather.

The Cadillac Man drove all night to his next appointment without stopping. It rained nearly the whole way but cleared up about an hour before sunrise. As he crested the hill there was a sign indicating a diner was coming up ahead. The Cadillac Man let up on the gas, engaged his right turn signal, and exited the highway.

Part II
The Detective

James stared out his window paying attention to nothing except the black Cadillac. It was the third time it passed by tonight, but he'd seen it before. The first time was after he'd had a fight at school.

He tried to explain to his parents how it wasn't his fault but was met with a backhand from his father followed by a month of being grounded. James had been looking out his window on that night as well, but through bleary tear-filled eyes. His left cheek was warm where his father slapped him and stung when he used his hand to wipe away the tears.

He was crying too hard and was too angry to really pay attention to anything, and the black Cadillac wouldn't have registered with him if it hadn't slowed down so much in front of his house. It wasn't uncommon for people to drive extra-slow down his street since the speed limit was only twenty miles per hour. Plus, there were usually groups of kids playing football or hockey in the middle of the street, which would slow any traffic down significantly.

It was dark out though, so no kids were playing, but still the Cadillac crept along slowing to a complete stop in front of James's house. At first, he thought it might be someone his parents knew and were expecting, but it only stopped for a moment before suddenly speeding away. The car raced down the street and out of sight with no regard for the posted speed limit.

James didn't think much of it even when he saw the same car drive by a week later, but when he saw it again two days after that he started to pay attention. Now he'd seen the Cadillac drive by four nights in a row, but this was the first time it drove past more than once in a twenty-four-hour period.

Tonight though, James was looking for the car because of the dream he'd had. The night before the Cadillac was in his dream, and so was the driver. James couldn't tell who was driving the car during his waking life since he only saw it at night, plus the windows were too drastically tinted to see inside regardless.

In his dream James was sitting at his window looking out at a street shrouded by darkness and twisted in the way dreams change the familiar. People and places typically become frightful parodies when projected through the subconscious lens, and James had many dreams in which he experienced these grotesque stand-ins for reality.

The street was quiet and empty in the dream, and James could see only darkness beyond the other side instead of Mr. Mere's house, which was directly across from his. In reality he would be able to see the house clearly, and on many occasions, James had unfortunately seen the older man walk past his unobstructed bedroom window naked.

James wasn't sure if Mr. Mere did this on purpose hoping to give some random passerby a cheap thrill, or if he was oblivious. There was also the possibility he was just an old guy who didn't care who saw him or not, because he wanted the curtains open at all times and that was that.

There was no house, or naked old men in James's dream though; there was just darkness. He knew he wasn't looking at a black wall erected to obscure his view either, because there was depth to this darkness. It looked thick and deep like it would take a long time to make it all the way through, but resistance caused by its consistency would make an attempt impossible.

The darkness wasn't advancing across the street toward him, but it was moving. It pulsed, and rippled like it was breathing, but stayed contained on the other side of the curb where James's old, naked neighbor's house should have been.

In the dream James started off looking through the window but found himself suddenly on the front porch sitting in one of the rocking chairs his parents kept there. A moment later the street lit up in front of his house from the headlights of an approaching vehicle. He knew it was the black Cadillac before it fully came into view, but instead of slowing down before passing by the car stopped right in front of the driveway.

James wanted to get up and go inside, but was unable to move from the chair, so he remained seated and waited. The Cadillac idled for a few moments before the door swung open, and the Cadillac Man stepped out into the street. He was tall and thin wearing what James remembered thinking was a very dapper suit. It was as black as the car itself, but different from the darkness across the street.

The thing that stood out most about the Cadillac Man was the shock of blond hair atop his head. It hung just past his shoulders and was lying across his eyes as he began to walk up the drive toward the porch. Everything inside of James was telling him to get up and run, but he had no control over his body. James could see the paleness of the man's complexion from where he sat since the extreme lack of color gave the impression it was glowing.

The Cadillac Man walked up to James, stood before him, and brushed the hair from his eyes. They were shiny and black with deep crimson marbling and stood out in a ghastly fashion against the Cadillac Man's ultra-fair complexion. James should have been terrified by this man, and in fact couldn't think of any circumstance in which he wouldn't be, but for some reason he wasn't.

Despite having seemingly no control over his body the presence of the Cadillac Man was calming, soothing even. James had never seen this man before yet there was air of familiarity about him like they'd been old friends forever.

"Hello James."

The Cadillac Man's voice was icy but smooth with an intangibly enchanting tone that left you wanting to hear him speak more words, any words even if they didn't make sense.

"I believe we are in the position to help each other."

James tried to reply but was still paralyzed. He wanted to ask what the man meant, but also wanted to know who he was, and why he was here? The Cadillac Man extended his hand, and James found himself suddenly able to move as he watched his own hand reach out to accept the stranger's handshake. He woke up as soon as their hands touched.

This was why James sat at his window tonight looking for the Cadillac, and watching it pass by each time wondering when or if the connection would be made. There was a good possibility he'd just dreamed this all up out of random instances his brain stored and put together in dream form with no context or direction, but he dropped that theory when he saw the Cadillac stopped in front of his house.

James stood and backed from the window keeping a close eye on the Cadillac. When the driver stepped out and James saw it was the same thin, blond, pale man he saw in his dream he was paralyzed either by fear, or an outside influence.

The Cadillac Man stood in the street next to his car looking through the window directly at James beckoning with a gesture of his hand for the boy to join him.

———————◆———————

Amelia wasn't ready although she'd spent the better part of the morning convincing herself she was. It wasn't like this was a surprise, or something that snuck up on her. This had been coming for some time, and now the day was here. Not even having prior knowledge and understanding of the 'how' and 'why' behind it all did little to assuage her fear.

She grew up knowing there was no such thing as a free lunch, and this day would eventually come. Amelia had told herself more times than she could count that she'd be ready for this and would even look forward to it the closer it got, but it was all lip service. She always knew in the back of her mind it was only a front to hide the fear from herself, or at the very least downplay its severity.

She sat in a booth alone at the *Roadside 55 Diner* aptly named for its location on the side of highway 55 where it served as an oasis of sorts since there were no other businesses for twenty miles in both directions. She'd arrived early and was on her third cup of coffee when she checked her watch wondering if she should call James just to check on him. When they spoke earlier in the morning, he told her he would be there at ten a.m. and it was only five after, so she decided to wait five more minutes before reaching out.

Amelia tried to suppress the thought of James standing her up, but each tick of the clock made it that much harder to block out. He wouldn't leave her there to take it all on alone, would he? She couldn't imagine James doing something like this, but they'd both done many things they never thought they would from the very start of their relationship with him, with the Cadillac Man.

Him not showing up would be tantamount to suicide, and he knew it. There was no running or hiding from this, because there simply was nowhere to run, and no place to hide. Once they'd met the Cadillac Man, he was tied to them, and would remain so until . . . she didn't really know when? It wouldn't be today she knew for sure. Today would be only the beginning of the *really* hard work.

Amelia thought there was a slight possibility it would

be all over once they completed their part, but she wasn't able to get her hopes up about it. Hope was something she'd let go of a long time ago.

She wondered if she and James would have had a different kind of relationship without the shared tether to the Cadillac Man? They went to the same elementary, middle, and high school, but if not for the single communality Amelia doubted they'd have been anything more than ancillary acquaintances. She ran in much different social circles than James who mostly kept to himself, but not because he'd been a social outcast.

He knew the Cadillac Man longer and had in fact brought him to her as a sort of broker of their relationship. Amelia used to think James would get some kind of break by bringing her in like they do at the gym where they entice you into forcing a friend to join in order to save ten bucks. She didn't think that anymore. Not after what she'd already seen and been through. Amelia was convinced there were no breaks as far as the Cadillac Man was concerned.

Her interaction wasn't as brutal as the relationship James and the Cadillac Man had, but he was vague and secretive when it came to any discussion regarding the matter, so she'd stopped trying to pry. She came to know the blond man in the black suit when she was seventeen, and while she could tell James had more of a history with him, she had no idea how far back it went?

James's parents weren't alive anymore by the time Amelia had come to know him, and he'd been left with a grandparent for a legal guardian. It didn't matter which grandparent because it was never true to begin with. It appeared that way on paper, but James had been on his own since his parents' death with only the Cadillac Man left in his life.

It made sense why he was so secretive and low-key at school and made sure he never drew any unnecessary attention to himself, or really any attention at all. She used to think he was a slacker burnout when she'd see him stare off blankly during classes not bothering to take a single note. Little did she know he was recovering from being out all night with . . . him. It also didn't matter if he paid attention to anything because his grades were already secured by the Cadillac Man. James could literally turn in a blank test with only his name at the top and receive an A.

She could've had a deal similar to his, but she was already halfway through her senior year, and the thought of being absolved of all schoolwork did not occur to her at the time of her deal. Back then Amelia would have gladly done all her work for the entire school year over again, or even three times just to be rid of him, of *them*.

The waitress filled Amelia's empty coffee cup for the fourth time breaking her from her fog of her thoughts.

"Were you ready to order any food, or you still good with coffee, hon?" asked the waitress who was entirely too young to be calling Amelia 'hon'.

"No thank you," she replied. "Just coffee is fine for now. I'm expecting somebody . . . "

Amelia trailed off as she looked back out the window just in time to see James's old Chevy pickup pull into the lot.

"Just let me know when you're ready."

The waitress moved to fill coffees for the patrons one booth over, and Amelia stared at the truck waiting for the door to open. She knew it was James, but she needed to actually see him to set herself at ease. The door swung open with a rusty screech she could hear through the window, and Amelia realized she was wrong.

Seeing James didn't make her feel better, and while she thought she was scared before it was nothing compared to the chilling fright she felt now. It was getting closer, and now *he'd* be here soon.

————————◆————————

Rebel hated his first name. It was more suited for a sci-fi

cowboy, or an overweight female singer from the nineties, but it didn't fit him at all. At least he'd told himself that over and over since he was a kid. Normally when someone isn't too keen on their first name they go by their middle name, but for him 'Rebel' was the lesser of two evils.

His middle name was Danger. While it may seem funny or cute to be able to tell someone Danger is your middle name, for Rebel it was adding insult to injury. His parents hadn't been weirdos, or hippies, or even especially freethinking, quirky people, and they both came from reserved, conservative backgrounds.

When asked they never had a particularly stirring story about why they decided to saddle their only child with the odd moniker. Rebel speculated it was their attempt at making sure their son lived a more exciting and adventurous life than they had albeit ill-conceived and misguided.

At the time they didn't anticipate how difficult it would be to live up to a name with such implications, or at least it was for Rebel. He was small, scrawny, and scared of just about everything, which was typically not indicative characteristics in a person called Rebel, or Danger, or Rebel Danger. Any attempt at going by a nickname was instantly disregarded once his real name was learned despite his preference.

He'd begrudgingly drug his name this far into his life and figured there was no sense in having it legally changed now. He was born Rebel Danger, and that's what it would say on his tombstone. Besides, he thought it helped him build character, and wanted to keep it so he'd always be reminded of what growing up with a name like his taught him about people.

Rebel Danger Hanover was his full name, but these days he went by Detective Hanover as often as possible. He'd been the youngest officer to make detective five years ago when he made the change, but since then there'd been two more who were younger than he'd been at the time. He was old news in that respect, and he didn't mind it one bit.

He wasn't on for another two hours, but Rebel went in early. He woke up with a bad feeling he couldn't shake and didn't know why, so he figured he'd get an early start. He had some reports to catch up on anyway, and once he fell into the flow of the day Rebel was sure the feeling would pass.

It didn't.

"Hey Hanover, what gives?"

The voice of his friend and fellow detective Michael Rain startled him more than anything but helped pull Rebel from his daydream haze. Detective Rain went by Mick, which was instantly accepted from the moment he said it.

My name's Michael, but you can call me Mick.

No one asked why or told him they liked *Michael* better. They just accepted it. Rebel wished it had been that easy for him to impress a preferred moniker on the people he met in his life.

"What's that?" Rebel asked leaning forward in his chair rubbing his eyes with his palms.

"I said what gives, Hanover?"

Mick placed a Styrofoam cup of black coffee on Rebel's desk before taking a seat on the opposite side. He had a cup for himself as well so heavily diluted with cream and sugar it hardly resembled coffee anymore. Rebel didn't understand how a person could drink coffee any way other than black.

"Oh, I'm just . . . catching up on these reports, and the—"

"My ass you are!" Mick chuckled after taking a long drink from his cup. "You've been acting like a zombie since you got here. You came in early to *catch up* on work, but you've been staring at the walls for the last hour and a half. You're still working on the same report you started with."

Rebel's eyes snapped down to the desk in front of him to see Mick was right. The report he'd started with was still there, and barely complete.

"I know you like to be thorough and everything," Mick continued, "but this is a little ridiculous even from you. So, like I said, what gives?"

The department wasn't big enough for the detectives to have partners, but Mick was as close Rebel could get.

"Okay, you got me," Rebel said dropping his pen on the desktop. "I really can't explain it though. I just have this . . . feeling I can't seem to shake."

"Like what kind of feeling?" Mick slurped the rest of his coffee-flavored milk down in one single gulp.

"Well, not a good one." Rebel leaned back in his chair ignoring the squeaking coil's desperate plea for oil. "If it was a good feeling, I wouldn't be so distracted by it."

"I've been distracted by good feelings before," Mick replied with a grin. "If you know what I mean, huh?"

Rebel paid no attention to the other detective's attempt at innuendo and continued.

"It's like I'm waiting for the other shoe to drop only I don't know when the *first* one did, or what it was related to?" Rebel stood, stretched, and walked to the window. "It's a feeling where you know what's coming is something you can't stop, but you try to convince yourself you can anyway. Does that make sense to you?"

"I guess I can sort of relate, only I haven't had a feeling like that just crop up for no reason. Did anything weird happen to you lately? Maybe something that seemed insignificant at the time?"

Rebel was staring out the window, his back to Mick, but didn't answer. It wasn't because he was contemplating or combing his memory for such an incident. While he'd heard the question it may as well have been in a foreign language for as much as it registered.

Rebel was paralyzed as he watched a familiar black Cadillac exit the parking lot of the police department and disappear down the street. Suddenly his bad feeling made a whole lot more sense.

The Cadillac Man

———————— ◆ ————————

Amelia decided she was going to talk to James as soon as class was over. Her original plan was to do it that morning before the first bell rang, but she'd lost her nerve as soon as she saw him wander up from the parking lot. He was scowling and muttering under his breath, so she let him pass by where she'd been waiting beside the tennis courts.

She chalked it up to him not being a morning person, and decided he'd be more receptive to her question in the afternoon. Now she was sitting in Chemistry, her last class of the day, and the only one she shared with James, watching the minutes count down until she'd be forced to do it, or let the entire idea go completely.

Amelia was barely hanging on to a 'C' average and should've been paying attention to the teacher's review for the upcoming midterm exam, but she couldn't focus. The entire class was feverishly scribbling notes trying to capture nuggets of facts they would use to cram with over the weekend except for Amelia and James.

Amelia held a pen but hadn't written a thing on the piece of paper in front of her. James didn't have anything out on his desk. He was sitting with his arms crossed staring at the teacher, and Amelia thought he might actually be sleeping with his eyes open if that was even possible.

Otherwise, she couldn't imagine being on the opposite side of that stare for any extended amount of time, and certainly not forty-five minutes. Amelia was trying to decide if James wasn't blinking, or he was but she couldn't tell because she was blinking at the same time when the bell finally rang.

Startled, she jumped in her chair eliciting snickers from those seated around her as they gathered their things to leave. She looked back across the room to James's seat and saw he was standing but stopped to stretch. Maybe he had been sleeping?

Amelia leapt from her desk and pushed past her more leisurely classmates to cut James off at the front of the row. Her voice caught in her throat as she got within steps of him, and the only word she could manage to push through her lips was, "Hey," which she said as she tripped and fell into him.

She grabbed James' shoulder, and he brought his arm around both catching her, and helping stabilize balance at the same time. Amelia stepped back knowing she needed to say something, but her words weren't working. There was a disconnect somewhere keeping her from being able to communicate. James didn't seem to notice at all and continued toward the door.

"Wait!" Amelia called out surprised she'd been able to reactivate her ability to speak. "I . . . I . . . "

James stopped and turned around.

"Are you coming?" he asked flatly.

"What? Where?"

"He told me you'd be coming around today. Follow me."

James yawned as he turned to leave the classroom, and Amelia dashed back down the row to her chair to collect her purse and backpack. She didn't bother to pack her Chemistry book, because whatever happened she figured she wouldn't be studying over the weekend either way. The classroom was empty now and Amelia shot easily through the desks pushing them out of the way for a more direct path to the door.

When she hit the hall her heart sank. It was packed with students pushing, shoving, and grab-assing their way to the exits and forty-eight school-free hours. She swung her head from one side to the other scanning the raging horde for James, but he was lost to her in the crowd.

She turned to go back into the classroom and happened to catch a quick glance of James's dark messy hair between two football players having a slap fight to impress a cheerleader who scrambled to get out from between the two of them.

"James! Hey!" she cried out as she worked her way against the flow of traffic trying to get to him.

He didn't turn around, or stop, or make any indication he'd heard her at all, but there was no way he couldn't have. Amelia didn't have time to be embarrassed about how loud she was screaming after a boy down the hallway. She was sure there'd be a juicy rumor circulating by Monday about her being a 'crazy bitch' because someone broke up with her, or something else along those lines all ending with her being the bad guy.

James was still a ways in front of her when he walked through one of the exits letting the door swing shut behind him cutting off her view.

"James! James!" she called in vain trying to push through the ever-swelling student populace working against her.

Three stoner guys, Amelia didn't know their names, stood in her way dancing like idiots and mocking her. *James! James! Oh my James!* Without thinking Amelia brought her knee up into one of the boys' groins, then stepped over him as he fell. She was able to sprint the last ten feet while the cackling laughter of his two friends bounced off the walls and chased her out the door.

She thought for sure she'd lost him. He had more than enough time to have disappeared into the student parking lot and would probably be driving away from the school before she made it out to the sidewalk. Amelia stepped outside surprised to see she was wrong.

James was standing at the end of the walkway on the curb waiting. He wasn't looking back, but she was positive he was waiting for her. She hurried the rest of the way down to where he was standing and looked at him for direction, for what she should do next.

James gestured to a shiny black Cadillac parked against the curb across the street from the school. He didn't say anything; he just motioned her toward it. Amelia began to walk to the Cadillac but stopped after a few steps and turned around. James was still on the curb.

"Aren't you supposed to come with me, or something?" she asked trying not to let fear show through her voice.

He shook his head not looking directly at her, but she'd already known the answer before she finished asking the question. Going to see the Cadillac Man was something she would have to do alone.

———————◆———————

When Rebel was still a patrolman, he would familiarize himself with old cold cases partially out of curiosity, but mostly because he wanted to study the different investigative techniques being used in the department. He had his sights set on detective since day one and used most of his free time preparing himself for the job he *really* wanted.

One thing Rebel would specifically look for the were tactics used by detectives that didn't work, or consistently yielded little to no results. Then, he would look for patterns throughout the unsolved cases of these erroneous tactics being used. He figured cold cases were unsolved for a reason, and a lot of times the reason was shitty detective work.

Rebel didn't want to be a shitty detective, and by the time he was promoted he'd familiarized himself with the best way to streamline a case and cut out the unnecessary, outdated techniques used in the past. This was why he moved up to detective so quickly, and also why the department was able to close two cold cases each over ten years old.

When he officially became a detective, he had the authority to do more than just study the case files, and he took action immediately. After a bit of re-investigating Rebel was able to find and put together evidence needed to close those cases. His detective work made him a hero in the department, but his quiet, cold demeanor kept his fellow officers at arm's length.

One of the cold cases he'd studied weighed heavy on

his mind for a while, and he would find himself thinking about it out of nowhere sometimes. Of all the files he'd gone through this one stuck with him, and he was becoming mildly obsessive over it.

It was a double homicide case involving a husband and wife killed in their home while their fourteen-year-old son was left alive, but in bad shape. This was no ordinary 'robbery gone wrong' killing either, this was a brutal slaughter. Their names were Todd and Vicki Forester, and their son's name was James.

From the start nothing about this case made sense, while from the outside looking in a crime as violent as this should be an easy solve. When an attack is as vicious as this one it's referred to as 'over-kill' because the damage inflicted is beyond excessive. In this case though, even that was an understatement.

There was no sign of forced entry, which typically means the victims knew the killer since they more than likely let them into the home. It could also turn out to be something as simple as the backdoor being left unlocked, so you never really can tell. The couple was found in their bedroom with Mrs. Forester in the bed, and her husband on the floor next to it.

He was decapitated; she was ripped nearly in half at the stomach. They were both cut open and eviscerated by an unidentified blade that was never found. Pathologists couldn't discern the type of weapon either only that it was dull. So dull it made it appear as though the flesh was torn apart, but there was nothing conclusive to prove it either way.

What was known for certain was there were pieces of them missing. Not just organs either, but random chunks of muscle and fat had been separated from the body by the same instrument used to open their bodies. It was also determined the Foresters were alive for the majority of the time they were being taken apart. It had to have been an unfathomably painful death for them.

The son, James, was in the living room covered in blood with a noticeably deep gash across his forehead. He was rushed to the hospital and was in and out of conciseness on the ambulance ride there before falling into a coma minutes after being rolled into the hospital.

An officer rode with the boy in case he became coherent enough to answer questions or reveal any information about the attacker. According to his report James did not respond, and his brief visits to consciousness were filled with mostly unintelligible muttering and moans. Mostly.

What the officer *was* able to decipher was what he thought sounded like 'cattle' or 'Cadillac'. The boy didn't say anything else discernible in the short trip to the hospital, and when he came out of the coma three and a half weeks later, he had no memory of anything.

It turned out the boy wasn't as badly hurt as first thought since most of the blood he was covered in belonged to his parents. This development made the boy a suspect but only briefly. It was quickly determined due to the physical amount of strength needed to carry out the attacks on his parents James would not have been able to perform them.

It was argued the boy might have used the element of surprise to initially subdue his parents before ultimately killing and disemboweling them, but there were too many unknowns regarding the theory, too many loose ends. The main glaring details being the pieces of the bodies missing were not found in or around the crime scene, but not for lack of trying.

The surrounding area was searched for weeks after as far as fifty miles out in some places without as much as a single trace of anything related to the killings found. The detectives briefly considered the possibility of a Satanic cult having used the body parts for a ritual, but again no evidence was found to give weight to the theory.

While James continued to claim he had no memory of

the attack or anything he said in the ambulance one of the detectives noted the boy was distant and detached during questioning. He didn't come across like he was trying to hide something, but rather like he was afraid to say what he knew.

The investigation started to slow down soon after and was eventually shelved to free up resources for new cases. His grandparents signed James out from the hospital, and while there was documentation to show this none of the nurses could remember him leaving, only that he had.

One nurse said she saw the boy walking through the hall with an elderly man while an orderly on the first floor stated he saw the boy walking across the parking lot with an older woman. He said the car they got into was black and appeared to be a luxury model vehicle of which he did not know. The examples listed were Lexus, Towne Car, and Cadillac.

Another element that ignited Rebel's interest in this case was an encounter he had with the Forester boy, James, during another investigation. He wasn't involved but happened to be in the crowd of onlookers along with dozens of other teenagers since the crime scene was at the local high school.

It seemed to be a bizarre suicide pact between three students that was enacted in the gymnasium after hours. They were found when the football coach showed up around six the next morning. The school was an absolute zoo for weeks afterward with the investigation and the media, which subsequently forced classes to be suspended for the rest of the year.

It wasn't just seeing James that inspired Rebel's rumination on the case, but there was an adjacent similarity between the two cases. The deaths at the high school had all the earmarks of suicide, but some strange findings from the autopsies complicated the theory.

Self-inflicted gunshots were initially ruled the cause of death, but then they found the two girls were missing their hearts. Actually, they were only missing from the girl's chests, but found in the boy's stomach. What was truly missing from the scene was *his* heart, which was not found in any stomachs or elsewhere.

This provided the possibility of a fourth person being involved who either backed out of the pact at the last second or had executed a very elaborate murder made to look like a suicide. The displaced and missing hearts were not a detail disclosed to the public in order to not cause panic, but also if there was a fourth person involved, they and the detectives would be the only ones to know.

This would help weed out suspects while hopefully leading to a quick apprehension as well. Stealing an organ from a human body is no easy feat, and the culprit would surely have left evidence in some capacity. If they were selling the heart on the black market that was another story since those cases tended to be very professional.

The detectives reached out to their informants on the street telling them to keep their ears open for anyone talking about a deal going down involving the sale of human organs particularly a heart, but so far no one was singing. They were either all *very* well paid, or whatever happened was far more secretive than they realized.

James Forester was four years older, but still hadn't outgrown some of the baby-face features Rebel recognized from the photos in the file. Seeing the Forester boy in person brought the details of the case surging to the front of the detective's mind easily usurping whatever attention he was dedicating to his current case.

Rebel started thinking about the old case so much in fact he used his current case, the one he supposed to be working on, as an excuse to talk to James. He planned to show up at the boy's residence under the guise of asking questions regarding the suicide school case. The detective was going to lead by saying James's name had been brought up in another student's statement as being a close friend to one of the deceased.

This wasn't true, but Rebel hoped to open with some questions regarding this false friendship, and then smoothly transition into asking James about what happened four years prior when he and his family were attacked. He knew it would be a sore subject and could potentially create a volatile situation, but he'd been in similar situations.

Rebel was confident he could maintain control of the conversation regardless of how angry or uncomfortable it made James feel. It was a risk, but one he was willing to take in order to find anything out to help end his obsession with the case.

The detective showed up at James's home on a Wednesday evening just on the other side of dusk before the night stepped in to take over. The only vehicle in the driveway was a red pickup truck, which Rebel quickly ran the plates of finding it was registered to James Forester. He stepped out of his unmarked car, grabbed his notebook and pen from the console, and slipped on a navy-blue windbreaker with the word DETECTIVE emblazoned in yellow across the back.

The porch light had been on since Rebel arrived, but the inside was still dark. There wasn't any other light showing through the windows he could see, but that didn't mean it wasn't lit up like Christmas in the back of the house. As he approached the door Rebel considered the possibility of James not being home, and it sunk a lead weight down through his bowels.

He hadn't even thought about not being able to talk to the boy tonight, and never considered the chance he wouldn't be there. Rebel could wait outside, but how long could he do that without drawing suspicion from neighbors? The last thing he wanted was some nosy neighborhood watch person to call in a suspicious vehicle parked outside one of the houses on their block.

He didn't feel like having to invent excuses as to why it was so important he talk to this kid especially since there was no mention of James in any statements, and he'd have a hell of a time explaining to his boss why he felt so compelled to talk to someone not involved in the case at all. It wouldn't take long for them to figure out what he was up to especially when they found out who it was.

Rebel wasn't supposed to work on any cold cases without either asking permission, or being assigned, and it would be particularly frowned upon for him to be doing it while working on an active investigation. He now wondered if he should have brought Mick along, but the less anyone knew about his unofficial investigation, the better. He would have to weigh out his options if it came down to it, but for now he decided to stick with his plan.

Rebel stepped up to the door and knocked loudly, but not 'police knock' loud so as not to immediately put the boy on edge. He let a few seconds pass before trying again, and the door opened mid-knock momentarily startling the detective.

"I'm Detective Han—"

"Hey," James interrupted before turning around to walk back into the darkened house.

He left the door open with Rebel standing out on the porch.

"Excuse me sir," the detective called after him, "My name is Detective Hanover, and I have some ques—"

"I know who you are," came James's voice from the end of the dark hall he'd disappeared down. "He told me you'd be coming tonight."

Rebel was slightly flummoxed and not prepared for whatever it was the boy was talking about.

"Are you coming in or what?"

James sounded further away now, and Rebel couldn't see more than a few feet into the darkness of the house. Everything inside him said not to go in. He was alone, he hadn't reported where he was or why, and doing so would be an even further breach of protocol. Still, something was drawing the detective in. He was overcome by the feeling he was supposed to be there only he didn't know why, or for what?

Every bit of his training and common sense screamed from within for him not to go into that house, and Rebel wished he had listened. Actually, he wished he'd never seen James that day at the school, and even that he'd never studied the cold case. In the end he wished he'd never become a detective.

Rebel ignored his instincts, which was uncharacteristic, and if you had come to him twenty-four hours earlier and said he was going to go against his gut feeling he wouldn't have believed it. After close to a minute passed his eyes adjusted to the darkness enough for the detective to see down the hall to where it opened into the living room. He could see James sitting in a recliner with light from what he guessed was a television casting a dull illumination across the boy's face.

Rebel put his hand on the butt of his holstered gun and stepped slowly into the house. When he was halfway down the hall the door swung slowly shut behind him. If it hadn't, he would have seen a black Cadillac pull up to the curb, and park behind his own vehicle.

———— ◆ ————

The day it was supposed to happen Amelia stayed home from school. Even though she knew it wouldn't *happen* until after classes had been dismissed for the day, she didn't want to see them during the day beforehand. She was nervous and was worried she'd act differently or seem suspicious.

She also didn't trust herself not to sabotage the whole thing by throwing a monkey wrench in the works. Amelia was getting exactly what she wanted, and had paid significantly to do so, but as the day approached thin spindly feelings of guilt and regret began to worm their way in. She was afraid if she were at school she might crack when she saw the three of them, and then start screaming 'get out!' and 'you'll die if you stay'!

Amelia already knew it wouldn't make a difference what she did, or who she told what to because there was no stopping what was already set in motion. He was very clear on the terms of their agreement, and the severity in his words was less than mildly implied.

Amelia didn't want to stop it though. Her anxiety from the buildup was playing hell on her emotions, but she knew at the core of it all it was what she wanted, and he was giving it to her.

He was very good at reassuring her, the Cadillac Man, and validated all the reasons she had for wanting them dead. He told her they deserved it just like she knew they did. Looking back on it, Amelia couldn't think of a more cliché high school reason.

Her recent ex-boyfriend Ben had been cheating on her with a junior named Jennifer who transferred into school at the end of her sophomore year. The two had struck up a friendship before summer break, and the affair started mid-July while Amelia was out of town at her grandmother's funeral. It continued the rest of the summer and had been going on the entire school year behind her trusting back.

She was being naïve though, and she knew that now. Looking back there were things she should have picked up on, clues dropped along the way, but the truth was she didn't see them because she didn't want to. It didn't help her best friend, Ashley, was feeding her bullshit the whole time, and quick to douse any suspicions before they had a chance to smolder into flames.

Ashley went out of her way to help hide the relationship from Amelia because as it turned out she was also a part of it. The three of them: Ben, Jennifer and Ashley, were all in a three-way, sex-romp of a relationship with each other. Without the constant misdirection of her closest friend Amelia might have figured it out, but the person she trusted the most in her life held sway over her perception.

The two had been friends since kindergarten, and had been through so much together, which was what made her betrayal all the worse. Amelia had been there for Ashley in sixth grade when her parents got divorced, and she threatened to kill herself by taking her mom's diet pills. Inversely, Ashley was there for Amelia when her parents ended up divorcing a year later.

The girls were inseparable always, and knew everything there was to know about each other, at least until recently. Learning Ashley was involved put the nail in the coffin for Amelia as far as the action she took was concerned. She'd had boyfriends before, even ones who cheated on her, which she was able to get through with the help of her best friend.

In this situation Amelia did not have Ashley to lean on, because Ashley *was* the situation, or at least a huge part of it. The heartbreak she felt over her friend's betrayal was too much for Amelia to take, and it broke her completely. Weeks later when she'd finally managed to pull herself somewhat together, she'd become hardened and bitter, and developed a coldness in her personality off-putting to even herself at times. She'd have work to change these things if she cared, but the truth was she just didn't. Amelia didn't care about anything anymore.

That's why it was easy. She'd turned her story of betrayal, with the help of the Cadillac Man, into the stuff Greek tragedies were made of. On the page it was romantic, but in reality, it was grisly, and vile, and evoked only feelings of terror with the realization she'd fully lost control.

The night it happened Amelia had been sitting in the living room of her mother's house just waiting. She was unable to focus on television or reading, and even listening to music irritated her, so she sat in the dark in silence.

The knock on the door was soft and quiet, but came off as deafening against the vacuum-like silence she'd been sitting in. Amelia jumped from the couch and held her hands to her mouth as her pulse began to skyrocket. Amelia's blood pressure shot up so quickly she felt lightheaded and would've most likely passed out if it weren't for the massive adrenaline dump happening simultaneously.

She was six feet from the front door before realizing she'd even started moving, and a moment later her hand fell on the brushed nickel doorknob. Amelia stopped and exhaled for the first time since moving toward the door, and took three, slow, deep breaths immediately after.

Without further hesitation she turned the knob and pulled open the door in one quick motion like pulling off a bandage just to get it over with. She expected someone to be there, expected *him* to be there, so when she saw no one, her heart quickened again. She heard the engine of a car driving away, but she didn't have to see it to know it was a big, black Cadillac.

Amelia looked down and saw a small wooden box on the welcome mat, but she wasn't surprised. She knew about this part of it as well, she'd known the whole time. She bent down and picked up the box holding it gingerly in her open palm, and then closed the door. Amelia didn't need to open the box to know its contents. Ben's heart was inside waiting for her.

———————◆———————

James looked over his shoulder when he stepped from his truck, which was a habit he'd taken up quite a few years ago. He recognized Amelia's tan Ford Escort among the sparse number of cars in the diner's small parking lot. She would say he was late, but he didn't know how it was possible for him to be late to his own funeral? Or hers.

He watched his reflection in the glass door grow large as he approached and ran his hand underneath his chin unaware how scruffy his face was until now. James was only twenty-two but looked like he was pushing forty. Lines around his eyes and mouth were creased and set, and there was the smallest touch of gray already lightening around each temple.

He hadn't paid attention much since his looks were low on the list of priorities, but Amelia noticed right away. It didn't seem as bad when she was looking at him in the parking lot through the window, but now that he was standing in front of her it was glaringly obvious. Amelia realized she'd been staring for a second too long unable to stifle the involuntary cringe of shock, so to stifle the awkwardness she stood and immediately embraced him in a non-reciprocated hug.

"You're late," she said into his shoulder before letting go and pulling away. "Are you feeling okay? You look . . . "

"Like shit?" he quipped sliding into the booth.

"No," she replied taking her seat across from him. "Sick. I was going to say you look sick."

"I haven't been sleeping," James said through a yawn, which the waitress took as a cue to place a cup of coffee in front of him.

"Haven't been sleeping?" Amelia chuckled motioning for her cup to be filled again as well. "For how long, the last four years? You just look really tired is all."

"Which is it?" James snapped blowing spectral-like steam across the brim of his cup before taking a tentative sip.

"What's that?"

"Which is it, sick or tired? First you said I looked sick, and then you said I looked tired. Which is it?"

"Both, I guess?" Amelia said into the menu she was pretending to read. "You look sick and tired."

James chuckled and sipped his coffee again.

"So," Amelia said with an unintentionally exaggerated nonchalance, "what are we going to do?"

"What are you talking about?" James was scowling now dropping the playfulness from his tone. "What are we going to do about what?"

"About *him*." Amelia still held the menu open in front of her, but her eyes were now locked with his.

"Oh," James said relaxing his posture, and placing his cup on the table to be refilled. "What are we going to do about *him?* Well, to put it plainly, nothing."

"Nothing?"

"Nothing. We'll do nothing, because there is nothing to do. Today's the day he's coming, as we've known the whole time, which we've *understood*. Soon he'll be here and that will be that."

"That will be *that*?" Amelia was fuming now, but James was unaffected by her scathing stare. "You're saying that's it? There's no . . . amendments? No renegotiation?"

"Renegotiation? You're not a free agent hoping to get a better offer from your league rivals, Amelia. We belong to him *you* belong to him. Period!"

Amelia held her tongue fuming as the waitress stepped up to the table to freshen their coffees.

"Were you two ready to order?" she asked having added a flirty lilt to her voice to which James was oblivious.

"I'll just have an English muffin please," James said, his eyes still holding Amelia's angry glare from across the table. "Toasted with butter on the side."

The waitress pretended to write the order down on the pad she was holding but was really adding to the doodle of her boss with a giant cartoon cock being rammed down his throat. She'd been working on it all morning and was pleased with the way it was coming along.

"And what about for you?" she asked looking up from the pad smiling at Amelia.

"The same."

Amelia said it like each word was its own sentence and slapped the flimsy laminated menu down on the table in front of her.

The waitress rolled her eyes while adding detail to the veins she'd drawn on the shaft of the very impressive dick before picking up their menus.

"I'll get that right out for you," she said stepping away.

"And keep the coffee coming," James called after her.

She smiled over her shoulder while quietly calling James a 'prick' through her teeth.

"Look," Amelia said sternly pulling the attention back to their discussion. "This can't be just . . . it. I've heard things."

He viewed her statement as nothing more than a thinly veiled ask for validation, which James let hang languidly between them in the dancing steam rising from their coffee refusing to give it to her. He wasn't biting at her poor attempt to trick him into giving up some information she thought he knew, but he was entertained.

"I've heard about something," Amelia finally continued. "Something you can do to change it, something you can do for him."

The waitress returned with their English muffins and set the plates in front of them before filling James and Amelia's coffees from the carafe she was also holding.

"Thank you," James said with a quick nod as she moved to the next booth to fill more coffee cups.

He picked up the top half of his English muffin and used the knife on his plate to smear it with butter.

"Okay Amelia," he said taking a big bite and chewing loudly with his mouth open. "Tell me what you know."

———————◆———————

James met the man he dreamed about, the Cadillac Man, when he was fourteen. The familiar shiny, black car pulled up to his house one night like he'd summoned it to arrive, and in a way he had.

He didn't recall leaving his house when the Cadillac Man beckoned to him from the street, but he must have because he found himself at the curb looking up at the pale, blond man. James wasn't scared at all even though he felt like he was supposed to. He instead felt the comfortable familiarity of a relative, or an old friend, so when the passenger door opened, he got in. It just felt like the right thing to do.

James pulled the door shut behind him and looked over to see the Cadillac Man was already in the driver's seat despite having just been outside, and on the opposite side of the car. The interior light faded slowly once the door was shut transforming the man sitting next to him into a shadowy silhouette.

The engine didn't make any noise as the car pulled from the curb, and James looked through the heavily tinted window surprised to see a fog had rolled in. Not 'rolled in' though because he hadn't seen it coming. This fog had been fully cultivated, and then dropped onto them. It was dense, and thick, and offered no visibility, or at least not for James. He couldn't see the houses, or the yards let alone the street in front of them, but the Cadillac Man continued to drive unaffected.

"I'm glad you called me, James." The Cadillac Man's voice was smooth and non-threatening, and James swore he sounded like someone he knew, but couldn't quite put his finger on it.

"Me?" James asked still straining his eyes to see through the windshield. "I didn't . . . I mean, I don't think . . . or, I don't remember . . . "

"You've only just now realized it," the Cadillac Man continued, "but call me, you did. Trust me."

James noticed how he'd held the 's' in trust a touch longer, and for the first time felt a sinisterness radiating from the man. Maybe he shouldn't have gotten into the car? He had no idea who this man was, or what he wanted from him, or even how the hell he could drive without being able to see the road, or anything else for that matter?

"Don't worry James," the Cadillac Man said. "There's nothing you can do about it now anyway."

———— ◆ ————

It was no secret Rebel hated his name, and everyone knew it. Outside of that no one particularly knew much else about him. Even Mick, who was the closest approximation to a friend he had, didn't know a lot about Detective Hanover's background. He was an extremely disciplined man who cared very much about being the best at his job and cared about little outside of doing just that.

Rebel wasn't trying to be some kind of 'Super Cop', and he certainly wasn't after quasi-fame or recognition as he preferred his name *not* be mentioned in the paper, or news broadcast when they reported on the success of a solved case. He never participated in press conferences opting to pass the responsibility to his peers. Mick was always up for it though. He'd dreamed of being an actor when he was a kid, and it was the closest thing to scratching that itch he'd ever get.

Law enforcement wasn't something that ran in Rebel's family. Typically, when someone displays that kind of high-level dedication and commitment it's because they feel they're picking up the mantle for someone close to them. It means more because it's more than a job for them it's a legacy. This wasn't the case for Rebel who not only had no cops in his family; he didn't even have a family member who served in the military.

His reasons were his own and guilt-driven rather than familial. It wasn't guilt exactly, but that was the closest adjective to it. Guilt is never simple, and often contains layers of other emotions with patchwork rationalizations woven throughout. Rebel's guilt stemmed from a different level where two distinctly different points of origins coincide in one place.

This unique version of guilt was what drove Rebel to work hard and excel at his chosen profession. He'd kept his secret for all these years never breathing a word of it to anyone and was smart enough to never write anything down regarding it. There was no such thing as a 'private journal' in the eyes of the law if you recorded the kind things Rebel kept secret within. It becomes 'Exhibit A' in an alphabet's worth of evidence against you.

Rebel was twelve the first time it happened. He was

playing with his friend B.J. who lived just up the hill from his house, and the two had found a hole in the fence of a construction site big enough to easily fit through. It was Labor Day weekend, and the job was shut down until Tuesday. The unsupervised site was too tempting for the boys to pass up the opportunity offered them by the hole in the fence.

Nothing in particular occurred to act as the catalyst for Rebel's actions, and the two were in fact having a great time. They were running around and climbing on equipment playing a game in which they were pretending to be secret agents infiltrating an enemy base. The thought just came into his head, and when no other thoughts came after to object, he acted.

The boys were hiding as they advanced through the site ducking behind steel girders, concrete mixers, and a seemingly endless array of machinery used in the construction process. Rebel was a little ways behind B.J. since his assignment had been to 'bring up the rear'. From his current post he watched his friend climb over an unfinished concrete wall between the rebar support rods jutting two feet out from the cement.

B.J. climbed the side of a scaffolding set up next to it and perched on a plank about twenty feet above the wall. Rebel snaked his way through stacks of roofing supplies, and the start of what looked like some very complicated plumbing work to get to the other side of the same scaffolding. He climbed silently and deliberately until he was on the same plank standing behind his friend.

B.J. had his hands cupped around his eyes to mime the pair of spy-binoculars he was pretending to look through when Rebel pushed him. He didn't say anything beforehand. He just pushed him. It wasn't an extremely far fall, but far enough for B.J.'s body to be impaled on the thin steel rods still waiting to be cemented over.

Rebel hadn't noticed it happen, but B.J. must have twisted around because his body was facing up. One of the rods had gone through the back of his head and come out the direct center of the boy's left eye expelling it from the socket. While badly damaged, what was left of it was impaled and slowly sliding its way down rod.

There were two more rods coming out from his chest, and another one that had gone right through B.J.'s groin. Despite the horrific context Rebel couldn't help but softly giggle at what he found to be hilarious placement. Blood started to push its way out from beneath the boy's punctured body, and Rebel watched it for a while as it started to pour down either side of the wall.

The breeze blew the smell of Labor Day cookouts through the construction site, and Rebel suddenly realized how hungry he was, so he climbed down from the scaffolding and went home.

He didn't notice it, but a black Cadillac drove by just as Rebel had slipped out through the opening in the fence.

———————◆———————

Amelia sat on her bed staring into the box open on her lap for what felt like at least an hour. It was empty now. She'd eaten the contents as soon as the door to her bedroom closed behind her wanting to get it over with as soon as possible. It was the final step, the last bit of instruction she was given for the task to be complete.

It wasn't as bad as she thought it would be. Eating Ben's heart. She expected to find a gory mess in the box, but it was quite a clean presentation. The organ was moist, but there was no blood left in or around it. The blood was his. Amelia grabbed the heart like it was an apple and brought it to her mouth.

The texture was foreign and felt odd in her hand like cold rubber and sandpaper, two things that weren't supposed to go together. Despite the texture when she bit into the heart Amelia found it was strangely tender and melted on her tongue like thinly sliced pork belly.

The taste wasn't as offending as she'd predicted either,

and was like unseasoned bacon with the smallest bit of sweetness on the backend like a touch of dessert that came with every bite. The unexpected pleasantness helped her to eat faster, and in six big bites the heart was gone.

Amelia briefly wondered if all human hearts tasted this way, or if the implication *this* one carried altered the true natural flavor? What if it was her palate that had suddenly changed? Was developing a taste for human organ meat a side effect of trafficking with the Cadillac Man?

Amelia closed the box, stood up, and walked over to place it on her dresser. There were no lingering aspects of the heart's flavor, and it was already only a memory as she peeled off her clothes and climbed into bed. She already knew she wouldn't be able to sleep but being in bed was comforting amidst the surrounding circumstances.

She'd already planned not to go to school the next day, so she didn't set her alarm, but she didn't think she'd be sleeping at all. Apparently sometime shortly after pulling the covers to her chin Amelia had fallen asleep. She'd been waiting for a wave of emotion to hit that never came, and in the anticipation, she'd dozed off.

When Amelia opened her eyes the brightness of the room told her it was far later than she usually woke up. She was confused as to if what happened the prior evening truly occurred, but a quick look at the box on her dresser anchored the events to reality. Amelia thought she should've been awakened by a phone call long before the sun was this high in the sky.

She couldn't imagine that no one would reach out to her about what she already *knew* had happened. Her mother surely must have heard, or Ashley's mom, or even Ben's mom. It didn't make sense otherwise.

Amelia left her room and looked down the hall to find her mother had already left for work without bothering to wake her up either. She went back, sat on the bed, and stared across the room at the box like she expected it to do something. In a way it did in that it made her think, which then reminded her of certain details.

One call she didn't expect to get, one she *knew* she wouldn't get, was from the police. He told her she wouldn't be connected in any way to what happened to Ben, Jennifer, and Ashley, which she took to mean as far as law enforcement was involved, and she wasn't wrong.

Amelia realized the Cadillac Man not only protected her from legal repercussions, but he'd also completely removed her from every aspect of their lives. It was as if he'd delicately cut around the parts of their lives involving her, and simply removed and discarded them like fat to the scrap pile. Ashley and Ben's moms didn't call Amelia with the terrible news because they had no reason to. As far as they now knew she hadn't ever been in their now deceased children's lives. This was why no one from the school called, and none of her other friends had reached out.

Amelia remained seated on her bed and let the totality of what exactly that meant sink in. She realized she had no idea what effects these changes could have on her life if any at all. She thought about movies and books involving time travel and remembered their ever-present warning about what manipulating the past could do to the present. This wasn't a time travel situation, but it made sense for the same rules to apply.

The thought was fleeting because the only rules that mattered in this instance were the Cadillac Man's, and nothing about them was going to make sense. Nothing else about her life would be changed aside from Ben, Jennifer, and Ashley being removed from it. In a sense everything else would be the same while simultaneously never being the same again.

Again, she waited to be overtaken by a deluge of emotions that remained surprisingly absent. She didn't feel sad, or mad, or confused, or anything else she expected to feel about the whole thing. She just felt nothing. Amelia continued to stare at the box for several minutes until her stomach started growling. She remembered the phantom taste of Ben's heart, and her mouth started to water.

———◆———

Rebel moved carefully down the hall of James's house toward the flickering light of the television. His gun was drawn now but was pointed at the floor. As he approached the end of the hall where it opened to the living room the detective could hear canned laughter from an old sitcom, although he didn't recognize which one.

Rebel holstered his weapon as he entered the room unsure of what to do next. He'd been caught off guard when James answered the door and was now unsure of how to proceed. The boy was just sitting there in a recliner staring at the television show. His face registered neither enjoyment nor distaste, but rather a resting apathy that seemed to be James's baseline.

James behaved as if he were alone despite letting the detective in barely over a minute prior. Rebel collected his wits and attempted to shake off the overall creepy vibe of the house by getting back on track.

"I need to ask you a few ques—," Rebel started noticing shadows moving across the wall despite the absence of a light source to create them. "I need to ask you a few questions about what happened at the school."

James moved his eyes as the only form of acknowledgment rolling them momentarily in Rebel's direction before returning to their fixed forward position. He did not reply.

"Now listen to me son I am an office—"

Rebel stopped when he heard the front door open, and then quickly close. James continued staring at the television while the detective slowly turned to look down the hall. It was too dark to see the intruder, but he could hear the slow and steady pace of their footfalls as they approached. A thin, blond-haired, man in a black suit stepped from the hall drastically changing the dynamic energy of the room.

Rebel felt a deep chill that triggered an involuntary shiver, and from the corner of his eye he saw shadows shifting against the wall again. James remained seemingly unaffected and had not altered his present behavior in any way.

"Hello again Rebel," said the Cadillac Man stepping closer to the small amount of light the television screen provided. "Or should I say detective?"

Rebel moved his tongue to begin forming a reply but found it and his entire mouth had gone dryer than he thought possible. He attempted to work up saliva while the Cadillac Man continued.

"I'm sorry I was running a bit late, but I trust James let you know I was on my way."

The boy muttered an indecipherable grunt and waved in the Cadillac Man's direction without taking his eyes off the screen.

"That's a typical teenager for you," the Cadillac Man continued. "Always glued to the television. James can be a little obsessive at times when it comes to his shows."

James grumbled to himself again without any additional movement this time, and Rebel attempted to speak for the second time.

"Wh—"He coughed but quickly regained composure. "Why did you come back?"

"Come back?" The Cadillac Man smiled showing teeth that gleamed against the low light of the room. "Didn't you realize? I never left."

Rebel heard something behind him, but it didn't come from the T.V., it was James. The detective looked over his shoulder to see the boy was facing him and pointing while rolling with laughter.

———◆———

James began his work with the Cadillac Man directly after his parents had been killed. When you want something very badly, and then actually get it there's an adjustment period that typically follows. The change in reality is so drastically affected it feels like it's not really the person's life. It doesn't take long but is typically essential, nonetheless.

There was no adjustment period for James to enjoy or regret getting exactly what he wanted. The Cadillac Man came the night after the funeral for them to start their work together. James saw it as him working *for* the Cadillac Man since his tasks had very little to do with them working *together*.

He didn't consider anything he did to be 'hard work', but it took more of his time than he liked, and there were no holidays, sick days, or paid time off. It didn't matter the day or the time, if the Cadillac Man needed him, he had to go. The majority of what he did was act as a sort of intermediary between the Cadillac Man and whoever needed to see him.

Most days the hardest part of his job was waiting around for someone to show up just so he could tell them 'Follow me'. The hours leading up to saying those two words could be excruciatingly boring making it seem even longer than it already was.

James didn't understand why sometimes he'd have to wait for hours while other times he would just walk around a corner and there they'd be, but he didn't ask. It didn't matter if he knew the reasons or not, because it made no difference. He didn't have a choice either way, and James wasn't particularly interested in the details behind what he was doing.

The Cadillac Man was very particular when it came to timing, and as far as James could tell his 'boss' didn't operate under the same rules of time he'd been saddled with. He knew when he was with the Cadillac Man a version of those rules applied to him as well. Sometimes James would be gone for what to him was weeks, but then the big, black Cadillac would drop him off at his house an hour after he'd left.

The Cadillac Man

It wasn't as if he ever time traveled in the sense of moving forward or backward, but the Cadillac Man seemed to move laterally through time. It was like he was able to see sections of time happening all at once and choose where to insert himself. He utilized his unique relationship with time to act with a swift efficiency that kept James very busy.

If the Cadillac Man's charm didn't take care of his schoolwork for him there would be no way he'd pass any class. James didn't have time to read a newspaper headline let alone whatever was considered required eighth grade reading at the time. Oddly enough he didn't care about this part of the arrangement since James would have quit school anyway or gladly flunked out. Grades, jobs, money; none of this meant anything to him anymore, because it wasn't important.

Nothing was.

James learned this on his first ride with the Cadillac Man when his life was essentially laid out for him. He told James he wanted him to know this, because it was part of the bond they would now share. He wanted James to know the truth.

There was no good in this world or any other; there was only evil. This evil was indiscriminate and acted like a tornado that devastates an entire block but leaves one house in the center of all the destruction untouched. It strikes down the good inflicting them with strife while the detestable rise to power and fortune. Evil has no allegiance, nor does it have any aversions.

There is no charm, or spell, or prayer that could deliver you from evil or somehow shield you from it. Every deity along with beings who call themselves angels, demons, and spirits of any kind are all agents of evil. They act as an extension of the 'greater' evil like a limb or a tentacle. They're part of evil, but are semi-autonomous coordinators, or choreographers if you will.

The Cadillac Man was one of those extensions.

"So, you see young James this is why nothing matters. Absolutely nothing."

This was what the Cadillac Man told him about on their first foggy drive when he was fourteen years old, and it made an instant and significant impact on him. He remembered it very clearly because of the physical feeling that accompanied the change within him.

He didn't have to let it sink in, or contemplate, or ask for clarity. The truth acted like an entity entering his body to rewire his whole perception of reality departing once its job was complete. For James it felt like a switch had been flipped, but off rather than on. There was a simultaneous loss of hope, faith, and optimism all at once when the switch was flipped.

The truth the Cadillac Man told him moved quickly through his system choking off all other thoughts or theories about the way the world worked. His eyes were opened, and his mind was fortified against lies contradicting what he now knew as fact.

James was glad he knew this truth though. He'd hate to have lived his whole life striving for what didn't matter. He wouldn't fall into the trap of molding his life in some specific way to achieve a specific goal. He let his aspirations wither on the vine and settled in for the ride. It might be long, but at least it didn't matter.

Amelia was more frustrated than she was angry. She hoped out of anyone James would at least listen without being so dismissive. Just because he'd known the Cadillac Man longer didn't mean he knew everything there was to know about him. James wore a snide smirk as he chewed another bite of English muffin waiting for her to continue.

"Look," Amelia started, "I don't know much about it except for what I heard. I was hoping you could help me put it all together."

"So, who is it?" James asked after pausing to sip his

coffee. "Who has revealed this particular piece of information to you?"

It was Amelia's turn to pause and sip her coffee.

"He did."

The remaining traces of levity drained from James's face, and his expression turned hard and serious. He'd lifted his mug to take a sip but stopped mid-way and placed it gently down on the table in front of him.

"He who?' James asked having drastically lowered the volume of his voice.

"You know who," Amelia fired back. "Don't play dumb James, it only makes you look more pathetic. Him. The Cadillac Man. *He* told me!"

The waitress stepped in with a fresh carafe and topped off Amelia's cup first then filled James's all the way to the brim.

"How's it going over here you two? Did either of you want anything else?"

Neither of them acknowledged her, and instead sat silently staring at each other across the table scowling like they were trying to win a contest for doing it. The waitress took the cue and moved to the next table, her smile unwavering. She'd just refilled their mugs with decaf and would continue doing so for the duration of their stay. She brewed a special pot just for them.

"What do you mean he told you? Told you what?"

James flashed back to the first conversation he had with the Cadillac Man and remembered what he'd been told. He was suddenly much more interested than he had been. He really did think he knew everything there was to know about the Cadillac Man, and the fact Amelia claimed to have been given a grain of wisdom withheld from him was unnerving.

"He told me there *was* something I could do," Amelia spoke slowly and carefully deciding how to best to word her response now that she'd clearly captured James's undivided attention. "He told me there was one thing I could give him to change everything."

"Liar!"

James didn't yell, but he'd raised his voice enough to draw the attention of patrons occupying the tables around them. Amelia noticed and attempted to cover by starting to laugh, which infuriated James further.

"Oh you, stop it," she said in a coy tone mimicking the playfulness of an actual couple as best she could. "You're so funny."

She sensed the hackles of the surrounding diners lower, and she shot James a look to which he was unresponsive. He clearly didn't care about anything other than what they were discussing.

"I'm not lying," Amelia finally said keeping her voice lowered. "Look, he didn't tell me what, okay? He didn't tell me *what* I needed to give him. I was hoping you knew something that could . . . I don't know. Help put it all together so we could find whatever it is and change everything."

The tightness in his face loosened, and James relaxed back into his side of the booth. He sipped his freshly refilled coffee, the smirk returning to his face. He was nearly a hundred percent sure Amelia was bluffing, and in doing so had hoped to trick him into giving up some secret information she believed he had.

"Well, you were wrong," he said lowering his voice, "because I don't know what the hell you're talking about."

"I didn't expect you to know the *exact* answer." Amelia rolled her eyes again. "I just wanted to see if asking might spark a memory of something you heard that didn't make sense at the time, and we'd make a connection somehow."

"It's a little late in the game to throw a hail Mary anyway, don't you think?"

Amelia took a big bite of her English muffin.

"When the hell else do you throw one?"

———————— ◆ ————————

Rebel snatched the jacket from the back of his chair with one hand and scooped his keys off the corner of his desk with the other.

"Whoa, what's going on?" Mick asked placing his Styrofoam cup on Rebel's desk as he stood up. "Where are you off to in such a hurry all of a sudden? Is something wrong?"

"Uh . . . no, nope," Rebel said slipping on his jacket as he headed out the door of his office. "I just . . . thought of something I forgot. A lead I was gonna follow up on, and I just realized I'm late."

"You want me to come along?" Mick asked following the detective from his office. "I have some reports to finish up, but I can push them off to the afternoon or even tomorrow."

"I appreciate it Mick, I really do," Rebel said over his shoulder as Mick caught up to him at the elevator, "but I can do this one by myself. Why don't you meet me for lunch later though?"

"Sure." Mick was obviously crestfallen not to have been asked along, but mostly because he was procrastinating his necessary paperwork. "Jackie's?"

"You know me too well." Rebel stepped into the elevator. "I'll be there by noon, quarter after at the latest."

Mick nodded as the silver doors slid shut between the two detectives, and he reluctantly started back to his desk where the dreaded reports were waiting. The detective stopped short suddenly and looked down at his hand confused as if he expected something to appear between his fingers.

"What the hell did I do with my coffee?" Mick asked out loud to himself.

He narrowed his eyes and chewed on the inside of his left cheek like he always did while trying to remember something. A few seconds later he shrugged and headed for the coffee machine to procrastinate further before being chained to his desk by reports.

On the other side of those elevator doors Rebel's heart raced as he descended to the ground floor. This was already taking too much time, and he hadn't gotten to the car yet. He knew realistically the Cadillac would be well out of his range of sight once he got on the road leaving him to pick a random direction, but Rebel had gotten lucky a few times in the past. He hoped this was one of those times.

He quickly walked from the elevator to the front doors looking straight ahead wearing a set stern expression crafted to dissuade fellow officers from interrupting his momentum. Whatever they wanted could wait until the afternoon when he would hopefully be in a more receptive state of mind.

Rebel pushed through the one of the glass doors leading to the parking lot while fumbling to get his sunglasses from the inside breast pocket of his jacket.

"Watch it, Hanover!" snapped another detective named Lewis as he narrowly avoided being hit by the door.

Rebel wasn't paying attention and had carelessly gone out through one of the doors clearly marked entrance. The bank of doors he should have used was to his right. He was startled and stumbled, but instead of reaching out to steady him Detective Lewis gave him a light shove in the opposite direction. Rebel's glasses hit the sidewalk a second before his foot came down on top of them as he caught his balance.

The other detective had already gone inside without bothering to see what the outcome of his efforts had been. Rebel didn't have time to worry about it and left his now destroyed glasses on the ground as he proceeded across the parking lot to his unmarked vehicle.

He pulled the keys from his outer jacket pocket as he stepped to the driver side door, but in his haste failed to grasp them with a firm grip. The ring of keys flew from his hand, hit the pavement, and slid underneath his car.

"Jesus Christ," he muttered as he got on the ground to retrieve the keys.

Rebel hadn't been this rattled since his first month as a rookie cop out on patrol. He stood, paused, and took a deep breath before slipping the key into the door. He accepted the fact he was most likely far too late to follow the Cadillac, but he still wanted to drive around just to clear his head and calm down.

He maneuvered the unmarked cruiser to the same exit the Cadillac had taken from the parking lot and turned out onto the street. While having the presence of mind to operate the vehicle Rebel was otherwise running on autopilot. Thoughts and scenarios flipped through his head like a slideshow on fast-forward too quickly to dedicate much time to any of them individually.

There were so many uncertainties he couldn't fathom, and more than a few *certainties* he didn't want to think about. Over four years had passed since the last contact he'd had with the Cadillac Man. It was at that kid James's house where Rebel showed up under the false pretense of seeking information for another case.

Rebel remembered the bad feeling he'd woken up with and his stomach suddenly cramped and twisted in on itself. He not only wanted to know why the Cadillac Man had come back, but why had he come to the police station? Had something else happened as a result of the man's unique and often creative influence, or was something *about* to happen?

Rebel realized he'd started biting the nail of his right index finger, and quickly pulled his hand away from his mouth. He'd broken the habit of biting his nails back in high school and was surprised at himself for the mechanical lapse into the dirty habit.

He wiped his hand on his pants as he slowed with the rest of traffic for the upcoming red light. Rebel was so inside his own head he sat for a full thirty seconds before he was aware of it, and even then, he couldn't believe it. The Cadillac was right in front of him.

———— ◆ ————

B.J.'s body wasn't found until the construction site opened back up on Tuesday morning, but it wasn't for lack of trying. Police and neighbors started a thorough search of the surrounding area Saturday evening when the boy didn't come home.

Neither B.J.'s nor Rebel's parents knew the boys had been together earlier in the day since they went out to play independently of each other. They hadn't planned to meet up even though it was typically a given if one of them was outside playing, the other one was with them, and because of this B.J.'s parents came looking for Rebel first.

Rebel had been home for several hours by then, and his friend's parents were genuinely shocked their son wasn't with him. When his mom told B.J.'s parents how long he'd been home for already the worry set in instantly. When Rebel added he hadn't seen his friend all day their worry escalated to panic. B.J.'s father called the police from there while Rebel's mother did her best to set their minds at ease.

When the cops showed up, they took B.J.'s parents' statements on the street in front of the Hanover family home, and neighbors soon began to wander over to see what was happening. When they found out a few of them left together to begin looking immediately for the missing boy.

The police asked Rebel a few questions but had no interest in the boy in regard to his missing friend. They asked how long he'd known B.J., and if they were good friends, and if he'd seen the boy any time during that day? Since he had nothing valuable to contribute to the investigation, Rebel didn't even register as a slight blip on their radar.

No one thought to check the construction site during the search because as far as anyone could tell it was completely locked down. No one noticed the opening in the fence big enough for a boy about B.J.'s size to fit through, or two boys, but they weren't looking for it either. Even after they found B.J.'s body in the construction site it was never officially determined how he'd gained access.

Rebel was at school when the body was found, and the principal came on the intercom to announce they'd be dismissing classes for the rest of the day in light of the sad news. The parents had been notified prior to the announcement and cars lined the street in front of the school hours earlier than usual. Rebel's mother's car was among them, and when he climbed inside, he could tell she'd been crying.

On the drive home she asked him if he was okay, and if he wanted to talk about what happened to his friend? Although he truly felt nothing either way about what happened to B.J. including his role in the boy's death Rebel realized he should start faking it so as not to seem suspicious.

"I'm just sad," he said looking at the floor doing his best to muster up some crocodile tears. "I don't want to talk about it right now."

Rebel managed to make himself appear to be crying, and his mother patted his leg for some assurance.

"Whenever you're ready to talk about it just let me know," his mother said stifling a sob as they drove the rest of the way in silence.

Rebel spent the remainder of the day in his room because he 'wanted to be alone', which was true but not for the assumed reason. He didn't want to have to pretend to be sad around his parents, but in his room, he could read and play while on the other side of the door they imagined he was heartbroken over the sudden tragic loss of his friend.

He did use the time in his self-imposed seclusion to think how he felt about what he'd done, or rather the lack of feeling. He knew it was wrong to kill, there was no confusion for him there, and he knew he was *supposed* to feel bad about having done such a thing, but he did not.

What Rebel *did* feel was an urge, the urge to do it again. It was small at the moment but was sure to only get stronger.

B.J.'s funeral was a hugely sad event attended by everyone from the neighborhood along with most of the student body and teachers from school. Rebel's parents volunteered to help B.J.'s parents with the event, and after the service when the coffin was lowered into the ground, he found himself alone at the graveside.

Everyone had either left or was in the funeral home where Rebel's parents took care of the business side of things while B.J.'s mother and father remained inconsolable. He didn't notice the mourner standing behind him until they spoke.

"He was a good friend of yours," came the voice from behind. "Wasn't he?"

Rebel was startled and nearly lost his balance when he spun around to see who was speaking to him. The man was tall and thin with astonishingly blond hair, and was dressed in a uniquely formal, three-piece, black suit. He wasn't looking down at Rebel, but past him into the dark hole where B.J. lay in a specially made wooden box for his small stature.

"Uh . . . Oh yeah," Rebel answered. "I mean yes, yes he was a good friend."

Rebel made sure to use his best 'I'm sad and miss my friend' voice to respond to the question. He was proud of himself for being able to remain in character, if you will, for the entire day.

"That's too bad," the man said. "It's hard to lose anyone especially if they're important to you."

"Yeah."

Rebel managed a sniffle with his response for effect, and the two stood in silence for a few seconds until the man spoke again.

"He was your good friend, but you killed him anyway."

Rebel felt like he'd been struck by lightning, and he spun all the way around aghast to face his accuser. His mind raced too quickly for him to register any of the possible scenarios churning through it. He looked at the man trying to remember if he'd seen him before.

Was this one of the officers he'd spoken to in the days prior to the funeral? He couldn't conjure any connection at the moment, but he knew it didn't matter anyway. Whoever this person was they knew exactly what he'd done.

"Don't worry Rebel," the man said through the hint of a smile.

Rebel's stomach flipped and churned as anxiety lit up the sensors in his brain. The man knew his name.

"I'm not the police," continued the man. "I'm . . . a friend, but I'm really more of what you would call a 'business partner.' More accurately, *your* business partner."

Stunned, Rebel remained silent. He wasn't sure what this man meant by 'business partner'? It was a term adults used, of which he had only a vaguely tenable understanding, but he was only a kid. As far as he knew he had no business let alone any requiring a partner for.

"I'm . . . I . . . "

Rebel tried to push words from his mouth that wouldn't come, because he seemed to have lost complete control over his tongue. He looked past the man, and across the graveyard to the funeral home hoping his parents would walk out at that moment.

"What's worse is that not only did you kill him, you liked it. You even want to do it again. You see a good businessman knows things like this about those they partner with, which makes me quite the ideal choice. Not that you have another one, mind you."

Rebel hardened at this statement and his fear instantly morphed into anger.

"What do you want?" Rebel chewed the words and let them fall from his mouth like undigested stones.

The man's grin stretched to a full-blown smile, which irritated Rebel further.

"Well," he began, "It has more to do with what *you* want. Like I said, you want to do it again, kill I mean, and you may not realize it yet, but you're going to want to keep killing. I can help you with this."

"Help me?"

"Yes, I can help you. Of course, for us to be partners you'll have to help *me* out as well."

"How am I supposed to help you?" Fear was starting to creep back in now, Rebel's momentary burst of confidence waning.

"Simple," the man answered. "You want to kill people, and I want people dead. You kill those specific people for me, and we both get what we want."

"I'm just a kid." Rebel's voice inadvertently cracked as if to drive home his point. "I can't . . . I can't . . . "

"Yes, you can. You can because I can make sure you get away with it, and that you always will, as evidenced with *this* particular incident." The Cadillac Man gestured to the open grave.

Rebel struggled to interpret what the man meant exactly, and he didn't want to say too much. No one was around the construction site, which was how he got away with it. It wasn't because of this stranger's intervention.

"You two didn't notice, but the construction site was littered with temporary security cameras set up to catch people stealing. They hadn't been set to record over the weekend thanks to a hasty exit by the foreman. Also, the police didn't find the break in the fence you snuck through not because it was overlooked, but because it no longer existed. You didn't think you were really that lucky all on your own, did you?"

Rebel swallowed against the lump forming in his throat doing his best to steady his emotions and keep from crying.

The truth was he *did* think those things and hadn't considered the possibility he'd been helped in some way. It did make sense, though.

Being a child Rebel's base understanding of the police was still black and white. If you committed a crime they came and took you to jail, and that was that. This was instilled in him through his parents, the school, and the media he consumed. In every movie he watched, and comic books he read the bad guy was always caught in the end, but more than that the cops would be onto them from the start.

Only since the incident with B.J. had this understanding been challenged, but he hadn't thought about it until what the stranger said forced him. Maybe there was something to what he was telling Rebel?

"I understand this is a lot to take in particularly under the current circumstances," the man continued. "Think about what I've said for now, and when it's time I'll come visit you again."

He turned and walked away toward a black Cadillac parked along the road running through the cemetery. The car hadn't been there until the moment the man started walking to it. From across the tombstones Rebel heard his name and looked to see his mother calling from the front of the funeral home. When he looked back the Cadillac was gone.

———— ◆ ————

Amelia chalked up her initial misunderstanding of what dealing with the Cadillac Man would be like to naivety, or more realistically wishful thinking. What started at first with ambiguous dreams eventually became the concrete thoughts of someone or something else being beamed directly into her head. The meeting brokered by James came next, and all the vague mystery of the Cadillac Man was erased by his actual presence.

She always knew there would be more to this although

it was hard to admit. There was no such thing as a free lunch, and there never would be no matter how hard she wished. Amelia knew the proverbial check would be dropped on her table eventually, and she would have to pay or be forced to. Either way the Cadillac Man would get what he was owed.

Amelia didn't have much interaction with him in the four years since his intervening on her behalf to solve help solve her problem. He did visit once on the one-year anniversary of their meeting, which was when he told her in very vague terms about something he wanted. He never actually *said* getting it for him would sever his hold over her, but it was clearly intimated. At least she strongly felt it was.

That was all he told her though. He didn't so much as hint to what this *thing* he wanted was, or if it was even something she could procure for him. She was left with a sprig of hope, and that was all she needed. Amelia held onto the possibility of one day finding what the Cadillac Man was after despite having no real information to go on. The thought was what helped her get from one day to the next.

It was a struggle to balance out her constant sense of dread when at any time the other shoe could drop. She fooled herself into believing the odds were better than they actually were. Amelia operated under the assumption she had a fifty/fifty shot daily between having to pay up or finding whatever it was the Cadillac Man wanted. In reality the odds were far slimmer than she would unfortunately come to realize.

Sometimes when she was home alone a feeling would pull at the pit of her stomach, and she would look out the window just as James's old red truck happened to pass by. She didn't think it was a purposeful intimidation tactic on James's part, but it wasn't just a strange coincidence either. James didn't look in the direction of her house when he passed, nor did he make any gestures indicating he was driving by for some specific purpose.

It was the Cadillac Man's way of making sure she knew he was always around. She felt sorrier for James since it seemed like he was connected to the Cadillac Man in a completely different way. She wanted to think he was just a gopher, but in reality, she knew James was more of a slave than anything else.

He was constantly tethered to the Cadillac Man, and at his beck and call regardless of what time it was. James didn't tell Amelia this, but he didn't have to. She'd seen some of it in the dreams she had before finally deciding to approach him. It was very clear her way to the Cadillac Man went through his personal valet, James.

At the time she didn't think much about James's connection to the strange and powerful man, but as time went on, she found herself thinking about it quite often. It was fear more than curiosity motivating the thought, as she often wondered if she was destined for such a life? Would she be the one to take over for James locked in servitude for an indeterminate number of years, or worse decades?

It was around the four-year mark when Amelia did find out what the Cadillac Man wanted, and it terrified her to be the one to give it to him. This was why when the day came, she wanted to meet with James early. She hoped he would know something different, or related, or even contradicting to what she now knew, but when his initial reaction revealed his ignorance to the fact her heart sank.

Amelia didn't want to do this at all let alone by herself. She didn't want the responsibility of actually acting on her knowledge. She didn't have a choice though, since this could, no this *would* be her only chance.

This raced through her mind as she sat in the diner with James across the booth from her. Then, he smiled as if he knew what she was thinking.

———◆———

Until Amelia all James had helped the Cadillac Man do was kill people. He didn't do the killing per se, but helped facilitate death on a regular basis making him just as responsible. He had no delusions regarding his role and was as matter of fact about it as if he were doing any other kind of physical labor job.

Amelia was also the first person requested by the Cadillac Man James knew personally albeit in an ancillary sense. James and Amelia weren't great friends, and they didn't run in the same crowds, not that James ran with any crowd, but they did go to the same school. While novel he didn't consider it to be that big a deal, but for some reason could not shake the nervousness he felt leading up to the day she was to approach him.

James didn't have much contact with Amelia after he brought her to the Cadillac Man. With the remainder of the school year canceled after the incident, *her* incident, he didn't have any reason to be around her otherwise. Since the Cadillac Man kept all suspicion from being aimed in her direction, he didn't expect much of anyone to see Amelia for a while, or even notice her.

James watched it happen to others and was hyper-aware when it was happening to him. The Cadillac Man didn't make you invisible exactly, but it was very similar. You could still be seen only not in a way that really registered with anyone, and it was often difficult to get the attention of someone standing directly in front of you. These side effects faded with time but never fully went away, or at least not for James.

Oddly enough he often found himself driving down Amelia's street past her house. James's comings and goings with the Cadillac Man would have him out and about at all parts of the day and night, but no matter what time it was he never saw her. He never caught a glimpse of her going inside with an armload of groceries, or getting in her car, or sitting on her porch.

Eventually James stopped thinking about it and passed Amelia's house without a second thought. It wasn't until four years later when Amelia herself reminded him. It was close to 2:15 in the morning when James was heading to his house exhausted from a night of ghastly deeds with the Cadillac Man, and he aimed his truck in the direction of home before zoning out.

He didn't realize he was on Amelia's street, or that it was Amelia who stepped off the curb to flag him down until he brought the truck to a full stop. Then, he caught his breath. He'd somehow managed to keep from fishtailing, and by a stroke of luck avoided hitting any cars parked along the street.

James stepped out of the truck, and Amelia was already walking down the street toward him. She told him she needed to talk to him, but she didn't want to talk tonight. She said something was going to happen. She said it was important and pressed a small, folded piece of paper in the palm of his hand before turning around and disappearing up the driveway back into her house.

James opened the note there on the street, and was suddenly gripped with the same nervousness he felt four years earlier when he took her to meet the Cadillac Man. The note simply listed a time, date, and the address of the diner. The words 'This is important' were written across the bottom of the page.

———————◆———————

After B.J.'s death Rebel started doing poorly in school, which was something a therapist told his mother was to be expected from a child his age experiencing the trauma of a close friend's death. A situation like this would be confusing, and difficult for him to reconcile according to the therapist, and it would cause him to be distracted for an undetermined period of time. Eventually, Rebel would process his emotions, come to terms with what happened, and be able to get himself back on track and moving forward.

The assessment made perfect sense to his parents, as he seemed to be displaying all the earmarks of what they'd been told to expect. For Rebel, this was just a convenient cover he used for the way he was *really* feeling. He was disinterested in his schoolwork and endlessly listless not because he cared anything about what happened to B.J., what *he* did to B.J., but because he was waiting for the Cadillac Man to come back.

He'd become consumed by the conversation they'd had at the cemetery and could hardly bring himself to think about much else. Rebel wasn't distracted as much as he just really stopped caring about anything unrelated to the proposed *partnership*.

The urge was getting to him as well, which only made him pine for the Cadillac Man even more. He'd thought a lot about what the man said and was quite interested in the idea of this protection being offered to him. The only thing Rebel worried about was if he could be patient enough to wait, but relief was granted just when he'd reached his breaking point.

It had been five weeks since the Cadillac Man sidled up next to Rebel in the cemetery, but he came back just as he'd promised.

It was a Saturday morning just after nine, and Rebel was alone at the park on the other side of the construction site where the 'accident' occurred. It was too early for any other kids to be out yet, which was just how he liked it. Every day since he'd killed B.J. Rebel found a way to walk by the construction site, which remained closed for over two weeks, and had only recently gotten back to business as usual.

He found by just walking past the site he was able to relive the incident in a more extreme and satisfying way than if he was thinking about it at home or school. He didn't know what it was, but he felt a sort of electrical charge when he was close to the construction site, and it excited him.

On the weekend days he'd taken to getting up early so he could walk by the site, and then sit in the park alone to revel in his memories. He found this practice comforting in that it provided temporary respite for his bloodlust while helping to extend his patience.

It had all been worth it when he saw the black Cadillac come down the street and pull up to the curb in front of the park. The sight alone was enough to put an indelible smile on his face and lift a weight from his shoulders he didn't realize he'd been carrying.

The driver side window opened just enough to reveal the familiar blond hair before the Cadillac Man stuck his hand out to wave the boy over, so Rebel leapt from the swing and rushed to the waiting car.

———————◆———————

James wasn't surprised by what was in the note Amelia almost caused a major accident to give him. He already knew he was supposed to be at the diner on that day at that time because the Cadillac Man told him. What did surprise him, or intrigue him rather, was why he was getting the message twice? It unsettled James in a way he hadn't been for quite some time, and he couldn't seem to shake the nasty feeling.

As far as he had been concerned it was business as usual and was supposed to be what James lovingly referred to as a 'pay up' meeting. He'd been a part of many of these, and they were always entertaining. Making the final payment on something like a house or car is an accomplishment worthy of celebration but making a final payment to the Cadillac Man was anything but.

The date, time and place were when Amelia was supposed to 'pay up' along with some detective who he barely remembered coming to his house at the end of his senior year, but it didn't matter to him. What mattered was this sudden deviation from a protocol he'd had ingrained in him for the last ten years.

It made sense for Amelia to know the things in the note since she would have been given the information from the

Cadillac Man in one way or another, but why would she think to bring James into it? She couldn't know he was already going to be there, or she wouldn't have gone to the trouble of conveying the information to him.

Maybe she was desperate and hoping he really knew something she didn't, something that could help her? But, now as James looked across the table at Amelia, he suddenly felt like the shoe was on the other foot. She was saying she knew something, or was told something, and while he initially believed she was bluffing he wasn't so sure now.

He was starting to think he should be the one trying to get information out of her. Then again this could be another wrinkle in the grand scheme of how the meeting was supposed to go down for Amelia. Each of the experiences James witnessed was unique, and while generally on the extreme side of the macabre he found them entertaining. There was a strong possibility this business with the note, and her supposed secret information was part of the Cadillac Man's bigger plan.

James decided to believe this was the case until he had reason to think otherwise. For now, he was going to pretend to go along with her story. It was almost time anyway.

———————◆———————

The next one came the very same day the Cadillac Man picked Rebel up from the park, and then the killing became quite regular. It was another easy one, but just as satisfying for him, nonetheless. It didn't feel like they'd been driving for long, but where they stopped felt very far away.

On the drive the Cadillac Man told Rebel again of his proposal to be business partners, and the boy excitedly accepted without further explanation. He was far too excited to pay attention to what else the Cadillac Man had to say but tuned back in for the parts about how 'nothing he did' mattered, and 'only evil existed', and there was 'no escape'.

This made Rebel happy to hear, but he was too anxious to focus on what any of it meant. He was going to get to kill again *finally,* and the anticipation consumed him. He felt like getting out and running alongside of the car just to settle down, but they had reached their destination.

They were in a suburban area like the one Rebel's family lived in only the houses were built in a completely different style. The detail made Rebel believe they'd traveled much farther than it felt. The car was stopped in front of a house with a woman on her hands and knees out front planting rosebushes.

Rebel only recognized them because his grandfather had rosebushes as well and was quite proud of the hard work he put into them cultivating them. When Rebel's parents put the old man in a home the new owners of his house didn't keep up with them and they all died. He assumed his grandfather died as well since he didn't see him anymore after that.

Rebel looked from the window to the Cadillac Man, but he continued to stare ahead as if he still needed to keep his eye on the road. He didn't have to say anything though, because the boy already knew what he was supposed to do, what he *wanted* to do. Rebel couldn't help but smile wide as he opened the door and stepped from the car.

He didn't close the door behind him. This wouldn't take long.

He started across the lawn heading straight for the woman who was on all fours obliviously working with her back to him. When Rebel reached the middle of the lawn he stopped and looked around the yard not knowing what he was looking for, only that he'd know what it was when he saw it.

His eyes landed on a piece of cinder block lying off to the side of the yard about six feet to his right. It had been broken carelessly leaving the edges sharp and jagged, but the weight was what he was after it for. It was heavier than he anticipated, and Rebel had to lift the chunk with both hands. It was awkward but he didn't have to carry it far, and he adjusted his grip as he continued the rest of the way across the lawn.

It happened fast because it had to since the woman was sure to see him in her peripheral, so there was no time to waste. Rebel quickened his step as he approached and lifted the piece of brick over his head.

He was right, too. The woman felt him coming and was turning to look when he brought the brick down hard against the side of her head. A tremendous explosion of skull-dappled crimson erupted from her temple, her skull rupturing against the force of the blow.

The woman's body went limp and crumpled forward pushing her busted head into the soil she had been lovingly tending to. Her limbs began to tremble suddenly but ceased as he reached for the brick again. He could see the pink of the woman's brain pushing through the opening he'd put in the side of her head, and knew she was done for.

It was time to go, and Rebel took a mental snapshot of the woman's broken head to revisit later, and then started back across the lawn to the Cadillac. A moment later he was back in his seat, and they were driving down the road.

The entire twenty-two second experience played on a loop in his head as they drove, and although quick it was enough to satisfy Rebel's urge for now.

———————— ◆ ————————

"Excuse me," Amelia said placing her coffee cup down on the table. "I need to use the ladies room."

"Don't take too long in there," James said as she stood. "You know how he is about timeliness."

She ignored the sarcastic remark and walked past the row of booths lining the front windows of the diner to the short narrow hallway where the bathrooms were. Despite the amount of coffee she'd been drinking Amelia didn't really have to go to the bathroom but wanted a minute or two alone away from James to clear her head and think.

She'd been put-off by James's attitude since he showed up, and it was only getting worse as their conversation continued. Amelia knew he'd been 'helping' the Cadillac Man for a while so maybe this was old hat for him, but she wished he would take this seriously. He had no idea how important today was, because he wouldn't act this way if he did.

She couldn't tell him either, she wouldn't dare. It had been made very clear to her what would happen if she did.

Amelia clutched the sides of the small sink and leaned forward inspecting her reflection for blemishes, food in her teeth, or anything hanging in or around her nose. Satisfied with the presentation she stood up straight, turned the water on, and began soaping her hands beneath the warm stream.

"I just don't know," she said to her reflection while rubbing her hands dry with a paper towel from the dispenser. "I just don't know . . . if I can go through with it."

Amelia sighed as she threw the balled-up paper towel at the trashcan connected to the wall, but it fell short bouncing off the side and falling to the floor. She bent to pick it up for a second attempt when she was startled by a loud bang from the stall directly behind her. She didn't think anyone was in there with her and was caught off guard by the sudden sound.

Amelia could feel her heartbeat pounding in her head, but her pulse quickly slowed back to normal. She felt embarrassed to have been talking to herself without realizing someone else was in the bathroom and decided to switch to decaf when she got back to the table.

Amelia bent back down retrieving the paper towel this time and dropped it directly into the bin when she heard the noise again, but now it was much different. It was louder for sure, much louder, and sounded like two pieces of metal crashed and scraped against each other. Whatever it was could not have been created by anything that should normally be in a bathroom stall.

It sounded like a miniature car crash.

"Hello," Amelia called out weakly. "Uh . . . Is everything alright in there?"

No one answered and her heart jumped back into jackrabbit mode. She paused before taking a tentative step toward the stall, and then took another one. The crashing sound came again, and Amelia covered her mouth to suppress her squeal. Then, the toilet flushed.

"Hello?" Amelia tried again before bending down to look for feet beneath the stall door, and there were none.

She stood back up, and the door slowly swung open a few inches. Everything in her was screaming to get out of there, to go back to the booth. She'd tell James about it, and he could check it out, but she remembered his attitude and thought differently.

He would probably chide her with some smart-ass quip, and say she was being paranoid and anxious. Amelia was going to have to do this alone, because whatever was happening was supposed to be for her anyway. Otherwise, some spooky shit would've gone down at the table with both of them, and not while she was alone in the lady's room.

Amelia reached out, touched her hand to cold metal door, and gently pushed it the rest of the way open.

The toilet was gone, and the entire inside was charred black like it had been burned from the ground up. The flimsy walls were buckled and melted, and the graffiti had all blended together to form an unreadable black spot. It looked like a small explosion happened where the toilet had been, but what Amelia heard was not an explosion.

In place of the missing toilet was a small wooden box exactly like the one the Cadillac Man gave her nearly four years ago. The one she ate Ben's heart out of. The box was open, and there was indeed a heart inside, but it wasn't his. Amelia realized the pounding in her head stopped, and she absently brought a hand to her chest.

Her fingers encountered something wet and tacky, and

she looked down to find a bloody jagged opening in her torso from which her own heart had been torn. Amelia's heart was in the box this time. It suddenly started to beat, and Amelia gasped before releasing a scream she was unable to hold back this time.

A second later the bathroom door flew open and slammed loudly against the wall, and Amelia spun around to see the waitress with a concerned look on her face.

"Are you okay? I heard a scream. It's not another rat, is it?" She was talking fast from the adrenaline rush.

Amelia looked back into the stall to see it was perfectly normal. The walls weren't charred black, and instead of her heart in a wooden box there was only a toilet. She turned back to the waitress but kept glancing over her shoulder just in case.

"Yeah, I mean yes. Yes, I saw a rat. It was a big one too."

"Goddamnit!"

The waitress groaned while anxiously looking back and forth across the bathroom floor in search of the offending culprit. Finally, she stepped back through the door and yelled down the hall.

"Wade! Wade, get out here we got another one in the ladies room!"

She let go of the door, and Amelia leapt to catch it before it closed completely and followed the waitress out. She didn't want to be in the bathroom alone anymore.

———————◆———————

Upon returning home after bashing in the skull of a stranger Rebel felt a calming confidence at twelve years old most people never experience in their entire life. He didn't feel guilt or remorse from what he'd done to the woman, and in fact thought fondly of the scene daily. He often pictured the glistening and swollen pink organ pushing through the hole he'd put in her skull like a sprouted sapling struggling upward toward the sun and would think about it for hours.

The memory alone was enough to excite his system imprinting the foundation for future sexual proclivities to be launched from. Rebel found he could conjure a variation of the rush he felt that day just by calling up the memory, but it didn't take long before the effect began to wear off. Like a junkie trying to chase their elusive first fix, Rebel was itching for more.

He was becoming desensitized and needed another kill to reinvigorate the intense pleasure he derived from the act. It was getting to the point where the memory he'd held so dear enraged him due to the frustration he felt. Rebel was very close to satisfying his need alone when the Cadillac Man showed back up just in time.

He was sitting in the park again, but this time it was evening after supper. Rebel wasn't there to reminisce though; he was looking for another victim and had been eyeballing a man shooting baskets alone at the concrete half-court across the park when he caught a sudden chill. Rebel looked from the man on the court to the street just as the black Cadillac was pulling up.

He didn't wait to be beckoned, or for the door to open, but instead leapt from the top of the picnic table he was sitting on and sprinted over to it. He was panting when he grabbed the handle and pulled, but the door did not open. Rebel waited a second figuring the Cadillac Man tried to unlock it at the same time he was pulling, but when he tried again it remained locked.

A small sparkler of panic ignited in his stomach and quickly shot up to explode like a bottle rocket in his chest. Rebel pulled the handle again this time hitting the door with the palm of his hand to communicate the intensity of his urgency. He yanked on the door handle with every bit of might in his small body and was on the verge of tears when the window slid down halfway.

Rebel let go and stepped back staring into the darkness of the vehicle waiting for an explanation.

"I told you to be patient, Rebel."

The Cadillac Man's voice flowed through the window to Rebel's ears with a patronizing paternal tone he didn't expect to hear. It was the same way his teachers and parents talked to him as a precursor of the punishment to follow. Rebel went to reply but caught himself before speaking. He'd learned from past similar situations that adding his own commentary only made it worse.

"I . . . know." Rebel said softly. "I was, I mean I have be—"

"If you were being patient then what were you about to do to that man?" The Cadillac Man interrupted gesturing in the direction of the basketball court.

Rebel looked at the ground. The grass was a deeper shade of green in the dark, and he dug into a small pre-existing rut with the toe of his left shoe.

"Kill him," his voice was even softer.

"What was that?"

"Kill him." Rebel looked back up at the Cadillac Man through the window. "I was going to kill him."

The Cadillac Man turned away looking through the windshield, and Rebel heard the click of the lock disengage. He hesitantly reached for the handle, pulled gently, and to his relief the door opened. He didn't waste any time and leapt into the passenger seat pulling the door closed hard behind him.

The window closed, and as the Cadillac pulled gently from the curb Rebel struggled to contain his excitement. The Cadillac Man didn't start speaking right away like on the last trip they'd taken and remained silent until they'd driven several blocks.

"Patience is an important part of our business partnership," he said finally. "Do you understand what I mean when I say that?"

"I do," Rebel replied staring straight ahead.

"I hope so," the Cadillac Man said pulling off to the side and stopping the car. "I'd hate for you to have to learn the hard way."

Rebel looked out the window and his heart sank. The entirety of his excitement was extinguished at once, and his body felt numb but heavy at the same time. They were back at the park in the same place he'd been picked up from only minutes ago.

He started to panic now unsure of what this meant. Was that it? Did his desire to kill without the Cadillac Man nullify their agreement?

Rebel reached for the door handle slowly hoping to be stopped.

"Rebel wait," the Cadillac Man said. "Don't get out there."

He eased his foot off the brake and the car moved fifty feet down the curb. The car stopped in front of the basketball court just in time to watch the man take a wild shot that sent his ball beyond the hoop to the edge of the wooded area behind it. The passenger door opened on its own this time, as Rebel watched the man going to retrieve the ball leaving his back to them.

"Take this," said the Cadillac Man handing Rebel a length of pipe.

Rebel gladly accepted the weapon, jumped from the car, and sprinted toward the man with the pipe raised ready to strike. He felt like he'd been shot out of a cannon and closed the distance between them quickly as adrenaline and excitement propelled him forward.

He was holding the pipe with both hands now, leapt the remaining few feet between them, and brought it down with every bit of strength he had combined with the momentum behind him. The pipe connected with the back of the man's head hard enough for Rebel to feel the sensation of his skull crunching travel up the pipe through his fingers.

The man grunted and dropped to his hands and knees immediately. It was too dark for Rebel to see the damage he'd caused, but he'd felt the blood spray back up into his face. This wasn't like the last time with the woman in the yard and wouldn't be as easy as 'one and done'.

The man groaned again and grabbed at the ground in front of him trying to pull himself away from his attacker. Rebel couldn't wipe the smile off his face if his own life depended on it. He derived a pure form of joy from watching the man struggle but took only a moment to revel before pouncing again.

Rebel hit him again but not as hard this time halting the man's attempt to crawl away. He brought the pipe down again and again until moans of pain were replaced by the squishy wet crunch of the man's skull buckling. Rebel continued hitting the man and imagined the sickening sounds of each impact were the notes he was using to compose a masochistic symphony, and then he heard laughing.

Rebel slowed his beating to listen and realized it was him. He was the one laughing, which only made him laugh harder as he continued mercilessly beating the dead man's pulpy swollen corpse.

Rebel's arms started to ache under his armpits, and his forearms were burning from the exertion. The effects of the massive adrenaline dump were slowly waning, and the pipe became heavier and harder to swing with any power behind it.

Rebel finally relented and bent over with his hands on his knees to catch his breath. The dark shadows of the dense tree line mostly hid the gory scene he'd created, but it wasn't too dark for him to tell he'd turned the man's head into a lumpy pile of wet red mush. He straightened up and turned to see the Cadillac Man was still waiting for him watching through the open passenger's side door.

The boy began to walk back to the car and could feel the soreness burrowing deeper into his arms with each step. When he reached the open door the Cadillac Man was holding his hand out for the pipe, and Rebel handed it to him bloody side first. The Cadillac Man didn't seem to mind as he accepted the makeshift weapon immediately tossing it over his shoulder into the backseat.

Rebel wasn't sure what to do next and stood on the curb waiting to be instructed to get in the car, but the Cadillac Man reached over and pulled the door shut. The window came down halfway again, and Rebel stepped up to the opening.

"Remember," the Cadillac Man told him. "Be patient. It's not a virtue, but a necessity."

The window went up leaving Rebel looking at his own reflection in the heavily tinted glass. His hair was a matted sweaty mess, and tiny blood drops dotted his face like freckles. He watched the car pull away from the curb and drive slowly down the street until it disappeared around the first bend.

Rebel left the park feeling like he was walking on air, as the electricity from the kill rushed in to replace his depleted adrenaline. He didn't know what time it was, but it felt a lot later than he was allowed to be out. He was worried about his parents, but the thought was fleeting.

He didn't have to worry about his parents. He didn't have to worry about anything as long as he remained working on the Cadillac Man's terms. Rebel walked right through the front door of his house with no fear. His parents were watching television in the living room, and neither looked back as Rebel crossed behind them on the way to his room.

"Reb, hon," his mother called freezing him in his tracks. "Don't forget to take a shower before bed especially since you've been out playing. I'm sure you're a sweaty mess."

"Do as your mother says," his dad chimed in to cut off any protests before they began.

His parents continued staring at the television, and Rebel smiled at how right his mother was. Not only was he a 'sweaty mess', but he was covered head to toe in bloody spatter.

"Okay mom," he called from the hallway. "I'll go take one right now."

"Thank you dear," she called back, but he was already in the bathroom with the door shut and locked behind him.

Seeing his reflection in the light was upsetting to say the least, and Rebel was glad his parents hadn't caught a glimpse of the state he was in. He didn't realize when he saw himself in the Cadillac Man's window that his hair wasn't matted from sweat, but from so much blood he worried it would turn his dirty-blond hair into a pinkish hue.

There was quite a bit more blood on his face he was unable to discern in the tinted window's reflection, which made his comparison to freckles seem ignorant and foolish. The blood on his face mixed with sweat to create stained red streaks down his cheeks and across his mouth. It looked like the very messy aftermath of eating a rapidly melting cherry popsicle, only instead of just his mouth the red stains were all over.

Rebel was also surprised at the amount of blood on his hands for having not actually touched the body with them. Like a pair of skintight gloves, it went from the tips of his fingers to his wrists, and nearly halfway up his forearms. He was prepared for the long shower he'd need to fully clean himself, but his clothes were another story.

His t-shirt and jeans were completely ruined and covered in blood to the extent there was no coming back from. He was going to have to get rid of them, but he wasn't very concerned about keeping his clothes clean. Rebel peeled off the blood and sweat soaked clothing and chuckled at his naked reflection now due to the contrast of the stained skin versus the unblemished parts that had been covered.

It took a good forty-five minutes for Rebel to fully scrub the stranger's blood from his body, and an extra fifteen to clean the tub out afterwards. He took the clothes to his room and buried them in the corner of his closet beneath his sleeping bag, and a pile of clothes he'd purged from his wardrobe because he'd grown out of them.

Rebel was tired and sore, but happy as he crawled into bed and fell asleep instantly. He dreamed about beating the man's head in, but instead of one man there were dozens all lined up along the tree line in the park. After destroying one of their heads with the pipe he moved on to the next one, and the next, and so on. He didn't tire in his dream like he had in real life, and when he woke up Rebel found he'd had his first wet dream.

The body, of course, was discovered early the next day since it wasn't necessarily hidden. Rebel stood around the corner from his parents who were in the kitchen quietly discussing the news to no doubt keep him from hearing.

It turned out the police did a search and found a schizophrenic homeless man living in the woods just beyond the tree line. Apparently, it was this man who found the body the night before, and had decided to play with the blood leaving his hands, face and chest stained red. When the police approached the homeless man, he started shouting about the blood sacrifice he'd made to the Old Ones to bring about the end of days.

The man clearly had mental issues, but he'd taken the blame for the murder and seemed to truly believe he had done it. Rebel wondered if the homeless man really had been living in the small wooded area of the park, or if he just suddenly found himself there via the Cadillac Man's doing? Even more, did the man go to sleep as a schizophrenic homeless person, or had he merely woken up as one?

The latter possibility made Rebel giddy to think of the many layers that went into separating him from his crimes. It gave him an inflated sense of importance to complement his newfound and thriving fearless confidence.

His parents didn't fill him in on the details of the aftermath, and only told him something bad happened in the park, but it was okay now because the police caught the person responsible. Rebel read all the details for himself in the newspaper after his father was done and left it on the kitchen table.

He took it to his room and read the article on the murder over and over, then slid the paper under his mattress to revisit whenever he pleased. There was also some speculation mentioned in the article about the homeless man possibly being involved in the death of his friend, B.J. The boy's death had initially been ruled an accident by authorities, but according to the article the case would be reopened to investigate the possible connection.

The only other thing his parents had to say about what happened was they didn't want him to go to the park after dark anymore, which he agreed without comment or argument. It's not like they would ever know if he went out to meet the Cadillac Man, but he didn't expect there would be another meeting for some time.

Despite his excitement on the night he killed the man in the park Rebel could tell the Cadillac Man was upset with him for not being patient. He could feel the anger rolling off the pale blond man in silent waves that crashed against his ego eroding its recent swelling. He figured there would be a period of growth he'd have to endure before the next meeting in order to show he could be patient.

Rebel wasn't happy about the possibility of an even longer wait before his next kill, but he was prepared to wait as long as he had to until the big black Cadillac came by to pick him up again. He hoped the vividness of his memories would be enough to hold him over, because like it or not they would have to.

Surprisingly, he was completely wrong, because the Cadillac Man came the very next night. Rebel wasn't in the park like he'd been the first two times, but only because he wanted to wait for the heat to die down before going back. The park was full of people on this particular night anyway participating in a candlelight vigil for the man he killed.

This time the Cadillac Man came to his house as if providing some kind of curbside death-dealing service. Luckily the boy's window faced the street, and he happened to be looking out just as the car pulled up. At first, he didn't think it was the right Cadillac, but when the door popped open, and he saw the hand reach out to beckon him all doubt was erased.

———————— ◆ ————————

It turned out Rebel was completely wrong in thinking he would have a long wait between kills, because after the man in the park the Cadillac Man came for him on a quite regular basis. The pickups weren't limited to the park and Rebel's house either but would happen anyplace at any time.

The Cadillac Man came for Rebel sometimes when he was walking to and from school alone, or even if he was at other friends' houses playing. He was picked up from a birthday party one time to push a man off a scaffold and dropped back off in time for cake and ice cream.

One time during the school day Rebel was called to the office to find the Cadillac Man waiting for him. They went somewhere completely foreign to the boy, and he didn't understand the language being spoken. The language barrier didn't stop him from sneaking into a running vehicle while the woman who owned it had gotten out to pick up her paper from the driveway.

Rebel slid the car into reverse and jammed down on the accelerator to run her down. He'd never driven a car before, but knew enough to move the gearshift into drive, run the woman over again, and put it back in park. He exited the vehicle just as the Cadillac Man pulled up, and he jumped in. A short drive later Rebel was back at school in time to take the math quiz he'd hoped to miss.

Another time Rebel was at the grocery store with his mother who told him to go pick out a breakfast cereal while she waited at the deli counter. He ultimately knew he would choose *Choco-Berry Blast*, which was his favorite and standard go to, but he still liked to work his way from one end of the aisle to the other taking in the extensive selection just in case something grabbed his attention.

When Rebel entered the aisle, he found more than the colorfully decorated boxes of sugar. At the entire opposite end of the aisle was the Cadillac Man holding up a box of *Choco-Berry Blast* lightly shaking it as if Rebel were a dog he was trying to entice with a box of bone-shaped biscuits. He was too young and too naïve to be offended by the gesture let alone come to the conclusion he should be.

Instead, Rebel felt the twinge of excitement in his stomach followed by the accelerated heartbeat he experienced every time the Cadillac Man showed up out of the blue. As he approached his beckoning 'business partner' Rebel thought about how odd it was to see the Cadillac Man in a setting like the grocery store.

The harsh buzzing fluorescent lighting gave the man's complexion an even lighter pallor than usual, and chunky streaks of his blond hair seemed white. His dark and steely eyes remained unchanged by the odd environment, and Rebel smiled up into them.

"Don't worry," the Cadillac Man said handing Rebel the box of cereal. "This won't take long."

Rebel never worried about how long it took, because it didn't matter since as far as he could figure the rules of time didn't apply when he was with the Cadillac Man. He wasn't even sure other people could see him when he was with the supernatural stranger. No one seemed to notice either of them as Rebel followed a step behind still clutching the box of cereal, but instead of heading to the front of the store to exit, they were going to the back.

The Cadillac Man passed through a pair of swinging doors against the back wall of the store semi-hidden off to the side of the long, refrigerated, dairy case. Rebel had never been in the back of a store before, and the dusty concrete floor lined with pallets of product wasn't necessarily what he expected.

The Cadillac Man led him down a narrow corridor that opened to a larger stockroom with shelving full of dry storage items stacked from floor to ceiling. At the far end of the room was a door with a small window next to it. From where he was standing Rebel could see it was an office of some kind with a man inside sitting at a desk presumably working.

He had no idea the man was the store manager, nor did he care. The Cadillac Man pointed to a forklift parked against the same wall on the other side of a section of shelves containing pallets of washing machine detergent. Rebel didn't wait for instruction; he already knew what to do. He handed the box of cereal to the Cadillac Man and scampered over to the forklift.

He jumped in the seat and looked at the controls and had no idea what to do with them, but luckily, he wouldn't need to. Rebel pushed a green button he guessed correctly would start the machine up, and he could feel the seat vibrate letting him know he was correct. The forklift wasn't loud at all until Rebel began to pull randomly on levers while spinning the wheel around.

He couldn't see it from where he was, but the commotion caught the attention of the manager who was getting up to come out and investigate. Unaware, Rebel kept playing with the controls until suddenly the forklift lurched backwards. Since the wheel was turned the machine spun out slamming the forks into the side of the large shelves as the manager was exiting his office.

"What in the hell is goi—"

The manager stepped from the office just as the shelves buckled sending hundreds of pounds of soap products directly on top of him. It happened so fast the man didn't even have a chance to scream or realize what was happening. The satisfying snap of breaking bones along with the growing puddle of blood was enough evidence for Rebel to know he'd done his job.

The collapsing shelves and resulting avalanche of product wasn't as loud as he'd thought it would be, or rather should be especially in such a large room with a metal ceiling and concrete floors. Rebel hopped from the forklift and took a moment to admire the growing blotch of crimson spreading out from beneath boxes of Tide, Cheer, and various miscellaneous generic brands of soap.

The Cadillac Man was across the room waiting, and he scampered over to him. He handed Rebel back the box of cereal, and they both walked back the way they came down the hall, and then exited through the same double doors as if they were coming from somewhere they were supposed to be.

Rebel turned to go in the direction of his mother and the deli counter while the Cadillac Man went the opposite direction and disappeared down an aisle without saying a word. It wasn't unusual for their meetings to end with them silently going their separate ways. They had an understanding, and the Cadillac Man wasn't one to make unnecessary conversation or chitchat.

Rebel walked up to the deli counter just as his mother was being handed the turkey, ham, and Swiss cheese she'd ordered, and he smiled holding up the box for her to see.

"Perfect timing," she said when she saw her son approaching. "Oh Rebel, you picked *that* one again? You might as well just spoon sugar into your mouth directly from the bag."

His mother said something similar each time he picked out a cereal, which was always the same, not that it mattered. She would have said it about any cereal he'd chosen, and she'd be right about every single one of them, but she never refused him his choice. Rebel tossed the box into the cart and followed his mother to the checkout lanes as three concerned looking store employees rushed past them barking 'excuse me' as they blew by anyone in their way.

"Sheesh, what's the big hurry?" Rebel's mother said to him. "Are they trying to put the produce out before it turns or what?"

She was making a joke, and Rebel acknowledged her by giggling with a shrug.

"I don't know. Maybe," he replied. "Hopefully it's a Twinkie emergency, because I could help with that!"

"I bet you could," she chuckled taking items from the cart and placing them on the conveyor.

While they were checking out Rebel watched a man who also appeared to be a manager answer the courtesy phone he'd been paged to pick up, and he saw the man's face go white seconds after pressing the receiver to his ear. All he did was repeat the word 'what' every few seconds in disbelief of whatever he was being told.

The man didn't bother to replace the phone back on the hook, and let it fall from his hand before he too sprinted to the back of the store. Rebel watched the telephone receiver bounce and swing from its coiled chord, which kept it from smacking the tile where it would most assuredly break. His mother didn't notice any of this at all as she made small talk with the cashier while completing their transaction.

They pushed their cart through the doors just in time to see an ambulance, fire truck, and two police cruisers speeding through the parking lot with lights on and sirens blaring. The ambulance pulled up on the sidewalk in front of the main entrance, and two paramedics leapt out and dashed past Rebel and his mother on their way into the store.

"I wonder what that's all about?" his mother asked as they maneuvered around the ambulance on the way to their car. "I hope everyone is okay."

Rebel shrugged and helped her load the grocery bags into the trunk. He knew if he were here with his father instead the two of them would stick around to see what was happening. His dad liked to talk to cops and fancied himself an armchair detective of sorts never missing a chance to chat up an officer if one was around. His mother had no interest though and was very big on reminding both Rebel *and* her husband to mind their own business.

As they turned onto the street from the parking lot two

more police cruisers raced past in route to the grocery store as well. Rebel's mother pulled off to the shoulder until they passed as she did when in the vicinity of any emergency vehicle, and she watched them in the rearview mirror for a few seconds before pulling back out onto the road. Her cheerful disposition changed suddenly, and the smile turned to a disconcerting look.

"I don't know what's going on, but I'm glad we left when we did," she said re-entering the flow of traffic. "There's too much emergency activity for it not to be something serious. I think we may have gotten really lucky."

Rebel nodded while pretending to be reading the back of the cereal box he'd retrieved from the bag before it went in the trunk. She was half right in that luck was involved, but it was he who had been the lucky one. An ordinary boring shopping trip had been turned into a wondrous rush of endorphins for Rebel who reveled in the kill the entire drive.

When they got home his mother told his father about what was going on at the store as they were leaving expressing her concern over what could have possibly happened. Rebel's dad said he hadn't heard about anything but would call around to see if he could find something out. He also shared his wife's sentiment about being 'lucky' to which Rebel agreed without comment.

It didn't take long for the news of what happened to circulate through the neighborhood that afternoon, and by the end of the day it was on the local news broadcasts although they seemed to know very little details. The official statement from police was at the moment they believed it to be a tragic accident but would need to conduct a full investigation before ruling out foul play completely. Rebel knew the investigation would yield no such evidence and would tell them not to waste their time if he could.

The dead manager's name was Robert Murphy, and it turned out he was a family man and very well-liked by the community. He'd been married for eleven years, and he and his wife, Ellie, celebrated their anniversary only one week before his death. He had three children, two sons, seven and five years old, and to really stick it in and break it off a daughter only three months old. She would never know her father.

Mr. Murphy was leader of the neighborhood Boy Scout troop, served as an usher at the Baptist church he attended, and singlehandedly organized the largest food drive in the community every holiday season. Looking at it all on paper you'd think Mr. Murphy didn't deserve to die not with all he had going for him, and what a great selfless person he was perceived to be.

Too bad it didn't work that way.

It didn't matter how many of life's boxes you checked, or people you helped, or the amount of money you gave away. The sword dangled above everyone's head just the same and dropped on a whim indiscriminately with no rhyme or reason. The fact humanity had fooled itself into believing their deeds and beliefs protected them against such chaos was for the best. Otherwise, every waking moment would be lived in constant fear.

The funeral was a week later, and the grocery store was closed for the entire day in observation. Rebel's parents attended the service along with a few of the neighbors despite not knowing Mr. Murphy personally, but Rebel stayed home. They didn't think it was a good idea to bring their son to the cemetery again after burying his friend only months ago, which was fine by him. The Cadillac Man picked him up while his parents were at the funeral so Rebel could cause a flock of sheep to rush their herder forcing him back into a running thresher.

The man's death was a magnificent sight with bloody pink strips flying like streamers at a parade as the spinning blades skinned him while pulling his body to pieces. As gruesome as it was Rebel couldn't help but laugh hysterically, and the image instantly became his new favorite thing. This was far and away the most entertaining kill yet, and while he would like to have had the moment captured on video his memory would more than suffice.

His parents were still gone when the Cadillac Man dropped him back off at home. After he'd showered and added his bloody clothes to the growing pile in the corner of his closet, Rebel sat on the floor in front of the television only he wasn't paying attention to what was on. He was watching a man being devoured by farming equipment on a loop in his head, and it was still just as funny.

He started laughing so hard streams of tears poured down his cheeks to his chin, and almost didn't hear the deadbolt turning on the front door.

Rebel stopped laughing immediately and flattened out the smile he'd been wearing for hours. A moment later his mother stepped into the living room while his father went to their room to change.

"We're home sweetheart," his mother said somberly. "It was a very ni—"

She stopped when Rebel turned to look up at her, and she saw his red face streaked with fresh tears. She knelt by his side, wrapped her arms around his neck, and hugged him tightly.

"Oh honey, it's okay, it's okay." She rubbed his back as she continued to embrace the boy. "What's wrong? Did something happen?"

Rebel hugged his mother back harder and buried his face into her shoulder.

"I was just thinking about B.J.," he whispered next to her ear adding a sniffle for effect. "I miss him."

———◆———

James ran his finger absently around the rim of his mug when Amelia went to the restroom and stared through the window out into the parking lot. He wasn't as concerned by her believing to have some ambiguous information he wasn't privy to as much as he was just bored.

He'd been awake for going on twenty-six hours and wanted to get this over with so he could go home and sleep. He'd done longer though with his record being thirty-seven straight hours of being awake, and that was without drugs. Of course, James was 'juiced up' when on official Cadillac Man business courtesy of his proctor, but even though he could stay awake didn't mean he still wasn't exhausted.

The waitress stopped at the table and began to fill his mug from the carafe she was carrying without being prompted. James was still looking at the window and glanced down at his mug as it was being filled, and quickly did a double take. The hand holding the carafe was now starkly different than the thin and delicate well-manicured one pouring refills up until now.

The hand was stripped of its former femininity replaced by enlarged knuckles sprouting coarse and curly black hairs, and yellow cracked fingernails with dirt-lined cuticles. The attached arm was pale to the extent of being albino and lined with purple and blue veins bulging through tissue paper-like white skin.

When James looked up at the waitress's face it no longer belonged to her, and he scooted back against the window. It was angular with high, sharp cheekbones emphasized further by a flattened upturned nose. Unnaturally yellow bloodshot eyes stared back at him as a smile stretched open wide showing off an uncomfortable number of pointy teeth. They were stained a complementary shade of yellow except for where they went crimson at the gum line.

Then, the smell finally hit him.

"Hello James."

This was no longer their waitress, but still wore her dress and apron. The oval white nametag pinned to the top of the apron said 'Jacobi' in what was most certainly blood. A small crooked heart was used to dot the 'i'.

"Jesus Jacobi!" James spat. "You scared the shit out of me. What gives?"

James was familiar with Jacobi, the Cadillac Man's manifested imp sidekick, but did not enjoy his company. He'd only dealt with the creature a handful of times, but it was enough to know nothing good happened when Jacobi was around.

"Nice to see you too," the imp hissed sarcastically. "Actually, I'm a little early, and when I saw your friend leave, I wanted to stop by and say hello. So, hello!"

James felt wet warmth on the front of his pants all of a sudden and looked down to see Jacobi continued to pour coffee despite having overflowed the mug. A translucent brown puddle consumed the majority of tabletop in front of James and was now flowing like a tepid caffeinated waterfall onto the crotch of his pants.

He tried to maneuver away from the overflow, but there was nowhere to go since Jacobi blocked him from exiting the booth. James pulled his feet up to try and stand, but they slipped off the wet slick plastic of the bench seat.

"Hey!" James called out as Jacobi continued to pour from the bottomless coffee carafe. "Hey! Hey! HEY!"

James looked up at the unresponsive imp, but Jacobi was gone, and when he looked back down the mess was too. The table was clean, his pants were dry, and his coffee mug was empty. From across the diner the waitress heard him yelling as she was coming from the bathroom and rolled her eyes assuming he was trying to get her attention.

"Just a moment please sir," she barked curtly, her tone now void of sugarcoated politeness. "I have a rat emergency to deal with then you can have all the precious coffee you want."

James went to explain himself but decided against it since whatever he said would most likely inflame the waitress further making things worse.

"Fuckin' prick," she muttered purposely loud enough for him to hear as she walked behind the counter on her way to the kitchen, which he did but chose to ignore.

The waitress pushed the swinging half-door, and

partially stepped in the kitchen while holding it open with her back.

"Wade," she called to her boss again.

A beer-bellied, tank-top wearing, sweaty man hollered back from a sizzling griddle spattered with eggs and meats in various stages of becoming a full-fledged breakfast. A cigarette dangled expertly from the corner of his mouth sprouting an impossible length of granny-ash seconds away from becoming an ingredient in an omelet.

"What! I'm busy!"

"We got another rat in the ladies," the waitress hollered back at him. "And it's a big one."

The man cursed loudly then continued stringing expletives together under his breath while moving piles of pink and yellow mush to the back of the grill with a spatula. The waitress ignored him as she grabbed the carafe of decaf coffee to refill James's mug with.

———— ♦ ————

James had been working with the Cadillac Man just over two years when he was introduced to Jacobi. It was dark when the car pulled to the curb, but still on the side of winter when the days are short, so it wasn't late yet. James was standing at the end of his driveway holding a greasy cardboard container of French fries with one hand while the other was buried in his jacket pocket. He brought the flimsy receptacle to his face and plucked out fries with his teeth.

It was cold, and he wanted to stay as warm as possible while he waited without getting grease on his fingers. The Cadillac Man didn't let James know he was coming ahead of time, but after the first few weeks he developed a sense for when his boss was on his way. He recognized the car by the headlights as it turned onto the block gliding silently up the street toward him.

James leaned his head back, poured the few remaining French fries into his mouth, and tossed the container over his shoulder. He heard it skid across the driveway behind him as it caught in the breeze and tumbled over into the neighbor's yard. James stepped to the street as the Cadillac slowed to a stop, pulled open the door, and jumped in the front seat.

They began to drive without saying anything having forgone the formality of greeting one another early on in the relationship. It was another understanding, which also went without saying, but this time James immediately noticed something was different about the car. Not the car really, but the atmosphere inside it.

There was a smell, but the kind of smell that came with a certain humidity attached, and James could feel the air thickening around him by the second. The Cadillac Man continued to drive silently, and James gave a sideways glance in his direction hoping to prompt an explanation, but one wasn't offered.

James tried to ignore the smell but there was a lingering sour undercurrent he couldn't seem to get past. He was about to say he needed to open his window when he heard the distinct sound of heavy breathing coming from behind him. He remained perfectly still while holding his own breath. The breathing got louder, and James felt a warm rush of air against the back of his neck. Gooseflesh activated across his back and arms as he realized the breathing wasn't getting louder; it was getting closer.

"Hey! What the hell man!"

James scooted forward in his seat slapping at the back of his neck and looked over his shoulder to confront the source. The backseat was dark and felt like it went back much further than the outside of the car made it look. Despite the shadows James was able to make out the form of someone leaning back against the seat, and now they were laughing.

"James, I want you to meet Jacobi," the Cadillac Man said without taking his eyes off the road. "Jacobi is another . . . helper of mine, so to speak. You needn't concern yourself with him, and before you ask; no, he is not human."

"Not human?"

James looked into the back seat again as the hidden passenger leaned forward into the light. He did his best to stifle his initial gasp when he saw what the Cadillac Man meant by 'not human'.

Jacobi was exceptionally pale and completely bald. A flattened-out nose was pushed back into the center of his long thin face constructed by an angled bone structure foreign to any human James had ever seen. The thing's eyes were jaundice-yellow pools being rushed from all sides by snake-like blood-red veins eclipsing the white beneath them.

"Nice to meet you."

Jacobi hissed a smile revealing too many pointy yellow teeth than should be possible to hold in one mouth. He chuckled again before leaning back into the darkness.

"We're going to drop Jacobi off," the Cadillac Man said. "Then, you and I have work to do."

James nodded and mumbled an acknowledgment, as he settled back in his seat while trying to keep Jacobi in his peripheral vision. He looked through the windshield and realized they were on a highway now despite not having been in the car long enough to even get out of the neighborhood. James wasn't shocked since he knew the Cadillac Man didn't operate under the same constraints of time and space he had to.

The highway was lined with trees up and down both sides, another indication they were nowhere close to James's home. Although, it was possible for them to be in a completely different time era, so there was really no way of knowing where or when they were.

The Cadillac Man signaled and slowed the car as they approached and took the next exit. The road curved off away from the highway with nothing of note in sight as far as James could see except for a truck stop about a mile down the road. The yellow sign with black letters stood out against the night sky, and James watched it mesmerized as they approached.

The Cadillac Man did indeed turn into the truck stop where James broke free of the sign's spell and looked out at the empty parking lot around them. There were no cars or trucks at any of the many gas pumps, but James could see lights on inside the small store through the glass doors.

Jacobi didn't say a word as he opened the door and exited the car. As he walked toward the doors James saw he was dressed like he worked there. The button-up shirt was typical of the kind clerks wore at gas stations, and the color scheme matched the simple yellow and black of the sign. Jacobi paused when he reached the door and turned with a smile to wave before going inside.

A sense of unease lingered with James after his first encounter with the Cadillac Man's inhuman helper, which he imagined was the intended effect of Jacobi's presence. If his being there was supposed to serve as a warning of sorts, James had no idea what the warning was?

Not knowing didn't lessen the effectiveness though, and he spent weeks walking on eggshells hoping not to inadvertently act against the mystery warning. James didn't ask any questions about Jacobi as they drove away from the truck stop, or any other time after that.

He felt like it was the Cadillac Man's way of putting some fear back into him at the time. As far as James knew the Cadillac Man could move in, around, and through time, so there was no reason to have the two of them in the car together. It wasn't like they were carpooling, and the truck stop had been on the way to their final destination. James had gone numb long ago, but for whatever reason his 'boss' wanted to him to remember fear especially when it came to him.

He told James Jacobi wasn't human, but had he been at one time? Did the Cadillac Man make him into whatever he was now? If so, was the transformation a form of punishment for failing to perform his duties to satisfaction?

These were the questions swirling in James's head while wondering if Jacobi's condition was a product of circumstance, or an inevitable result of working with the Cadillac Man? Was it only a matter of time before he looked in the mirror and saw a similarly horrific face looking back, or would he have to cross the Cadillac Man to earn such an 'honor'?

Almost three years went by before James encountered Jacobi again, but this time the Cadillac Man brought him to the white-skinned demonic-looking creature in a parking garage.

"We need to make a stop," the Cadillac Man told him after they'd been driving for a few minutes. "It won't take long. Oh, and you can say hello to an old friend while we're at it."

James shrugged noncommittally like usual, but inside he was on high alert. This was another anomaly in his career with the Cadillac Man, which gave him good reason to be nervous. They never made stops on the way to where they were going, but what really concerned him was the 'old friend' comment.

James didn't have friends now let alone ones in the past who would be considered 'old', and he was afraid of what he may encounter. Was the Cadillac Man truly taking him to see someone from his past, and if so, was it an actual living person, or was it someone he helped kill come back as a living-dead ghoul? Why not? James didn't have any kind of contract, and it wasn't like the Cadillac Man was an upstanding trustworthy entity. He was very much aware that any time the big black Cadillac picked him up it could be his last ride, and not because they were going to his retirement party.

James shifted in his seat when they pulled into the multi-leveled structure but maintained a calm demeanor despite the raging pit of nerves writhing in his stomach. He didn't recognize where they were, but the modern looking vehicles told him they were in or around the present time period.

The first level was completely full as was the second and the third, although James was pretty sure they weren't looking for a place to park. They bypassed the fourth and fifth levels, which also appeared completely full, but when they reached the sixth level there wasn't a car on the entire level. In the middle of the large open space James saw someone on their knees with their back to them.

They were leaning over something in front of them with their head down almost against it. The Cadillac Man steered the car in the person's direction giving James a better look at the back of the pale baldhead he knew belonged to Jacobi. On the ground in front of the creature was a body, or rather what was left of one.

Jacobi was bent over the unidentifiable carcass using his sharp yellow teeth to rip muscle from bone like a wild animal devouring its fresh kill. The car slowed as they approached, and he looked over his shoulder in acknowledgment of the Cadillac Man's arrival. Jacobi's face was completely covered in blood. The red was deep and vibrant against his ultra-white complexion, and if James weren't looking at the mangled corpse the blood came from, he would've thought it was fake.

The car stopped about six feet away, and Jacobi reached inside the ruptured torso and ripped out a rib before he stood up. The jarring crack was followed by a wet suction sound wholly unique to anything James had heard before in his life. Jacobi stood with the rib to his mouth and walked to the car picking tissue from the bone along the way.

Jacobi wasn't wearing a shirt and his chest was slick and shiny with blood like his face. It appeared he'd been wearing a pair of coveralls unzipped so the top half dangled behind him like a cape for his ass. The sleeves drug the ground leaving two parallel running streaks of blood behind him.

The driver side window slid down seemingly on its own as James didn't see the Cadillac Man push any buttons, and Jacobi leaned into the open space flashing an uncomfortable crimson-stained smile. James could already smell him.

"Nice to see you again James," Jacobi snarled punctuating the greeting with a bite from the rib directly after.

James nodded and quickly looked away. Through the windshield he had an unobstructed view of what was left of Jacobi's meal. It was mostly a pile of wet bones since a gnarly assault of Jacobi's razor-sharp teeth had expertly extracted the majority of flesh. There were scattered chunks of unidentifiable organ meat, and a few feet of small intestine on either side of the body either discarded or set aside for later.

The skull was bare, and the face was bashed in. The cracks between the broken parts stood out in places where the space was big enough for bits of brain to show through. The ribcage was mostly intact but appeared to already have lost a few of the ribs before the one he'd watched Jacobi remove. The organs left in the ravaged cavity were a pile of indistinguishable mush.

James could tell there weren't enough 'pieces' left to make a full human, and wondered if they'd been removed elsewhere or had already been eaten? He didn't want to think about either scenario and lowered his gaze to the floorboard at his feet.

The Cadillac Man and Jacobi had been talking the whole time, but all James could hear was gibberish since what was being said was not for him. Jacobi took a final nibble from the rib before handing it through the window to the Cadillac Man who quickly slipped it into the breast pocket of his jacket. It poked out from the top like the tip of a grizzled and morbid cigar.

"I'll see you around James," Jacobi said in English signaling the end of his conversation with their mutual employer.

"Whatever."

James tried not to look in the creature's direction but couldn't help a brief yet disturbing glance in which his eyes locked with the deep-set, burning-yellow pools in Jacobi's face. It was only a moment, but the image was permanently tattooed in his memory, and would present itself to him randomly at times in the future without having been provoked.

The window went up by itself, and Jacobi returned to his meal. The Cadillac Man made a wide U-turn to send them back in the direction of they'd come. He maneuvered the vehicle slowly down the twisting ramp to the first floor exit, and James seethed inside fighting hard to keep his comments regarding Jacobi from breaking his front teeth out to escape.

"Stop worrying about Jacobi," the Cadillac Man said as he steered through the garage exit and made a left. "You needn't concern yourself with him now. In the future you two may make a great team, but not now. Not for a while."

James knew the Cadillac Man could read his thoughts, but he didn't think about it all the time. He'd remember in the future to work on being more guarded while the two of them were on one of their drives. He couldn't protest, but he didn't have to agree with the Cadillac Man's prediction regarding his relationship with Jacobi.

"Team?" James huffed and crossed his arms against his chest but kept his eyes forward as he spoke. "I doubt it. I don't want to be part of a team with whatever *that* is."

He hooked a thumb over his shoulder for emphasis, but quickly returned his arm to his chest. When the Cadillac Man didn't respond James looked over to see he was grinning while slowly shaking his head. James resigned himself to silence for the rest of the drive, and the Cadillac Man followed suit as neither cared to continue the conversation.

It was dark when they arrived at their destination,

which turned out to be a construction site. The Cadillac Man pulled the car against the fence on the far side of the site away from the main part of the street running in front of it. He gave James a very specific set of instructions regarding what he was to do at the site, which consisted of him moving certain pieces of equipment in very specific ways, and into very specific places.

James stepped from the car, and it drove off when the door closed behind him not to return until he was done. As he approached the fence a small opening tore across the chain link directly in front of him, so he crawled through and got to work.

Despite his best efforts James could think of little else than the fluorescent yellow eyes glowing horrifically out from that blood-soaked face, and later when he was back in his home, he didn't sleep because of it.

————————— ◆ —————————

Amelia slid back into the booth across from James still frazzled, but immediately distracted by the equally unsettled look on *his* face. Their eyes met for a moment before falling to their respective coffee mugs as the waitress stepped up to refill them.

"Really sorry again about –" The waitress gestured with her head in the direction of the bathrooms while mouthing the words 'the rat'. "I got Wade on it though, so you know."

She flashed a quick grimace while running a finger across her neck to communicate Wade's intentions for the supposed rodent before glowering down at James.

"What about you?" Her apologetic tone turned flat to match her expression, and she started walking away before James had time to wave her off.

"What the hell was that all about?" James asked reflexively sipping from the cup despite having had his fill.

"I should ask you the same thing," Amelia fired back still on edge from her experience in the bathroom.

They both sipped nervously from their coffees while continuing to avoid eye contact acting as if the other weren't there. James caught a lingering phantom whiff of Jacobi's distinct sour stench and jerked his head around to look over his shoulder.

He didn't see any sign of the creature, and now his nostrils were filled with the smell of bacon, eggs, and coffee along with a various sundry of other requisite breakfast foods filling in the blanks.

"So, let me guess," James said turning back around to face Amelia. "There was no rat in the bathroom?"

Shaking her head, she brought the mug down from her mouth to the table and lingered on it a few more seconds before finally bringing her eyes up to meet James's.

"No," she said softly. "There was no rat."

"But it wasn't nothing either, right?"

"Yes," Amelia replied bringing her voice to a normal volume. "What happened out here while I was in there? Did you . . . see something too?"

"More like *someone.*" James took another quick look over his shoulder that did not go unnoticed from Amelia. "But I imagine it was to create a shared unease between us. It could just be distracting us from something else?"

"You saw someone?" Amelia's eyes darted from one section of the diner to another unsure of what she was even scanning for. "Who? Was it *him*?"

"No, no, no, but he's getting close."

"What do you mean by distraction? What could we be being distracted from?"

James paused for a sip of coffee before answering Amelia's question.

"That's the whole point of a distraction. Whatever we were supposed to be distracted from must've already happened."

———— ◆ ————

The Cadillac Man's frequent visits with Rebel kept up for quite a while before they began to gradually taper off. The amount of time between kills grew longer and longer over a stretch until eventually they stopped altogether.

The Cadillac Man hadn't said anything about severing their business partnership the last time Rebel saw him, and while he wouldn't know what to look for, he was fairly certain he hadn't been given a 'sign' of some kind either. The odd thing was Rebel didn't really care anymore, and in fact the thought had even slipped his mind.

He no longer felt the mounting anticipation that used to fill the torturous gaps of time between meetings with the Cadillac Man, and the *urge* he'd fed so frequently seemed to have abated without warning. Rebel remained apathetic regarding the killing he'd done, and the concept of remorse still eluded him. He simply no longer experienced the nagging insatiable pang directing his every motivation toward its fulfillment.

One morning Rebel tried to remember how long it had been since his last ride with the Cadillac Man, and realized he'd lost track. He also tried in vain to recall his last kill, but they all ran together in his head. Was it the older man he'd clubbed in a shitty bar bathroom before drowning him in the urinal, or had it been the woman he'd electrocuted while she was in the shower?

He remembered being excited to see a woman naked but was so consumed with the act itself her nudity barely registered. It couldn't have been the man he pushed in front of the bus, which killed him while triggering a major traffic accident resulting in three additional deaths, because he'd remember something so significant.

The more Rebel tried to remember the more everything seemed to run together with one kill becoming indistinguishable from another. These experiences, once indelibly crystallized in great detail within his memory bank, were now fuzzy, far off, and deteriorating by the day.

He used to sit for hours dwelling on his deeds while

watching them play out in his mind's eye exactly as they'd happened, but now the ability had left him. Some days he would second-guess whether any of it really happened or existed only within his morbidly vivid imagination?

Rebel often found himself vacillating on this idea until the theory was put to bed completely when he found a wooden box the Cadillac Man had given him in the beginning. He was cleaning out his room at the end of his senior year in high school and came upon it back of the bottom drawer of his desk. It was buried under years of unfinished homework and unopened letters addressed to his parents from the school.

The box was a physical touchstone tying him to a definitive past, but it didn't improve his memory any, so while he couldn't deny committing those acts he could no longer recall the specifics. Rebel started to purposely think more about the Cadillac Man after reaching this realization in hopes the thoughts themselves could invoke him one more time.

It wasn't because he wanted a final thrill, or even to reignite the former frequency of their meetings, but really, he just wanted a chance to say goodbye. Rebel had spent a great deal of time during his formative years engaging in activities with the Cadillac Man, far more than his own father. The least he could do was stop by just to say 'thanks for everything kid. I'm proud of you, have a nice life'.

He didn't come back though, and Rebel didn't think about him anymore focusing instead on what he wanted to do with the rest of his life. He felt empty and incomplete without a clue, an idea, or direction. Whatever he did Rebel wanted it to be something he could throw himself into wholly. Something he could let consume his life to distract him from the permanent numbness he was left with otherwise.

The decision to join the police academy was impulsive but held no sway on his choice. He didn't care what he did, and being a cop was something he knew would require long hours, overtime, and offered any number of security side jobs. By the end of his first week at the academy he decided to become a detective as quickly as possible after graduation.

One thing he'd retained from an incalculable kill count was a keen eye when it came to crime scenes due to his extensive experience in creating them. Rebel was able to see things in a case from a completely different angle to help fill in the blanks, which was exactly why he was so good with cold cases even before being promoted.

The Cadillac Man rarely crossed his mind anymore but nursed a growing resentment in Rebel when he did although he wasn't sure why. They didn't owe each other anything, not even the goodbye Rebel thought he needed, but still the animosity grew.

In the far, deep, furthest reaches of Rebel's mind was the idea his detective work was as close as he'd get to atoning for the things he'd done while acting simultaneously as a slap in the face of the Cadillac Man with every case he solved.

———————◆———————

"Goddamn, mother fucking, bastard-ass rats."

Wade muttered to himself while pushing mounds of sizzling eggs and meat to the back of the griddle where it was cooler. He didn't want any of the orders to burn while he stepped away to dispatch another rat. The rodent issue was starting to become a real pain in his ass, but he'd gotten good at bashing in the bastards' heads so it wouldn't take long.

He rested the spatula upside down on the counter next to the flattop and walked over to the red plastic milk-crate in the corner of the kitchen where he kept his 'killin' tools'. Wade didn't like to specify them as 'rat killin' tools', so as to not be pigeonholed when it came to what he killed with them.

He selected a hammer from the pile of makeshift

weaponry, which also included a rubber mallet, a meat tenderizer, and another larger hammer. The items were caked in blood and fur like medals of achievement, and morbid tally marks for each kill. Wade wiped the head of the hammer on the front of his apron leaving a deep red streak amongst the grease and food stains.

"Goddamn rats," he said through clenched teeth as he gripped the hammer tight and exited the kitchen via the swinging door on his way to the ladies' room.

He walked behind the waitress as she picked up the last meal, he'd plated from the handoff plane under the mostly warm warming lamps.

"Try not to be so loud this time," she said to him over her shoulder.

Wade grunted and continued toward the bathrooms anxious to deliver death to another pain-in-the-ass rat so he could get back to cooking. He disappeared down the short dark hall and paused at the door to the ladies' room.

He put his ear as close as he could to the door without making actual contact listening for sounds he would deem as 'rat related' but heard none. He placed his non-hammer carrying hand flat against the door and pushed slowly scanning the room as the aperture widened. Wade stood at the entrance propping the door open with the side of his foot, and made one more long, slow sweep of the room looking carefully for any evidence to point him in the direction of his enemy.

He held his hammer at the ready and stepped into the restroom letting the door swing shut behind him. Inside it was silent save for the dripping faucet and a running toilet, both of which he was supposed to have fixed already. Wade stepped forward keeping his head on a swivel and his hammer poised to strike but saw no sign of the rat.

He'd dealt with enough of them to know just because he couldn't see them didn't mean the culprit decided to vacate on their own. Having the odd ability to squeeze themselves through almost any crack or crevice gave rats quite the advantage, but Wade was confident he'd be able to sniff out its hiding place and carry out the execution.

The surly short-order cook headed slowly in the direction of the sink where the receptacle for used paper towels was filled to overflowing. Wade had caught more than a few rats rooting around in the bottom of that trashcan and decided to begin his search there. He lifted the hammer as he approached but changed course when he heard something come from the stall.

"I got you now you furry little bastard," Wade said through a smile as he approached the origin of the sound.

A moment later the noise came again, and louder this time. It sounded like pieces of sheet metal being smacked together and was followed by the unmistakable plop of something dropping into the toilet. Wade remembered the last time he went to kill a rat when it was still in the toilet, he turned the bowl into porcelain shards in the process. The rodent surprised him when he'd checked the stall, and he just started swinging his hammer without thinking.

He killed the rat but destroyed the toilet in the process and the ensuing mess was such a pain in his ass Wade swore to himself he'd never go after a rat in the toilet again. The water had to be turned off for it to be fixed, which meant the diner was closed during the installation costing him even more money. Wade didn't like to lose money.

The new toilet he'd installed on his own dime was barely three weeks old, and he scrambled to put together a plan on the fly to get the rat *out* of the commode. Wade took a quick look around the small dingy room for something to inspire an idea when he heard splashing in the stall followed by the clicking sound of claws on tile.

He smiled knowing his job had just gotten easier and continued toward the stall.

"I'm comin' in there to getcha'," Wade sang out. "I hope you rememb—"

Wade stopped when he saw the tail roll out from under the stall door like a snake uncoiling. It wasn't the sight of the tail that stopped him, but the size. It was thick like a fire hose, and the section he was seeing was at least three feet long with who knows how much more hidden from his view?

"What the hell?"

Wade crouched to take a closer look but kept two feet of space between him and the impossibly large rat-tail. For a moment he thought it might be a practical joke but even with a closer look he couldn't be sure. The tail was either real, or a prop from a movie, because it looked way too good to be something someone from around the diner whipped up to scare him.

He reached out with the hammer to give the tail a gentle tap to better gauge its consistency, but the tip flapped to the side avoiding his attempt. Wade flinched, dropped the hammer, and fell back on his ass. He flailed to right himself and return to his feet but continued stumbling until his back hit the wall.

The end of the tail flapped back and forth smacking the tile in quick wet slaps while the rest slithered side to side. Wade's breath came hard and fast, and he could feel his heart beating up in his neck just below his ear. He gave a quick glance in the direction of the door not wanting to take his eyes off the tail for too long.

The bathroom was small, but the door felt like it was a hundred miles away. Wade wanted to run, but his legs refused to respond. His panting became labored as tightness worked across his chest like his lungs were in a vise.

He leaned hard against the wall and clutched at his chest trying to slow his breathing despite the heavy gasps. The hammer lay inches from the writhing tail where it did Wade absolutely no good. The tip of the tail came down on the hammer and pulled it closer as if it knew he was thinking about it. The end of the tail curled back and whipped itself at the hammer sending it sliding across the floor where Wade, having suddenly regained control of his limbs, lifted his foot and brought it down on the tool to stop it.

He looked up just in time to see the tail curl back beneath the stall door and out of sight. Wade hesitated only a moment before bending down to pick up the hammer then shot back up ready to strike. It felt good to be holding the weapon again, and it reinvigorated his motivation to finish what he came to do.

Rat or not, Wade was going to hit whatever was in the stall with his hammer until it was a mushy pile of blood and hair. He gathered his nerve and stepped toward the stall just as the door flung open banging hard against the inner wall. It sounded like a rifle report, and Wade closed his eyes, turned his head, and reflexively brought his hands to his ears still clutching the hammer tight.

When he opened them back up, he saw someone or something standing in the open stall. It looked like a person only bald and pale enough to almost glow in the low light of the windowless bathroom. Its face was distorted by jagged dramatic angles jutting frighteningly from each side flanking a flat nose that appeared to have been shoved back into deeper into the skull. Its eyes were a blazing shade of yellow with both cat and reptile-like qualities to them.

It was wearing in the same dress and apron the waitresses at the diner wore, which somehow intensified the overall frightfulness of its appearance. Wade couldn't read it from where he stood, but the name tag pinned on the top left of the apron said Jacobi.

"How dare you?" Jacobi's tone was sarcastic and sinister. "This is the ladies' room!"

He broke out into a fit of shrill raucous laughter, which gave Wade a good look at what was essentially a mouth full of small knives in place of teeth. Other than that, he had no idea who or what he was dealing with. A sudden spark of anger triggered a surge of courage in the short order cook, and his body language adjusted to his new frame of mind.

He'd come into the bathroom to kill a rat, but now had to deal with some freak who'd been doing creepy things in the ladies' room stall. Wade had seen weirdos like this come through the diner before, and it wouldn't be the first time he'd had to remove one forcibly.

It typically occurred when rock and roll bands on tour would stop on their way in or out of town, and there'd been more than a few dustups when opposing biker clubs would show up sat the same time. Wade had been through them all and lived to tell the tale, and this carnival-freak-looking, drugged-out, albino would be no different.

"What the hell you think you're doin' in there son?" Wade growled as he stepped confidently toward the stranger in the stall, the hammer raised and ready. "I think it's time for you to go on back to whatever sideshow you came from."

Jacobi put his hands on his hips and cocked his head while Wade closed the distance between them.

"Oh, I'll be out of your hair soon enough," Jacobi said in a sugary tone. "I just stopped in for a quick bite."

Wade lunged forward intending to deliver a blow to the flat space between the stranger's inhuman yellow eyes, but the hammer fell from his hand before he could bring it down. He was confused, and numb, and a sudden intense ringing in his ears rattled his equilibrium.

He was very hot, and then very cold, and didn't know where he was or what he was doing? The 'weirdo' was smiling, his face covered in blood. Wade looked down to see blood streaming down the front of his own chest and realized something wasn't right.

He looked back up at the grinning creature who'd moved too fast for Wade to process that a bite had been taken out of his neck. Wade's body folded to the ground, and Jacobi pulled him the rest of the way into the stall then closed the door.

---- ◆ ----

Rebel followed behind the Cadillac Man down the hall and watched him enter one of the rooms through a door on the right. He'd come to James's house under the pretense of following up on an investigation and didn't expect the Cadillac Man to show up, although he really should have.

The cold case regarding the murder of James's parents stuck with him because it had all the earmarks of the Cadillac Man's influence. The supposed suicides at the high school did too, and he should've realized it was only a matter of time before his old 'business partner' popped back up. None of it truly clicked until Rebel followed the Cadillac Man into a room in James's house.

The part of his brain where he'd compartmentalized his past cracked down the middle and flooded his mind with detailed memories he'd thought were far away, and long forgotten. Rebel never denied to himself what he'd done in the past, he felt no reason to, but having it all come back in that moment was almost too much to handle.

His head was spinning from the onslaught, and he closed his eyes while massaging the bridge of his nose to alleviate the overwhelming pressure. The room was mostly empty save for a few cardboard boxes, some empty beer bottles, and a wadded-up flamingo-covered shower curtain tossed in the corner.

The Cadillac Man stood before Rebel for the first time in years, and still held the powerful commanding presence he'd been intoxicated by as a child. His unblemished appearance remained exactly as it had been, and the shock of blond hair was also untouched by time.

"Hello again Rebel," the Cadillac Man said smiling down on the adult version of his old business partner. "It's time again."

An opiate-like wave of warmth rolled up and down his body, and he reveled in its familiar embrace. The case didn't matter anymore; none of them did now. Rebel's true sense of purpose was restored. The Cadillac Man had returned, and it was time to get back to work.

————————◆————————

The four years bookended by Amelia's meetings with the Cadillac Man were lonely for her. She had no relationships last longer than a date or two, and only recently had she realized the last steady partner she'd had was in high school, and she'd had him killed.

It had nothing to do with her feelings over what Ben had done to her, or what happened to him, or what she arranged to have happen to him. Amelia really felt nothing about his death or her part in it. She suspected her lack of relationships was a direct result of her knowing the Cadillac Man.

His poisonous touch had withered her capacity to care about the people she'd affected by their covenant, which in itself was an unexpected result. Although Amelia couldn't imagine her life would be much different if she'd been forced to deal with the emotional toll of what she knew she'd been responsible for.

She certainly hadn't been happy since then, but she wasn't depressed either. More than anything else she was just plain bored. Amelia tried to find jobs to distract herself with but could never hold them for longer than a few months. Every time she thought about college, or secondary education of any kind, she couldn't get past the overwhelming feeling it was all a waste of time. At least it would be for her.

Amelia used to love to read, but after the Cadillac Man she lost the spark of intangible delight she derived from books and hadn't finished a single one she'd started in four years. She tried to force herself to keep reading, but never got farther than halfway through anything she attempted despite the length or subject.

Amelia would read a page and then end up staring at

it for sometimes minutes at a time without proceeding or rereading. The motivation to turn the page was lost to such an extent Amelia found it hard to remember what it was like to be propelled forward by a story. She used to be able to get lost in a book for hours without realizing it. If she could spend even one hour trying to read a book now she'd be lucky to get through four pages.

She tried to date, or rather there were several men who tried to date her, but like reading and other things she used to delight in, seeking a relationship of any kind was lost on her. Amelia was caught off guard when men approached her in her day-to-day life to make quick small talk before asking for her phone number. The whole experience felt foreign and intrusive as if she were a long-married woman who'd forgotten what it was like to be courted.

She chalked her disinterest in the first few men she'd gone out with up to there being no chemistry between them but soon realized this was the case with everyone. No matter who she went out with or tried to get to know in a romantic capacity Amelia felt nothing but indifference.

If she went on more than one date with anyone it was out of guilt since she knew the result would be the same no matter how many times she went out with the same person. Amelia didn't become depressed, nor did she mourn her ability to feel anything toward a potential mate.

She didn't care about things like finding the right partner or being married by a certain age in order to settle down and start a family like she had when she was a young girl. Amelia's life post Cadillac Man was full of ambivalence, apathy, and an overall numbing of her capacity to care about anything she may have deemed important had she not crossed paths with him.

About the only thing she *did* feel was anticipation. Every waking moment of her life Amelia felt like she was waiting for something to happen. Maybe the Cadillac Man was supposed to come back? Maybe she already knew he was?

Sometimes she'd be dreaming and wake up in the middle of the night with the overwhelming feeling something she'd been waiting for was finally making its way to her. Amelia tried to find tasks to occupy her time with, but would often find herself sitting doing nothing with no idea how long she'd been doing it?

Amelia couldn't see her life getting any different until whatever was supposed to happen happened. Until then she'd live a numb unsettled existence riddled with holes of missing time.

———— ♦ ————

The waitress ducked to look through the opening at the handoff plane into the kitchen for Wade, but he'd yet to resume his post. She grumbled her way over to the swinging kitchen door and held it open to get a full view of the entire space to see if he was at the fridge or the sink, but he wasn't there at all. She couldn't imagine he'd still be dealing with the rat since he was so boastful about how 'quick and efficient' he was at killing rats, but maybe he'd met his match with this one?

The food Wade had moved to the back of the griddle with the intent of coming back to finish was starting to burn quicker than the exhaust hood could keep up with. Smoke was starting to roll up over the sides of the stainless-steel industrial hood when the waitress opened the door.

"Goddamnit! Wade!" she called out racing to the stove. "Where the hell are you?"

She snatched the spatula from the counter and began turning off burners while scraping burning food off the grill top. There was nothing salvageable from what he'd left cooking, and she moved the trashcan closer to discard the blackened crusty chunks.

"Goddamn you," she grumbled while trying to scrape off charred chunks stuck to the grill. "All you had to do was one thing, one thing. Kill a fucking rat, is that so hard?"

When the flat top grill was free of blackened bacon debris, and scorched egg whites, and all the burners were off for sure she stormed from the kitchen. The waitress proceeded dutifully around the counter passing by customers waiting for their food without making eye contact, as she proceeded directly to the ladies' room.

"Hey dick for brains," she called approaching the door. "You almost burned the goddamn place down!"

She pushed open the door to find the room empty with no trace of Wade or the rat, but still called out again.

"Wade? Hello? Wade?"

She turned to leave when she heard something and caught the door before it closed.

"Wade? Don't pull that 'I'm gonna scare you' shit on me. You need to quit messing around and get back to the kitchen!"

No verbal response followed, but she did hear the noise again that drew her back in. It was coming from one of the stalls and sounded like a metal rake being scraped against the blacktop.

"Wade? This shit ain't funny."

She was angry, but a little creeped out and it showed unintentionally through her tone. When the sound of her own voice decayed, she was answered once again by the same scraping sound from the stall. The emerging fear was quickly overtaken by frustration as the waitress stomped across the tiled floor to the stall in question.

"Okay, very funny dipshit," she said as she slapped the door with her palm to open it, "Now get back to wo—"

The stall was empty. There was no sign of Wade, a rat, or more importantly what had been making the sound. Her anger leaned in the direction of confusion for only a moment before bending back immediately.

"Goddamnit Wade!"

The waitress stormed back to the door, through it, and stepped across the hall to check the men's room.

"Wade? You in there? Hello? Oh, goddamnit!"

She huffed and started back the way she came, her frustration mounting with each step.

"Excuse me, miss?"

One of the diners tried to get her attention when she breezed back by but was roundly ignored as she continued unabated. The waitress approached the counter and smelled it a step before she heard the unmistakable sizzle of orders being cooked on the griddle once again. She had no idea how Wade could have gotten back to the kitchen without her seeing him? The diner wasn't that big after all.

The waitress paused and looked over her shoulder at the patron who'd tried to flag her down.

"One sec hon," she said with a sweet lilt through a sugary smile in a saccharine-drenched combination sure to give even the gruffest customer a cavity. "Food's comin' right up."

The smile melted back to a scowl like sugar in the rain as she continued to the kitchen prepared to give Wade an ear-beating for ruining all the food because he took so long. If she missed out on her tips because *he* fucked up, she was going to take it out of his ass. She was sick of suffering for the mistakes of a barely competent short-order cook with a face only a mother could love, and the waitress burst into the kitchen to tell him just that.

"Jesus Christ Wade! Where in the hell were you? I went back to the lai—"

She stopped when she realized something was wrong with Wade, or maybe not wrong but different. It took her another moment to realize the difference was the person in the kitchen wasn't Wade at all. It was someone or something else.

The stranger was wearing a dress that from the back was very similar to her own, and they were bald with paper-white skin stretched across a deformed skull.

"Wh—" she stammered. "Who are you?"

"What's the matter? Don't you recognize me?" said the impostor at the grill before turning around to face the waitress. "It's me, your old friend Wade!"

It was Wade's face looking back at her across the kitchen, only it wasn't attached to Wade anymore. The now saggy unanimated flesh of the cook's face was draped over that of the stranger's with beasty yellow eyes looking back through the wide empty openings.

The flesh was jagged and moist around the edges most likely due to the method of removal, and there was a red spot on the apron where blood had dripped from the chin. The waitress's vision fluttered, and for a moment she thought she might faint, but surging adrenaline kept her conscious.

The stranger removed Wade's amputated visage from his own and slapped it down on the grill face up eliciting a loud and satisfying sizzle as pockets of fat popped sporadically. She watched the face hit the griddle and saw what else had been cooking when she walked in.

There was an entire arm with hand intact, palm down, and burned crispy black all along the underside. Next to it was a mostly mangled and skinless ribcage with whatever meat left hanging off in thin jagged ribbons. Laid out in a row on the far side of the flat top were very plainly a human heart, liver, and the thin pink cylinder of Wade's pathetic dick.

She was struck with the thought of all the times he'd tried to put the moves on her and was glad she never gave in seeing as he didn't have much for her to work with.

The waitress brought her eyes up from the frying face of her friend to the spike-toothed sneer of the man-like creature who'd just been wearing it. His blindingly white complexion was obscured by smears of red that stood out against the bright background.

He smiled and his teeth were like individual candle flames coming together to form an inferno of a smile. She became so transfixed by its hypnotic flickering she didn't realize it was coming closer.

Teeth like fire ripped into the soft-skinned throat of the waitress, and the heat burned the underside of her chin as the flame's devastation spread across her body until it was so hot, she couldn't feel it anymore.

———◆———

The tint on the back window of the Cadillac was too dark for Rebel to see through, but he could feel the Cadillac Man looking at him in the rearview mirror. He knew Rebel was in the car behind him right on time just like he was supposed to be.

Rebel didn't realize how hard he was gripping the steering wheel until his fingers started to throb. He eased up and flexed the digits a few times waiting for the light to turn green. When it did Rebel's stomach exploded with the sensation of anticipation and excitement like when he was a child. He'd all but forgotten the feeling and the intensity with which it drove him to complete any task given by his old business partner.

He'd also forgotten how the sensation would not abate until it had been resolved with violence like the final note needed to cap off a melody. It wasn't out of the ordinary to experience this kind of feeling when the Cadillac Man came around, but this was different.

Rebel had never followed behind in his own car, but if he weren't supposed to, he wouldn't have seen the Cadillac leave the lot from his office window. He certainly wouldn't have ended up directly behind it seeing as how long it took to get to his own vehicle. This particular instance was different and unexpected but intriguing nonetheless, and Rebel was anxious to see how this hand played out.

He followed along leaving a car-length or so between them and thought about when he and the Cadillac Man were in a room together at James's house some time back. His old partner told Rebel it was time again.

Rebel hoped it meant they were getting back to business as usual meeting with the same frequency from when he'd been younger, but this wasn't the case. It started off well enough that very night with a ride in the big black

Cadillac, and his first kill since he'd become a police officer. He hadn't even killed anyone in the line of duty, although there were a few times he could've and been perfectly within his right to do so.

The old adage of 'it's just like riding a bike' came to mind when Rebel used an eighteen-pound bowling ball to smash in a man's face on the night of his reunion with the Cadillac Man, and it was true. You never forget. It was more than just muscle memory though; the act reignited an instinct gone dormant with the long absence of his business partner, and with it came back the forgotten fuzzy memories in crisp full detail.

All the scenes he'd committed to memory and rolled back over and over in his mind as an endless form of entertainment when he was young became clear again the moment that bowling ball kissed the sleeping stranger goodnight for good.

It was easy and over rather quickly, and Rebel figured the Cadillac Man was purposely easing him back into the old habit while he wanted to dive in headfirst. Although he was sitting in the passenger seat of the Cadillac now as an adult, he felt like a child again. The seat itself still seemed too big for him to fill, and he wondered if it was by design or just in his head? He wouldn't doubt if it were an enchanted aspect of the vehicle in which the passenger was made to feel small next to the imposing figure of its pilot.

The ride was spent in silence, and despite the excitement and myriad questions running through Rebel's head he was starting to nod off. He fought off sleep as long as he could until finally relenting unwillingly allowing his eyes to close. As soon as his eyelids touched Rebel snapped them open, but he wasn't in the Cadillac anymore.

He was in a strange house, in a strange room where a stranger was sleeping in their bed. Momentarily startled by the jarring change of scenery Rebel nearly dropped the bowling ball he didn't realize he was holding. When he looked down into the iridescent-green swirling pattern on the ball and knew exactly what he was to do.

222

When he was a child the Cadillac Man had supplied a weapon or two for him and made sure a door or two had been unlocked, but Rebel had never just woken up where he was supposed to be. Rebel wasn't a fan of blacking out and losing swaths of time, but more importantly he didn't like not knowing what happened during that time. More specifically, Rebel didn't like not knowing what happened to *him* in particular.

He didn't let it occupy his mind much longer having rationalized it as a way for the Cadillac Man to make it easier to get Rebel back into the groove. He didn't want to think there could be nefarious reasons for this missing time, although he'd be foolish not to lend some credence to the idea.

He knew the rules of time didn't apply to the Cadillac Man and witnessed evidence of this many times. It was nothing for them to be driving along, turn down a street, and find themselves decades in the past, but he was always conscious. Rebel had never, for lack of a better term, 'teleported' to a destination and/or time period for a kill. While this vexed him it was what came after that worried him more.

Rebel brought the bowling ball down and heard the satisfying crunch of bones breaking in the man's face as they collapsed puncturing the delicate tissue of the brain. He closed his eyes and turned his head to keep blood from spraying in his face, but when he opened them was in the driver seat of his own unmarked police vehicle parked in front of James's house.

It was morning, and there was no sign of the Cadillac Man, or any other evidence to indicate what became of the rest of his night. Rebel was wildly unsettled by the entire experience until he saw the image in his head of that bowling ball resting in the concave bowl the sleeping man's face had become.

He decided to look past what made him uncomfortable about the Cadillac Man's new methods for now but swore to bring up the next time they met. It was a promise not kept and long forgotten by the time the Cadillac Man finally came back for Rebel.

———————◆———————

James didn't want to believe Amelia really knew something he didn't, but when Jacobi showed up his conviction began to wane. As much as the Cadillac Man seemed to be a creature of habit operating under his own strict and self-enforced guidelines for doing business, the presence of the albino imp was a wildcard meaning there was a possibility all bets were off.

He didn't know what the purpose for Jacobi's involvement as far as the Cadillac Man's business went. Years ago James thought the man-like creature had been used as a sort-of scare tactic meant to re-instill or re-affirm a healthy fear to keep him in line when he was younger. If the intention was the same today it worked, because the old fear began to creep back now that he knew Jacobi was there.

He sipped his coffee and leaned back in the booth attempting to appear relaxed and noticed Amelia doing the same. It had been almost two full minutes since either of them had said a word, and James decided to break the silence by trying to pry deeper into what she may or may not know.

"So," he began, "did ol' mister tall, pale, and blond ever ask you anything else out of the ordinary? I mean, besides this supposed ambiguous 'thing' he claims to want."

Amelia knew what James was doing, but she wouldn't be tricked into giving information up especially information she didn't have. She didn't understand why he was trying to be sneaky about it and was offended by his thinking she could be so easily manipulated. She would love for them both to willingly offer *any* information either of them had in hopes they could piece together the mystery behind their shared situation.

There was one thing she wouldn't tell James regardless, but only because it wasn't her place. He'd find out soon enough anyway. This was why Amelia knew sharing information between them wouldn't, or rather couldn't occur.

"Out of the ordinary?" Amelia began. "I would say that's a blanket statement applicable to anything he would say or do."

If he was going to play games with her, she was going to play right back.

"Okay, ha ha," he replied shifting his posture again suddenly feeling unable to sit still. "You know what I mean. Out of the ordinary for this . . . most *unordinary* situation we happen to be in."

Amelia smiled behind her coffee mug at the temporary flummoxing she'd inspired in the usually ice-cold and unaffected James before she put it down to answer.

"Well, I don't really know," she said, "or actually I'm not sure. I haven't had that much one-on-one time with him, so I'm not sure I have enough context to know the difference. I kind of thought just about everything he told me was strange."

James sighed letting his irritation and loss of patience start to show through the cracks of his straight-faced demeanor.

"Fine," he said smacking his palm flat against the table. "What about me?"

"What about you?"

"Me." James leaned across the table. "Did he ever say anything to you about *me*?"

Unprepared for the direct question Amelia's heart sank into the bubbling acidic cauldron of her stomach. She wasn't as good as James at maintaining a poker face, and she knew he was able to perceive the involuntary change in her expression when she hesitated before answering.

"I . . . I don—"

"He did, didn't he? Don't bullshit me, Amelia! If he told

225

you something about me, you need to tell me. Tell me now!"

Even if she wanted to tell him she couldn't, and especially not now. It was too late. Things were in motion and had gone too far to be changed now. She decided to fire back with a question of her own attempting to deflect the pressure.

"What happened to you when I was in the bathroom?"

"What?"

"Something happened," Amelia continued sternly. "You were all sorts of frazzled when I sat back down, and you just tried to play it off. So, what was going on, huh? What'd I miss?"

"Me?" James's tone turned defensive and accusatory. "Hah! I should ask you the same thing. When you came back you looked like someone rattled the shit out of your cage. So, Amelia, what happened to *you* in the bathroom?"

A charged silence hung between the two of them growing heavier by the second waiting to be dispersed by the next one to speak. James's eyes dared her to answer while Amelia's hardened gaze taunted him to keep going. It lingered a moment longer before being broken by someone else entirely.

"Order up!"

A platter was dropped on the table between them with a loud smack startling away the mounting aggression and toppling the mostly empty coffee mugs. On the platter was a dead rat the size of a raccoon on its back with his stomach cut open, and the skin pulled back. Steam was billowing from the freshly cooked innards of the giant rodent. Also on the platter was the crispy face of Wade garnished by a smorgasbord of diced organ meat.

Amelia screamed, and they both squirmed back in the booth to get as far from what was on the table as possible. James and Amelia looked up to see Jacobi smiling through his blood smeared face. He was still dressed like a waitress only now his apron was covered in blood and nearly blotched out the writing on his nametag.

"Bon Appetit!" beamed the freakish being. "Eat up before it gets cold."

————◆————

The Cadillac Man swung the big black car into the parking lot of the diner and pulled it into a spot close to the door, but he didn't get out right away. He was right on time as usual, and as far as he could tell everything seemed to be moving along. He knew Rebel wasn't far behind and would be pulling into the lot in the next twenty-seconds, so he waited a little longer.

The Cadillac Man needed Rebel to see him leave the car and enter the diner. If not, the detective would stay in the parking lot over-thinking things, but Rebel wouldn't be able to resist following him in once he'd actually seen his old business partner.

He pushed open the door, and Rebel's unmarked white cruiser turned into the parking lot as the Cadillac Man's left foot hit the asphalt. The vehicle slowed abruptly upon entrance, which meant Rebel had indeed seen the sharply dressed man. An unmistakable coif of platinum hair danced around his head in the wind like white flames.

Rebel drifted slowly towards a parking space on the opposite end of the diner as far away from the Cadillac Man as he could get. The only other vehicles in the lot were a newer model white sedan and an old red pickup truck, which were parked along the same row. Aside from that the diner didn't appear to be open. A dusty sheen across the windows lining the front of the shotgun-style restaurant kept Rebel from being able to see if anyone was inside, but there were lights on at least.

The Cadillac Man stepped from his car, stood, and used his hands to smooth down the front of his jacket. He approached the door, and reached out for the silver cylindrical handle, but paused before he entered. The Cadillac Man looked back over his shoulder across the lot at Rebel's cruiser, smiled, and winked.

---◆---

When Jacobi dropped the gore-covered platter on James and Amelia's table the diner shook, or to be more accurate it shifted. It was as if the space around them became warped and caused the walls of the structure to bow slightly. Things became fuzzy for a moment and snapped back into sharp focus just before the temperature dropped by ten degrees.

Amelia gasped for breath to scream again but the sudden disorientation forced the air from her lungs. She looked across to James who didn't appear as concerned about the situation as she thought he should be. She wanted to leap from the booth separating herself from the sickening sight, but Jacobi stood at the head of the table blocking her exit.

Amelia looked back to James and saw his lips moving, but she couldn't hear what he was saying.

"What! What!"

Amelia felt like she was screaming, but her voice came out as a whisper. James held his palms up, and though she saw he was still speaking there was no sound. There was suddenly a tremendous rush of air followed by the sound of the diner door closing, and then she could hear just fine.

"—alm down, okay! Just calm down!" James had raised his voice as he continued to get through to her.

"I can . . . I can hear you now," Amelia said at a normal volume, her breath catching in her throat.

James put his hands down and nodded but couldn't hide his expression of aggravation. She glanced down at the eviscerated rat on the tray then back up at him wondering how he wasn't completely freaking out. Maybe he was used to this kind of thing from all the time he spent with the Cadillac Man? The only thing she'd experienced anywhere close to this was eating her old boyfriend's heart, but it was in no way as wretched as what sat on the table between them.

It was a memory she'd worked daily to bury deep in her mind trying to trick herself into forgetting it happened. Besides, it was over four years ago, and since then her interactions with the Cadillac Man were ethereal, dream-like, and romanticized. Apparently, she had been getting the mystical teen-drama treatment, while James was living a *Cannibal Holocaust* version of their shared co-conspirator, which would explain his indifference.

"Wh—what is this? What is going on?" she finally managed.

"Exactly what we came here for." James shrugged shooting a disdainful look up at their new 'waitress'. "You gotta get your hands dirty at some time, and it looks like your time has come."

Amelia looked past James over his shoulder and saw the Cadillac Man was standing at the door inside the diner watching them.

———◆———

James turned around in the booth and followed Amelia's sightline over to the Cadillac Man. He noticed the diner was now empty of the other patrons and had taken on a worn down dirty look. They were still in the same diner only they'd been bumped over into a different pocket of reality.

James experienced these 'shifts' before, but it was never explained to him *exactly* what was happening, and he didn't ask. He knew better. If he needed to know the Cadillac Man would tell him, and he was just happy to come back from wherever this place was when his work was finished. James rarely stayed for the entire ordeal in instances like these, but he had a feeling he wouldn't be given an early exit today.

Whatever this was all about, he was in it for the long run.

He turned back around but could hear the Cadillac Man's footsteps as he walked past the empty booths to where they sat. James heard the door open again and turned around to see another man enter the cafe. He looked familiar but James wasn't sure why until the man un-holstered a pistol from inside his jacket.

It was the detective who'd met with the Cadillac Man at his house years ago just before he'd graduated high school. James hadn't seen the man since then, and didn't expect to, as was the norm with almost everybody he'd encountered as a result of his obligation. The newcomer leveled his weapon in the direction of the four of them, but the only one to flinch and throw their arms up was Amelia.

"Freeze!" The detective slowly approached the booth with his pistol at the ready. "Nobody move until I get this all figured out."

"Detective." The Cadillac Man put his hands behind his back and turned to face him. "Rebel, that won't be necessary."

"Look, I don't know who these people are, and whatever . . . " Rebel gestured to the bloody demon with the dress on. "Whatever the hell *that* is, but I wa—"

Rebel stopped when he realized his police-issued thirty-eight-caliber revolver was now a banana. He lowered his arms, tossed the banana over his shoulder, and relaxed his posture. The Cadillac Man pulled his hands from behind his back and held up Rebel's pistol making a show of it for all to see before tucking it away in his jacket.

"Tsk, tsk Rebel," the Cadillac Man said waving his finger. "Have you forgotten our conversation about patience already?"

Rebel did remember despite the number of years gone by, but he also knew time didn't work the same way for the Cadillac Man. He very well could have come straight to the diner directly after the conversation happened.

"Ye—yes," Rebel replied, the bravado of authority now gone from his voice.

"Hmm." The Cadillac Man looked down at the buffet of body parts on the table and motioned for them to be taken away. "Jacobi, please?"

The costumed, blood-spattered, pale-skinned creature bent to pick up the tray but paused first.

"Don't worry," Jacobi said to James and Amelia, "there's plenty of leftovers. I'll put a doggy bag together for you!"

Jacobi cackled as he lifted the tray of cannibalistic cuisine. His laughter could still be heard after he'd pushed through the swinging door separating the kitchen from the dining area.

James and Amelia went to stand, but the Cadillac Man stepped to the head of the table and motioned them to stay seated, which they slowly and reluctantly did.

"Hello Amelia," he said with a smile. "Are you ready?"

———————◆———————

The last time Amelia saw the Cadillac Man wasn't too long before the meeting at the diner. It was also when he'd told her what he wanted, and what she'd have to do. More importantly he told her what he would give to her. She'd agreed right away in the moment, but only now had the gravity of that agreement set in. The carrot he dangled to motivate her was too good to pass up.

The Cadillac Man told Amelia he could make her feel again.

No longer would apathy and indecision rule her life if only she agreed once more to his tempting terms. Naturally, she'd jumped at the chance to bring anything but indifference back into her existence. Amelia accepted deciding not to think about what she would have to do until the moment was upon her.

Finding herself in that moment now she regretted not taking time to better prepare herself. Amelia didn't expect other people would be around not to mention an albino, nightmare, monster thing thrown in the mix.

She was completely and utterly unprepared mentally, and she hadn't even remembered to keep the proper tools for the job on her person leaving them in the glovebox of her car instead.

She slowly looked up at the Cadillac Man until their eyes met, and he reached inside his jacket removing a small, plain, silver dagger with a simple black handle. It reminded her of something from a *James Bond* movie, something a spy would have hidden in his boot or holstered to his ankle.

The Cadillac Man smiled and placed the dagger on the table in front of Amelia with the point facing at James.

———————◆———————

The time for thinking was over.

The only thing left to do was act, and so she did. Amelia grabbed the dagger, lunged across the table, and plunged it into James's throat. He'd barely time to register the Cadillac Man had put a knife on the table, and now it was in his neck.

James didn't realize how lucky he was, nor would he. Amelia put enough power behind her strike to push the dagger all the way through his neck and out the back severing his brainstem killing him instantly. He didn't suffer. There was no useless gasping for air as his lungs filled up with blood while they waited for him to drown or bleed to death, whichever came first.

Perhaps the quick death was a parting gift from the Cadillac Man for his years of service, or maybe James had just been 'lucky', so to speak? Either way he was just as dead, which meant Amelia had done what she'd been asked. The Cadillac Man told her he wanted James dead, and he wanted her to kill him. In doing so she would be untethered from the entity that held intangible agency over her.

Amelia's life hadn't been affected by the Cadillac Man the same way James's or Rebel's had. She hadn't been relegated to the position of personal assistant at the mercy of his beck and call daily, nor was she picked up out of the blue to act as a secret assassin. Amelia's subjugation was specially tailored to be personally devastating.

When she'd eaten Ben's heart Amelia felt nothing about what she'd engineered to be done as she was promised. She didn't know the numbing of her senses did not exclusively apply to this single act. She didn't understand the only thing she would be able to feel for the rest of her life was impending dread always waiting for something to happen, but never knowing what, or how she would be affected by it?

Whatever reluctance she'd felt leading up to the act was gone in that single moment. As soon as the short thin blade pierced James's neck and came out the other side her reward was granted in a rush of indescribable emotional pain all at once. Not over what she'd just done, but from every emotion she should have felt over the last four years flooding her body in that single instance. She was crippled by the surge of feelings she thought she missed bombarding her formerly dormant receptors.

Amelia looked up at the Cadillac Man smiling down on her and knew she'd made a huge mistake.

———— ♦ ————

James felt nothing beyond a momentary sensation of pressure as the dagger initially punctured his throat. He hadn't thought anything of it when the Cadillac Man pulled the blade from his jacket, and in fact hadn't been paying close attention. The detective standing behind him made James nervous, and he'd tried to split his focus between what was happening at the table while keeping an eye on him as well.

In actuality it wouldn't matter if he had given his complete attention to Amelia and the Cadillac Man, because he couldn't have stopped it anyway. James would've confirmed the notion to himself if he'd been alive a second longer.

Despite the efficiency with which he'd been dispatched James felt only one thing in his final fractured moment of life. Relief. The vast, floating, empty void of death would change that, but before it could James felt the weight, he'd been saddled with by the Cadillac Man lift away. He felt like he did when he was a kid back before the dreams started, and the big black car pulled up in front of his house.

He felt more alive in the moment just before his death than he had in years, and then the feeling was gone, and so was James.

---- ◆ ----

The stabbing was incredibly jarring in the moment, but the aftermath was anticlimactic. There was no attempt made to retaliate, no screaming or moaning, no thrashing about in the throes of death. James was just dead. It was like when a child's toy is abruptly switched off during play bringing an immediate halt to its function, only there would be no change of batteries for James.

His heart stopped almost immediately, and without it pumping blood trickled from the wound after its initial spray. James's body slid over on its side slowly leaking blood like a dripping faucet. Amelia was barely aware of where she was anymore as the barrage of emotional pain unrelentingly continued.

She buried her head in her hands and closed her eyes tight trying to gain some semblance of control over herself but wasn't able to stem the tide. Amelia felt a hand patting the top of her head as if she was a child, or a dog who'd learned to sit. She didn't need to open her eyes to know it was the condescending touch of the Cadillac Man to whom Amelia truly was a pet and always had been. There wasn't enough capacity within her mind to fully process the realization on account of the relentless onslaught of compounded sadness.

The only thing she could do was accept it since there was no changing course now. Amelia knew she'd relegated herself to servitude the first time she climbed into the big black Cadillac four years ago, and no amount of denying or rationalization could change that.

She had no idea how she was supposed to go on like this, or how she'd be able to live her life in a constant state of unabated emotional distress. She couldn't, and she wouldn't. Amelia preferred death to a lifetime in her present state, and now she realized there was another reason for her being at the diner that day.

———————◆———————

A wave of euphoria crashed into Rebel exciting his senses and igniting his pleasure receptors at the site of Amelia stabbing James. The technique and lack of hesitation was something he hadn't seen in any other person aside from himself and was inadvertently aroused at the sight. He adjusted his stance to account for the sudden erection, which partially abated to half-mast as if in anticipation of impending intercourse.

"Well done. Amelia," the Cadillac Man said giving her a patronizing pat on the head. "I knew you wouldn't let me down."

Amelia responded in sobs; her head buried in her hands with no regard for the blood on her fingers. The scene held an intangible sense of beauty for Rebel, which helped stoke the fire of his excitement. He took a step forward and to his left for a better view of James's body now slumped over on its side. The Cadillac Man bent over the body, leaned in, and retrieved the dagger from James's neck. The sound of the blade slipping from the wound was soft and wet like stepping in mud with galoshes on.

Rebel had only ever killed by himself, and never *actually* witnessed another person commit such an act of brutal savagery even in his police work. Being a detective meant he showed up for the aftermath of a crime and was familiar with the mild excitement derived from that, but this was something else entirely. This was like murder foreplay, and Rebel found himself just short of being worked into a frenzied state.

The Cadillac Man removed a black handkerchief from

a pocket in his jacket and wiped the blood from the dagger before both disappeared back into his coat. Rebel was so intently focused on James's body and Amelia he almost forgot the Cadillac Man was there until he spoke.

"So, Rebel," he stepped back from the table and turned to face the detective. "What are you waiting for?"

Rebel snapped from his trance confused thinking he missed the first part of the question. He looked at the Cadillac Man for clarity but was met only with a smile. Disorientation came over Rebel as suddenly as Amelia had stabbed James, and he saw crisp vivid memories from his kills as a child. They were just as detailed as they were back then when he would muse on them for days at a time while waiting for another visit from the Cadillac Man.

The kaleidoscope of death spun the warped psychedelic scenes across his mind's eye for what felt like hours, but in reality, was only mere seconds. Rebel felt as if he'd slipped into a dream state, and when the memories finally began to dematerialize the detective returned to his senses struggling to shake the haze.

Something was wrong.

Not wrong necessarily but different and unfamiliar, so he equated it as 'wrong' until better able to make the determination. Rebel blinked away his foggy vision and looked up at the Cadillac Man anticipating further clarity regarding the question, but that wasn't right.

The blond stranger had always been taller than Rebel but only by inches not feet. The height disparity wasn't the only difference Rebel noticed when he looked down at his own body.

His hands were markedly smaller as were his feet, which were now stuffed into a pair of old high-top sneakers instead of the loafers he'd walked in wearing. He had on a pair of blue jeans and a t-shirt in place of the slacks and button-up that comprised his daily uniform. Rebel vacillated between confusion and anger struggling to understand when he heard the Cadillac Man's voice pointed at him from above.

"Well?" The Cadillac Man said smiling down on Rebel. "I said, what are you waiting for?"

Then, it hit him.

Now Rebel understood what happened, and the ecstatic excitement he'd felt at seeing James stabbed returned with heightened fervor. He'd quite literally reverted to the child who climbed into the car with the Cadillac Man for the first time all those years ago. Rebel's lips split apart into a wide toothy smile that tightened his skin until his cheeks sore.

"Have at it my boy." The Cadillac Man stepped aside with a grand sweeping gesture in Amelia's direction.

She lifted her head for the first time since stabbing James and looked at Rebel puzzled through bleary red eyes.

"Hey," she started, "where'd the kid come fr—"

But Rebel was already upon her.

———— ◆ ————

Rebel made a mess of Amelia, and by the time his adrenaline began to wane the woman was in pieces.

He'd used his hands mostly since it took a while to come to his senses enough to consider a weapon. Rebel felt like he'd cleared the space between him and Amelia in a single leap taking her completely by surprise like she'd done with James.

Despite having the body of a child Rebel found he still had the strength of a man, and one who was stronger than he'd ever been regardless of age. His small spindly fingers clenched handfuls of Amelia's hair tightly, as he brought her head down against the table over and over until her forehead caught the edge and a wide gash split across her swollen brow.

Blood poured in a red waterfall down her face causing further disorientation beyond the repeated blows to the

237

head. He pulled Amelia to the floor, and while struggling to remain conscious she attempted to resist, but it was no use. Even if she weren't already injured the young boy version of Rebel was imbued with more than enough strength to overpower her.

Amelia managed a peek into the boy's eyes through the bloody film coating hers when he was holding her down and, and she saw the wild animal that was his urge looking out from behind them. Whatever it was that drove him to kill was in complete control of the body in which it resided. She didn't see much after, but not because she was granted a quick relatively painless death like James. The boy gouged her eyes with his thumbs and continued to apply steady pressure until they burst in the back of her ocular cavities. From outside Rebel felt them pop, but Amelia was able to hear the organs rupture like firecrackers in her skull.

She took a long time to die, and in the course endured an incredible amount of pain of which she felt every bit. This was by design of course, another aspect of her ironic reward for killing James. While in and out of consciousness she felt nails on tiny fingers dig into the soft flesh of her belly until they'd managed to break the skin.

Little fingers dug into the fresh cuts both widening and deepening the eight single wounds until they became one. The sensation of Rebel's thin digits burrowing through the layer of fat and muscles until penetrating her completely felt like drill bits being carelessly piloted by a novice carpenter.

Amelia heard the ripping sound before she felt her stomach being torn open by the child's bare hands. She'd never heard the sound of tearing flesh, and it reminded her of ripping fabric. When she was a little girl Amelia's grandmother taught her to sew and stitch just as she'd been taught, and the woman would use her hands to tear swaths of fabric from larger pieces for her to practice on.

Amelia went into shock once Rebel opened her up, and

most of what she was able to feel after was translated into pressure. The boy grabbed handfuls of innards and pulled until they became disconnected from the inside of her body. He pulled so hard her back came up off the floor until stubborn pieces of tissue stretched thin enough to snap.

Amelia danced between death and awareness as the blood-lust crazed boy pulled out her intestines like a magician pulling a never-ending handkerchief from their coat pocket. If her eyes hadn't been turned into milky puddles in her skull, she would have seen Rebel take several bites from her small intestine while removing it while the Cadillac Man stood over the boy smiling.

For a moment she felt lighter as he continued to remove her insides, but she'd misinterpreted what was actually emptiness. Rebel worked his nimble fingers beneath her ribcage and pulled it open with minimal effort as if he were cracking a lobster claw.

Her sternum broke apart with a loud and satisfying snap, which to Amelia sounded exactly like what she imagined breaking another person's bones was *supposed* to sound like. The tearing of her skin along with the wet sucking noise of her organs being removed were foreign and unsettling, but her chest-plate being broken open sounded just like it did in the movies. Amelia found this bit of truth comforting amidst her savage disemboweling.

She was close to death, and knew it too, but still vaguely aware of what was happening, as something kept her from being able to let go completely. When she felt the boy reach between her lungs Amelia understood why she was still barely alive. The powerfully nimble fingers gripped her pathetically murmuring heart, and Rebel started to pull.

The 'other shoe' Amelia had been waiting for finally dropped as the boy stood with her heart in his hand. As Amelia drifted away, she heard the wet mastication of her heart being eaten until she was too far gone to hear anything at all.

———————◆———————

Rebel wasn't told to eat the woman's heart, but the compulsion was too strong to resist. He'd never eaten parts of his victims before, but he'd never felt compelled to do so until now. He pictured himself a savage warrior devouring the hearts of slaughtered foes. He was celebrating a great victory in an archaic way meant to show power over those you've defeated even in death, and he reveled in what he hoped to make a new tradition.

Amelia's heart was tender with a uniquely satisfying flavor, and Rebel devoured it with the same frantic abandon he'd used to obtain it. He consumed the entire thing in seconds and felt a pang of regret when he found his hands empty again. Rebel didn't dwell though, because this was just the first of what would be many going forward. He'd eventually learn to slow down and savor the flavor of his conquests, but for now he would gorge himself.

He nearly forgot the Cadillac Man was there until he heard the laughter behind him and whirled around thirsty for approval. Rebel smiled up at him and couldn't help but speak first.

"Did I do good?"

The Cadillac Man chuckled again, reached down, and tousled young Rebel's blood-speckled hair.

"I don't have to tell you things you already know now do I, Rebel?"

"Nope!"

He beamed up at the Cadillac Man finding the hair tousle endearing rather than patronizing as it had been with Amelia. He stood waiting for further instructions, but when silence hung between them for a beat too long Rebel felt something change again like a sudden charge of invisible static ghosts.

"What's wrong Rebel?"

The Cadillac Man's smile was eerily whimsical as he

stepped forward encroaching on the distance Rebel tried to put between them.

"What . . . what are we gonna do next?" Rebel asked trying to make it sound genuine, like he didn't have an inkling something may be wrong. "I'm ready to get back t—"

"Rebel, Rebel, Rebel," the Cadillac Man said shaking his head slowly shining his devious delight down on the boy. "What have I told you about patience?"

Rebel's mouth went dry, and his legs felt as solid beneath him as the pile of human-mush he turned Amelia into. The enhanced strength that surged through his small body as he ripped the woman apart emptied out through the bottom of his feet like dirty water down a bathtub drain. The ability he was left with now matched with his current stature.

This wasn't right. This wasn't how it was supposed to happen. He and the Cadillac Man were business partners, and Rebel wanted the two of them to get back to business. It was why he'd been changed back into his child-self, wasn't it? So, things would be just like they were when they started, right? It was the only scenario Rebel could picture until this moment, but now he saw a much different version of what his future held.

The Cadillac Man took another step forward prompting Rebel to retreat but suddenly found his back against the booth behind him. All he wanted was to do something that made him truly happy, the *only* thing. It would be too late by the time he'd realize happiness wasn't real but merely a trick your mind plays to keep you from running into traffic.

Regardless of whether he killed one person or a million the trick didn't work on him anymore. The veil had been permanently lifted, and 'happiness' was something he would forever lack the ability to contemplate let alone feel. Working with the Cadillac Man tends to break all the *spells* your reality has over you to reveal the bleak uselessness of existing.

"I'd like my old body back," Rebel managed weakly. "My adult body. I can be much more effective if I ca—"

"No, Rebel I don't think so," the Cadillac Man said, but this time he stepped back and away from the boy. "Things will be much . . . easier if you stay at this current size."

"Easier? Easier in what way?"

Rebel smelled the smoke before noticing the haze collecting around the ceiling and followed it with his eyes to the kitchen door. The Cadillac Man called over his shoulder to the bleach-skinned creature that drug James's body away with him.

"Jacobi!"

The swinging door burst open, and Jacobi stepped through giving Rebel a quick look at the flames engulfing the kitchen behind him. Red and orange tongues of fire licked around the frame as the door swung shut to tease the inferno's inevitable spread.

Jacobi's dress was nothing more than charred scraps clinging to parts of his body, and he tore them away as he walked around the counter. By the time he got to the Cadillac Man the dress was gone, and the creature was wearing nothing but blood and soot stains. There was a smooth flat area where genitals should have been; further emphasizing that while Jacobi appeared somewhat human, he was decidedly not.

The imp servant's face was a stain of slick red, and his mouthful of yellow fangs was pink from being used to rip apart flesh, muscle, and viscera some of which was dangling from the side of his mouth like a worm from a hooked fish. Jacobi's demonic yellow eyes gleamed through the slits of his narrowed lids exerting an invisible force that kept Rebel's back pinned against the booth.

"As I was saying," the Cadillac Man continued. "Your current size will make things easier for Jacobi here to finish you in one bite."

Rebel got but a glimpse of the swirling serrated spiral of teeth in the unhinged jaw of the creature before it was upon him.

———— ◆ ————

The Cadillac Man headed for the door as the smoke grew darker and thickened around Jacobi and Rebel. The creature took the boy into his mouth all the way to his knees before biting down. Smoke obscured his view of the child's legs flopping over on the floor, but the Cadillac Man heard two wet thwaps when they landed.

There was a tremendous gushing of blood from Jacobi's mouth as he whipped his head back to swallow, but the smoke was far too thick to see the beautiful ruby geyser's eruption, or revel in its artful aftermath. The Cadillac Man pushed through the door and paused to dust off his jacket before getting into his car. Smoke-blackened windows kept him from seeing inside the diner, but he could hear the alabaster demon shrieking as he backed out of the parking space.

In the rearview mirror he saw the dancing orange glow of the first flames to find their way to the roof as he swung a wide left turn out onto the two-lane highway. When the Cadillac Man put a few more miles between him and the diner he saw the black pillar of smoke curling around itself as it scratched its way up into the sky escaping the confines of the small restaurant.

The Cadillac Man didn't bother looking up when the explosion happened. He was already far enough away to have hardly heard it, but what he did hear was a cacophony of sharp-edged sirens stabbing their shrill tone through any other sound.

A parade of emergency vehicles coming the opposite direction sped by in a whirling cloud of dust and exhaust unaware the party they were going to was already over. The diner would be a pile of smoldering rubble by the time they got there, and not a big pile either.

The Cadillac Man continued far beyond the sirens' warbling decay and disappeared into darkness as it chased dusk from the sky.

Part III
The Family

"**I don't know**. It still ain't lookin' exactly right."

Angie's southern twang was quaint and endearing to people who didn't have to hear it on a regular basis. Between the accent, her feigned aloofness, and the fact she was easy on the eyes made it easy for her to get away with most things.

Her cousin, Brie, was among the small percentage that found everything about Angie insufferable, but if it weren't for her, they'd all have gone down a long time ago, the entire family. Brie figured this was why most everyone else tolerated her, but if other members of the family felt the same seething annoyance, they hid it much better than she.

"How about now?" Brie called back across the lawn to her blonde bubbly cousin. "Any better?"

Angie squinted, pursed her lips, and tapped her index finger against them like making a ridiculous face was the answer to the question she'd been asked.

"Move the left arm up a tiny smidge," she finally replied.

Brie sighed loud enough for her cousin to perceive her annoyance from the other side of the yard, but Angie just smiled on. For reasons she didn't explain, but was never asked to, Angie liked the bodies to be positioned into poses of subjects in different paintings from the Baroque Era.

Brie had no idea how her cousin came to acquire this particular 'fetish' since she didn't go to school past the sixth grade and never expressed interest in any kind of art, Baroque or otherwise. It was another of the many mysteries about Angie that made her so damn likable, so manipulative. She wasn't one of those 'know nothing know it all' type of people either, although Brie knew a few of those too. Rather than spout surface level bits of information about a topic, Angie would display in depth knowledge as well as her point of view on countless topics a girl like her had no business knowing anything about.

Brie looked down at the picture in the open book at her feet and studied the position of the arm to which her cousin was referring. The painting was called *Apollo and Marsyas* by the artist Bartolomeo Manfredi. It depicts Marsyas, a half-man half-beast character, who is tied to a pole while Apollo flays his skin off for thinking he could beat the god in a music contest.

The image was a grim depiction of man's perceived punishment for arrogantly challenging a higher power, a sentiment that still rings true amongst the naïve and closed-minded centuries later.

Brie loosened the knot in the rope around the man's right wrist and pushed the arm up, so it appeared as if his hand was on his hip. He groaned as she repositioned him but made no attempt to resist. They'd beaten the struggle out of him long before tying him to the cement pillar in the backyard. Uncle Rory was the one who put it there when the two girls were still quite young, but he'd told them and anyone else who would listen all about it after he had a few drinks in him.

The pillar was as thick as a lamppost and twelve feet tall, but only six of the feet were visible. The other half was buried in the ground where it was cemented into a three-hundred-and-sixty-pound concrete block for what he referred to as a 'precautionary measure'. Uncle Rory said it was to help keep it anchored in place, as if someone or something had the ability to yank it out of the ground.

That was when they were kids, though. Now, the girls understood why the added reinforcement was needed, and were glad their uncle added it no matter how many times they had to hear him tell the same story.

One thing Uncle Rory *didn't* talk about when it came to his precious pole was the symbols he'd carved along the entire thing including the part buried in the ground.

Brie pulled the rope tight around the man's torso to keep the arm in the position Angie desired. His skin was a smattering of psychedelic bruises in brilliant shades of purple, red, and yellow, and the ropes were cutting crisscross gashes wet with blood around his wrists and arms forming tiny crimson tributaries.

The man wheezed and spit when Brie secured the rope again, and his puffy, cracking lips trembled as the blood he coughed up dangled like grotesque licorice whips.

He started to say something. "Plea—"

"How about now?" Brie called cutting him off.

Angie smiled wider and gave two thumbs up.

"That's just perfect," she chirped.

Angie pulled around the crossbow slung on her back and lifted it to take aim when the cousins heard the guitar coming from the front of the house.

———— ◆ ————

Pap was the oldest left among them, and he'd earned his place at the table. He spent most of his time these days drinking with Rory and Boyd or sitting on the porch plucking his old guitar.

The family could tell when things were getting serious from the way Pap played. If he was pickin' and grinnin', and mostly noodling about there wasn't much to worry about, but when he clamped down and played with an urgency of furiously fierce precision the family knew to come running.

Pap was the most sensitive to visions out of everyone, always had been. He'd been born with a keenly heightened sense, which grew sharper with age. There may be some snow on his roof and a few more wrinkles here and there, but the old man hadn't lost a step when it came to his discernment and intuition.

Every member of the family owed their lives in one way or another to Pap multiple times over, because of the advanced warning he was able to give them. It wasn't something he held over them, or ever even mentioned. He knew what part he played in the family and owed just as many life-debts as anyone else, but that was why everything worked so well. They were a team, a cohesive unit unable to function without all its parts. They were a family.

And by god they would *stay* a family. Pap would do anything in his power to make sure of it, but today he was scared, and the rest of the family could feel it in every note that sprung from the sound hole of the battle-worn acoustic guitar.

Fear.

They all felt it as they hurried to follow the beautiful fear-charged notes to the front porch.

———————•◆•———————

Rory opened the second of the two cans of Pearl he'd brought over to the workbench so he wouldn't have to stop what he was doing to get another beer. The only problem was when he brought two beers he drank twice as fast, which defeated the entire purpose of the forethought.

The second beer was already half empty after only one swig, and Rory had yet to finish arranging his tools let alone start any *actual* work. And now the second can of Pearl was gone. Rory crushed it in his hand and dropped the can in the empty bucket at his feet where the first one landed not long before it.

He turned around, walked the ten feet separating him from the refrigerator, and opened it with a sigh basking in the soft white glow of the comforting light within. The fridge was stocked with more beer than you'd think a man could drink in an entire month, but you'd be wrong.

Rory removed just one of the gold and white cans this time and stepped back from the refrigerator to let the door swing closed. He could see the girls through the window to the left of the fridge and couldn't help but smile watching Brie adjusting the ropes around the man tied to the pole.

He took a swig of beer and made a mental note to tell them the story about how he made the pole back when they were just babies. As far as Rory knew Angie and Brie were always as happy to hear it, as he was to tell it. He chuckled musing over his favorite parts, as he sauntered back over to his workbench.

Rory and Dwayne built the small workshop a few years ago in a corner of the expansive backyard. Things were getting to a point where they needed the extra space to keep up, so the two worked a few fifteen-hour days in a row to get the small structure up. The shop had paid for itself countless times over since then and was worth every bit of the extra effort.

Dwayne was good with electrical work, so he wired the place up before running a line from the house to provide the juice. Rory was no expert plumber, but he knew enough to install a shitter and a couple sinks. They got the refrigerator when it became apparent a tremendous amount of drinking would occur there and making the walk across the backyard to the house every time another beer was needed was out of the question.

Rory took another small sip of Pearl determined to be more judicious with this one and went to set it on the workbench when he heard the guitar. He brought the can back to his lips, tipped his head back, and poured the rest down his throat.

———◆———

Dwayne pulled the string on the lone bare bulb at the bottom of the stairs, but the pale-yellow light did little to illuminate the basement. He made a mental note to replace it with one of a higher wattage to better cut through darkness so thick it could have been a physical entity.

The basement used to be the place where he, Rory, and occasionally Pap would do most of their work as far as fixing and building were concerned. It was used for storage now since the workshop had been built, but there was still a few 'special' projects Dwayne insisted remain relegated to the underground cover of darkness the basement provided.

He stepped across the cold dark room to the old workbench against the far wall where he and Rory spent countless hours toiling away, but now the space was all his. He didn't mind working alongside the man he referred to as his brother, but there was something about working alone in the quiet stillness Dwayne found extremely cathartic.

He flipped the switch for the light over the bench, and it flickered a few times before the filament in the fluorescent bulbs burned brightly in stark contrast to the dull glow at the bottom of the stairs. Jars containing various specimens Dwayne collected lined the four shelves on the wall above the bench, and the light added an eerie glow to the yellow-green liquid inside.

The weapon he'd been working on the day before was on the bench where he left it, and Dwayne shook his head after giving it a cursory look. Angie was getting harder and harder on her weapons lately, which were perpetually in need of upkeep or repair. He didn't mind the work, nor would he ever complain.

The only reason any of them were still alive was because of Angie *and* Brie, so Dwayne would gladly fix the same small issues over and over. Pap liked to preach how the family's continued success relied on them coming together as one cohesive unit, but Dwayne knew the girls carried the three of them on their backs.

He would never say any of this to Pap, of course, and

while he hadn't talked to Rory about it either, he didn't think he had to. If Rory wasn't already actively thinking the same thing it was only because he was fighting hard to suppress what he already knew. Sure, the roles Dwayne, Rory, and Pap played were important and crucial, but he'd already considered the notion that the girls may be better off on their own.

Putting sturdy and reliable weapons in the girls' hands meant his walking meat-sack would live another day. Although, with the intensity ramping up in the last few months Dwayne hoped their luck wouldn't run out. He put the thought out of his mind directing his full attention on the task at hand.

For the life of him he couldn't understand why Angie preferred to use such primitive weaponry when there was an endless slew of modern counterparts, with more being made all the time. But Angie was like that. She had her way about things, and if it kept working no one was going to question it. It was like her thing with the paintings.

Brie had fewer discriminating tastes and was a crack shot with the .38 she kept on her hip, along with most any pistol, and some rifles. She'd taken to guns more than her cousin, but not to be outdone Brie still practiced with the older weapons as well. She'd rather be put on the pole herself than let Angie have one up on her, and she'd always been that way.

It was a one-way rivalry though, as Angie seemed unaffected by the competitive spirit of her cousin. She let her talents come naturally and strengthened them from there, whereas Brie attacked every challenge intent on checking the box then moving on to something else. Her unbreakable discipline paid off as she was proficient with more weapons than the three men combined, but Angie's mastery came with little to effort.

The same intangible quality was responsible for the endearing effect she had on folks, as well as stoking the flames of fierce competition in Brie. It was healthy rivalry amongst family members who otherwise loved each other very much, or at least Dwayne hoped so. He'd never actually talked with either of the girls regarding how they felt about each other.

He'd spaced out thinking about it for a moment until the guitar pulled him out of his daydream. The notes tumbled down the stairs like busted slinkies adding more weight to the pit in Dwayne's stomach when they reached the basement floor.

"Shit."

Dwayne flicked the light over the workbench off and hurried up the stairs.

———————◆———————

Pap and the rest of the family had been fighting the same battle since any of them could remember, but their enemy was much, much older. The business of exterminating evil was not a nine to five job, there were no holidays or paid time off, and death was the only means of retirement. They were only five people, now, with finite lifespans up against an ever-strengthening, ageless, regenerative foe, but the family did their fair share of damage.

They did what they could to dispatch these denizens of evil hoping their efforts caused damage to the actual source, never knowing for certain. They weren't even sure it could be killed. Still, the family stood strong and undeterred regardless, and if they couldn't stop the inevitability of evil; the five of them would at least be a humungous pain in its ass while they were alive.

The family lost many years and many lives cutting off the creeping tentacles of evil one by one only to see them sprout anew overnight. Still, they had something inside that wouldn't let them quit. As far as the members of the family were concerned it was better to die young fighting the evil, than live a long life watching it happen.

Pap used to believe the family's work made a difference, but as he grew older came to find it was untrue.

He knew Dwayne and Rory felt similarly. They didn't say as much, but they didn't have to.

None of them wanted to admit it to themselves let alone each other that what they did was tantamount to using thimbles of water to put out a forest fire. They'd all come too far to stop, and wouldn't know what to do if they did, so like those before them they carried on. Besides, the girls hadn't come to this realization yet. As far as they knew the family was kicking the living shit out of evil and had been for so long it was finally on the run.

They interpreted the rise in the activity and increased attempts on the family's lives as evil using the last of its strength to throw haymakers hoping to do whatever damage it could while sliding down the ropes to the canvas. The truth was evil had only gotten stronger and more cunning with the passage of time, and if anything was flaunting its ever-growing power by rubbing it right in their faces.

No one was in a hurry for Angie and Brie to become embittered by the truth, as they would eventually come to it on their own time, and in their own way. For now, the three men would go into battle temporarily convincing themselves they were making a difference and wishing so hard for it to be true. They'd seen too much though, and despite wanting to revert to the mindset of their youth, the girls' current mindset, they *knew* hope existed only in fairytales.

Dwayne was the closest to the porch, and therefore arrived first bursting through the screen door having accidentally opened it using excessive force. It smacked the wall with a crack like a .22 rifle report, and while Dwayne startled himself, Pap didn't miss a beat. He remained bent over his guitar plucking the strings intently with the fingers of his right hand, while the fingers of his left bent and stretched across frets to form chords at the same time.

Angie and Brie appeared a moment later sprinting around the house from the backyard leaping up the porch steps two at a time. Angie was still carrying the crossbow, but the pointed bolt it had been loaded with was back in the forehead of the man tied to the pole. She'd taken the shot and still beat Brie to the porch by three steps who was already stewing over it.

Angie and Brie were catching their breath when Rory ambled around from the opposite side of the house.

"You're gettin' slow fat boy," Dwayne teased Rory patting him on the belly while he sucked air next to him.

"Fuck off," Rory managed between gasping breaths. "You were practically on the porch already."

"You're both slower than shit anyway, so drop it already."

Brie whispered harshly back at them without mimicking the playful tone between the two. Dwayne rolled his eyes, and hoped the girl learned to lighten up some soon. She took everything so damn serious the girl could suck the fun right out of most anything designed to bring joy, and his hope was she took on an outlook more like Angie's before life *really* had a chance to beat her down.

The sound of the guitar ceased abruptly as Pap laid his hand across the strings halting their vibration. The older man leaned the guitar gently against the porch banister and stood from the rickety rocking chair roundly known as 'his seat'. His gaze remained fixed on the horizon where the property line touched the sky for a few moments before turning to face the rest of the family.

Pap wanted to make sure he hid his fear well enough to not be detected by any of them, but as soon as he met Dwayne's eyes, he knew he'd failed.

"Well," Pap started. "It's him. He's coming, and this time he's coming for us. No games. No mediators. No bullshit."

"Who the hell'd be smug enough to do that?" Brie fired off.

"Check yer tone girl," Dwayne said softly but sternly

254

from behind the girl. "You damn well who. The Cadillac Man."

————◆————

Anton stepped from the office and slipped easily into the flow of workers walking to and from meetings, or the bathroom, or whatever the hell else people did in an office. He didn't know, and he didn't want to know. Anton had never worked in an office before and didn't see himself doing so in any possible version of his future.

He certainly didn't work at the office he was in now and was mildly put-off by having to blend in by wearing a shirt and tie. They'd be stripped away soon enough once he got to the car, and at least he didn't have to wear clothes like this every day like the rest of the saps in this place.

Mr. Benkin didn't have to worry about wearing a tie everyday anymore, but would no doubt be buried in one forever relegated to his capitalist costuming even in death. With the shape Anton left him in there was little hope for an open casket, so they'd more than likely burn the poor son-of-a-bitch. Being burnt to ash had to be far better than spending eternity in the ol' corporate noose.

He headed toward the elevators picking up his pace as the doors started to close. A man inside saw Anton rushing to make it and his arm shot out causing the doors to slide back open.

"Thanks," Anton said stepping into the elevator.

"No problem," the man answered with a smile.

The doors slid shut, the elevator began its descent, and the two faced forward in silence. Anton sized up his fellow passenger out of habit, and noticed right off how similarly they were dressed, almost identical. The man wore black-framed glasses slightly too big for his face, and a goofy grin spread crooked below his nose. He had the kind of smile that made a face extremely punchable, achingly so even, and Anton found himself fighting the urge.

"Mondays, huh?" The man said out of nowhere "Am I right?"

He didn't turn to face Anton when he spoke, but only leaned slightly in his direction keeping his eyes on the brushed sliver doors. Anton said nothing as the floors ticked slowly by as indicated on the digital display above the door. The elevator came to a stop on the ground floor, and Anton stepped through the door before it fully opened.

"Okay pal you have a good one!" The man called after him as the doors slid shut again.

Anton stopped and turned around. The man hadn't gotten off the elevator. There was no lower floor than the one they were on, and the button for the ground floor was already pressed when he'd gotten on the elevator. Why would the man ride the elevator all the way down if he weren't getting off? The interaction wasn't odd enough to give it a second thought though, and Anton dismissed his over-analyzation of the situation. He was still keyed up and on high alert after all, and never would he be able to relate to the mind of a corporate drone.

He needed to get to the car, take off the half-a-monkey suit he was wearing, and hit the road. On to the next one. Anton caught his reflection in the passenger side window as he approached the classic black Cadillac and started loosening his tie as he opened the door and climbed inside.

————— ◆ —————

Nobody in the family ever talked about the Cadillac Man, although they all thought about him more than they'd like to admit. It was jarring to hear Dwayne say his name out loud in the same way some people feel when they hear the word 'cunt'. Brie would rather have a hundred 'cunts' whispered in her ear than *that* name even once.

Pap heard Dwayne and nodded.

"Yep, 'fraid so."

The family primarily dealt with the people in league with the Cadillac Man and those like him, but they were human. The Cadillac Man himself was an entirely different story. He was part of the evil, one of its many far-reaching

256

hands, and if he was indeed coming for the family, they'd be right to take it damn seriously.

Once a normal person connects themselves to a being like the Cadillac Man it's forever. There was no removing evil's mark, which is why the family did their best to quickly dispatch those who'd been touched by it before they did too much damage. The 'damage' being them killing innocent people, and a lot of them.

Throughout the years the family had taken down hundreds of these human denizens no doubt saving countless lives but dealing directly with who they trafficked with was a rare occurrence. They all saw this coming though, knew it was coming, but there's no way to ever be prepared.

Hearing rumblings about the Cadillac Man having it out for the family wasn't new, they were warnings mostly sputtered desperately as the last words choked from his many servants. The family didn't believe the halfhearted threats, and never would they show fear, but they couldn't ignore Pap.

"So . . . what are we gonna' do?" Rory piped up. "What's the plan?"

Pap squinted back out at the horizon with his hands on his hips, and spit over the banister.

"That I don't know, but I reckon we better figure it out pretty goddamn quick."

———◆———

Olivia didn't take the extra time she used to anymore. She didn't savor or try to drag anything out longer than necessary. It wasn't that she was getting bored, or becoming desensitized, but it was more about just being efficient. At least that's the way she preferred to view it.

She didn't eat them anymore either, not if she didn't have to, for no reason other than she'd just lost her taste for it and had even cut most meat from her diet in general. It didn't mean she'd gone soft or lost a step, if anything it helped sharpen her talents. On rare occasion she would partake willingly without pushback, but only as another way of being efficient. Olivia didn't argue with the Cadillac Man, to do so was self-defeating and endlessly frustrating.

Olivia never complained and wasn't going to start anytime soon. She knew what the deal was, knew exactly what she was getting herself into, and was in it for the long haul. She no longer had a choice in the matter, and rather than attempting to ward off inevitability welcomed the fate chosen for her. Besides, she liked it.

Olivia didn't know she enjoyed killing so much until she'd been forced to perform the act. She wasn't squeamish and was never one of those girly-girls who shied away from blood and horror movies. She'd just never thought about death and killing in this way. It was like refusing to eat vegetables as a kid without trying them because you heard they were gross only to discover as an adult vegetables are one of your favorite things.

She didn't like it enough to do recreationally apart from what the Cadillac Man requested of her, but when the time came, she was more than happy to rise to the occasion. The old saying, *if you love what you do, you'll never work a day in your life,* was quasi applicable since she took great personal joy in carrying out any killings the Cadillac Man tasked her with.

Olivia reapplied her lipstick, checked her face again for any errant spatter she may have missed, and stepped over the widening puddle of blood on her way out of the bathroom. There were customers milling around the convenience store attached to the old truck stop now, and a line of irritated confused customers had begun to form at the counter.

"Hey lady," called one of the impatient-looking men in line. "Is the clerk back there or what? I need to pay for my shit and get back on the goddamn road!"

"And I still need my receipt," added a waiting woman, her eyebrows knitted in anger. "I need it for my expense report, because I'm not paying out of pocket for this shit."

Olivia paused to feign surprise. "Unless he's hiding somewhere in the ladies' room, I didn't see another soul back there." Her voice was soft, her tone light and coy, she knew how to work a room.

The customers' attention turned from her to each other, and they loudly complained hoping to pull the clerk out from wherever he was hiding. Olivia strolled up the candy aisle, stepped through the line without saying excuse me, and exited through the glass door. Nobody noticed the small trail of blood she left from having unknowingly stepped partially in the puddle with her right heel.

The black Cadillac sat idling by the door waiting right where she knew it would be.

———— ◆ ————

Carla hated Jacobi. *Hated* him, or at least she referred to it as a 'him'. The truth was she didn't know what exactly Jacobi was other than some kind of imp or devil-man sidekick to the Cadillac Man. Jacobi was more of a gopher or glorified assistant able to be called for or banished on a whim. He was no sidekick; Jacobi was a little bitch as far as Carla was concerned.

The smell was already starting to bother her, and she opened her driver side window more than halfway. Jacobi may have been able disguise himself by taking on seemingly any appearance, but there was no disguising his scent. It reminded her of the dirty turtle aquarium she cleaned daily the summer she worked in a pet shop when she was seventeen. It made her gag, and so did Jacobi.

Carla didn't understand why the Cadillac Man kept sending Jacobi with her to play some secondary role, as if she couldn't handle everything on her own? Didn't he trust her? What did he think she was a screw up anyway?

She thought she heard Jacobi snickering over the rush of air from the open window, but when she glanced over, he wasn't even smiling. Carla wondered if the Cadillac Man's lackey silently loathed their forced time together as much as she did. Maybe the two were always paired together because both were viewed as weak links?

They were like the Abbott and Costello of the Cadillac Man's army: too stupid to be sent out alone, but not stupid enough to work well as a team. The only thing good about having Jacobi with her were the extra 'talents' he brought along like his super strength, and ability to look like other people. Despite not liking the scaly alabaster-skinned creature, Carla had to admit there was never a dull moment.

His mood was erratic with him cackling like a hyena one minute, and the next be in a full-blown rage ripping the heads off anyone in arms reach for no reason other than he could. Carla also relished the fear he induced when revealing his true form to their selected victims. He didn't always break out the whole monster-face thing, but when he did it never failed to evoke the desired reaction. Having Jacobi's disgustingly horrific face be the last thing a person ever saw made the kill even sweeter despite having nothing to do with her.

Carla still liked to eat them whether she had to or not, which was difficult at times since Jacobi could dismantle and devour a body with a speed and skill she'd never possess. Regardless, it still became a competition between the two of them both trying to eat the lion share of their victims.

She also resented the fact that *she* had to drive the two of them on these excursions, which was the most annoying aspect of their whole partnership. In the beginning when she'd first started with the Cadillac Man, he personally chauffeured her to and from all the 'gigs', but suddenly it all changed. Carla found herself paired up with a monster she had to hoof all over town in her own car.

If she'd fucked up somewhere along the line, she wasn't aware of it, nor had it been brought to her attention, but it felt to her like she was being punished. Carla didn't bring it up despite how badly she wanted to but managed to bite down hard on her tongue anytime the temptation arose.

260

She'd learned the hard way that asking even one question was one too many. She wouldn't make the same mistake twice.

Carla slowed to a stop at a red light, and without the rushing air to carry it out the window; the sour fish tank smell filled the car.

"Oh Jesus!"

Carla covered her nose and mouth with one hand and turned the air conditioner up to its highest setting with the other. Since Jacobi's window was still closed all, she succeeded in doing was pushing the smell around the cabin with a high-powered blast of lukewarm air.

Now Jacobi *was* laughing, and he was laughing *at* Carla. The streetlight reflected off his disgustingly misshapen, pointy, yellow teeth until she slammed down on the accelerator propelling them forward and banishing his maw back to the darkness.

"Fucking swine," Carla snarled as they sped down the darkened street with Jacobi's laughter echoing in the night behind them.

———◆———

Unfortunately, Pap had no additional information to offer the family as far as when the Cadillac Man would strike, or even an estimate as to how much time they had to prepare? Pap wasn't sure there was anything the family *could* do to prepare that would make any difference, but he kept the thought to himself.

All he knew was the Cadillac Man was coming for them, and it was not going to be good. The Cadillac Man wasn't the only extension of evil out recruiting humans to help spread the randomized chaos evil thrived upon. There were others they'd come to know about through Pap's discernment but none as daunting in comparison. The others didn't have the staying power of the Cadillac Man and would often disappear for long stretches of time after having been thwarted.

Not him though. The Cadillac Man was *always* an ever-present threat to the family and reminded them often that while he may be watching from the fringe, he was still watching. Pap's constant awareness of their lingering enemy was truly unnerving but far better than being taken by surprise.

This was the smallest the family had been for quite a while, and Pap figured they'd at least have a few new members by this point, but no such luck. The girls had been the latest additions and the only members who'd actually grown up in the family. Pap figured it put Angie and Brie at a disadvantage when it came to experiencing any normal kind of life outside of the unnatural chaos they dealt with on a nearly daily basis.

All the other members of the family had a very different kind of life before they picked up the mantle to join the fight. Hell, Pap himself had been in the army, got married and divorced, and was running his own barbershop before he became a member. He knew what it was to be young and make stupid mistakes with no serious consequences while learning how to grow up.

Angie and Brie were experiencing a different kind childhood where the consequences of even the smallest mistake could be death. In his more optimistic musings Pap hoped the possibility for Angie and Brie to move on at some point and live a normal life existed though he knew it was mostly wishful thinking.

The only 'moving on' anyone did after joining the family was moving from the house to the cemetery. Even if it were possible for the girls to leave and strike out on their own how would they adapt? They'd been raised learning to fight and kill, and Pap just couldn't see how they could come back from that.

Along with all the good things the girls were missing out on, they were spared the experience of being crushed by the world and having their spirits broken. This was why the two of them, Angie especially, were able to fly so easily in the face of evil with unabashed, but also unchecked confidence.

Dwayne and Rory were fearless as well, but in their own way. Despite the two having let go of their fears long ago they remained tethered to them by a thin fiber left overlooked. They were still able to remember what it was like to be afraid, to have the fear inside them. Angie and Brie were unable to relate to the concept in the way the three grown men did, and the quality served the girls well.

One thing Pap didn't do before joining the family was play guitar. The closest he'd come in his life to playing an instrument was changing the station on the radio but was suddenly struck with an impulse to pick up the guitar when he started having dreams about playing in odd settings like a mountaintop or floating on a raft in the middle of the sea.

He found the guitar the day he moved into the family house. Pap didn't know if it had been placed there purposely, or somehow materialized, but there it was in the back of the closet of the room he'd chosen for himself. It was old and worn from being well played for many years before the instrument came into his hands.

He held the guitar by the neck and sat down on the edge of his bed to examine the instrument. Certain areas of the dark mahogany fretboard were worn light blonde from where fingers had rubbed countless times in the past to form chords. Pap sat the guitar across his lap balancing the curve in the body on his knee attempting to imitate what he'd seen actual musicians do when playing.

He brushed his thumb gently across the strings and listened. Pap had no idea how to tune a guitar, or what it would sound like if he did, but for some unknown reason his ears told him it was already tuned up. He wrapped his fingers around the neck, and his fingers sprang into action as if moving on their own until Pap realized he was indeed controlling them.

He stretched and contorted his fingers to form chords, which he plucked with his right hand, or strummed with his thumb. He started to hear the notes in his head a split second before his fingers responded to play them, and as he continued to play images came to life before his eyes. They didn't make sense, and moved too quickly for him to register, but the longer he played the clearer the pictures became.

This was the first time he saw the Cadillac Man, but had no idea who he was, or why such heavy dread fell upon him when he did? As he continued to play, Pap saw the Cadillac Man standing over a pile of corpses as if presiding over it. The last thing he saw that first time he played the guitar was the family's house with the Cadillac Man standing right out front.

His fingers fell from the frets sending up an off-tune whine from the strings, and his shoulders shuddered as a chill gripped his entire body. Pap didn't know why what he saw unnerved him so badly, but it left a heavy ominous air around him. It was his first premonition, and while he hadn't honed the discernment of his visions, he knew whatever he'd seen did not bode well for the family.

Pap grew in his new ability and was soon able to translate the horrific scenarios he saw in his head to help the family navigate battles which would otherwise have been calamitous for them. He couldn't save everyone though, and it took a while to adjust to that aspect. No matter how hard he practiced or concentrated the ability he'd been given just didn't work that way.

Pap came to terms with his limitations but was never fully at peace. He knew the things he'd seen helped save the family countless times over as well as given them the upper hand in most confrontations, but he couldn't guarantee their safety, and it burned him up inside. Anytime the family returned minus a member regardless of it having nothing to do with him, Pap couldn't help but take it personally.

He took responsibility for every life lost in the family since he'd joined and endured his self-imposed suffering in silence. He chose not to seek the commiseration of his other 'relatives', because he knew they'd tell him he had no reason to feel responsible. They'd try to convince him to let it go, and say the dead didn't blame him, but he didn't want to let it go. He would carry the weight on his shoulders right on into the grave.

Pap knew if anything happened to Angie and Brie it would break him. He could not silently suffer their loss, and the wave of guilt and sadness he'd kept dammed up in his soul for years would burst loose and crush him. Pap hoped to be long dead before anything happened to those two.

This morning in his vision he saw the family house much like he'd seen it the first time he picked up the guitar only now rivers of blood poured from the windows and out the front door in frothy crimson waves. The Cadillac Man was facing away from this house this time, and he was smiling.

———◆———

Carla parked the car in an alley and leapt out immediately after turning off the ignition to escape Jacobi's smell. She was going to have to wash her hair in tomato juice to strip the rancid scent from her long curly coif. Jacobi took his time, as usual, and Carla was already almost to the fire escape ladder by the time he opened the car door.

She sighed and crossed her arms against her chest waiting for the albino imp to saunter over. No matter how many times she'd seen him go through one of his 'transformations' it was still unnerving to watch. His face began to shift and contort like white modeling clay someone was trying to stick their fingers through from the other side. When the features began to take shape and harden in place Carla threw her hands up in frustration.

"Goddamnit Jacobi!" She tried not to raise her voice, but frustration got the better of her. "You know I fucking hate it when you do that."

"Do what?" Jacobi said in his new voice through a smile.

"That!" Carla barked emphatically gesturing at his new face and body.

She was looking at an exact replica of herself. Usually, Jacobi turned himself into her for no reason other than to get even further under her skin only this time it was necessary. It didn't mean she liked it any better though and was disgusted having to look at her face on Jacobi.

"Just get the ladder down so we can get on with this already," Carla said nodding toward the fire escape.

If she were alone Carla would have to find something to stand on to reach it, two or three somethings. This was one of the rare times it came in handy having Jacobi along with her since it was nothing for him to jump all the way up to the roof if he wanted.

She stepped back as he positioned himself under the ladder before leaping to pull it down. Carla kept her eyes on the ground not wanting to catch an accidental up-skirt view of herself. Jacobi had no visible sex organs normally, but Carla didn't know if they came with his transformation and was quite positive she didn't want to know.

She didn't like that the Cadillac Man had her wear a dress to this one, but it wasn't for her to know his reasons, which was annoying in and of itself. Granted, she didn't *need* to know the reason behind anything to do her job, but she still wanted to.

She felt since she was going to be the one killing a person, she should at least know *something* about the reasons behind it if for nothing else than to satisfy her curiosity. The Cadillac Man didn't do things that way, and despite her frustration Carla knew better than to bring it up to him.

The ladder slid down low enough for her to reach, but Jacobi was already climbing upward. They were here to pay a visit to an artist who had a studio space in the building and was now supposed to be on the roof working on a sculpture.

Jacobi was already halfway up the building by the time Carla made it to the first landing, but she didn't care if he made it to the top before her. She had to be there to start the whole thing off, so he would just have to stake out his hiding spot and wait. She climbed each ladder slowly due to the shoes she had to wear, but at least thy were flats. She couldn't remember if Jacobi had been wearing a pair when he began his ascent not that it would slow him any.

As she approached the ninth and final story before the roof, she saw Jacobi waiting on the platform.

"If you were moving any slower, you'd be going in reverse," he said as she climbed onto the platform with him.

"Get fucked," she said with a venomous nonchalance that accompanied her everyday inflection. Carla gestured up the last ladder leading to the roof. "He up there?"

"Yep," Jacobi answered in a pitch-perfect imitation of Carla's voice.

"So . . . What the hell are you waiting for?"

"It seems things have become slightly more complicated," Jacobi answered as Carla shoved him aside to climb the ladder.

"What the hell is that supposed to mean?" she asked making her way up the rungs. "If he's up here let's just do this, and get th—"

Carla paused when she heard it, but it was hard to tell exactly where it was coming from? She took the last three rungs slowly, and the noise grew louder with each one. At the top she slowly peeked over the edge to see a party happening on the roof, and not a small one either.

She cursed under her breath and scanned the scene trying her best to stay out of sight. Carla saw their target right away because he was standing near something large covered by a red sheet. There were several small spotlights arranged in a circle for the express purpose of highlighting whatever was under the covering.

The artist wasn't up on the roof *working* on one of his

sculptures; he was unveiling it. There were easily a hundred people milling about in all arrays of fancy garb, which made having to wear the dress a little easier to understand. Carla made her way back down the ladder so the two could revise their plan, which had really been just sneaking up behind him while he was sculpting, or whatever, and taking him out. This situation, however, called for an *actual* plan.

"There's a goddamn party going on up there," Carla said stepping down onto the platform.

"How'd you put that one together?' Jacobi mocked sending her frustration level soaring.

"Cut the shit, okay," Carla snapped much louder than she should have and immediately adjusted. "Stop being an asshole, and let's figure this out."

"What's there to figure out? We can walk right up to him, rip his head off, and split. It's not like we'll get caught."

Jacobi had a point. Carla didn't know how, but the Cadillac Man had a way of making things go away like videos, witnesses, and even police. It was easy for Jacobi to say since he wasn't human and couldn't give a shit about discretion, but it wasn't the same for her. This was exactly the kind of 'sloppiness' she'd been warned about in the past, and now she couldn't help but think the job was set up this way to see how she'd handle things.

It was a test, or at least she viewed it as one, and for all she knew Jacobi could be in on it attempting to coax her into making mistakes. Her face went flush at the thought, and she wouldn't put it past the pasty shape shifter to try and take her down a couple pegs.

Carla wasn't going to be able to trust anything Jacobi said, or suggested they do for the rest of the night. This was completely on her, and she was going to have to come up with a feasible plan, but one she could execute alone if indeed her partner pushed her toward failure.

"Well?" Jacobi piped up.

"No, we're not doing that," she snapped. "Just let me think for a second."

Jacobi started chuckling but Carla blocked him out. She knew they had a finite amount of time to get this thing done, so she needed to think fast.

"Okay, okay," she finally said. "How about this? We climb the ladder and slip into the party. I'll sidle up to the guy and aggressively hit on him saying things like I'm his biggest fan, and meeting him was my dream, and how I've had a crush on him for so long.

"I'll feed his ego, get him all worked up, and tell him to meet me in the bathroom in three minutes where you'll be . . . as me. Then, you can take him out inconspicuously, and I'll follow in behind to help."

"Help? Help whom? Me?" Jacobi scoffed.

"Just shut the fuck up and get up the—"But Jacobi was already up the ladder creeping over the edge onto the roof.

Carla heaved a heavy sigh of frustration and shot up the ladder after him. It wasn't hard to slip over onto the roof because of the shadow cast by a large catering tent just beyond the edge. Jacobi was already gone, and Carla could only hope he'd follow along with the plan and not go rogue just to make her look bad. Of course, it would also make *him* look bad, but he wasn't concerned about that as much as she was. He had nothing to lose.

———— ♦ ————

Angie sat cross-legged on the bed scribbling furiously into a notebook as Brie paced the floor in front of her spouting ideas. They'd left the porch after Pap's announcement mostly because they could tell the three men wanted to discuss some things amongst themselves without the two of them around. It had been Brie's idea for the two of them to brainstorm a plan to take down this Cadillac Man that had everyone shaking in their boots.

Brie robotically spat ideas for a plan, but Angie only wrote down a third of them and even then, it was in a shorthand all her own only she could decipher. She mostly doodled random images like flowers, hearts, and pictures of severed heads with arrows sticking in them like morose pincushions.

Angie wasn't one for plans really, but she understood how important it was for the rest of the family to have an idea of what they're going to do before they do it. Of course, she always agreed with whatever plan was dictated or mapped out, but only as a show of solidarity in the moment.

It wasn't like other members of the family made *bad* plans or ones she disagreed with. Angie just had a knack for making the proper adjustments in the moment particularly after taking in the surroundings getting the lay of the land.

"Are you getting all this?" Brie snapped.

"Word for word," Angie smiled continuing her macabre doodles.

Angie wasn't as worried as she knew she should be about the Cadillac Man, and the possible raid on the family home, but she didn't get nervous about most things. She possessed a calm metal clarity that allowed her to see solutions where others saw only problems, which was why she wasn't big on setting plans in stone.

For her family members having a plan was a security blanket, which Angie thought provided as much actual safety as one. When the shit hit the fan, she was quick on her feet seemingly able to dodge blows before they were thrown. The ability to not see but rather sense something a second or two before it happened was one she'd honed well growing up in the family.

"What do you think about that one?" Brie asked. "It might be one of the better options."

"I absolutely agree."

Angie answered without hesitation though she had no idea what her cousin said or had been saying for the last several minutes. It didn't really matter, because she knew

Brie could never trust her notes anyway and would most likely re-write all her ideas anyway unless Pap or one of the uncles already had something up their sleeves.

Brie was far more analytically minded than her cousin and needed the structure of a plan to work within, required it even, and thrived best within its guidelines expertly executing it to the letter. Brie was an extreme Type A personality who had her entire day laid out before leaving bed in the morning with a place for everything and everything in its place.

Angie was the exact opposite seeming almost too laid back for her own good, which might be more accurate if she wasn't a member of the family. To call Brie high strung would be an egregious understatement, but despite her often over-bearing bristly demeanor Angie never lost patience with her cousin.

They balanced each other out, and worked together better than a well-oiled machine, they were like two halves of the same person intimately familiar with each other's unique nuances. One thing they both knew, though Brie would never admit it, was they absolutely needed each other. They were like two keys in a submarine needing to be turned at the same time to launch a nuclear warhead. Pap, Rory, and Dwayne knew it too, which was why they went to great lengths to keep the girls safe most of which the two weren't even aware of.

Angie may have been laid back, but she was extremely perceptive, and while she knew the other family members were legitimately worried, not scared but worried, she had not the slightest flutter of a butterfly in her tummy. She never did. Some would say the quality was a true sign of bravery, others would say it was just plain foolish.

The bedroom door wasn't closed, but the girls were too wrapped up in what they were doing to notice Dwayne had stepped into the doorway. He knocked lightly on the doorframe so as not to scare them, but Angie and Brie were startled enough to jump anyway. Angie even emitted a high-pitched *Yeep*, but quickly covered her mouth already giggling at herself.

"Jesus Christ Uncle Dwayne," Brie sputtered, as she'd clearly been more taken by surprise than her cousin. "You're lucky I didn't have my Luger strapped on, or you'd be one dead duck, you know that?"

Any other time Dwayne would have sarcastically egged her on while ripping on her for being such a scaredy-cat, but his demeanor and tone were serious.

"Pap wants you girls to come downstairs," he said flatly. "We have to show you somethin'."

————◆————

"Where the hell are we going?"

Anton watched unfamiliar scenery fly by through the window, which didn't necessarily mean something was wrong since he rarely knew where they were going or coming from, but this was different. He didn't know how or why but the Cadillac Man was exempt from the laws of time and physics.

Anton had been dropped off for jobs where as soon as he stepped from the big black car it was painfully obvious he wasn't in the present anymore, at least not *his* present. It was easy to tell if he was in the past since the cars and buildings were dead giveaways. Anton found it much harder to discern if he was in the future as it wasn't quite so obvious. The Cadillac Man never took him to the distant future, or if he had nothing changed enough for him to notice.

More than a few times Anton was immediately unsettled upon arriving at the Cadillac Man's chosen destination for him. It felt almost like he was sick to his stomach but not quite. He didn't know for sure because he didn't want to ask, but his theory was in those instances he'd entered a timeline in which he didn't exist, and he shouldn't be there.

It took him a while to come to this conclusion as a

possibility because the differences were subtle, nearly imperceptible. People's demeanor, body language, and even at times their appearance was what tipped him off. Anton attributed the unnatural queasy feeling to his own biology rejecting whatever universe or dimension he'd stepped into. His body knew it didn't belong there and was most likely actively trying to pull Anton back where he belonged one cell at a time.

Of course, these were only theories as he knew better than to ask questions, which was why the one he'd just asked surprised even himself. The Cadillac Man kept his eyes on the road ahead of him and said nothing. Anton sunk in his seat a few inches like a child who could feel the impending scolding they were about to receive, but it did not come. They drove in silence for the next few minutes before the Cadillac Man finally spoke.

"Anton." The way he said it sounded like the start and finish of an entire sentence. "I have something special for you to do, something important. Something only someone like you can handle."

The Cadillac Man exited the highway and turned right at the first cross street they came to. The only thing on the street up ahead was an old truck stop and nothing else.

"Okay," Anton said. "I can dig that. What's the job? Is it up at that gas station or something?"

The Cadillac Man remained silent as he slowed the car and made the right turn into the truck stop. Anton's head was on a swivel trying to take in the surroundings he assumed he would be working in. The Cadillac Man pulled the car up close to the door to the small store and slowed to a stop, but when Anton went to get out the door was locked.

Before he could try again a sharply dressed attractive woman stepped out of the store and into the parking lot. Anton paused to take in another good look when he noticed she was walking in the direction of the Cadillac. Confused, he glanced over at the Cadillac Man who was still looking straight ahead deadpanned. When he looked back the woman was within three feet of them, and a second later she was opening the back door and getting into the car.

"Hey," she said casually as she shut the door behind her. "Is this the guy?"

The Cadillac Man now turned to face Anton flashing a sly smile.

"Anton, this is Olivia. Olivia, Anton."

———————◆———————

Olivia was an elegant young woman with a knack for killing and the inclination to boot. In the case of nature versus nurture, upbringing had nothing to do with her predisposition for murder. Most children tend to be a product of their environment when such things like atrocious crime and murder are concerned, but she was an exception.

She'd come from money, though wasn't snobbish about it, but she did enjoy nice clothes and was quite particular about how she presented herself. She didn't have to try to be pretty since the genetics of her Nordic father and southern beauty queen mother set her up nicely in that department. Olivia used the effort she didn't have to put into her face or body to give extra attention to fashion and style.

The clothes and shoes she wore were expensive, but she didn't worry about overspending on clothing or anything else. Olivia grew up with the best of everything from clothes to education, and cars to houses. Her mother required she take etiquette classes every summer to make sure she was the most proper of all the other proper young ladies, but even then, Olivia was putting on a show.

She learned the way her parents wanted, or rather expected her to act and imitated the behavior to the letter but it was all an act. None of it *really* mattered to her. This was more than the typical pre-teen/teenage pushback every kid gives their parents for forcing them into something.

Olivia didn't rebel against her parents, or obstinately refuse to model the behavior she was being made to learn. She just didn't care but it wasn't only that, Olivia didn't care about anything and hadn't since she could remember. She wasn't unhappy and was quite content growing up, but nothing ever resonated with her.

Olivia didn't feel connected to anything, which she was completely fine with until meeting the Cadillac Man. She connected with him to such an extreme Olivia forgot what it was like to feel nothing for all those years, to have no passion in her life whatsoever.

The Cadillac Man made her feel the passion she didn't know she'd been missing and gave her purpose. With him, she had direction and something by which to define herself. It was quite liberating especially since Olivia was unaware she needed to be liberated at all.

Olivia didn't know her life had been preordained, and unbeknownst to her was simply following the path laid out. She, like many children before her, belonged to the Cadillac Man from birth thanks to her mother's arrogance and vanity. She'd traded away her responsibility by promising Olivia to him not only before she was born, but before she was even conceived.

Olivia's mother, Loretta, grew up in Georgia with an affluent family steeped in southern pride and history. She'd been being groomed by her own mother to be the near-perfect southern belle she'd eventually become, but that was the problem. Loretta was only 'near-perfect' despite the amount of time and money spent on etiquette lessons, private tutors, and a litany of beauty care specialists and products.

She was missing an intangible element unidentifiable by her mother or any of the experts at her disposal. Loretta's mother was well regarded throughout the entire state for her beauty and charm and expected her daughter to follow in her footsteps.

No matter how hard Loretta tried she always fell just

short of her mother's expectations who didn't hesitate to communicate her disappointment on a constant basis. One day while walking home from one of her classes on being a proper southern lady a black Cadillac pulled up beside her and everything changed.

Soon, Loretta was at the top of all her charm school-esque classes, winning every pageant she entered in Georgia, capturing attention on a national level. Suddenly, she could do no wrong in the eyes of her mother only her mother wasn't there to see any of it.

There was more to it than Loretta simply trading away a child she wasn't going to have for over a decade, as there were more immediate sacrifices to be made. Friends and relatives fawned over her sudden success, and at the same time lamented the mother who would never get to see it. Of course, there were rumors and fantastical stories passed around about why Loretta's mother suddenly disappeared, but none of them were close to the truth.

It was speculated she'd run off with a rich baron from a foreign land she'd been secretly carrying on a relationship with for years, or she'd grown tired of her life and lifestyle and moved somewhere under an assumed identity to start completely over. Some thought she'd taken her own life and would eventually show up face down in one of the nearby bodies of water.

A small faction of people close to Loretta's mother held the belief she'd been a victim of foul play, but despite their insistence the theory wasn't given much credence. There was simply no evidence to support it, so the police didn't pursue the possibility for very long.

The Cadillac Man told Loretta no one would see her leading her mother into the woods behind their property to show her some bones she'd found. Loretta's mother explained they were most likely from a long dead animal and *not* a person but said she'd go with her daughter to reassure her. The Cadillac Man said it would be easy to split the back of her mother's head open with the hatchet left hung from one of the low hanging branches, and he was right again.

Loretta pointed to a pile of brush where she said the bones were, and when her mother bent over for a closer look she struck. The rest of her instructions included rolling over the body, hacking open her chest, and eating her mother's heart before returning home. She thought this would be the hardest part of her task, but it was surprisingly easy and the most enjoyable.

A unique sense of satisfaction fired through her system and Loretta burned with a new sensation of life as she brought the small hatchet down again and again against the breastplate until it finally cracked apart. The heart was warm, and heavier than expected. She kept waiting for it to start beating again as she held it in her hands, but there was no life left in the organ.

The meat was tough and chewy, but it didn't stop her from ravenously devouring it like a starving feral child. Blood and saliva poured from the sides of her mouth and rolled down her chin as she sucked the juice from each ventricle greedily unable to swallow fast enough to keep from spilling. The blood felt rich and velvety on her tongue and tasted like the sweet biscuits she enjoyed on Sundays with her tea.

She left the body there as instructed, and of course as promised it was never found. Not even a trace. Loretta looked back before exiting the woods and caught a glimpse of what she first took for a ghost standing over her mother's body, but its form was much too opaque for an apparition. Whatever it was, its body was white like eggshells, and the thing had yellow eyes that seemed to glow in the darkness of the woods.

The instant Loretta stepped from the woods she felt it, the change. Suddenly, whatever had been holding her back evaporated while other aspects of her were now heightened. There wasn't any one thing she could put her finger on as being different since the sweeping change was comprised of many smaller changes within her.

She felt confidence like she never had before, and a level of fearlessness no one was supposed to ever be able to reach, nor should they. Things looked brighter and sharper suddenly, and although she checked several times to make sure she hadn't actually grown Loretta felt taller. And so, whatever intangible element she'd been missing she now had an overabundance of bought and paid for with the blood of her mother, and the sweat of her unborn daughter.

If Olivia was able to feel anything for her mother she might have been devastated to learn of Loretta's pre-natal betrayal, or maybe she would've taken just as much delight in it? Perhaps Olivia and Loretta would've become a devious duo cutthroat in the pursuit of their desires while devoid of the ability to feel for those they'd hurt or wronged?

Olivia would never know she was a product of her mother's selfishness. She'd never know the sole purpose she existed was to continually feed what was the insatiable, bloated, perpetuation of evil by way of acts perpetrated according to the whims of the Cadillac Man. But no one ever does.

————◆————

Carla smoothed down her dress, caught her breath, and composed herself before slipping out from behind the catering tent to blend seamlessly into the party. Despite her rising anger level, she donned her trademark killer smile and strode confidently through the huddled groupings of people's personal cliques like she belonged there, like she'd been there the whole time.

As she crossed the party, accepting a drink from a server's tray along the way, Carla scanned for any sign of herself lingering elsewhere on the roof. She couldn't explain why she had a sinking feeling Jacobi was going to fuck her on this one. She just did.

While it was nothing new for Carla to feel a constant

low-grade wariness of being double-crossed by him at all times, this was different. Instead of the slow and constant smoldering in the background this was sharp and piercing. It was like something hooked to her guts and pulled down with all its weight. She took a long drink and told herself it was just nerves.

Carla approached the still unrevealed statue, and its soon-to-be late creator giving a quick glance around before stepping up to tap him on the shoulder. She could only hope Jacobi stuck to the plan, but she was used to having to think on her feet with him.

Carla's smile was dazzling, this much she knew, and she was so well put together no one would ever guess she'd just climbed nine stories up a fire escape on the side of the building. This was why she was confused when the artist turned around with a smile that quickly dropped upon seeing her.

"Hello there," Carla said in her best sultry tone determined not to be thrown off by his initial reaction.

Sometimes it took a second for the person she approached to take her 'all in' when she caught them off guard. Carla was stunning and completely self-aware enough to know it was her best weapon.

"Oh . . . hi," the artist said, his eyes darting from side to side. "Again."

Again. *Again*? Again! She was right to have been extra-suspicious of Jacobi since he'd clearly not stuck to the plan, and now Carla found herself thrust on stage without knowing any of her lines. Thankfully, he took the lead.

"What are you doing back so soon?" He stepped in and spoke low, the fake smile back on his face. "I thought we were meeting in the bathroom in five minutes?"

"Oh," Carla chirped with feigned aloofness. "That's right."

Carla was furious. Jacobi stuck to the plan, only he was doing both parts of it and neither of them well.

"So . . . " The artist's eyes cut the room in half again as

he let the word hang. "Like I said earlier my wife is around here somewhere and I don't wa—"

"Someone's in there," Carla cut him off, purring the words soft and coy. "Do you see the big tent across the roof over my shoulder? The catering tent."

His eyes slid from hers, and he nodded as they leapt right back.

"Meet me there instead," she whispered. "On the back side of it."

The artist glanced in the direction of the tent again and gave a quick nod. Carla winked before she turned to make her way to the other side of the roof, and the new impromptu rendezvous spot. Jacobi tried to screw things up, tried to make her look incompetent, but she'd beat him at his own game this time. Maybe after this the Cadillac Man wouldn't make him go everywhere with her anymore?

Carla didn't want to put the cart before the horse though. She needed to pull it off first before Jacobi had a chance to interfere, and either screw it up or steal her thunder. There would be plenty of time to gloat on the drive back, but for now she needed to focus on the task at hand.

While she truly believed Jacobi was stupid, she knew he wasn't *that* stupid. When the artist didn't show up in the bathroom after five minutes, he'd get suspicious and go looking, so Carla wouldn't have much time alone behind the tent. She'd need to act fast and was already putting together a plan as she ducked into the darkness behind the tent.

Carla positioned herself at the edge of the roof next to the fire escape where she planned to pull the artist close for a kiss, but hip toss him off the building instead. The ledge was at the right height to help knock him off balance, and they'd be far enough from the ladder he wouldn't be able to reach out and catch himself on a rung. Once he went over, she'd race down the fire escape, rip his heart from his chest, and eat it on her way back to the car. If

Jacobi wasn't already there waiting he'd have to walk back, or fly, or jump, or whatever hell he did?

After a minute Carla heard shuffling from the side of the tent where the artist slowly made his way around the corner, his hand on the canvas to guide him while his eyes adjusted to the darkness. She could tell he wasn't able to see her at first, so she cleared her throat to let his ears point his eyes in her direction.

"Over here," Carla sang softly in her hypnotically flirtatious timbre.

"Are you sure this is . . . safe back here?"

He moved to her slowly whipping his head around to see if they were potentially visible by way of some hidden angle.

"Trust me," she called softly. "No one can see us."

She could sense his growing arousal as he moved to quickly close the gap between them and adjusted her stance to receive him into her arms before tossing him across her hip and off the roof in a single fluid motion. It happened so fast that by the time Carla realized something had gone awry, she was already falling.

Just as the artist was passing in front of the ladder Jacobi shot up from the side of the building, his cartoonishly large mouth open wide, his jaw unhinged to show off the obnoxious amount of impossibly sharp teeth. The giant mouth snapped shut around the artist's entire head, and the teeth slid easily through the soft neck flesh.

Jacobi dropped from sight while the artist's headless body took two more steps before falling into Carla and sending them both over the edge tangled together. His neck was situated beneath her chin as they fell, and warm surges of blood erupted hot and thick into her face from the heart's last few beats. She inadvertently swallowed a mouthful, which pissed her off because it only made her hungrier.

Under different circumstances Carla would be lapping at the wound until the body was bone dry and then eat the bones, but now she was preoccupied with figuring out how to survive falling nine stories.

The now headless artist's arms were wrapped around Carla's midsection, and she wrapped her own arms around the torso locking her hands together behind his back. She used the body's dead weight to spin them into a barrel roll she hoped would complete one revolution before the jumbled mess of their bodies hit the pavement.

It wasn't a sure thing, but it was the only chance she had to possibly survive. If she timed it so she was on top when they landed the body would take the brunt of the impact and *hopefully* somewhat break her fall. She wouldn't walk away unscathed regardless, Carla knew that, but bones healed, and she'd always been a big believer in 'walking it off'. Jacobi really screwed her this time, and she resolved if she lived to use whatever strength left in her body to rip the pale scaly imp apart.

As soon as they began their twisting descent Carla realized they were spinning too fast. There wasn't enough time to make another half-turn, which meant she would be the one to hit the ground first. She shrieked but not out of fear or panic, but rage for what Jacobi had done to her. Whether or not her falling off the side of the building was part of his plan didn't matter now. Carla closed her eyes and took morbid solace in her final thought that at least being dead meant she didn't have to see the ugly fucker ever again.

Her momentum ceased suddenly followed immediately by the sickening squishy pop of organs bursting through split skin, and the crackling crunch of bones being pulverized by way of an abrupt halt in inertia. Carla didn't feel anything right away, and a moment later when she still didn't feel anything figured she'd been lucky enough to die before the pain could register.

Carla smiled and opened her eyes. The expression quickly deflated to a grimace when she saw the big black Cadillac parked a few feet away from where she was being held in the arms of Jacobi. He'd assumed his normal disgusting form, but still wore the same dress as Carla.

"Jesus fucking Christ, Jacobi!" she roared and smacked at his arms where they were holding her. "Put me down you creep."

"Whatever you say," Jacobi smiled.

He let go and she dropped the last three feet to the ground landing in the warm sticky slop of artist's pulpy remnants. Now the sound she'd heard made sense. Jacobi had plucked Carla out of the air while the headless corpse continued to fall, and now she was sitting in the puddle of human stew she was a pussy hair away from being an ingredient in.

"Goddamnit."

Carla mumbled shaking mingled fluids from her arms while trying to navigate standing up in the slop pile without slipping. Jacobi's cackling bounced between the walls of the narrow alley carrying the biting laughter to the streets both in front and behind them. He offered his arm to help Carla up and she slapped it away, which made Jacobi only laugh harder.

The sound of a car door slamming silenced the laughter and snapped both of their attention to the car in front of them. Carla almost forgot it was there after being momentarily overwhelmed by the fact she was still alive. The Cadillac Man had exited the vehicle and stood in front of the car staring at them. Carla started to lift her arm when Jacobi snatched her by the wrist and yanked her to her feet.

Her mind was racing as to how she was going to explain their current scenario. It was obvious the two of them had taken care of the target, but things were never supposed to get *this* messy. Carla took a breath and went to launch into an impromptu reimagining of the last half hour when the passenger side door of the Cadillac swung open along with the back door on driver's side.

The man who stepped out of the passenger side was dark skinned, medium build, and was wearing a white undershirt with khaki slacks. At the same time a woman stepped from the back seat dressed in a stylish designer-brand dress and matching heels with legs that seemed to sprout all the way up to her neck. She looked like she was prepared for a night on the town, while the man looked like he'd just finished his shift sacking groceries.

"Who the hell are these assholes?" Jacobi barked before Carla could say anything.

The man who'd exited the passenger side of the Cadillac took a step forward and folded his arms across his chest before he spoke.

"I was about to ask the same thing."

———————◆———————

Dwayne turned from the doorway of the bedroom where the girls were cooking up plans and went downstairs to wait with the other men for Brie and Angie to join them.

"Shit, I hate being interrupted," said Brie shaking her head. "Now I lost my whole train of thought. Did you get that last part down? I wanna pick back up there later."

She went to look over the top of the notebook to double check, but Angie snapped it shut before Brie could catch a glimpse. She'd been doodling a picture of herself riding a Pegasus while throwing daggers down at tiny troll-like figures on the ground below them.

"Yep," Angie said with a smile. "Word-for-word just like you said."

She left the notebook closed on the bed, leapt off, and followed Brie out of the room.

"Wait," Brie was halfway down the stairs when she turned around. "Did you bring the notes? We can run some of the ideas by Pap and get some feedback."

Angie didn't have time to make up an excuse before Uncle Dwayne called from the living room.

"Quit wasting time and get down here."

He didn't sound angry, but it wasn't the usual playfully sarcastic tone in which he spoke typically. Normally this would have prompted a scathing remark from Brie, but even she picked up on the seriousness and kept her mouth shut. The girls continued downstairs, through the hall, and met the rest of the family where they were gathered in the living room.

Both Angie and Brie could tell from the grim faces the men weren't delivering good news, and the enormous gravity of the situation was fully realized in that moment. Typically, when the family gathered to plan an attack there was at least *some* levity involved. It was serious business, they all knew that, but you could still expect a few jokes cracked by the uncles at each other's expense.

Brie masked her concern easily and took the lead, as usual, by speaking first.

"So, what's the deal? If we're already working on a plan let me go get my notes, because Angie and I ha—"

"Sit down Brie," Pap interrupted. "They'll be plenty of time for your . . . notes later."

Brie fell back on to the couch heaving the impatient sigh of a petulant child while Angie elected to sit on the floor with her legs crossed, her smile unwavering despite the air of seriousness.

"Until now the family has faced only the people who've been tapped to carry out certain acts to perpetuate and further strengthen the behemoth that is evil," Pap started. "In our entire history the family has never faced one of the limbs of evil, the ones it extends into the world we exist in. The fact it's reaching out specifically for us makes it even worse."

"Never?" Angie asked. "Even like way back years ago when the family started?"

"Never," Pap answered.

"Why is that?"

This time the question came from Brie, the lingering attitude now absent from her voice.

"Well, it's sort of complicated," Rory piped up, "but I guess sort of not, too."

"What the hell is that supposed to mean?" The sharp edge returned to Brie's tone with the question.

"Take the pole for example," Rory continued.

"Oh, come on," Brie moaned. "Not the pole story again."

"No, no, no, I'm not gonna tell the whole story again."

Angie could tell the man was trying to tamp down his frustration, and she wished her cousin would lighten up a little. Brie always meant well, but her demeanor wasn't helping in this situation.

"The symbols carved *into* the pole are part of it," Rory continued slow and easy. "They help 'ward away' evil, or at least they're supposed to anyway. I copied them exactly from the family bible."

The 'family bible' wasn't the kind you took to church but rather a historical document precious to them all. Since the family began, they'd kept detailed records in their bible recording every engagement with the enemy. It included what worked, what didn't, what they'd learned and planned to implement in the next confrontation, along with countless notes containing valuable knowledge meant to aid the family for generations.

The girls had never seen the inside of the family bible but witnessed Pap writing in the massive tome many times. It was the job of the family's appointed elder to keep the bible safe, as well as updated. Ever since Brie and Angie could remember the duty had belonged to Pap.

"So, the pole protects the house from evil?" asked Brie. "That's it?"

"And what did you mean by 'supposed to'?" chimed Brie.

"No, that's not 'it'."

Rory stepped over to the mantle where a large portrait of someone Brie and Angie never met had been hanging their whole lives. He reached out and grabbed the sides of the frame before gently lifting it up and away from the wall. Behind it a large chunk of sheetrock was missing to reveal a wall of red bricks, each bearing a different symbol the girls recognized from the pole.

"You see," Rory said still holding the painting and gesturing with his chin, "the walls of the house are lined with another layer of brick behind what you can see on the outside. Each is marked with a symbol taken directly from the family bible, which claimed they would keep the house and those in it protected."

"But?" Brie tossed out.

"*But*" Rory mocked, "it's never been tested, at least not by us, and we have no idea if these symbols really do have power to them. There's never been any large-scale attacks on the house, not to mention we've never dealt with something of this magnitude before."

"Sure," Brie shook her head, "that makes *a lot* of sense."

"What's that mean?" Angie asked genuinely.

"It means," Pap took the reins again, "we haven't seen it work. Sure, it could be working, but this is the first time we'd be facing something like *him*."

They all knew he meant the Cadillac Man.

"For all we know he could burst into flames or explode the second he walks through the door . . . "

"But you do know. Don't ya Pap?" Brie's voice was soft again.

The old man looked at the floor and nodded his head. The girls looked from Pap to their uncles who'd leveled their collective gaze toward the ground.

"It's bullshit." Pap finally said. "All of it is bullshit."

Angie and Brie exchanged puzzled looks that flashed concern as Pap sighed and massaged the bridge of his nose with his thumb and forefinger. Then, he took a deep breath and told the girls what he'd already told the uncles, everything he'd been holding back.

———— ◆ ————

The Cadillac's backseat was far larger than it looked or

should have been but was just one of the many anomalies contained within. Such as being able to pass freely through time forward, backward, or even laterally. The Cadillac Man and the vehicle he'd been named for, his trusty steed if you will, weren't bound to laws of physics, or impeded by dimensional boundaries.

Evil darkened the entirety of existence across all planes with its thick inky shadow. There was no such thing as hiding from it. Safety was a myth, and no one was exempt.

Jacobi and Carla were made to sit in the back with the well-dressed woman whose name was Olivia. From the outside it looked like it would've been a tight squeeze for three adults to ride comfortably, or rather two adults and whatever Jacobi was.

Thanks to the unique and unexplained abilities of the car there was plenty of room for all three of them to recline comfortably with at least a foot of space between them. It wouldn't have mattered to Jacobi if he had fifteen feet of space, and a partition to separate himself from the other passengers. The very fact he was being made to sit in the backseat was insulting regardless of any luxuries it provided.

Jacobi didn't understand why the Cadillac Man let any of his filthy human cattle ride in the front seat at all. They were nothing but mindless meat puppets whether they realized it or not. They were all destined for the same fate, but Jacobi would still be around, and he'd always come back. The front seat should be designated for him only, and even if he weren't in the car humans should *always* ride in the back.

It wasn't up to him though even back when it had been just the two of them. Jacobi couldn't remember what time or realm he'd been yanked from by the Cadillac Man to become his 'assistant', for lack of a better term. He wasn't anything like what the Cadillac Man was, but still a far cry from anything close to human. Jacobi wasn't an imp, or any iteration of a demon, or angel, or any other mythological creature, but one thing for sure, he was durable.

There were others in the same business as the Cadillac Man who'd plucked members of his species from their lives for this very reason. Jacobi was like having the ultimate utility player on your team. Not only could he play any position, but he was also practically invincible. He'd been shot, stabbed, blown up, run over, and burned to a crisp several times, but always found himself waiting on the same street corner over and over for the Cadillac Man to pick him back up.

When it was the two of them, they'd sowed large swaths of chaos everywhere they went, but then the Cadillac Man started experimenting with using humans as a means to spread the evil he existed only to proliferate. He didn't have to be as hands-on if he used them and could have many working at the same time to feed evil steadily rather than in short bursts.

Jacobi wasn't bothered by having to work with humans at first. It was fun for him to know he'd be ripping them apart sooner or later while subjecting them to unspeakable acts of horror. The novelty wore off quickly though, and he was soon tired of this new arrangement.

Humans were far too cocky for being such delicate and fragile creatures, and Jacobi found their arrogance both offensive and foolish. Yet, he found himself perpetually chained to one in some way or another as the Cadillac Man cycled them through. He felt like an animal trainer or a babysitter most of the time now, not the crucial role he believed himself to have in the overall plan.

What that plan was exactly, Jacobi didn't know, but believed he was more important than the humans who'd been brought into the mix. They were weak, soft, and completely disposable, and he was none of those things. He came back. Jacobi always came back. He didn't know why or where he went, but it didn't matter to him.

Now he was sitting in the backseat with *three* humans

in the car, which was three too many as far as he was concerned, and while unusual Jacobi was too annoyed to be curious choosing to fume in silence rather than ask questions. It wouldn't matter anyway since the Cadillac Man didn't answer until he was ready.

Whatever they were doing Jacobi didn't like it already, especially if it involved him working with multiple humans. Even if it meant he got to eat all of them in the end, it just wasn't worth it to him. A thought suddenly occurred to Jacobi that derailed the disdain train he'd been riding through his mind.

What if this was it? What if someone or something was going to eat *him* at the end? He recalled the last time any change occurred in his routine with the Cadillac Man was when the humans started being used. While he wasn't happy with the way his responsibilities had been amended, Jacobi was kept by the Cadillac Man's side, which may have contributed to his inflated sense of confidence.

For the first time since he'd started Jacobi felt nervous. There'd never been four people in the Cadillac Man's car at one time, but now suddenly it was a regular carpool to the office. Something was different. Something was changing, and the fact the Cadillac Man hadn't said a word since telling them to get in the car, while not entirely unusual, gave Jacobi further reason to worry. Riding in silence was normal, but this silence had weight that sat heavy in his lap and leaned hard against his chest.

Jacobi shifted in his seat, looked out the window, and prepared himself for the worst.

———◆———

Angie was alone in the living room standing by the mantel studying the exposed brick shown to her and Brie by their uncle earlier in the day. The portrait used to cover it was on the floor leaned up against the wall, but Angie promised to replace it when she was done. The family's meeting had been over for an hour and a half, and she'd been standing in the same place since staring and thinking.

What Pap had to tell them wasn't received well by Brie, and though he didn't say it, Uncle Dwayne's hardened expression showed he felt the same way. The betrayal they felt showed heavy in their eyes, but Angie was neutral to the whole thing.

She'd watched her cousin's face contort with rage as Pap spoke, mostly listening while impatiently waiting for her turn to talk. What she had to say was laced with misdirected hostility and rhetorical questions mainly settled around the symbols in the bricks.

"How in the hell do we not know if it works?" Brie was supposed to be working on not raising her voice at inappropriate times, but she wasn't working very hard. "Isn't that what the whole stupid book is for, so we know what works? What else are you not telling us about what's in there?"

"Now, you watch it Brie—"

Dwayne took a strong firm tone with the girl, but Pap raised his hand to signify he would handle it. He knew there'd be questions, and he knew Brie would ask most of them. He'd prepared for this.

"Brie," started Pap, "You have every right to be upset and want answers. I'm not sure I have them all, or any for that matter, but I'll share what I have."

"The symbols," Brie snapped sitting down on the couch again. "Why?"

The old man paused and ran his hand over the cover of the old family bible as if it were psychically telling him what to say before he said it.

"Unfortunately, there are no hard and fast rules to what we do. Back when the family started, they wasted many years and many lives figuring that out. Every charm they sought, every text religious or not, every spell, along with an endless line of deities was all for naught.

"Each and every avenue of hope explored ended in the

hands of evil, because that's all it was, that's what all of it was. Anything ever dreamed up or passed down as a deterrent was created by evil to put people right back on the path to it even when they think they're walking away."

"So, wait," piped up Angie. "Does that me—"

"Yes." Pap cut her off firmly. "Before you ask, yes. It means none of its real, none of it. It's all a trick, and it always was."

"Does that mean the symbols are a trick too? Like, as in definitely?" Angie's voice was chipper as always despite the grim atmosphere.

"Like, as in he knew the whole time?" Brie mocked her cousin's tone with added bite.

Pap dropped his head again, and then looked over at the uncles standing off to the left of him. Rory met his gaze, but Dwayne kept his eyes locked on the floor trying hard to mask his own feelings on the matter.

"Years ago, when I first came into the family," Pap said turning back to face the girls, "I'd become fast friends with the elder at that time and ended up spending a lot of time with her. Her name was Bethany. Of course, I didn't know I'd be the elder of the family myself someday since there's really no way to know how long any of the members would last.

"When I took over the ol' helm, so to speak, some said my time with Bethany had been purposely guided by a spirit. Preordained so she could pass her knowledge on to me knowing I would one day take her place, but I didn't think so. It was just chance like anything else, but I could sense the glimmer of hope within them as they expounded on their theory. I didn't have the heart to rain on their parade."

"But isn't that why you're in charge of the book?" Brie's tone was still stilted in anger despite her attempt to suppress it. "So, you can tell them the truth about things like that? Things that inspired false hope?"

Pap lowered his eyes again and sighed heavily before looking back up to continue.

"Yes and no, but it's more complicated than that."

"Doesn't seem so complicated to me."

Brie's steadily increasing frustration turned her face beet-red. Angie knew her cousin despised secrets and took it personally when information was kept from her. Even when Pap or the uncles told her it was for her own good, she'd fire back about how *she* was the one who knew what was good for her.

Occasionally they'd invent situations to gently tease Brie about it whenever she got wound too tight. They'd pretend there was some big news they were keeping from her, and once she was about to lose her mind one of them would reveal the secret as something incredibly banal like bananas were on sale two for one, or that it was going to rain later in the day. There were no jokes or teasing now though, this was deadly serious.

As Pap explained what he meant by things being more complicated Angie could sense waves of anger radiating not only from Brie, but both the uncles as well. Neither Dwayne nor Rory was as transparent with their frustration as Brie, and while Angie had good reason to be upset as well, she wasn't. She understood the reasoning behind his actions, and besides nothing could be done about it now.

The long and short of it was the symbols never did work and weren't going to start anytime soon. It was Bethany who was tricked into believing in the symbols, although she wouldn't reveal to Pap how she was fooled or by whom. He now knew by way of his intuition it was the work of the Cadillac Man. She'd already recorded all the information into the family bible long before discovering it was a farce, and was so fraught she confided in him, and him only.

The family members at the time had already finished the bricks for more than three quarters of the house when Bethany was made aware of her error, but she still let them finish the job. While the sense of hope it provided was hollow, it was hope nonetheless at a time when the family needed it badly.

They'd suffered significant losses just before Pap joined the family, and while he couldn't fully relate to their sense of sadness, he felt it cloud the air of every room in the house. The Cadillac Man had sent a stark-white, scaly, man-like monster after the family who ripped four of the members apart with its bare hands like they'd been paper dolls.

Why the creature didn't finish them all off at the time was a mystery. Their morale was so fragile Bethany couldn't bear delivering further bad news especially since the surviving family members had thrown themselves into making these bricks thinking it a surefire way to remain safe as long as they were in the home.

Pap agreed to keep Bethany's secret for the sake of sparing the surviving family members another demoralizing blow. At the time it seemed like the right thing to do, but he'd regretted it ever since particularly his part in perpetuating the false information.

After a while there was no one left who'd been there during the making of the bricks, and the only one who knew about it was Pap until Rory took the portrait off the wall in the living room one day. He was attempting to straighten it but accidentally knocked it down and discovered the patch of exposed brick. Pap could've nipped it in the bud right then and there, he should've at least. He opened his mouth with the intention of telling Rory the truth, but instead out came the same fantastical story Bethany told many years prior.

So, a false confidence settled over the family yet again, and Pap sat back and let it happen. After a while his visions started to show him why he shouldn't have, but it was too late to go back and change anything, too late to stop it.

Pap used to wonder why the Cadillac Man and his monstrous-looking sidekick hadn't finished off the entire family way back when he had the chance, but now he knew exactly why. He'd marked the family years ago, so he could come back to get something from them in the future, something they didn't have until now and it was time to collect.

Angie traced her finger along the grooves of the symbol in one of the bricks. She thought they were beautiful despite the unfortunate story that went along with them. She'd come to terms instantly with Pap's withholding of information, as she understood the importance of hope. Pap told her, Brie, Rory and Dwayne how the Cadillac Man put his mark on them, and was coming to get something from them, but claimed he had no idea what it was. Only he did, and Angie had no idea why he was lying again, but Pap had his reasons. After all this he couldn't bear to tell them it was the family itself that would be collected.

"Angie, goddamnit!" Brie had gone to review the notes her cousin and found doodles and gibberish instead. "What is all this shit? You didn't write down a goddamn thing I said! Get up here!"

Angie stepped back from the wall, lifted the portrait, and smiled as she hung it back over the mantel.

"Coming," she sang as she skipped from the living room.

———————◆———————

Dwayne had gone back down into the basement after the meeting with both he and Rory forgetting about their collaborative work planned for today. What else could he do, really? He knew something like this was coming eventually, he always knew although it didn't matter. It was one of those things you could have an entire lifespan to prepare and still not be ready when the day finally came.

Dwayne *did* believe Pap when he said he didn't know when exactly the Cadillac Man's attack on the family would come, but only that it'd be soon. As far as he was concerned it had already started. Just knowing they were officially *on the clock* as it was tantamount to engaging in battle. Their guard now had to be up at all times while keeping an eye out over their shoulders as they readied themselves trying to prepare with whatever time there was, which wouldn't be enough regardless.

He was upset with Pap for keeping information from the rest of the family, but Dwayne chose to throw himself into his work to keep from stewing on it though couldn't shake the thought entirely. The crossbow on the workbench in front of him still needed to be reassembled, and seeing it made him think about the girls. Angie and Brie would be key in their beating the Cadillac Man and any cronies he had in tow. There was something special about those two, all of them knew it, and the thought reinvigorated his focus.

Dwayne cared very much for Pap, which was why it was hard to be angry with him, but he'd need time they didn't have to get over it. He knew the old man meant well, but now there was a good chance they'd be riding his good intentions all the way to hell. There *was* harm in letting them believe they were protected inside the house regardless of the rationalized justification.

All these years instead of laboring under this false belief they could have been working on trying to find something that did protect them, and if that 'something' didn't exist at least they'd know.

They could've explored other ways to fortify themselves against attack; they could've spent weeks or months concocting plans to defend the home from any number of assaults. Maybe then the situation wouldn't seem as bleak and desperate as it did now?

Nothing could be done about it now, and Dwayne knew any amount of dwelling was a waste of energy regardless of the amount of mindshare dedicated to the thought. Every bit of focus from all five of them was needed for what they could do now, not what they *could've* done years ago.

His fingers ran nimbly across the weapon as he continued to reconstruct it taking special care with certain areas and aspects to ensure the crossbow wouldn't malfunction. After double-checking his work Dwayne cleaned and polished the weapon before hanging it on the wall by the stairs. He retrieved the crossbow she used as backup and took it to the workbench to check it out.

It didn't need fixing, but he still took it apart and reassembled it with the same care given to the one he'd just repaired. He cleaned it just as thoroughly when through before taking it across the basement to hang next to its mate. Dwayne was halfway back to his bench when he thought he heard something and stopped.

He stood still holding his breath and listening, but it didn't happen again. He wasn't sure if it came from upstairs, or outside of the house, or if he'd really heard anything at all? It sounded like something was dropped or maybe fallen over. He remained still for another few seconds before slowly making his way back to his workbench silently still straining his ears to listen.

He set back to work this time to make the custom bolts the crossbows fired even though there was a good amount already stockpiled. It was an item he made sure to make every week regardless of whether they were needed. Dwayne figured they could never have too much ammo, but now he wondered if all the ammo in the world would even make a difference?

This wasn't going to be like any other mission the family had been on since his time with them. They weren't going out and stalk their targets, take them by surprise, and maybe drag a few back to tie to the pole for target practice. The pole. They poked fun of Rory for telling the story over and over, but he was damn proud of it and felt like it was his personal contribution to the family's safety. Now they knew it was just a waste of eight bags of concrete, and the time he spent meticulously creating small molds for some symbols while others he carved by hand.

He'd never say it, but Dwayne could tell Rory was hurt to learn the truth. After the meeting Dwayne watched him go out the back door, and assumed he was headed back to the workshop. He decided he'd leave him be in there for a while to let him get over it in his own way but would check on him in another half-hour or so.

If Rory still felt like he needed to talk about it, Dwayne would listen. The man deserved at least that, but he deserved it most from Pap. The conversation would never happen though, which at the moment was for the best. The last thing they needed was to start arguing when it was imperative they work together.

For all Dwayne knew that could even be a part of the Cadillac Man's plan? Maybe he'd planted the deception years ago in order to create dissent amongst the family now, and once they were distracted going at each other's throats he'd strike catching them completely off-guard.

The thought made him physically shiver, and he quickly pushed it from his mind for fear he'd accidentally manifest it. If the theory were true, it meant they never had a chance. Not just the five of them, but the entire family from its inception making everything they'd done, every single hard-fought victory, ring hollow. If the enemy could manipulate them across time, then what other unknown failsafe holds did evil have on them?

Dwayne began humming to distract himself and directed his focus sanding the point at the end of the bolt in his hand making it as sharp as possible. The bolt and sharpening stone dropped from his grasp when he heard what sounded like a car crashing into a brick wall.

Dwayne tensed up and remained still listening to the subsequent banging that followed the crash decay. Was this it? Was it happening right now? The noises were so violent and jarring what else could be happening? The family was being attacked.

A moment later Dwayne had two handfuls of bolts with both crossbows slung over his shoulders, as he raced up the stairs.

———◆———

Rory wasn't as good as Dwayne at tamping down his emotions. He'd always been far too sensitive and had worn his heart on his sleeve quite prominently since he was a child. He just couldn't help it.

He was one of those people who wanted to look past obvious shortcomings to find the good in everyone. Even after he joined the family and learned there was truly none to be found, Rory had a hard time letting the old way of thinking go. He preferred to look at it like there were people with good in them out there; they just hadn't met any of them.

He'd seen enough to know he was being foolish, but keeping the thought tucked away was sometimes the only thing that motivated him on the bad days. This was a different kind of 'bad day' though, because he felt betrayed by one of his own. It was the kind of betrayal you couldn't help but take personally, and as softhearted as Rory was it devastated him.

When they dispersed from the living room after the meeting, he mumbled something about being in the workshop, and headed out the back door. He'd forgotten the project he and Dwayne were supposed to work on, which was just as well since Rory needed to be alone. He needed to process.

He closed the door behind him when he entered the shop and made a beeline for the beer fridge. He reached in, pulled out two cans of Pearl in each mammoth callused paw, and took them over to his workspace. Rory put down the cans and swept his arm across the area knocking everything to the floor with the single motion.

There was a loud metallic clang and a series of pops and pings until his tools along with pieces of the would-be project settled across the cement slab floor. He didn't know what it was going to be anyway, Dwayne was supposed to tell him. Rory couldn't give a shit less now and arranged the four cans of beer in the center of the workbench opening them all one after the other.

Rory brought the first Pearl to his mouth, and a few seconds later was taking the fourth can from his lips having emptied them all. He swept the empty cans to the floor as well, went back to the refrigerator, and repeated the entire ritual. As the cans clattered across the floor again, he looked up and through the window Rory could see the pole.

The man Angie had been shooting at was still tied to it with three crossbow bolts sticking out of his torso. He'd been out there for a while, and the ropes had loosened some turning the man into a drooping version of the figure from whatever one of those paintings Angie liked. Rory never understood art, or at least not in the way Angie did.

If he saw something he liked, well; that was that as far as he was concerned. He wasn't motivated to find a deeper meaning in the work or decipher some hidden meaning the artist had cleverly included about god or their mother. Rory didn't consider cultural significance, or demarcation points in history related to the art he liked. He also knew most likely the kind of art he looked at didn't have any of these things to offer anyway.

Sometimes he wished he could see things the way Angie did, or even Brie. She may not let on through her tough exterior but was also just as in tune with art as her cousin. Pap had his whole 'guitar' thing, and while Dwayne was no connoisseur, he was more artistically inclined than Rory by far.

At times this made him feel like the odd man out, like he was just a big dumb ox good for handling the heavy lifting and not much else. This was one of those times. Rory was halfway to the pole and closing in quickly before realizing he'd even left the shed. A moment later he was using his signature strength to rip the man from the pole without cutting the ropes first.

One quick horrific scream escaped his mouth before Rory snapped his neck, as the smoldering remnants of life were mercifully extinguished. It wasn't like either of the girls to leave anyone alive on the pole. They traded off one-for-one as far as who would do the tying and who would do the shooting, but they would both bury whatever they had left when they were done in the garden. The 'garden' was just a corner of the backyard where the family buried the poor bastards unlucky enough not to die before Angie and Brie could bring them back and tie them to the pole.

They just got distracted same as Dwayne, same as himself, having dropped what they were doing when they heard Pap's guitar. No, that wasn't true. Angie and Brie weren't distracted after the meeting; they'd just redirected their focus on protecting the family. Dwayne wasn't distracted either and most likely in the basement preparing as many weapons as possible before the coming siege.

The other members of the family responded in the appropriate analytical way not letting their emotions get the better of them. It wasn't that they didn't show their anger, all except for the seemingly eternally unfazed Angie, but it was how they were able to handle it. Dwayne and the girls could compartmentalize their emotions and switch into problem solving mode at the drop of a dime.

Rory had no idea what the three of them were doing now, but he knew it was productive. Meanwhile, here *he* was the only one so distracted he forgot what he was even doing but didn't forget to power-drink eight beers. Now, he was ripping an arm from the socket of the man on the pole, which provided the slack in the rope needed to remove the body entirely.

He threw the broken body across the lawn and stared razor-edged rage beams at the pole wrapping the rope around his arm to keep it from tangling, and then he threw that to the side as well. Maybe Rory was too sensitive for his own good, and probably just as dumb. He may not be able to see art correctly, or come up with any good plans, but he could destroy the pole.

It was the one thing he'd contributed to the family completely of his own doing. He knew the girls hated to hear him tell the story of the pole over and over, and while he acted like it was part of an ongoing inside joke, it was one he truly enjoyed telling. It made him feel proud of his accomplishment, his contribution. The same swell of pride he'd felt just looking at it from the window of the workshop.

Now, standing three feet away boring a hole through the pole with his stare, Rory felt no pride. He felt disdain. He felt foolish for taking such satisfaction in what amounted to a worthless effort, and the emotion re-aggravated the still tender sting of betrayal. Rory couldn't deal with feeling these things all over again whenever he looked at the pole now. He was going to have to destroy it.

Rory stepped back and scanned the yard for an appropriate tool to accommodate the job. Outside of a few shovels and a rake, which were far from being substantial enough to do the job, the yard was free of any heavy-duty tools. He spun around, stomped back to the workshop, and disappeared inside for only a moment. When he stepped back out, he was holding his sledgehammer.

It was truly *his* sledgehammer as it had been made by Dwayne just for him as gift to mark Rory's one-year anniversary in the family. The heaviest sledgehammer you can buy in a store weighs twenty pounds, but the one made for Rory weighed thirty-five. It was the heaviest Dwayne could make it while keeping the hammer balanced.

The long snakewood handle was stained with blood of past enemy encounters and bore more than a few nicks and dents for being made from one of the strongest woods in the world. The weapon was otherwise in immaculate condition, as Rory cleaned it directly after use religiously. He and Dwayne didn't know each other as well back then, and Rory valued the gift highly seeing it as a symbol of the respect the family had for him.

Not just anyone could earn *that* respect, and he took it seriously. The hammer meant he was accepted. He was here to stay, and not only that; he was an important part of something bigger, and this was physical proof of it. It was undeniable.

Rory stepped up to the pole and brought the hammer back to destroy one thing that lost its meaning with another whose self-implied sentiment now rang empty. The first swing was mighty but did little damage to the pole aside from sending a few small chips flying.

He wasn't surprised since he'd reinforced the pole when he built it to prevent the very thing he was trying to do. Rory's aim had been to make it indestructible, or at least a huge pain in the ass to do any damage to.

The steel rebar within the cement strengthened the integrity of the pole and coupled with its tremendous girth along with the density of the concrete made it difficult to destroy by design. Rory knew this better than anyone, but continued to bring the hammer back and strike the pole several more times. Winded, he dropped the massive sledgehammer on the ground and bent over with his hands on his knees to catch his breath.

The buzz he caught before launching his attack numbed him enough to get maybe three or four more swings than he could've done sober, not that they did him any good. Not even using his tremendous might to propel the colossal hammer's head against the pole was enough to do any significant damage.

Dust and small chunks of stone settled around the base of the pole, and Rory sucked wind while staring down at the pitiful fruit borne of his effort. He looked up the pole again and was struck suddenly with another idea. Rory snatched up his prized sledgehammer, took it back to the workshop, and came out with a cold Pearl in each hand both of which he consumed quickly.

He left the empty cans on the ground where he dropped them and walked around to the backside of the shop. A while ago he and Dwayne built a small shed behind it used primarily to store the family's yard equipment, along with a few bulkier weapons and some traps. Rory pulled open the doors and worked his way through the equipment to reach what he was looking for.

If anyone else had been in the backyard at the time they'd have been able to hear him long before they saw. The engine on the riding mower was loud, but with the amount of power in the thing it should've been much louder. The mower had been a longtime passion project of Rory's and was a quasi-prototype of an idea he'd had for a weapon.

He'd excitedly worked up some rough plans before presenting his idea to Pap and Dwayne, but the attempt was amateurish and mostly hard to decipher. Rory thought he'd done an excellent job of describing his idea to them since they were having trouble translating it from the page, but the two of them still struggled to grasp his vision. Dwayne remarked he thought part of it looked like a riding lawnmower, and that must've been what put the idea in Pap's head.

He told Rory he could use the family's mower to build a model of his idea to scale, the only caveat being he needed to make sure it could still be used to mow the grass. As long as it continued to perform its primary function Rory could use the mower for his idea as he saw fit. He accepted the deal but grumbled about having to tweak many things in order to adapt it properly.

It turned out there weren't many changes Rory needed to make at all, and in fact the incorporation of the riding lawnmower improved his overall concept. Another stipulation added by Pap was Rory would now have to mow the lawn every week further emphasizing the importance of making sure the thing still cut grass.

He wasn't a huge fan of yard work, but the added stipulation was a small price to pay. One of the reasons he upgraded the motor was so he could cut the grass faster, but more power was a welcome addition all around. While a lot of the 'weapon' aspect of Rory's design centered on the blades underneath, he'd reinforced the body, and mounted an enormous steel cowcatcher to the front.

Rory gunned it and the engine roared as he came

around the workshop taking the turn on two wheels. He shifted his weight to balance the machine as he straightened out and pointed it in the direction of the pole. Rory opened the throttle wide and gritted his teeth as the mower increased in speed. The pole became a physical manifestation of the feelings he needed to release so he was going to drive his riding lawnmower into it.

The impact sounded like a small explosion that no doubt scared the woolly shits out of the rest of the family inside, especially with being on high alert and all. The cowcatcher wasn't welded as well as he thought, and it crumpled off to the side during the collision doing virtually no damage to the pole. The engine block took the brunt of the crash and folded back into itself.

The pole still stood, but there was one bit of noteworthy damage. About a foot above the point of impact was an oval-shaped divot the size of a fist stamped with candy-red spatter.

Rory was on the ground unconscious beside the wreckage of what he'd turned the riding lawnmower into while blood pouring from the gash in his head pooled around the pole.

———————— ◆ ————————

Brie practically ripped the notebook apart flipping through page after page of her cousin's scribbles and childish doodles. She didn't understand Angie at all, and lately the disdain she felt toward her cousin was taking longer and longer to abate. The girls weren't sisters, and they weren't cousins either, but despite not being blood related they grew up together and developed a healthy sibling rivalry. It was Brie who carried it through to the present day.

She would never admit it, not even to herself, but deep, deep down she loathed Angie. Brie was someone who approached the pursuit of a new skill with a serious mindset and made it a point to fully educate herself as she worked toward its mastery. Her cousin was much more laid back and approached new learning experiences with a nonchalance Brie found insufferable.

Angie was good at everything she attempted from the start, but the things that truly captured her interest she excelled at. What burned Brie up most about her cousin's uncanny expertise was that she didn't even care. When the two were first learning to shoot rifles for the first time it was Brie who practiced for hours with her weapon while Angie barely touched hers at all.

When it came time to showcase their progress with firearms to the family Brie stepped up to her mark and displayed the excellent shooting posture she'd practiced for hours without even pulling the trigger. Smoothly, expertly she squeezed rather than pulled firing off three successive shots that struck just along the perimeter of the bull's-eye.

Angie cheered her cousin on, and even tried to give her a high-five on her way to the mark, but Brie did not engage or acknowledge. She remained laser focused and took her place off to the side between the uncles as Angie stepped up to take her turn. She lifted the rifle up to aim, and the weapon looked awkward and uncomfortable in her arms.

She hadn't practiced how to stand with the rifle, or how to hold it, not to mention her ignorance of the 'squeeze, don't pull' rule. Angie giggled and lowered the rifle so she could tie back her hair.

"Sorry ya'll."

If Brie could've rolled her eyes any harder it would have been audible, and she unsuccessfully tried to stifle her impatient sigh. When Angie brought the rifle up to take aim again, she looked foolish as if the idea of a firearm was foreign to her, but only for a moment. With an imperceptible fluidity everything about the way she'd been standing shifted into an expert stance.

She rang off three shots and lowered the weapon before anyone, except Brie of course, realized she'd pulled the trigger. All three shots hit the center of the target striking within millimeters of each other.

"Well, look at that," Angie bleated in her sweet southern accent.

She wasn't trying to be sarcastic, or tongue in cheek, and had no intention for her remark to come off like she was rubbing her marksmanship in her cousin's face only Brie didn't see it that way. She didn't buy Angie's aloof purity for a second and viewed everything she said through a filter of the derision Brie believed lurked just below the surface of her southern-fried cousin.

She didn't have any proof, and never witnessed Angie acting sinister or stuck-up. In fact, Brie didn't think she'd ever even seen Angie angry, or the least bit upset. She remained unflappable under any circumstance, and somehow maintained a constant steady coolness, which seemingly kept her on a perpetual even-keel. Despite Angie's unique character trait Brie remained forever waiting for the other shoe to drop, and it would be revealed her cousin wasn't so great after all. Maybe she'd even turn out to be a liability?

Frustrated, Brie took the notebook over to the wastebasket in the corner, tore out every page Angie touched despite what she'd written, and let them drop into the trashcan at her feet. When she was done the notebook was considerably thinner from having more than half its pages removed, and she took it over to her small desk next to the door.

She sat down, unclipped the pen Angie had been using, and flung it at the trashcan where it clattered off the side bouncing halfway back across the room. Brie didn't even want the pen Angie wrote with to touch the pages of the notebook again deeming it tainted by the girl's touch.

She took one of her own pens from the center desk drawer, and opened the notebook recently purged of Angie's foolishness to fill with actual intelligent ideas to protect the family. Brie paused, put the pen back down, and got up to close the bedroom door, which she slammed.

She wasn't going to call for Angie again, and quite

frankly hoped she wouldn't come regardless. Brie didn't want her help, nor did she need it. Not only was Angie not great at coming up with plans she was even worse about sticking to them. There'd been countless crucial situations in which Angie completely abandoned the plan in favor of 'feeling her way through it'.

The rest of the family viewed Angie's approach as valuable crediting the girl with having saved their lives many times by going with her gut, but Brie saw no value in having a loose cannon amongst their ranks. One of these days she was going to get herself killed, or worse the entire family. Brie sincerely hoped it would be the former.

She began to note bullet points from what she could remember of the ideas she'd been dictating to Angie, and before long stopped stewing on the feelings she harbored toward her cousin. Her thoughts turned to Pap, and what he'd told them. Brie attempted to brush it off, citing she didn't have much faith in 'magic symbols' anyway, but she did have faith in Pap, which was much harder to push away.

He said he'd meant well, which could've gone without saying, but his judgment was supposed to slice through well wishes and spare no feelings. Hurt feelings you could recover from, but there was no recovery from being dead. If none of the family had been led to believe they were somehow protected from attack within the walls of the house they could've found an *actual* solution.

Not to say they wouldn't be able to now or in the near future, but time was a luxury for the family no more. According to Pap they could come under attack at any moment now unless there was something else, he was keeping from them. It was almost disorienting to think about, and even Brie's thoughts and energy seemed scattered as opposed to the laser-focus she was typically able to employ.

Even now her mind wandered so much she couldn't remember where she was going with her plan and huffed as she ripped out the page. Brie wadded the paper and threw it in the direction of the trashcan but didn't bother watching to see if she'd gotten close. She stared down at the blank page trying to force ideas through the shroud of rage ensconcing her mind, but instead her thoughts continued to vacillate between Angie and Pap. Brie still didn't want to be angry at Pap and did the best she could to direct most of the emotion toward Angie.

She set to writing again, but before the pen touched paper Brie heard a banging noise coming from outside and cursed it for breaking her concentration again. The banging didn't go on for long, and Brie figured one or both uncles was outside working on something to help save the family's ass. Her room was on the front side of the house, so she could also hear random notes from Pap's guitar work their way up from the porch below.

Normally, she wouldn't have noticed the guitar since it was nearly ever-present, but since she'd come back upstairs from the meeting the familiar twang made her stomach drop, and her asshole pucker. It was quiet enough to tell he was just noodling around practicing more than anything else, as it wasn't the usual intense and intricate music that came with his visions.

Pap was no doubt working his fingers across the strings attempting to coax another vision, perhaps one with better news, but it didn't work like that. His second sight possessed a kind of sentience unable to be accessed at will as if it were as simple as making a phone call.

The visions came along in their own time and were never late but were also never wrong. Brie wrestled with accepting there was a possibility Pap had already been shown the outcome, and in continuing with his theme of inspiring hope, had elected not to tell them what he'd seen. It was quite feasible for her to think he'd seen the family horribly slaughtered by this Cadillac Man, and thought if he didn't acknowledge it there would be a chance they could prove the vision wrong.

Brie was lost in thought and didn't hear the droning engine sound, but the crash that followed nearly startled her out the chair, and she leapt up immediately at full alert. The guitar had stopped, and she heard the pounding footfalls of someone running up the basement steps. A few seconds later, she heard screaming.

———————◆———————

The Cadillac was silent inside for the entire drive save for the occasional audible sigh from Carla. All of them, even Jacobi, had questions, but they knew better than to ask. Outside the scenery appeared as amorphous blobs bleeding in and out of each other.

Nothing was in focus to provide any sort of context, so the passengers were unable to tell if they were traveling extremely fast or passing through some foreign plane of existence on the way to their destination. It wasn't a new experience for any of them, but the ride was lasting far longer than usual.

Suddenly, objects outside the windows became sharp and discernible to everyone in the car. They were on a two-lane road with trees lining the right side while the left was clear. It was dark, but the soft pink glow barely visible along the horizon meant it hadn't been night for long.

The Cadillac Man slowed and made a wide swinging left-turn into the parking lot of a small Dairy Queen. It was an older building with a walkup window like ones that existed in outdated movies and tiny country towns, of which they found themselves in the latter.

The Cadillac Man parked and exited the vehicle without a word. The interior was now a much a closer version of reality, and for the first few seconds the four sat in silence waiting to see if anyone knew what to do or was brave enough to take a chance.

"What the hell is this?" Carla turned to Jacobi. "Do you know what we're supposed to do now?"

Jacobi didn't know though, which upset him greatly,

and offered nothing but a shrug and a grunt in return. Anton turned around in the front seat to find Olivia looking into an open compact touching up her makeup while Carla and Jacobi argued like siblings on a road trip.

"Fuck this," said Anton as he pushed the passenger side door open, stepped outside, and slammed it behind him.

The other three sat for a beat before Jacobi followed suit and exited the vehicle with Carla close behind. Olivia checked her makeup one more time and put the compact back into her purse before nonchalantly stepping out of the car. They didn't see the Cadillac Man at first, but Anton spotted him across the parking lot. He was standing next to one of the three tables arranged to the side of the small square building holding a vanilla ice cream cone, which appeared to glow against the stark contrast of his suit.

Anton, Olivia, Carla, and Jacobi crossed the dirt and gravel parking lot slowly with no one in a rush to be the first one there. They tried to hide the attempts of their darting eyes as the four instinctively scanned to familiarize themselves with the lay of the land. If this were the end, they'd all run off in different directions and hope one of them got lucky.

If this were to be the case though, *none* of them would be lucky. In fact, luck hadn't been the best of friends with any of the Cadillac Man's reluctant troops. When they were in six feet of the table, and he still hadn't said a word Anton, as usual, piped up first.

"Are we here for an ice cream social? Is this our reward for being good little boys and girls?"

The sarcastic smile wilted when Anton saw an eyeball peer out between creamy-white lids from the center of the ice cream. He flinched at the sight and the eyeball blinked but didn't open back up again.

"I'm lactose intolerant," Carla announced with a tinge of adolescent sulk in her voice. She folded her arms against her chest further intimating immaturity through body language.

"I actually could go for something," Olivia said staring over at the order window contemplating her choice of sweet treat.

Jacobi lurked a few feet behind the three of them and peered through the space between their heads trying unsuccessfully to catch the Cadillac Man's attention via eye contact. His long-time employer had a way of being able to look at all of them without seeming like he's looking at any of them.

"There'll be plenty of time for that later Olivia."

These were the first words the Cadillac Man said since picking up Carla and Jacobi, and the sound of his voice snapped them all back to attention. He gestured to the table for them to sit down, and reluctantly they complied. When they were settled the Cadillac Man continued.

"I have a different kind of task for you, all of you, which requires your working *with* one another against a common . . . enemy, if you will."

None of them had ever heard the Cadillac Man say 'enemy' when it came to a job, or any other time for that matter. It was possible Jacobi knew better, but as far as Anton, Olivia, and Carla knew he had no enemies, or at least none who posed an *actual* threat. The unsettling notion of someone or something confident enough to oppose the Cadillac Man passed subconsciously between them.

The wind shifted, and Jacobi caught a whiff of something familiar, something that jogged his memory. Suddenly, he knew exactly where they were and why. Now, the Cadillac Man did make eye contact with Jacobi before continuing.

"A little further up the road is a small sleepy town, and in this town is a family who've been quite troublesome for more time than they deserve to be. The four of you are going to help me kill them."

None of them believed they heard him right, and the confusion delayed their comprehension. The Cadillac Man had tasked them all with killing many, many people for him, but the way he was phrased it using the word 'help' made it sound like it was something he couldn't take care of himself. The three humans looked around amongst each other waiting to see who would verbally acknowledge it first, but none of them would take the 'question bait'. Luckily, Jacobi spoke up spurring the conversation along.

"The family? *The* family, right? Now I know where we are, I thought I could smell it, smell *them*." Jacobi smiled as he drew out the word 'them' like he wanted to savor it for as long as possible. "Is it . . . time?"

Anton was getting impatient and didn't appreciate the vagueness with which the two seemed to be talking over the rest of their heads. He looked impatiently from Jacobi back to the Cadillac Man, and swore he saw the ice cream cone he was holding blink again.

"What the hell are you talking about? What family?"

Anton turned back to Jacobi and leveled the question at him in a flimsy attempt to circumvent the 'no questions' policy of their mutual employer. The pale imp smiled sarcastically and looked past him.

"The family has changed over time, their numbers always in flux," the Cadillac Man said, his tone a warning for Anton to be patient. "Since their inception this family has been on a crusade against myself and my associates to put a stop to our work. They in fact believe they've done well through the years to stem my personal tide of evil, and I let them believe it as I was the one who led them to that belief. I fostered it, nurtured it."

The wind shifted again, and the smell of French fries tumbled the short distance from the small building to the table, and Olivia's stomach grumbled. If she'd known this was going to be a long night, she would've grabbed the least disgusting food item at the truck stop for the road to tide her over.

The Cadillac Man was talking, but she was too distracted by hunger to pay attention. Olivia hoped he was telling the truth about them having time to order something from the tiny window of the Dairy Queen before they went to visit his family, or whatever it was he was blathering on about. The longer she had to wait, the further her mood would sour, and it was already starting to turn fast.

"The family is only five total at the moment," he continued, "and I do not intend on letting them grow any larger. Before they're finally snuffed out though, they will know there was never any hope to be had, and not one single thing they did mattered at all."

———————◆———————

Dwayne burst through the backdoor into the backyard crossbow drawn and ready to fire, as Pap came running through the house from the porch falling in right behind. It took a moment to figure out what they were looking at as both men's heads were on a swivel scanning for would-be attackers.

When Dwayne saw Rory laid out next the pole and the heap of twisted metal the mower had become, he let out a tremendous scream. Pap ducked and covered his head thinking the scream was to warn him of an incoming attack. Angie leapt from the back door and was sprinting after Dwayne when Pap lifted his head to see what they were running toward.

Brie stepped from the backdoor with her trusty sawed-off shotgun in hand, and a Glock hanging from the side of both hips. She cocked the shotgun and called to Pap who was only a few feet ahead of her. He still wasn't completely convinced they weren't running headlong into a trap and was still scanning the massive property for any sign of danger.

"What's going on?" Brie asked approaching Pap from behind. "What was that noise? What happened?"

The old man was startled and turned with a jump relieved it was only Brie.

"Damnit girl, you scare the shit out of me!" He turned back to the chaotic scene Dwayne and Angie were heading for. "I'm not sure yet but keep an eye out."

When the other two reached Rory they called back to Pap and Brie to come help, and Pap's old legs were pumping away before he realized he'd started running. He'd only gotten a few feet before Brie blew by him at a full sprint able to move completely unencumbered by weight of the guns around her waist or the one, she was carrying.

Of course, the girl had practiced running with more than that, and was extremely disciplined when it came to her weapons. Brie regularly ran drills the uncles regularly put together for her and was in constant competition with herself to make better times despite the size and/or weight of the various firearms she fancied.

Pap arrived last to where the group was gathered and was shocked by the amount of blood around Rory's head. Dwayne was on his knees having taken his shirt off and was using it to stem the gushing blood from the crooked gash running up the center of Rory's head, but the thin fabric quickly reached its point saturation and was doing little to help.

"What the . . . "

Pap looked from Rory's bloodied up body to the crashed mower, then saw the stained red divot in the pole, and was able to ascertain what happened. The family wasn't under attack, at least not yet, and Rory's wounds had been unintentionally self-inflicted.

Pap looked back down and caught a glimpse of the man's forehead after Dwayne wiped it down before it was covered in blood a second later. There, perfectly etched into Rory's skin was the symbol from where his head smacked the pole. His massive skull might've taken a good chunk out of the pole, but the pole bit back and left its mark on its creator turned destroyer.

Angie had already taken it upon herself to bolt over to the nearby workshop for rags and the first aid kit and was already back with armfuls of the supplies just as Pap reached them. Dwayne threw the blood-soaked shirt to the side and used a few of the thicker rags Angie brought. They worked much better to help slow the bleeding, but Rory was in bad shape.

"He needs help," Dwayne said applying continued pressure on the wound with the shop rags. "We need to stop the bleeding and get him stabilized soon, or he's a goner."

The mention of the possibility Rory could be a 'goner' shook Pap at his core, and his legs momentarily became jelly. He was close enough to the cracked-up mower to lean on and keep his balance, but the weight of his current reality threatened to drive him into the ground like a tent pole spike. It was happening. It was already happening, and it was his fault. The Cadillac Man wasn't even there yet, and the family was already down a man, a man who may possibly already be a *goner*.

If he hadn't lied about the symbols to begin with there wouldn't be a pole, and if there wasn't a pole Rory wouldn't have been so hell-bent on tearing it apart when he learned the truth. There was a very real possibility Pap's actions had already caused the family's downfall, and now it was all starting to play out.

The thought was too much for the old man to take, and his vision blurred as the frantic shouts of Dwayne and the girls faded into the background until it was so far away, he couldn't hear it anymore. By that time, he was on the ground next to what was left of the mower.

———— ◆ ————

They were all back in the car except for Olivia who the Cadillac Man finally allowed to have a quick bite to eat, but in a way, he could benefit from as well. He stood just outside the open driver side door watching the door on the side of the tiny building waiting for it to open.

The Cadillac Man had dropped the ice cream cone he'd

been holding after directing all but Olivia to go back to the car. He hadn't taken a single lick. Anton paused to look down at the quickly melting pool of ice cream speckled with pieces of the now broken cone it once sat upon.

The eye opened again in the center of the slowly spreading slop, and Anton instinctively brought his foot down on the puddle hard. White splotches speckled the bottom of his pant leg from where the ice cream splashed up onto them, and when he took his foot away the eyeball was of course gone. He cursed when he saw his pants but picked up his pace not wanting to appear as if he were lagging. Anton was back in the front seat trying his best to clean melted ice cream from his pants with the half of a tissue he found in his pocket.

Jacobi stared out the window impatiently waiting for Olivia to hurry up and finish. The screaming stopped what felt like ages ago, and his view through the order window had been entirely obscured with blood from the inside. Now that he knew what they were going to do Jacobi wasn't as bothered by being teamed up with humans.

He had intimate knowledge of the family having been up against their many iterations throughout the years. The Cadillac Man didn't share with Jacobi his plan for the family, and in fact never intimated the possibility of there being one. Jacobi knew there had to be though. He could smell it even back then. It made no sense otherwise for the Cadillac Man to drag out toying with the family for so long when he could easily have snuffed them out at any time unless there was a reason for it.

While Jacobi may have had the inkling of there being reason *and* a plan, he had no idea what either could be, and was beyond anxious to find out. He'd seen what the family was capable of several times firsthand, and was also excited at the prospect of Anton, Olivia and Carla being killed off very quickly, but Carla especially so.

There had to be more of a reason for the Cadillac Man to specifically bring *these* three humans aside from using them as living shields, or some other form of crash test dummy? It was unfortunate these humans were most likely integral in some way, but there was no use worrying about it. Jacobi was completely consumed by the anticipation of what was about to unfold.

Finally, the steel door on the side of the small restaurant burst open and banged hard against the wall with the crack of a rifle report. Olivia strolled out licking a vanilla ice cream cone noticeably spattered with blood like she'd added strawberry sauce as an afterthought.

Carla was getting restless and mumbled a mostly inaudible *about time* when she heard the door. The first thing she noticed wasn't the glimpse of horror Olivia was responsible for visible through the open door, but that she was wearing a completely different outfit. It was every bit as trendy and fashionable as what she'd been wearing prior to entering the Dairy Queen, but most importantly it was clean.

There was too much blood in too small a space for Olivia not to be covered head to toe in the stuff, yet here she was in new unsoiled clothing with matching designer heels. Seeing the ice cream cone made Carla wish she'd gotten one as well. The addition of blood kick-started her salivary glands, and her stomach emitted an embarrassingly loud gurgle.

Jacobi shot Carla a disgusted look to which she responded by putting her middle finger in his face.

"Fuck off," Carla told him, but she had little venom left with which to charge the phrase.

She was tired and even more grumpy and hoped they would be granted some magical second wind before they went after this family the Cadillac Man seemed to have a hard-on for. She didn't know about the other two, but Carla and Jacobi were picked up straight from already doing a job, and she was starting to feel the exhaustion. She halfway wondered if she should run over to the shack-style Dairy Queen and grab a basket of fries or maybe a pre-made burger from under the heat lamps to eat on the way?

Ultimately, Carla decided it was probably best to stay in the car and wait until she got home. She didn't know who this 'family' was, or anything about them beyond the cryptic pseudo-description given them by the Cadillac Man only a few minutes prior.

Olivia sauntered across the gravel parking lot to the car like she was walking a fashion show runway. Killing and eating parts of the two teenage girls with the unfortunate luck of working closing shift at the Dairy Queen was not what she had been craving necessarily, but it did the trick. Olivia made quick work of the girls with the efficiency she'd honed when it came to killing.

While she nibbled at the hearts and other various organs to appease the Cadillac Man, Olivia spent the majority of the short time spent inside the restaurant eating actual food. Not a lot of it, but enough to sate her craving for the greasy fast food whose scent had been teasing her since they'd first arrived. While the blood on her ice cream was a nice touch, it was not intentional.

She'd wanted just the plain vanilla as a sort-of palate cleanser, but on her way to the door one of the eviscerated teenager's severed heads rolled off a prep table and landed in one of the many puddles of blood, which splashed red spatter all over her simple sweet treat. Olivia was within three feet of the Cadillac and let the cone fall to the ground having only taken a few licks. Carla watched it splatter across the gravely lot lamenting its premature discarding.

With Olivia in the car the Cadillac Man slid back behind the wheel, and the vehicle's engine roared to life without the turn of a key or press of a button. The Cadillac itself was less of a car, and more of an actual part of the Cadillac Man like an appendage, or vital organ. He had complete control over the car that was his dominion.

He exited the parking lot kicking up gravel with the rear wheel that shot all the way to the blood-filled shack where it bounced off the steel door like buckshot. The car was silent for a minute, and then two prompting the passengers to again anxiously hope one of them would take a chance and speak up. Luckily, they didn't have to because another minute later the Cadillac Man finally spoke.

"Listen very carefully," he started keeping his eyes straight on the road ahead. "This is the plan."

————————•◆•————————

He could hear the music but could see nothing through the thick darkness around him. Pap knew the sound of his guitar when he heard it; of this there was no mistaking, only it wasn't him playing it. The tune was familiar, but only because it was a variation on what he'd been playing a few hours ago. It was thematically similar but wound off in its own direction.

He tried to look around, but his head was stuck in a fixed position, and when he attempted to move found there was no sensation in his limbs. Pap wasn't sure he even had a head or limbs to move at all anymore? At the moment he felt like a disembodied consciousness whose body was somewhere else for the time being. Off in the distance a pinprick of light pushed through the suffocating darkness and began to widen steadily like the aperture of a camera. The music grew louder, faster, and the momentum of its intensity matched the growing circle of light.

He began to see the movement of shapes begin to come into focus until the darkness was gone, and Pap was looking down with a bird's eye view on the scene currently playing out in the backyard. He saw himself on the ground with Brie leaning over him attempting to shake and slap him awake with Rory only a few feet away with Dwayne and Angie doing their best to tend to him.

A rapid flutter of notes came from the spectral soundtrack, and Pap's view changed starting with pulling way back until he was looking down from at least a hundred feet in the air. He could only watch as his view began to roam past the house all the way out to the road.

The guitar was chugging along in with a galloping riff

as the blacktop of the two-lane road flew by beneath him like he was watching a movie with the film sped up. Pap's point of view was gaining in speed until he reached the outskirts of town where he began to slow significantly.

He was seized with panic when he saw the black Cadillac turn from the parking lot of the old walk-up Dairy Queen. The Cadillac Man was on a direct route to the house, to the family, only this was no premonition. Pap was very much aware what he was watching was happening in real time, which meant only five miles of winding country road separated the Cadillac Man from the family.

The music raced to a crescendo and Pap's vision turned to a blur, as he was being yanked back down the road, over the house, and careened back down into his unconscious form lying in the backyard. He struggled to will himself awake quickly, but the fog couldn't lift fast enough for him. When his eyes fluttered open, he saw Brie still crouched at his side lightly slapping at his cheeks with one hand, while the other still held the shotgun in a firm grip.

"Pap, Pap!" Brie's tone was reflective of concern, and out of character for the young lady. "Wake up. Are you okay? C'mon, wake up!"

He opened his eyes and did his best to push the fog aside and return to full alertness, and noticeable relief passed across Brie's face. Pap could hear Dwayne and Angie speaking quickly talking about whether they should move Rory into the house, but the two of them wouldn't be able to move his massive bulk alone. He pushed himself up on his elbows and swatted away the hand Brie extended to help him up.

"Never mind me," he shouted. "Help them get Rory into the house!"

"Shouldn't we call an amb—"Brie started.

"There's no time, no time!" Pap struggled to get the words out as he rolled over onto his knees. "They're coming."

"You already told us that." Brie's tone was again laced with the familiar iciness it was typically packaged with.

"Now," Pap said finally managing to get to his feet. "They're coming now!"

This caught Dwayne's attention, and he looked up from tending to Rory for the first time since arriving by his side.

"Wait. Do you mean like NOW, now?"

"Yes! Yes!" Pap was yelling but couldn't help it. Every second counted, and he needed to convey a sense of urgency. "There's no time to explain now. The three of you get Rory into the house and be as careful moving him as possible. Lie him on the couch, then Brie and Angie, I want you to start barricading the doors and windows with whatever you can."

"What about you?" Angie said standing and looking concerned. "What are you going to do? Are you even okay? Did you hit your head when you fe—"

"I'm fine! Don't worry about me," he fired back cutting off the girl's well-intended questioning. "I'm going to bring as many weapons and tools we need in from the workshop while we still have time. I have a feeling it won't be easy to gain access to it once we get hunkered down inside."

The girls passed a nervous look between them, but Pap's tone registered its grave seriousness with Dwayne, and he urged them to get moving.

"You heard him, girls," he said waving them over to help him with Rory. "Let's get your uncle inside, we don't have much time."

He really had no idea how much time there was before whatever was going to happen happened but trying to discuss it right then and there wasn't going to get them anywhere. While they all now had good reason to question the legitimacy of Pap's claim after what he'd revealed earlier, there was a desperation fixed to the older man's voice Dwayne had never heard before. He could seek further clarification later, but for now he felt it was best to get them all into the house.

Pap nodded before turning to run for the workshop, as Dwayne, Brie, and Angie positioned themselves around

Rory preparing the best way to transport the man. Dwayne lifted Roy's shoulders and hooked his arms beneath while Brie and Angie each grabbed a leg. They lifted on the count of three, and Rory released a troubled groan as they raised him off the ground.

Since he hadn't made a sound since they found him Dwayne decided to take this as a good sign, as he strained to haul the man's hulking mass across the yard. He could see the strain on the girls' faces as well, but they weren't about to drop their uncle.

Pap burst through the door of the workshop, and nearly tripped on the cans, tools, and miscellaneous parts strewn across the floor. Luckily, he was able to catch himself on the counter just to the right of the entrance. The mess confused him, and at first, he thought he was too late thinking the shop had already been ransacked.

When he noticed the abundance of empty Pearl cans amongst the mess he immediately knew better, and suddenly the scene outside along with Rory's condition made a lot more sense. Pap knew the ol' boy was too sensitive for his own good, and prone to outbursts or irrational behavior. He was kind of like a child in that way, a child in an enormous body, but he always meant well. Rory's heart was always in the right place from which there was no deviation.

Pap opened one of the tall metal cabinets next to the counter he'd caught his balance on. He pulled out two large canvas bags, unzipped them, and placed them on a smaller workbench outfitted with wheels. Rory fixed it up to roll around for extra space needed at his own main workstation, or as a way to move his project across the shop from Dwayne in case the two got to drinking and picking on each other. Pap knew it was actually another product of the man's over-sensitivity.

Rory could dish it out but only pretended he could take it, and he wasn't all that good at pretending. The workbench on wheels allowed him to separate himself from Dwayne to stem the tide of playful insults, as well as hide his face to keep from telegraphing his *actual* hurt feelings. Rory knew Dwayne loved him and would do anything for him.

He knew these were just jokes birthed from an unbreakable fraternal bond much like the sibling rivalry type of relationship Brie and Angie shared from being raised like sisters. Brie administered most of their traded insults, but Angie was unflappable even when her cousin cut a little too close to the quick with her remarks.

Rory admired her ability to remain unaffected in the face of insults often pushed past the point of being 'playful'. He'd heard girls could be far more vicious with each other growing up than boys were, and Rory witnessed this injection of added venom between the girls constantly. It was mostly one-sided with the brunt of front-loaded verbal attacks being launched by Brie at her cousin.

Rory didn't pretend to understand the contentiousness of the girls' relationship, but he knew without a single doubt that no matter what was going on between them, Angie and Brie unequivocally had each other's backs come what may. Rory felt the same way about every member of the family. He knew in his heart they felt the same about him, but there was a deeply buried insecurity in the back of his mind making him think the family would never *fully* accept him. He just couldn't shake it.

He never voiced this feeling of doubt and never would, but Pap didn't have to be told to know. He could see through Rory's big tough-guy façade to the child inside locked infinitely in a wrestling match with doubt. Pap hoped the man would pull through and dismissed any negative thoughts of Rory's current condition to focus on the task at hand.

There were rifles and shotguns hanging along the far wall, and Pap crossed the shop kicking a path through the trash along the way. He took a weapon in each hand before walking back through the newly cleared path to retrieve the rolling bench. Pap put the two guns in one of the bags, and quickly pushed them over to the wall where he took two more, put them in the bags, and then took two more.

He ripped open a cupboard filled with ammo and started grabbing boxes tossing them in with the guns. Pap looked around for the crossbows, but they were all missing, and he sincerely hoped they were already inside. He thought he remembered seeing two of them slung over Dwayne's shoulders when they ran out into the backyard, but he couldn't be sure. His mind was moving a million miles a second and everything was a blur.

He did find some batches of freshly sharpened crossbow bolts in the cylindrical cases Dwayne used to store them, and in the one of the bags they went as well. There was a drawer with several knives, mostly to be used as tools in the workshop, but there were two nine-inch, serrated, hunting knives Pap discovered mixed in, and so they too went in the bags.

Pap spun in a circle scanning the workshop for anything else that could be used to defend the home and themselves, but he was starting to feel overwhelmed again and had to catch his breath. A sudden, lightning strike-like image of the Cadillac flashed across his mind. The Cadillac Man was still on his way, and he was getting closer.

There was no more time for Pap to rummage through the workshop for weapons, and he'd have to settle with what he'd gotten so far. The handguns were already in the house along with several swords of varying size and weight, but all sharp enough to split a single hair. Pap remembered how he would pluck a hair from Rory's head when he wasn't paying attention, and then demonstrate to him the sharpness of one of the blades.

Rory's always laughed and went along with it, but now Pap felt a pang of guilt with the memory. He zipped the canvas bags closed and hoisted one over each shoulder by the attached straps. Both bags were painfully heavy, too heavy for Pap to be carrying alone under normal circumstances, but they were far from normal now.

If Dwayne, Angie, and Brie could muster the strength to carry their behemoth uncle across the lawn to the house, he could do the same with the supplies they needed. Pap took a few steps shifting the weight of the bags to allow for the most economical of movement and rushed for the still-open door. Something leaned against the wall to the side of the door caught his eye, and he couldn't believe he'd completely missed it when he'd entered. It was Rory's hammer.

Pap bent to pick it up being careful to maintain the balance he'd achieved with the bags on his on his back. He grabbed hold of the hammer with both hands, and something shifted in one of the bags throwing off the delicate equilibrium he'd managed to achieve. Pap threw his right shoulder back to help restore his balancing act and was able to keep himself from going headfirst into the wall.

Pap rose slowly holding tight to the heavy hammer using his knees and not his back to hoist the added weight. He wouldn't be any use to anybody if he messed up his back, and he refused to be a victim of stupid mistakes. He stepped out onto the lawn and cut a straight line across the yard taking careful steady paces on his way to the back door of the house.

He no longer felt the burn in his muscles, and the extra-large hammer felt weightless in his hands. Something changed suddenly in Pap, and he found himself laser focused with the pain in his muscles having been reduced to a faraway inaudible drone. He didn't know if it was adrenaline, or stupidity, or something else that put him in this new state? Suddenly, he recognized the return of what had been absent from him since that morning. His confidence.

Pap was halfway across the yard when the guitar music stared to play in his head again, only this time he didn't let it distract him from his current task at hand. Pap picked up his pace, and the music followed suit.

———— ◆ ————

It didn't take long for the Cadillac Man to go over his plan since there wasn't much to it. He told them the specific parts of the house he wanted each of them to gain entry and attack from, and said he'd outfit them with weapons when they arrived. The last bit of information, and certainly the most unpopular part of the plan as far as everyone else in the car was concerned, was the Cadillac Man himself would *not* be joining them. Not at first.

He said he would be back to finish what he was sending them in to start, but when that would be was not intimated or disclosed, and of course no one was going to ask. After that, no one said a word for the rest of the short ride opting instead to stare blankly out the windows at a sea of pine trees race by on either side of the road.

The sun was down now, but the trees were so tall they blocked out nearly the entire sky anyway. Visibility was limited to the narrow space directly over their heads not quite as wide as the road itself. It cut a jagged path that grew narrower the farther they went until it was dark enough to suffocate in. The Cadillac's headlights cleaved through the chokingly thick night, but there was nothing visible outside of the beams of light they cast.

Anton leaned back against the headrest and closed his eyes, but not because he was trying to sleep. Sometimes he liked to imagine what his life would be like if he hadn't been tasked to deal death by way of an entity he didn't understand and didn't want to. He would play a game with himself where he would think about this invented life just before heading into a job and motivate himself by pretending the life would be his reward upon completing whatever ghoulish task he'd been charged with.

He was smart enough not to entertain this notion as a possible reality, but it was a good thought exercise and helped him to focus on the task at hand. The majority of his mini fantasies centered on what type of job he imagined himself to have had he'd gotten a choice in the matter, and not been predestined to do whatever this was. Sometimes Anton put himself in the role of a top executive, or a high-stakes investment banker, and even the mayor of a major city.

He liked the notion of holding a particular amount of power over large numbers of people, plus he liked the certain amount of fear someone in a position of power can strike in a person. Anton liked it when people were afraid of him.

Despite his fascination with fear and manipulation, most of the time he would imagine himself working just a regular everyday job. A banal nine to five where his actions held little to no significance or sway, and any real responsibility was non-existent. These particular fantasies focused him the most.

Tonight, Anton imagined he sacked groceries at a local store where the entirety of his interaction with other people would be boiled down to the question, 'paper or plastic?' His only responsibility began and ended there, and that's just all there was to it.

The Cadillac Man told Anton he was to attack from the front by basically forcing his way right through the front door. It wouldn't be as easy as all that though and would more than likely be serving as a distraction for one of the others to gain access undetected. He'd more than likely have the brunt of the family's defensive effort leveled at him in only a few minutes time, but right now he was far away in his head putting groceries in a bag without a care in the world.

———————◆———————

Dwayne and the girls managed to get Rory through the back door, down the hall, and onto the couch in the living room without dropping him. The effects of their exertion didn't hit until they'd put him down, and it took longer than they all would've liked for them to catch their breath.

Brie's arms tingled all the way up to her shoulders, and her legs burned from hefting the weight for the entire distance without stopping or slowing in pace.

Angie's arms were like jelly, but she recovered faster than her cousin and uncle, and was already looking for something heavy enough to barricade the front door with. Aside from having locks on the door, the only other form of built-in protection were the iron bars on every window installed years ago by one of the more paranoid family members.

Whoever they were was long gone, but Angie thought they'd be pleased to know their anxiety-inspired labor ended up being extremely helpful. If whatever was supposed to happen was coming as soon as Pap thought, it was there'd be no time to board the windows or secure them otherwise. They'd be sitting ducks and might as well just leave all the doors open for even easier access.

Angie rushed for the front door to make sure it was at least locked, which it wasn't, and she threw the deadbolt into place. It wasn't like they were one of the three little pigs in a house made of straw though, which Angie took into account.

The original front door of the house had long since been replaced by one very similar only it was made of steel, and three-and-a-half-inches thick. It was anchored into a reinforced steel frame beneath the wood, so even if the door weren't barricaded it would still be a right bitch to breach. Another thing Angie thought while studying the exposed brick behind the portrait earlier was while the symbols didn't provide any protection, the bricks they were carved into truly did.

The outside of the entire house was already made of brick, and while it wasn't the original intent, the extra layer of brick would still serve as protection, although not the enchanted kind. Plus, the bricks with the symbols were wider and thicker than the norm, which should provide extra-added strength to the family's beloved house.

Angie turned to scan the hall, but the two small tables behind her weren't substantial enough to hold the door back if it were to be broken down. Brie stepped out into the hall from the living room and called down to her cousin.

"Hey, come help me with this."

Angie rushed back to the living room where her cousin was pulling the large wooden table away from the wall, which would work perfectly. Uncle Rory made it after he broke the other one he, Dwayne, and Pap used to play cards. Rory had lost more hands in a row than he'd have liked and pounded on the table in frustration letting his emotions get the best of him once again.

The strength behind his wrecking ball of a fist was more than enough to bust through the table turning it into kindling. Angie remembered when it happened, and how Uncle Dwayne had laughed but Pap was upset. He raised his voice standing up as close to Uncle Rory's face as his height allowed him and scolded the man like he was a child.

Pap yelled for Rory to get his temper under control, or he was going to get them all killed some day. Thinking about it now the statement seemed eerily prophetic. Afterwards Pap refused to play cards with Rory no matter how many times he apologized. He stopped asking after a couple of weeks and started disappearing out to the workshop after supper a few days in a row.

That Saturday night after they'd eaten, and the kitchen was clean Rory slipped out the back door claiming he'd be right back. A few minutes later he kicked open the back door and brought in the table having to enter at a creative angle to keep from banging the doorframe. Rory presented the table to Pap as a peace offering to make up for the one he'd smashed with the added promise of never letting his emotions get the best of him again.

The men embraced, and Pap told Rory he didn't expect him to change overnight, but as long as he kept working on it everything would be fine. Afterwards the men moved the table into the living room and played cards on it until the sun came up. The best feature of the table, which Rory kept to himself, was he'd built it to be so strong not even *he* could punch through it.

The table was the absolute best thing to barricade the door with quickly, but it was heavy as hell, and after carrying their hulking uncle's dead weight their strength was too sapped to move it very far. Dwayne was at the couch by Rory's side cleaning and dressing the man's head wound with more first-aid supplies he'd retrieved from the kitchen.

"Uncle Dwayne give us a hand with this, will ya?" Brie shouted while continuing to strain with the awkward weight of the table.

Dwayne looked over his shoulder at the girls, saw what they were trying to do, and leapt up to help. The three of them struggled with the custom-made piece of furniture down the hall, and together managed to angle it against the front door in a way they felt the barricade would work best. No sooner had they gotten the table into place they heard the back door slam shut from the kitchen. Dwayne jumped slightly and tried to play it off while Brie drew both pistols from her hips, spun around, and trained the barrels on the opening to the kitchen at the end of the hall.

Every muscle in Dwayne's tensed up in anticipation of an impending attack, and he cursed himself for not having a weapon on his person. The crossbows were on the living room floor next to the couch where they deposited Rory, and he'd absentmindedly left his lucky dagger in the basement to the side of his workbench.

He glanced to see Angie was also unarmed, and his hope was Brie's aim was steady and true enough to offer enough cover for them to get back to the living room where their weapons waited. The rushed shuffling across the linoleum grew louder as the intruder approached the opening, and when they saw Pap step into the hall loaded with bags on his back and holding Rory's giant hammer they ran to him.

The three of them were so keyed up and frazzled they'd momentarily forgotten their patriarch wasn't already in the house with them. The older man was beet-red, and sweating through his shirt, but showed no outward signs of exhaustion. The look on Pap's face was one of determination, grit, and raw fury. Angie and Dwayne each took one of the weapon-filled bags from the man, but he held tight to the hammer.

"How is he?" Pap asked referring to Rory. "Is he awake? Is he alert at all?"

"Groaned a couple times, but that's about it," Dwayne shook his head as he answered.

"Well, I guess that's better than nothing."

Pap looked down the hall past them, and saw the table, the one Rory made for him, shoved up against the door at an awkward angle. He found himself struck with sadness and guilt at the sight of it, and wondered if the tabletop would ever see another card game again? Pap quickly compartmentalized these emotions to be dealt with later if there was indeed a 'later' for the family.

"The table was a good idea," Pap said as the four of them entered the living room. "If anything can hold the door it's that. Now, girls hurry and do the same to the back door but use the kitchen table. It's not as sturdy, but it's probably the next best thing."

Angie immediately sprinted for the kitchen while Brie, hesitant to holster her pistols, followed cautiously behind. Dwayne was already crouched over the bags emptying the items Pap collected and organizing them in piles on the floor.

"This is a lot of firepower," Dwayne remarked at the number of high-powered rifles. "You think we'll need this much?"

Pap looked over at Rory's unconscious hulking form spilling over the sides of the couch. Blood was starting to push through the bandages Dwayne used to stem its flow, and the red bloom was quickly spreading. From outside came the distinctive sound of car doors slamming shut.

"No, I don't." Pap answered turning back to face Dwayne. "I think we'll need a lot more."

———————◆———————

The Cadillac pulled away the moment they'd exited the vehicle, and Jacobi removed the large canvas sack from the trunk. Anton watched the car continue down the winding two-lane road before disappearing around a sharp curve to plunge deeper into the inky black night. When he looked back, he realized he was alone.

The others wasted no time disappearing off to the parts of the house they'd been instructed to attack and left the open bag of weapons lying on the side of the road a few feet away from him. Anton was glad, as he had no desire to make small talk with any of them. He didn't want to get to know them, and he for damn sure didn't want them to get to know *him*.

Anton crouched next to the open bag to see what had been left for him to play with. He removed a blade that when unsheathed resembled something between a machete and a serrated hunting knife, which he felt was quite fitting. Anton preferred to use a blade with his bare hands coming in a close second.

The only other item left in the bag was a small black box with two red wires sprouting from either side attached to what looked like a small lump of putty. On top of the box was a single red button.

"Well, I guess I'm not gonna have too hard a time getting in," he said to himself.

Anton stood and kicked the empty bag away from him toward the street. He attached the sheathed blade to his belt and studied the box in his hand again before deciding to carry it. He only needed one free hand to pull the unique weapon from his hip in case he met any resistance crossing the yard to the house, but from where he stood at the road the coast looked mighty clear. Still, Anton was too smart to let his guard down. He hadn't survived this long being cocky, and he for damn sure wasn't going to start now.

If the Cadillac Man was sending four killers in *before* him to settle some personal beef with whoever this 'family' was, Anton knew better than to think this would be a walk in the park. This family was different; they were special. The Cadillac Man intimated as much at least, only he made no mention of why this was.

Anton didn't care though. As far as he was concerned this was a job like any other, and he aimed on coming out the other side with his life regardless of how tough these bastards were. Wind swept through sending a rustle through the trees, and Anton started walking across the expansive lawn on his way to the house.

————— ♦ —————

Jacobi and Carla were paired up yet again for the Cadillac Man's planned assault on the family's home much to chagrin of them both. Jacobi didn't understand why he wouldn't separate them in order to expand their points of attack by one, but he kept his mouth shut despite his internal rage over the matter.

The two of them had been instructed to make their breach into the house through the entrance to the basement, which was on the back side of the house. Personally, Jacobi knew damn well he could handle this feat all on his own and didn't see how Carla would be effective in this task. Carla felt the exact same way.

Not only did she agree Jacobi could handle their instructions all on his own, but she *also* didn't see how she could make her own significant contribution to the overall mission if she was once again practically shackled to the smelly albino imp. She'd already decided to break off on her own once they'd gained entry to the house, and if confronted about it after the fact Carla would just blame it on Jacobi. He would make the same claim of course, and the situation would devolve into a 'he said, she said' battle.

Hopefully, their standard childish bickering would keep the Cadillac Man from probing the issue any further.

Carla's ultimate best-case scenario she could hope for included Jacobi being killed on this mission, and quickly preferably upon their initial entrance. He'd end up coming back of course, he always came back, but his return would come much later giving Carla her own moment to shine independently from the beast.

For the rest of their short ride to the family's house Carla imagined Jacobi opening the doors to the basement only to find out too late it had been rigged with explosives. Even better, maybe the property would be rife with landmines, and Jacobi would make his explosive exit before reaching the back of the house? Carla couldn't help but smile at the image of Jacobi being blown into the air, and coming back down as bloody and burned, unrecognizable, flaming chunks.

The only advantage she saw to having Jacobi with her was his prior knowledge of the family as well as their property. She noticed his excitement when he realized where they were, and what that meant back at the Dairy Queen. At the very least she could exploit his familiarity for her own benefit, but if Jacobi happened to get blown up before he was of any use in that regard, well; she wouldn't mind it too much at all.

When the Cadillac Man stopped to let them out Carla's first impression of the house was lackluster. All she saw was a classic, old-style, two-story house directly in the center of a larger than necessary piece of land. The property was clearly very well attended to, and the grass was short and neat.

There weren't any trees, or at least not any on the front side of the house, but there wasn't much of anything in the yard at all. Carla imagined it was by design to leave would-be attackers like themselves with no cover, and no place to hide. From inside the house, you'd be able to see someone coming in any direction from way far off, which would give the family the warning needed to prepare themselves.

They were too far off to be able to see any detail in the

windows, but she imagined at that very second someone was watching them. They were being sized-up by their enemy while standing completely exposed out in the open. This was clearly one of the reasons for the Cadillac Man having them attack different areas of the house, but wouldn't they be seen walking around to the back? Carla would be sure she stayed several paces behind Jacobi just in case.

After the bag of weapons was removed from the trunk and the Cadillac drove away things started moving very fast. Jacobi dropped the large canvas bag on the side of the road, his selection in hand, and kicked it over to Carla. She saw he was holding an oddly shaped sword and was now fastening its scabbard across his back.

Carla plunged her hand into the open bag and came back with a gun belt that looked like she'd pulled it right out of the old west. Bullets lined the front and back bandolier-style, and two silver six-guns were tucked snugly into holsters on either side. She strapped the belt around her waist without giving the bag a second look and walked over to Jacobi as she fastened the buckle.

Without a word Jacobi broke out into a sprint across the massive yard, and without missing a beat Carla was a step behind him. It wasn't the first time he'd done this to her, and she now had to foresight to expect it. The two angled their approach to go around the house from the right side, and as they got closer Carla had to force herself to not steal a look at the front window.

She couldn't afford to take her eyes off Jacobi for any amount of time regardless lest he pull one of his many tricks to sabotage her like he'd done at the party with the artist only hours ago. Carla wasn't going to let him do that to her again, and she dug in staying right on the back of Jacobi's heels as they rounded the corner into the backyard.

———— ◆ ————

When Jacobi and Carla took off running Olivia approached the bag and peered down into the opening. She looked over to Anton who was turned watching the taillights of the Cadillac grow smaller and dimmer the farther away it got. She bent over and pulled two items from the bag meant for no one else but her.

In one hand she held a small silver dagger with a four-inch blade connected to a handle made of polished black stone. With the same hand she'd grabbed a silver-plated Derringer revolver modified to hold six bullets, which were already pre-loaded. In the other hand Olivia held the familiar round shape of a makeup compact; it too was made of shiny slick silver.

Olivia looked up just in time to see Carla and Jacobi disappear around the back of the house. She turned and crossed the road to the side opposite the house where the darkness at the tree line made her practically invisible. She saw Anton turn back from the watching the Cadillac drive away and realize he was alone. He looked all around clearly confused as to the whereabouts of the people he'd exited the vehicle with.

Olivia remained still and silent as Anton's eyes passed over her twice, but he was unable to perceive her form through the cover provided by thick opaque darkness. She watched him reach into the nearly empty bag and remove something similar looking to a sword only not as big, and another item she couldn't see that was small enough to fit in his palm.

Anton situated the weapon attaching the sheath to his side by way of his belt and stood on the side of the road for almost a full minute staring across the grassy field at the house until he finally started walking toward it. When he was far enough away Olivia opened the clutch purse she'd been carrying since being picked up at the truck stop, emptied its contents at her feet on the side of the road, and pulled out the thin strap she usually kept tucked inside.

She deposited the three items she'd taken from the bag,

closed the clasp, and slung the purse over her shoulder and across her body to keep both of her hands free. She wouldn't need the weapons until she was inside the house, and Olivia preferred using her bare hands anyway.

On the off chance she was attacked on her way across the property, she would gouge out their eyes and remove most of their face with only her long, slim, dexterous fingers. The land surrounding the house was flat and barren of any form of cover, so she didn't anticipate a surprise attack. Out of habit, and a good one, Olivia looked both ways before crossing back over to the side of the street the house resided on, and without breaking stride continued down the slight incline from the road to the front yard.

Olivia was comfortable wearing high heels in any situation if the proper designer tag was attached, but the ground was soft and practically swallowed them with each step. She paused to kick them off and continued leaving her shoes behind. She wouldn't be able to wear them once she got to the house anyway, so shedding them now was just as well.

Anton was far enough ahead of her to also nearly be swallowed in darkness, but she was still able to see his silhouette stand out against the house as he approached. Olivia could tell he'd slowed as he got closer to the front porch, because she was starting to catch up to him. She wasn't going in the front though and adjusted her route to take her around the side of the house opposite of Carla and Jacobi, but she wasn't going through the back either.

The Cadillac Man's instructions were for Olivia to enter through the roof, and that was all he'd said to her. Granted, he wasn't extremely elaborate with his instructions to the others, but with her he was especially succinct.

Olivia, you'll go in through the roof was all he said to her about it. He didn't offer any reason, nor did he give the slightest clue as to how she was to go about getting up there. This was par for the course as far as Olivia's relationship with the Cadillac Man went, so the difficulty level of her assignment and lack of instruction came as no surprise. Just like at the Dairy Queen earlier in the evening, he could never let anything just be simple when it came to her.

It was as if every challenge given her was designed to purposely frustrate and push her closer to a mental and emotional breakdown. Olivia remained unflappable though, just as she was as a child, just like always. She didn't know if the Cadillac Man was doing this to make her stronger, or he truly aimed to erode her resolve enough to drive her mad? It didn't matter to her either way though.

Olivia was no closer to madness presently than she'd been the first time he used her, and she'd already determined she hadn't gotten better at killing people, but rather just become more efficient. This was just another job to her, and she assigned no difficulty level to them despite the Cadillac Man constantly ratcheting up the intensity.

Anton had stopped at the foot of the steps leading up to the porch. He was fixated on the small object in his hand he'd taken from the bag, and Olivia slipped past unnoticed on her way around the side of the house. She'd already figured out how she was going to get to the roof.

———————◆———————

"How many?"

"It looks like only four."

Dwayne was peering out the side of the living room window trying not to move the heavy curtain as he scanned the front of the property. He knew they shouldn't be able to see movement in the window all the way from the road but wasn't taking the chance.

"And . . . him?" Pap's voice wavered despite doing his best to keep it from cracking.

"No," Dwayne shook his head still looking out the window. "No, looks like he just let four people out of the car then took off, and in a hurry too."

"Are you sure?" Pap was loading ammunition into one of the rifles he and Dwayne had leaned up against the wall.

"Black Cadillac, right? Yeah, it drove away. It's totally gone."

"He'll be back."

Dwayne turned from the window as Brie and Angie rushed back into the living room.

"We locked up the back door and used the kitchen table along with the chairs to brace it as best we could," Angie said. "You're right though Pap, it's nowhere near as sturdy as the other table."

Neither man said anything for a beat, and the girls instantly keyed in on the new level of tension.

"What's wrong?" Brie asked flatly looking from her uncle to Pap.

"They're here," Pap finally said.

He locked a round into the chamber of the rifle in his hands, leaned it against the wall, picked up the one next to it, and began to fill the magazine. He moved much quicker this time but didn't sacrifice a bit of precision for speed. He'd practiced loading and unloading rifles countless times in preparation for this very day, and he'd be goddamned if he let nerves or haste compromise his ability.

"What the—"Brie's voice uncharacteristically cracked as she leapt to the side of the window opposite Dwayne filling her hands with her pistols in the process. "Why didn't you say something sooner? What are we up against? How many of them are there?"

"There are four of them," Pap said already loading another rifle. "And they're still at the road, so don't start panicking just yet."

"I only see one," Brie snapped pulling her face back from where she peeked through the curtain. "And they're walking toward the house right now."

"But I just looked ou—"Dwayne pulled the curtain to the side to see Brie was correct. "What the? She's right, but where'd the rest of 'em go?"

Dwayne turned reeling, his wide eyes locking onto the fixed intensity of Pap's stern stare. It didn't make sense that the four people he'd seen standing at the road became one in a matter of seconds, but what he saw at that moment in Pap's eyes showed him the family was up against something truly dreadful, and nothing about it, *absolutely* nothing, would ever make sense.

The Cadillac Man had come for the family, and the fact this could very well be their end finally settled in with Dwayne. They were in their own home, but not even that offered much of an advantage against what was coming.

"He's almost to the porch," Brie called without taking her eyes from the window. "If this fucking glass weren't so goddamn thick, I could shoot through it, and take him out right now."

"That *fucking* thick glass is what's keeping you from getting killed," Pap fired back. "You don't think he would've already tried to do the same if he didn't know better? Now get back from the window and come over here!"

"Now he's standing at the bottom of the steps," Brie said ignoring Pap's order. "He's just staring up at the door, and it doesn't look like he has a gun. All I see is what looks like a blade of some kind strapped to his side, but that's it."

Dwayne turned to look again too and shuddered as he confirmed what she saw.

"Shit! She's right. He's just standing there, though. I see the blade too, but he keeps looking down at something in his hand. It's too small to tell what it is from here. How the hell did he cross the property so damn fast?"

The resolve in Pap's face fractured for a moment, but Dwayne watched the man's expression quickly harden back to one of smoldering intensity. Pap hadn't expected the Cadillac Man's lackeys would be able to move so quickly, but he wasn't surprised. Their enemy would be pulling out all the stops, and it was time for the family to make a stand even if it meant they died trying.

Pap pushed the notion away refusing to let thoughts of death murky the brilliant clarity of mind he was currently experiencing. He continued to load the rifle in his hand, but this time slung the weapon over his shoulder by the strap instead of returning it to the wall.

Angie had been quiet since she and Brie returned, and Pap only now realized the girl was silently preparing. She'd attached two of the leather cylinders Dwayne fashioned to hold crossbow bolts to her belt so one hung from each hip much like Brie's pistol holsters. He noticed she'd already tied the sheath containing her favorite hunting knife to her left calf, and while he couldn't see it Pap knew she'd already tucked a small concealable dagger in her right boot.

She smoothly loaded bolts into one of the crossbows Dwayne had fixed up for her without the slightest hitch in her movement. Angie was calm and focused in her actions like she was getting ready for target practice and not about to engage in all-out battle.

Pap was proud of both girls, but he was especially impressed with Angie's ability to remain completely unaffected by the stress of any situation. He himself had a firm grasp, but it came with years of experience and practice while Angie's ability was one of inborn instinct. Her already highly impressive skills would only grow stronger with time, and even if he had to die trying Pap would do everything in his power to make sure she got that time.

"He's coming up the steps," Brie called.

She stepped back away from the window now pointing both gun barrels toward the center of the bar-covered bulletproof glass. Dwayne was next to her in an instant with hand on her left arm shaking his head.

"Come on Brie," he said pulling her arms down so both barrels pointed at the floor. "Pap *just* told you not to! If you shoot that window all you're gonna do is waste bullets and let that son-of-a-bitch know exactly where we are in the house!"

342

A long moan crested into what sounded like a sob but turned into an extended groan instead from the still unconscious Rory on the couch in front of them. The four froze catching their breath in their throats as they looked down at their fallen giant. A moment later their eyes snapped back up to the window as the heavy footfalls of their visitor crashed against the wooden deck like miniature explosions. Instead of approaching the front door they heard the man walk past the window away from the well-barricaded entrance.

"Get back here you two," Pap snapped trying to keep his voice down. "Now!"

Dwayne and Brie kept their eyes on the window as they stepped to the back of the living room where Pap and Angie were waiting. Seconds later the footsteps stopped, and the family heard the unmistakable jangling of strings from Pap's guitar. He forgot he'd left it out in the porch when he'd heard the crashing sound and ran to the back to investigate.

The visitor strummed across the open strings letting the sound ring out to its natural point of decay, and then did it again. Just knowing someone else was holding his precious guitar burned Pap up in the same way it would a man to find his woman in bed with someone else. The thought further hardened his resolve and struck him with the overwhelming urge to spill this man's blood. He had no business putting his hands on that guitar, and Pap was determined to make sure he let him know personally.

They heard the man on the porch begin to play the guitar forming notes and chords into a structured melody rather than just open strumming. The song didn't last long, but every pluck of the strings was like a dagger in Pap's heart until what came next. The abrupt end of the song was followed immediately by the crashing sound of wood splintering apart, and the off-tune whine of six steel strings being released of the tension holding them in place.

The crash came again and again as the man brought

the guitar down against the porch banister until the aged instrument was a pile of useless scraps not even worth using for kindling. The family couldn't see Anton smiling down at the broken bits of guitar lying in the yard, nor did they know he'd pulled down his zipper and was urinating off the side of the porch onto the remnants.

They all took the destruction of Pap's guitar personally, but for him it was heartbreakingly devastating. He didn't dare let the emotion show but didn't have to for the rest of them to understand what Pap was feeling. Destroying the guitar was an unnecessary slap in the face insult not only to the current family, but all the members who came before them.

The guitar was a powerful important symbol now turned into a declaration of what these people's intentions for the family were. As far as all were concerned this act signified the throwing down of the gauntlet.

The footsteps worked their way back across the porch toward the front door, as Dwayne busily armed himself with two of the more powerful rifles Pap brought in from the workshop. He double-checked their clips and slung a bullet-laden belt over his shoulder to wear across his body. He lifted his shirt and fastened another smaller belt containing daggers for throwing just above his waist and tucked a Glock like the ones Brie carried into the back of his pants.

Three sharp knocks came from the front door, and the family moved into the hall weapons drawn. It may take him a while to break through, but they'd be ready to greet him when he did. He knocked again and was answered by the intimidating sound of weapons cocking.

"Hello," the man called from the other side of the door. "I know you're in there, but don't get up. I'll use my key to let myself in."

"Key?" Dwayne looked to Pap who continued staring at the barricaded door. "What's he mean, key?"

Pap heard an almost inaudible click, but not from

tumblers turning in the locks, followed by a soft beeping. His eyes went wide, and he turned pushing Dwayne, Brie and Angie back down the hall toward the kitchen.

"Back!" He shouted. "Get back! Get ba—"

Suddenly, from the backyard came a tremendous explosion, and the floor shook beneath the family's feet.

———◆———

Jacobi stopped suddenly and Carla ran right into him. She fell backwards landing hard on her ass with the butt of both pistols digging up into her sides. Jacobi's body was solid muscle, but not like human muscle. No matter how jacked a person gets there's still some give to their bulging bodies even when they flex as hard as they possibly can.

Jacobi's body felt like it was made from stone, and was like running headlong into a brick wall, a scaly, rotten-smelling, brick wall. Carla was only momentarily stunned though, and quickly scrambled back up to her feet with not even an offer of help from Jacobi. In fact, he hadn't even turned around to acknowledge she'd fallen, or that he was the cause of it.

"Goddamnit you piece of shit!"

Carla cursed the imp and dusted dirt from the back of her bare legs still pissed off she was in a dress. She would almost rather have found a pair of pants in the bag for her rather than any weapons, but at least she was in flats and not the kind of heels Olivia was wearing. Carla didn't know how the woman walked around in them at all let alone in a situation like this. Jacobi was still and hadn't turned around yet.

"What is it?" Carla asked annoyed at being ignored. "Hello? You hear me dipshit? What the hell did you stop f—?"

The wind shifted and cicadas shrieked from the darkness around them joined by a chorus of chirping crickets as if they were participating in a cryptic game of call and response. It blew Jacobi's stink back into Carla's face, and she caught a mouthful of the rancid odor while in mid-sentence. She stepped to the side and bent over hacking to keep the scent from sticking to the inside of her lungs, but it did little good. She'd taste the creature's rank for hours to come.

"You want to make some more noise?" Jacobi looked over his shoulder at Carla, his words dripping in snide sarcasm. "We might as well have sent them a registered letter saying we were coming two weeks ago for as stealthy as you are."

Carla was bent over was spitting now and lifted her hand from her knee extending her middle finger in response to Jacobi.

"Fu-ck . . . you," she managed between coughs as she straightened up wiping her mouth on the back of her hand. "What are you looking at anyway?"

But now she saw the small building at the corner of the property Jacobi was staring at, as well as the wreckage of what looked like a small tractor next to a lamppost several yards to the left of it. In the dark she couldn't tell exactly what the crumpled metal thing was, but it was obvious what happened to it occurred shortly before they'd arrived. There was something else too. Someone had been hurt.

Carla could smell the blood on the ground from as far away as they were even with Jacobi's stench still lingering, which meant there was a lot of it. If she could smell blood then Jacobi certainly could, and now his sudden stop made more sense. It appeared as though the family was already a member down before the fun even started.

"Dead?" Carla asked regarding the person whose blood they both smelled.

"No," Jacobi answered still intently focused on the workshop across the yard. "Not dead, or at least not yet, but they probably wished they were. That's a *lot* of blood."

"What's up with that building?"

Carla stepped up next to the creature adjusting the gun belt again, tightening it another notch.

"I'm not sure?"

Carla looked over her shoulder at the back of the house behind them and saw where the slanted door to the basement was off to the far right. It appeared to be made of steel or metal at least, and even in the dimness of the night she could see the welding from where she stood. The door had been welded around the entire seam, and even the hinges were melted down to smooth, immovable, metal lumps.

Jacobi was strong, but she wasn't sure he'd be strong enough to pry open a heavy metal door welded to its frame. Carla didn't understand why they couldn't just go through the back door since it was right there, but she knew better than to wonder for long. She turned back to tell Jacobi about the door, but he was already halfway to the workshop.

"What are you doing?" Carla called jogging to catch up. "We're *supposed* to go in through the basement."

"I know," Jacobi said flatly approaching the wide-open door. "And we will. I'm just creating a little diversion first."

———————◆———————

Olivia was more than halfway up the wall and clung to a divot in one of the bricks looking for what her next move would be. The dagger was clenched between her teeth. She'd found plenty of footholds in the old weathered brick, so it hadn't been hard to get as high as she was only now she found herself stuck. The toes of her left foot dug into the small opening of space weather and age had worn into the outside brick while her right dangled free.

The fingers on her left hand gripped a gouge similarly sized to one her toes had found, and Olivia pressed the side of her face up against the wall to better spot a gash or cranny her right hand could reach. Then, she would be able to pull herself up higher, but the brick was smooth and flat in both directions. She was starting to think she might need to climb back down and start over when she saw a perfect groove three feet up the wall to her right.

It was too high for Olivia to reach up and grab, but she knew what she'd have to do if she didn't want to start again from the bottom. She braced herself close to the wall digging in hard with the single hand and lone foot, and slightly bent her knee. Using all the might she could muster, Olivia pushed off and up. She shot her free arm upward and managed to catch the small opening with the tips of her fingers. Her right foot easily found the crevice her left hand had been clinging to, and the momentary stability allowed her to adjust her grip.

Gravity refused to be defied further, and she felt its nagging tug working to pull her off the wall and to the ground. Olivia opened her mouth, the dagger dropped into her open left hand, and she closed her fingers around the smooth black handle. A fraction of a second later she'd buried it in the wall to the hilt and held tight against the nagging pull.

Clutching the handle of the dagger, Olivia saw the next three moves she'd need to make to put her on the roof. She didn't think, she just reacted moving in one swift blur of motion the rest of the way up. A moment later she was standing on the roof, hands on hips, looking down at where the dagger's handle jutted out from the brick.

It was much further out of her reach than she'd anticipated, and retrieving it was not an option. She shrugged and walked up the slight slant of the roof toward where the opening for an attic window had been boarded up years ago. Olivia wasn't worried about losing the dagger since the gun and compact were still in the purse she wore slung across her body.

When the explosion happened, Olivia realized how easy this was going to be, and doubted she'd need all six bullets.

———————◆———————

Carla followed Jacobi into the small workshop and immediately tripped over something on the floor. She fell against Jacobi's back for the second time in a matter of minutes reflexively grabbing onto his shoulders to catch her balance. She quickly pushed herself away but not before swallowing another mouthful of stench.

"Are you going to be doing that all night?" Jacobi was sarcastic as usual. "Because, if you wanted feel me up all you have to do is ask."

"Oh, shut up."

Jacobi snickered as he walked down the middle of the shop, and Carla kicked one of the empty Pearl cans at her feet. She was trying to hit Jacobi in the back of the head with it, but the crushed aluminum cylinder flew wide left.

"So, are you gonna tell me what we're doing in here or what?"

"Someone left here in a hurry." Jacobi said ignored her question while gesturing from the open cabinets to the trash strewn across the floor. "Looks like they grabbed whatever they could carry in one trip before locking themselves in the house. We must have just missed them."

Carla walked to the wall and looked at the hanging rifles that had been left behind. She only gave them a glance though because she and Jacobi wouldn't need them, but Carla found it funny the family thought these weapons would be of any help to them. She crossed to the refrigerator while Jacobi was in a far corner digging through a cabinet tall enough to nearly scrape the ceiling.

Carla opened the fridge and was pleasantly surprised to find it stocked with beer. It was cheap beer, but beer, nonetheless.

"Bet they wished they would've grabbed some of these too," Carla said to herself removing a Pearl from one of the shelves.

The can was extra-cold, and when she popped the top and brought it to her lips, she found the liquid inside to be colder still. This was how Carla liked her beer especially if it was cheap. The colder it was, the smoother it went down since the temperature masked the skunky taste of large batch beer made from subpar ingredients.

Carla tilted her head back and surprised herself by how quickly she drank it not realizing how thirsty she was until this very second. She let out a low growling belch and opened the fridge again to retrieve another.

"Well, well, well." Jacobi's muffled voice came from the cabinet his head was buried in. "I think this'll do just fine."

Carla opened a second beer and let the fridge swing closed on its own behind her as she headed in his direction taking long swigs from the can. Jacobi had pulled something big from the cabinet, but his body hid what it was as he stood over it adjusting something.

He stood and slung what looked like a futuristic jetpack over his right shoulder to the side of the sword already strapped to his back. Carla walked up and tossed her now empty can to the side where it clattered across the floor with the rest of the scattered trash. She recognized the flamethrower immediately and was already shaking her head as he buckled the safety strap across his waist like a seatbelt.

Carla's vast knowledge of weaponry was surprising to most people, and not something they expected from the tough yet fair Latina girl. The Cadillac Man wasn't surprised by it though and was in fact a strength he tapped her to use on many occasions. Her father had been a weapons specialist in the military and forced his daughter to learn all about them as a child. The twin pistols she took from the bag and was currently wearing on her hips were nearly identical to the ones her father gave to her on her eighth birthday, which she knew was by design.

While other girls her age were having tea parties and playing with dolls, Carla was in her backyard or on the range with her father learning how to shoot. Instead of going to slumber parties and joining the Girl Scouts she learned how to take apart, clean, and put back together her weapons. Still, even with all the training and familiarity she had with guns, Carla preferred ripping people apart with her bare hands.

350

Jacobi turned to face her holding the 'gun' of the flamethrower with both hands. He was smiling. It was obvious now he'd seen the steel door to the basement welded shut, and Carla was fairly sure of what he was planning, but she *positively* sure it wouldn't work.

"Please don't tell me you think that thing is going to melt through steel," she scoffed. "Do you have any idea how hot the flame would need to be to pull something off like that? Even if that thing has been modified it's still not possible."

She stood confidently in front of the creature knowing he knew that she knew what she was talking about, but Jacobi was indifferent as usual.

"I *know* this won't get hot enough to cut through the door," he said with a touch of venom in his voice, "but the temperature will weaken the steel enough for me just kick it in."

Carla clenched her teeth in frustration because Jacobi was right and had once again upstaged her expertise with a workaround plan. She had to admit it was a good idea though, which pissed her off even more, but if they were going to go in through the basement as ordered this would most likely grant them access.

"Yeah." Carla bit back her anger as much as she could, which wasn't enough to really make any difference. "Yeah, I guess that would work."

"I know it will," he fired back quickly, his self-assured tone throwing gas on the flames of Carla's irritation with him, "but first I want to have a little fun."

"What about the diversion you were talking about?" Carla rolled her eyes and wished she'd brought another beer over from the fridge.

"That's what I mean by 'fun'."

Jacobi pushed past her and kicked cans and other trash out of his way as he headed for the door. Carla sighed and followed behind again, but not before grabbing one more beer from the fridge before she went outside. Jacobi had already lit the torch at the end of the barrel and slowed to a stop about fifty feet from the small building, which was well in range of the flamethrower's reach.

Carla opened the beer and sipped at it as she reached Jacobi, but then stood several feet behind him. He looked over his shoulder at her flashing a smile full of pointy yellow teeth, and she rolled her eyes taking a long drink from the can. Jacobi leveled the barrel of the weapon at the workshop and pulled the trigger.

A tremendous burst of orange and yellow erupted from the end cutting the space between Jacobi and the workshop with fiery precision straight through the open door. The heat was intense, and Carla stepped back even further dropping the can to the ground to shield her eyes with both hands.

The structure caught fire instantly thanks to the napalm mixed into the fuel of the flamethrower. This is what made the weapon so dangerous in combat particularly when used on people rather than a structure. The fire spread quickly consuming the small building, but Jacobi held down on the trigger much longer than necessary.

He finally let go and the stream of fire ceased instantly, the last of it leaping upon the already fiery fray like latecomers to a dog pile. Jacobi turned around with the look of a petulant child reveling in its own obstinace.

"Now, you see," he began, "that was fu—"

Neither of them expected the explosion, and the force sent Jacobi flying back into Carla taking them both to the ground where they slid another fifteen feet with him on top of her.

He'd only planned to set the building on fire to act as an intimidatingly destructive backdrop to the ensuing battle, but he didn't know about the canisters of fuel on the backside of the workshop used for the now destroyed mower among other things. Although a surprise Jacobi had to admit it was a pleasant one.

"Get—get the fuck off me!"

Carla struggled for the breath needed to voice her demand. The wind had been knocked out of her, which was only a good thing because it kept her from breathing anymore of the stink, but she was having a hard time finding her voice. Her ears were ringing, and she wasn't entirely sure she hadn't been injured with Jacobi's massive heft pinning her to the ground.

He rolled off to the side without a sarcastic comment, which surprised Carla, and she pushed herself up into a sitting position gasping to pull much needed air into her lungs. The flames roared and rolled up into the sky disappearing into black smoke that was invisible against the night sky.

Carla started to feel her body for injury and winced when she touched her right side where at least one rib was broken amidst several she could already tell were cracked.

"Well," Jacobi said still lying on his back in the grass beside her. "I wasn't expecting that."

———————◆———————

Anton stood at the front door of the house holding the black box in his hand deciding how best to place it. He could hear the idiot family members right inside especially after he busted the guitar on the porch banister. If they were smart at all they would change their position while they had the chance if for nothing other than to prolong the inevitable.

He finally decided to balance it on top of the doorknob before pressing the red button and turning to walk back down to the lawn. He heard the soft beeping of the explosive device behind him and kept walking until he couldn't anymore before turning back around.

Anton estimated he was close to twenty-five feet away and decided to keep taking steps backward to increase the distance between him and the impending blast. He wasn't extremely familiar with explosives, and he wasn't sure how big the blast was going to be. He didn't imagine it would need to be all that powerful just to blow open a door, but there was really no way of knowing.

He heard an explosion and felt the ground shake beneath his feet only the explosive charge he'd set hadn't gone off yet. The sky lit up casting a moment of semi-daylight across the property, and Anton stepped back again to see the house backlit by what was obviously fire, and a lot of it.

He momentarily forgot about his own impending explosion when the fireball in the backyard ignited the sky until it went off a moment later as if in response to it. Anton had taken his eyes off the door and the explosion pelted him with splintered wood fragments despite his distance from the porch.

He crouched covering his face and head until the spray of shrapnel stopped before standing to survey the damage. He had no idea what happened behind the house, but it wasn't his problem. Anton was supposed to go through the front door, so that's what he was going to do. It was hard to see the opening he'd created through the smoke and dust, but as he got closer it settled and he could see another issue he'd have to deal with.

The door was gone having been blown to pieces, but whatever the family used to barricade it with along with a portion of the ceiling that had collapsed created a new obstacle for him to deal with. He heard gunshots from beyond the blockade, but if they were meant for him the shooter couldn't get the bullets through the newly formed barrier. They must have realized and gave up their attempt, because no additional shots followed the initial burst.

Anton examined the interlocking rubble looking for a weak spot when he thought he heard a choked off scream coming from the left side of the house followed by a thud like something hitting the ground. He decided it was related to whatever exploded in the backyard and went back to figuring out a way through the debris.

———— • ————

The first explosion confused and disoriented the family since they were expecting it to come from the front door, which was why Pap was pushing them back down the hall to the kitchen. When he realized it came from behind the house, and in the direction, he was moving the family in Pap froze. Dwayne, Angie, and Brie's heads were all on full tilt swivel as they individually tried to discern which direction they were being attacked from.

"What the hell was that?"

Brie was yelling now with one gun pointed at the front door, and the other aimed into the kitchen.

Angie stood with her back against her cousin's ready to fire the crossbow in whatever direction was needed first. Dwayne rushed through the kitchen to the barred over bulletproof window and stuck his head beneath the curtain.

"Holy fuck!"

"What?"

Pap found his wits again and stomped toward the window to inspect the backyard for himself. Dwayne pulled his head out from behind the curtain; the color was drained from his face.

"They blew up the workshop." Dwayne's voice was steeped in disbelief despite having seen it with his own eyes. "The backyard is on fire."

Pap thrust his head beneath the curtain and had to shield his eyes from the sudden brightness. The fire was at the far end of the property but was burning with such intensity it lit the entire yard. Pap was about to turn from the window when he saw something in the yard, two somethings actually.

It suddenly clicked what he was looking at, and a rush of excitement burned through him hotter than the flames outside. There were two bodies lying in the middle of the yard about seventy or so feet from the workshop turned inferno.

"There's two of them lying in the grass," Pap couldn't help but speak quickly. "I think they hurt themselves blowing up the workshop. It didn't look like they were moving."

Before Dwayne could pull the curtain aside to look again the second explosion occurred, this time from the front door as Pap had been anticipating. The floor beneath them shook as the house shifted from the force of the blast, and all four of them lost their footing.

Brie scrambled to her feet first and started firing both guns blindly through the cloud of dust billowing down the hallway toward them. Despite wanting to reload and continue firing she didn't want to waste ammo either, so Brie pulled her cousin to her feet while waiting for the visibility to improve.

Behind them Dwayne helped Pap stand up after being knocked back against the bars on the window. A gash was bleeding freely from the side of his head. In the living room on the couch Rory still lay unconscious but was now buried under debris.

———◆———

Olivia saw the first explosion shortly after climbing to the roof and paused to watch the swirling tower of flames twist in on itself while continuing to climb higher. She was able to feel the intensity of the fire's heat even from where she was all the way across the yard and on top of the roof.

She watched the fire for a moment before continuing up the slant of the roof to her chosen access point, the boarded over attic window. Olivia admired the destructive force of fire, and how something so beautiful could be so dangerous and hard to control. She felt like she could relate.

She knew Jacobi and Carla had gone around back, but had no idea why they would blow something up so far away from the house? With Jacobi involved though, it didn't come as a surprise. Olivia reached the window and bent to take a closer look at what she was dealing with.

A quick glance told her the boards weren't nailed but screwed and bolted into the framing of the window. The wood was thick too, and her intuition told her it would be doubled up with another equally thick piece of wood bolted on from the inside as well. It wouldn't be a walk in the park to get through, but Olivia had found ways to penetrate worse in the past.

She was already falling backward before the second explosion registered with her, although she didn't know which direction it came from. The shaking of the house had knocked her from her feet, and she landed on her back before tumbling head over heels off the side of the roof.

Olivia saw the ground rush up to meet her, and then she saw nothing at all.

———◆———

Brie and Angie moved back into the kitchen from the hall to where Dwayne was picking Pap up from the floor. He was dazed but refused to let the fog linger and forced it from his head. Dwayne was trying to get him to stand still so he could look at the cut in his head, but Pap pushed him away and moved the curtain to look out back again.

"They're gone," he said, then turned back from the window and said it again. "They're both gone!"

———◆———

Carla pressed against her side and lightning bolts of pain struck with burning fury at the point of contact. She was right about her ribs being broken and cracked, but her tolerance for pain had always been high, and she had in fact broken ribs on both sides in the past. Carla could tell from the sensation this injury wasn't as bad as the ones she'd experienced in the past, and she achingly maneuvered herself into a standing position.

Jacobi had already stood up and stepped over her on his way back across the lawn to the house, and she turned to see he was blasting the welded steel door with the flamethrower standing very close so as to increase the temperature quickly. Carla was limping up behind him when another explosion sounded from the front side of the house.

Jacobi let go of the flamethrower's trigger and looked around confused as Carla's response mimicked his own. She thought she saw the house itself rock slightly when the blast came but wasn't sure if she was just still shaken up from the third and most brutal of her collisions with Jacobi. Carla's first thought was whatever happened was the work of Jacobi as well, but when he turned back to her the look on his face told her otherwise.

"What was that?" Carla spoke first. "Was that . . . did we do that one too like setting off a chain reaction, or something?"

"I don't think so," Jacobi shook his head. "Or at least I don't see how we could've unless there's tunnels running underneath the property, but I know at least *I* would have found the entrance if there was one in that piece-of-shit workshop back there."

Carla glared through slits of anger at his insinuation as if she were incapable of having discovered anything of use to them.

"Oh, like you're so smart and perceptive?"

Carla cut her retort wincing from the pain in her side caused by raising her voice.

"Yes," he replied. "Yes, I am so smart and perceptive. We didn't cause whatever happened out front. Who was supposed to be out there again? Was it Anton?"

Jacobi didn't wait for an answer, but instead went right back to blasting the door with heat from the flamethrower. Carla thought she heard a scream come from the side of the house and turned quickly aggravating her injury once again. Instinctively she reached for her ribs, which only made them ache more from her touch. She needed something like a piece of fabric or cloth she could tie around her torso to at least keep her ribs from moving too much.

Carla didn't hear anything else, and assumed it was the whoosh of projectile flames playing tricks on her hearing. A moment later the flamethrower stopped, and the night was silent again save for the crackling of burning building behind them. Jacobi shrugged the flamethrower from his shoulder, tossed it to the side, and stepped even closer to the now glowing hot basement door.

Without hesitation he lifted his right leg and brought it down squarely on the tilted steel barrier with the tremendous force his otherworldly strength provided him. The door buckled down in the center breaking the welds that had been holding it in place. Jacobi repeated the action once more bringing his foot down in the same place where the door buckled in, and this time it bent in half having ripped completely from the welding.

The twisted hot steel fell inward and slid down the stairs into the basement as if laying out the red carpet to welcome Jacobi and Carla into the family home. Jacobi didn't wait for Carla as per usual and continued down the steps without so much as a look back or a gesture to follow. She expected this from him, but it still burned her up inside, which was a good thing now since her anger helped dull the pain in her ribs.

Carla rushed up to the opening hoping now that they'd gained entry the rest of the job would be over soon. Smoldering scorch marks ran down the stairs from the door, and smoke wafted up making it impossible for her to see into the basement. For a moment she thought Jacobi had caught the basement on fire with his stunt, but then she heard him call through the thinning smoke.

"You waiting for an engraved invitation?"

There was impatience in his typical smug tone now telling Carla he was just as anxious to get this done as she was. When she stepped through the smoke into the basement Jacobi was at the base of the stairs leading up to the house, sword drawn, and listening. Carla noticed a sheet covering an air compressor in the corner, and she snatched it up ripping a section off before discarding the remainder to the ground.

She wrapped the piece of sheet around her midsection three times before tying it off all the while biting back the pain. It hurt like a bastard, but at least now she could move a little easier. Done, Carla drew her pistols and joined Jacobi at the base of the stairs.

"Shhh." Jacobi put a finger to his lips. "You hear them? They're practically on top of us."

Carla could hear the family just up the stairs, but it wasn't hard since they were shouting. She nodded her head and cocked back the hammers on her silver pistols. A second later Jacobi was dashing up the steps with Carla once again a step behind.

———— ◆ ————

Anton studied the debris blocking his way as if it were a puzzle. He wanted to create a path big enough for him to fit through, but not so small and tight that he would be a sitting duck wading through it all. He knew he needed to act fast but wanted to be careful not to injure himself so as to not be compromised before even making it into the house.

He knew there was an easy way to do this while expending the least amount of energy; he just needed to see it first. Then, he did. A crossbeam jutted from the top right corner of the opening the explosion had created. The ceiling just beyond the door had collapsed from the blast causing the beam to fall down and forward where its momentum was stopped by the splintered remnants of the table and door all reaching the same point at the same time.

Anton got closer and looked underneath the portion of exposed beam, thoroughly scanned the left and right side as well, and knew exactly what to do. The beam was acting like a lynchpin of sorts that if moved would start a chain reaction dislodging the wreckage around and below it.

Anton grabbed both sides of the beam and tried to move it side to side to create more space, but it wouldn't wiggle as much as he wanted. For his plan to work he needed to move the beam down and to the right just enough to start the avalanche. He let go and took a few steps back.

With a slight running start Anton leapt up and wrapped his arms around the beam as if he were putting it in a headlock. He used all his weight to pull down and to the right and was able to move the busted lumber enough to make all the pieces it held in place fall away. Anton let go and watched as his plan worked, and a moment later he was looking at an opening large enough to more than accommodate for his size. It also provided him a clear view inside.

Smoke and dust still hung heavy in the hallway, so he couldn't see more than a few feet in front of him, which meant whoever was on the other side of it had the same range of visibility. They wouldn't be able to see him coming until it was too late. Anton pulled his blade from its sheath and stepped through the debris into the house.

---◆---

They heard the crash come from down the hall, but the fresh cloud of dust and smoke it kicked up hampered their view. Dwayne turned to the kitchen table propped up against the back door and started pulling to un-wedge the quickly made barricade.

"No," Pap said grabbing Dwayne by the shoulders trying to ignore the pain in his head. "What are you doing?"

"They're coming through the front!"

Dwayne shrugged Pap off and kept pulling at the expertly placed table unable to free it from whatever the girls did to make it so secure. If he had looked down, he would've seen the product of Angie's quick thinking. They'd stuck one end of the table under the doorknob but were only able to place it at only a slight angle due to the limited space.

Realizing they didn't have anything to brace it, Angie pulled one of the emergency toolboxes out from under the sink, and quickly nailed the feet of the back two legs to the kitchen floor. She was proud of herself for how good it held when she saw her uncle struggle with it.

"And where do you think those two in the backyard went, huh!" Pap was shouting still pulling on Dwayne to stop. "They didn't just leave. I guarantee if they're both not already at that back door now, they're only a few steps away."

What Pap said clicked with Dwayne, and he let go of the table. He slung one of his rifles around to the front and held it with both hands as if he expected the door to burst open right then.

"Upstairs," Pap said trying to usher them all back down the hall. "We have to get upstairs, now!"

"What?" Shrieked Brie. "Isn't that the exact opposite of what we should be doing in this situation?"

"They're coming from both ways, and we'll be trapped in the hallway if we don't move now. The stairs are the only way to the second floor, and if we get there first, we can pick them off as they try to come up. There's no time for this, just go!"

Pap and the girls made their move down the hall with Dwayne a few feet behind, but before he could step out of the kitchen the basement door flung open blocking his way. Suddenly standing in front of him was a man-like creature with yellow eyes and no pigmentation holding a sword. Just behind him was a woman brandishing two pistols that looked like they'd come straight out of an old spaghetti western.

The other three didn't realize Dwayne had been cut off, and assumed he was right behind them as they rushed to the stairs. When they passed the opening to the living room Pap saw the couch where Rory had been laying was completely covered in wood and sheetrock from the partial ceiling collapse the blast at the front of the house caused.

His stomach sank, but he couldn't stop and prayed the girls hadn't seen. They both had but knew they couldn't stop as well although tears were already forming in Angie's eyes.

They were feet from the stairs when the outline of someone coming through the settling dust appeared. Brie turned her pistols on the shape and fired.

"Get upstairs," she called. "I'll cover you from behind."

Brie continued to fire as Angie and Pap slipped behind her and up the stairs, and a moment later she was following them shooting over her shoulder in the direction of the front door.

———◆———

Dwayne was holding the rifle but wasn't prepared to shoot when the basement door burst open cutting him off from Pap and the girls. The first slash was more confusing than it was painful. He watched the albino creature bring the blade down in front of him, saw it come back wet and red, but the shock of being sliced from shoulder to groin wouldn't let him believe it was his own blood.

The pain came when he took a step forward, which pulled the half of his body on the right of the wound away from the flesh it had been seconds ago connected to. It made a sound like someone shoved their whole fist into a jar of Vaseline, and blood gushed from his torso like a bucketful of the stuff had suddenly been kicked over. Dwayne knew something wasn't right, but the signals in his brain were misfiring.

He went to lift the rifle and defend himself, but his hands were empty. Dwayne didn't realize the rifle had dropped from his hands and clattered across the kitchen floor when he'd been sliced. He also didn't realize he wasn't raising his arms. The strange intruder struck again this time slicing horizontally across Dwayne's abdomen, and while this he felt it immediately, he lacked the ability to react.

So fast.

That was the only thing Dwayne could think as his innards spilled from the new wound splashing down around his feet creating waves in the ocean of his spilled blood.

It just happened so fast

He was on his knees now looking up into the hideously pointed smile of his attacker, his killer, readying another strike. Just before the blade reached his neck separating his head from his body Dwayne realized the family was doomed.

———————◆———————

Anton sat leaned against the wall in hallway next to the stairs holding his left bicep where the bullet had gone through. He should consider himself lucky, but he only felt foolish. He'd managed to dodge nearly the entire rash of gunfire only to be hit in the arm by the last errant bullet the girl shot over her shoulder without aiming.

What made it worse was rather than passing cleanly through his muscle the bullet struck and shattered bone leaving the bullet lodged in his arm, and it was bleeding like a son-of-a-bitch. Anton knelt down, dropped his knife in front of him, and used his uninjured arm to pull his shirt over his head and off. He gripped a section with his teeth and pulled ripping it down the middle, then moved his bite down and repeated the action. He continued to use his good arm along with his teeth to tie the strip of fabric around the wound pulling as tightly as possible. Anton's nerves shrieked as the bullet was pushed deeper into his tissue, and for just a moment he felt lightheaded.

His mounting rage cleared his mind and helped to ignore the pain. A moment ago, this had only been a job, one in a long line of many, but now he was taking it personal. Anton had never been injured on any of his jobs with the Cadillac Man before, and his focus was rattled. He vaguely wondered if he'd be put down like a lame horse even if he still did the job and survived?

Regardless of what happened today Anton vowed to himself he'd break the neck of the little girl who shot him. After that, he didn't care what happened. Anton snatched up his knife with his right hand and rose slowly to his feet to avoid a disorienting head rush. He stood still and listened but could hear nothing coming from up the stairs.

He figured if they were smart, they'd be holed up in one of the bedrooms preparing for their last stand but could assume nothing so he cautiously approached the base of the stairs. Anton stepped lightly not wanting to let them know he was coming, and when he'd reached them, he stood still again to listen. There was still nothing but silence being transmitted from the top of the stairs, so Anton lifted his right foot and brought it down gently on the first step.

A door slammed down the hall, and he snapped his head to the side to see Jacobi and Carla entering the opposite end of the hallway. Before he could turn back a crossbow bolt sank deep into his left eye penetrating his brain. Anton's death was instant, and much quicker than he deserved.

———— ◆ ————

"Let me at least get a shot off on the next one before you chop their head off," Carla snapped as Jacobi wiped the blood from his sword with a dishtowel.

He ignored her as usual tossing the towel in the sink before pushing past to close the basement door. Without the obstruction they had a clear view down the hall and saw Anton at the foot of the stairs.

"Hey, isn't tha—"

He turned to them, and his eyeball exploded in his head. Translucent yellow and red ropes of slimy fluid rocketed from the hole in his face in spurts forced out by the pressure escaping his skull. Anton's body pitched backward and balanced on his left heel for only a moment before falling to the ground.

As he fell Carla could see the end of the crossbow bolt sticking out of his head, and suddenly understood what happened. Jacobi of course had already figured it out and was shifting into a defensive posture. She quickly stepped back, crouched down beside the wall, and trained her pistols on what she could see of the staircase. It was down the hall on the left, and closer to the front door than it was to the kitchen.

Part of the opening and the bottom two steps were all Carla could see from where she'd positioned herself, and she found her eye wandering to the opening across the hall, the living room. It was possible someone was in there waiting for her and Jacobi to rush to Anton's aid to spring an ambush on them. If that were indeed the case these people underestimated the total lack of loyalty amongst their attackers.

If Jacobi were to be shot in the head repeatedly by a crossbow right now Carla would spit on him before helping, and she'd be damn happy to be rid of him. She pictured his face filled with crossbow bolts twisting his features, rupturing his visage, and silencing his smart-ass mouth. Carla suddenly wanted this to happen very badly and found herself watching Jacobi from the corner of her eye so if it did happen, she wouldn't miss it.

She entertained her fantasy for only a second or two before going back to scanning the opening to the living room for any movement. Anton's motionless body lay at the foot of the stairs while blood rolled in smooth viscous waves from his mangled eye socket down the side of his face to join the puddle growing around his head. Carla looked from the body to the stairs, and back to the body before returning to the darkened opening of the living room.

"Where did that shot come from?" Carla spoke softly in case someone was closer than either of them expected. "Was he already hit before you closed that door, and we saw him?"

Struck suddenly with the realization the shot could have come from behind them, Carla whipped her head around to look over her shoulder back into the kitchen. She saw the eviscerated body of the man they'd encountered upon bursting through the basement door, his midsection flattened out from the now lack of organs. She could see yellow marbling in the exposed layer of fat lining the man's stomach where Jacobi's blade had expertly split him down the middle opening him up like a pig being slaughtered. His head lay on its side atop a messy pile of his still warm insides.

Jacobi appeared to be sniffing at the air when she turned back to him, although she didn't know how he could smell anything beyond his own fetid stink?

"Well?" Carla was losing patience again.

"They're upstairs," he finally answered. "That's for sure."

"So, should I cover you while you rush up there?"

She pictured the creature rushing up the steps only to make it halfway before falling all the way back down minus a face. Jacobi shook his head and shot a scathing glance across the hall at Carla as if he knew what she was thinking.

"Wasn't Olivia supposed to go in through the roof?" He stated more than asked the question. "Once they run into her the distraction will provide all the cover, we need to get up there and finish them off. All we have to do is wait."

———— ◆ ————

Olivia opened her eyes or tried to at least. She had only a vague grasp on where she was, and what she was doing there, but there was fogginess keeping the information just out of reach. Her head was pounding, and there was a constant whooshing that sounded miles away.

Her eyelids fluttered once, then one more time before their weight became too much for Olivia, and she sunk back into warm darkness.

————— ◆ —————

It was Angie who noticed Uncle Dwayne wasn't with them once they'd reached the second floor and rounded the corner. When her cousin came running up behind them alone Angie knew immediately something was wrong, and once they locked eyes Brie knew it too.

"Uncle Dwayne," Angie spouted breathlessly. "He's still down there!"

Pap reached for Angie's shoulder to pull her back, but the girl was too fast, and he came away with only a fist full of air.

"Angie, wait!"

She ignored Pap and dashed back around stopping short to peer around the wall at the top of the stairs. Angie saw a growing shadow cast by someone approaching the base of the steps, and as badly as she wanted it to be Dwayne it was obviously not.

She raised her crossbow at the ready bringing it up to her face, and situated the butt against her right shoulder. Her hands were cool and steady, and her breaths were deep and even as she watched the shadow get larger with each step the intruder took. Angie saw the tip of his nose come past the wall into view and pause, but she stayed herself patiently waiting for a clear sure shot.

A moment later the man's entire head floated slowly into view filling the sight of Angie's weapon. She squeezed the trigger smoothly and gently just like she'd practiced. The man turned his head like something down the hall had caught his attention just as the bolt was fired, so instead of finding its way to his brain through the man's ear it found entry through his eye socket.

Angie saw the bolt find its mark and quickly pulled back behind the wall out of view. She heard other voices from downstairs and strained in vain to make out what they were saying, but the sound was too low and muffled.

She went to take another slow surreptitious look, but Brie grabbed her arm and pulled Angie back down the hall away from the stairs.

Brie put a finger to her lips and nodded toward the stairs indicating she heard the voices too. Once they were about fifteen feet away, she spoke, but only in a hushed whisper.

"What did you see?" The desperation showed through Brie's softened volume of her voice. "Did you see Uncle Dwayne?"

Angie shook her head.

"No, but I got one of 'em."

"You hit one of," Pap grasped for the word he wanted to use but came up short. "Them?"

"No," Angie said stiff-jawed. "I killed him."

Pap didn't have to ask if she was sure, because if Angie said she'd killed someone you could rest assured they were dead. He wanted to believe Dwayne was alive and hiding somewhere, but his intuition wouldn't let him. If he were still alive, he'd be up here with them, or making a hell of a lot of noise downstairs. Pap couldn't mourn now though; he needed to fight back and keep the girls safe so Dwayne's death wouldn't be in vain.

"I can hear someone else down there." Brie had edged her way back down to where Angie had been perched to the side of the stairs. "It sounds like two people, but I can't tell. Could be more."

Pap waved her back over to him as his mind scrambled to come up with a plan. He knew he needed to get the family upstairs to save them in the moment, or at least most of them, but beyond that he wasn't sure what the next move was? He was already finding holes in his original loosely structured plan of picking off their would-be attackers as they came up the stairs and was struggling to think of how to amend it.

There was no way for him to guess what kind of weapons or firepower these people had, and what was to stop them from spraying bullets up the stairs to keep the family back while they just waltzed on up uncontested. He and the girls would be sitting ducks, and it would be all his fault. Pap looked up and down the hall deciding what the best way to defend themselves would be.

They could split up into different rooms, and whoever the intruders attacked first the other two could easily come up behind to take them out, but he knew immediately it wouldn't work. Again, he didn't know how many of them were out there, and there could be enough of them to attack each room at the same time easily overpowering them individually. Plus, the plan involved putting them all at risk.

They could go further down and around the corner into the next hallway on the left and attack from there, but they would have little to no cover. Pap quickly decided the best thing to do was to hole up in one room together, take cover, and hope to get the drop on the fuckers who aimed to take them down.

"This way," Pap motioned Angie and Brie further down the hall away from the stairs. "Follow me."

He was pointing to the closed door at the end of the hallway facing them, the door to Rory's bedroom. The three of them experienced a simultaneous pang of sadness as they raced to the room, entered, and immediately shut the door behind them. As far as any of them knew Rory was either dead or dying by now, and it felt strange to disturb the man's personal space despite their current predicament.

Angie caught an errant whiff of her uncle's cologne and started to tear up again. It was a piney musk called *Woodsman*. It was the same cologne she'd bought for him for Christmas when she was twelve years old from the drugstore, because that was as far as she could ride her bike, and it was cheap enough for her to afford on her allowance.

She remembered how her uncle was sincerely excited

to receive the gift, told her how much he loved it, and that he was going to wear it every day. And Rory had worn the inexpensive fragrance every single day since then always purchasing the same brand and bottle when he ran out. He didn't have to do that, but Uncle Rory didn't have to do any of the things he did. He genuinely wanted to.

She snapped from her memory when Pap flipped the mattress off the bed where it crashed into the dresser, and then started trying to lift the frame.

"Come gimme a hand with this," he said struggling.

Angie wiped her eyes on the back of her hand and rushed over to help Pap.

———————◆———————

"How much longer do you want to wait for her?" Carla asked in a hushed, but obviously annoyed tone.

She and Jacobi had been waiting at the end of the hall in front of the kitchen in silence for almost ten minutes but had yet to hear anything from upstairs that sounded like a struggle of some kind was ensuing.

There were a couple of loud thumps they heard coming from almost directly above them, but it was easily distinguishable as furniture being moved or toppled over. There was no screams or gunfire, and Both Carla and Jacobi were well acquainted with the sound of a human body hitting the floor, which was not what they were hearing.

"I don't know?" Jacobi finally answered. "Not much longer though."

Another much quieter thump sounded above them like someone was trying to set something heavy down as gently as possible.

"What the hell are they doing up there, gymnastics?"

"They're building a barricade," Jacobi said flatly.

"A barricade? No, they've got to be up to something else. I thought this *family* or whatever was supposed to be a bunch of bad mother fuckers or some shit?"

"They are."

"How come they're up there hiding already? Why was it so easy to get them on the run? It seems like the Cadillac Man could take them out on his own if this is as much fight as they're gonna put up."

"What about him?"

Jacobi nodded down the hall at Anton's motionless body. The blood puddle he lay in now spread from one side of the hall to the other and had already begun to congeal as indicated by its darkened hue.

"Lucky shot?" Carla shrugged.

"There's no such thing as luck," Jacobi looked from Anton's body to the base of the staircase and back. "It's how you react to the moment you're in that dictates your success. Luck is an illusion."

"What about back there?" Carla nodded over her shoulder at the mostly disassembled body in the kitchen and huffed. "You're telling me *that* wasn't luck? We walked right into the guy and surprised the shit out of him, literally! We didn't know we'd catch him alone like that, so how is *that* not luck?"

"But we *did* catch him alone," Jacobi snarled, "and in that moment we were both given the same opportunity to react to the sudden circumstances. He was holding a rifle, and posed just as much of a threat, but when it was time to react, he simply did not. I did. There was no luck involved."

Things like this reminded Carla of how much she absolutely loathed Jacobi. His arrogance was off the charts as evidenced by his statement, and the constant condescending way in which he was forever talking down to her was a ceaseless grating on her nerves.

Carla felt like she was always only a pussy hair away from emptying both of her pistols into his head. She pictured his face mangled by crossbow bolts again, and it helped tamp down her anger but not much.

"O-o-o-o-kay," Carla exhaled. "How do you suppose we

react to *this* particular moment, or is the moment not here yet? Oh wait, did it already happen? Did I miss the moment, or is the moment happening right now?"

The pops were muffled but loud enough to be recognized as gunshots. Three of them came in quick succession, and then stopped. Carla went to look up to locate the direction of the shooting, but her head and neck refused to work together.

There was a sharp pinch in both shoulders, and while she heard the consecutive thumps of her pistols hitting the floor, she didn't feel them drop from her hands. Her head hurt suddenly, and everything below her neck was cold and numb. Thick warm sweat ran down the sides of her face only it wasn't sweat. Carla's eyes were still open, but darkness was closing in from all sides, and for a moment from the corner of her eye she saw Jacobi looking at the ceiling.

Someone upstairs had fired three shots into the floor, and all three found their way to Carla striking her through the top of each shoulder, as well as down through the top of her head. She slumped against the wall still in her crouched position, and Jacobi watched the life go out in her eyes before the realization of what happened could set in.

"*That* was the moment," Jacobi said chuckling as he worked his way to the stairs with his back against the wall.

———◆———

The road was suffocatingly dark, and the trees lining both sides had reached across the lanes tangling together in their growth to create a tunnel of foliage. Even when the sun was out very little of its light was able to penetrate the thick groupings of leaves that sprouted between interwoven branches. This wasn't an uncommon phenomenon and was the case for many heavily wooded roads in far out rural areas particularly if seldom or never traveled.

This road though, the one the Cadillac Man was currently traveling, was the darkest of them all. It was so entirely overwhelming the car was completely invisible save for the headlights, which would appear as nothing but two faintly glowing floating orbs.

It was the punishing kind darkness typically found at sea when low-hanging black clouds against a starless night sky turned the ocean beneath your ship into opaque ink. You wouldn't be pulled up into it, or drug down beneath, but instead crushed to death between it, this darkness. It could drive a man mad were he to find himself lost out in it.

This was where the Cadillac Man thrived, and if it were possible for it to be any darker it would happen with his presence. This was the kind of darkness the Cadillac Man spread as one of the many tentacles Evil had thrown into the world leaving a trail of death and destruction as they were raked across the planet.

This was the darkness he put into men to grow until they filled to capacity and exploded. Then, he'd move on and do it all over again, and again, and again until the darkness, *his* darkness, was all there was left.

This road ran in a large oblong circle, and in a few minutes the Cadillac Man would drive out of the deep darkness to an uninhibited view of the night sky. Two miles beyond that point he would pass the small square-shaped Dairy Queen with the walk-up window where he'd stopped with his passengers earlier in the evening. Soon, he'd be back at the family's house where everything would be coming to an end.

———— ◆ ————

Pap and Angie turned the bedframe on its side leaned the mattress against it before dragging a very heavy chest of drawers, which Rory constructed himself, across the room. They tried to gently turn it over onto its side, but Pap's grip slipped, and his side of the dresser dropped the last six inches to the floor. Angie maintained her grip and swung her side around to form a triangle-shaped barricade with the bedframe.

They were so focused neither of them noticed Brie in the far corner of the room on her hands and knees with her ear to the floor like she was in the old west listening for the sound of approaching horses. When the shots were fired both Pap and Angie were completely caught off guard, and dove for cover behind the makeshift barrier.

Angie popped up quickly with her crossbow to her face preparing to counter their assumed attacker but lowered the weapon when she saw her cousin through the sight. Brie was looking at the floor while smoke from the barrels of her guns climbed up her wrists and curled around her forearms like sentient sheer fabric. Pap also saw it was Brie and pulled his rifle back from a space a space he'd created in the barrier to offer cover while shooting.

"Jesus Christ, Brie!" Pap's newfound anger was a product of his ever-mounting frustration, and he instantly regretted raising his voice at the girl, though she didn't seem to notice. "What was that? Why don't you just open the door and tell 'em where we are?"

He looked over at Angie and could tell from the quick glance shared between the cousins that Brie's actions served a purpose. The two of them came out from behind the barrier to join Brie on the other side of the room. At her feet were three fresh bullet holes through the floor in a straight line separated from each other by approximately six inches. This was not as easy to do as it may seem, and the precision Brie honed from years of practice with her weapons was undeniable.

"Well?" Pap asked as he approached, but Brie put her finger to her lips to shush the old man.

"I could hear them," she finally said after several seconds past. "I could hear at least two of them talking right below me. It sounded like they were arguing, but I couldn't tell."

"But you could tell where you were shooting?" Pap couldn't help but blurt out the question, his frustration getting the better of him once again. "What if one of your uncles was down there?"

He immediately regretted bringing up Dwayne and Rory, and even more so for positing the possibility Brie had just shot one of them. Pap needed to get a hold of himself, and he knew it but was struggling to get out from under the crushing feeling of failure. He needed to be focused for the girls; he needed to lead them out of this. He didn't need them disengaging, because he couldn't stop projecting his own insecurities onto them.

A stilted heavy energy hung between the three of them and took longer to dissipate than Pap would have liked, which only made him feel more shameful.

"I could hear them," Brie answered still looking at the floor with one ear cocked listening for signs of her success or failure. "When I put my ear to the floor, I knew I was directly above them, and once I pinpointed exactly where the voices were loudest, I took a shot. Well, three actually."

"I think it worked," Angie said after another moment of listening. "I don't hear anything. No moans, no screams, nothing. You must've got 'em clean, or at least one."

"That, or I hit neither of them, and just gave up our position like Pap said."

"No, I think it was a good plan either way," Pap piped up before more guilt could creep in. "I'm sorry for yelling and . . . well, I'm sorry. Somebody needed to take action, and I'm proud of you for trusting your instincts just like we taught you to. I—I just got a little off-track earlier, but I'm back now. Again, I'm sorry."

The girls nodded somberly, and Angie squeezed Pap's shoulder in acceptance of his apology. They didn't blame the man for coming undone. The family had been thrust into complete chaos in a matter of moments from which seemingly no amount of training or preparation could save them.

Brie crouched suddenly and held up her hand to signal for quiet once again. She slowly lowered her head closer to the bullet holes in the floor, and the look on her face showed she was straining to hear.

"I think I heard something again," Brie whispered up at Pap and Angie. "Listen."

All three strained their ears now trying to pick out any break in the surrounding silence no matter how small, but none could be detected. None of them had any trouble hearing the door burst apart as a sword sliced through it a moment later.

———◆———

Jacobi was relieved to be rid of the 'dead weight' he considered Carla to be. Under different circumstances he would shake the hand of whoever fired the shots and express his deepest thanks for what they'd done for him. Circumstances being how they were though, he was still going to have to slaughter his self-professed savior along with their associates.

His back was to the wall, and he held his sword at the ready when he approached the opening to living room just in case Carla's hunch was correct. When nothing happened, he looked back at Carla's crumpled corpse still propped against the wall in an awkward crouched position.

Jacobi shook his head and chuckled softly at the look of utter surprise now permanently frozen on the woman's face and studied it for several seconds wanting to preserve the image in his mind so he could visit the memory again and again. He continued sliding his back against the wall until he was close to the bottom of the stairs where he had to take a wide step over Anton's body and spilt blood.

Doing so took him away from the wall and left him momentarily open to attacks from the top of the stairs. He replayed the image of Anton's eyeball exploding when struck by a crossbow bolt he wasn't expecting, which to Jacobi meant he was either being sloppy, or whoever got him had an angle on him he couldn't see. If so, it was possible one of the family members was *still* stationed at this 'invisible' angle waiting for just enough of Jacobi's head to appear in the open before putting a bolt in him as well.

He turned to face the stairs before stepping over the blood, and kept his eyes trained on the darkened staircase for any sign of movement. Once he was on the other side of the blood Jacobi immediately hugged back against the wall taking himself out of the possible line of fire, although he wasn't as worried as he had been a second ago about an attack coming from the top of the stairs.

If there had been a shooter lying in wait, they would've taken a shot at him as soon as he came into view. Carla underestimated the family commenting on how 'easy' she found the mission to be, but Jacobi knew better, and Carla; well, she learned the hard way. They may have the family back on its heels now, but that was subject to change, and he knew it. Jacobi had dealt with past generations of the family and knew the cunning strength they possessed.

He held his position, remained still, and listened. He could hear voices only they weren't coming from the top of the stairs, but through the bullet holes in the ceiling. Judging from where they were in the hallway he could surmise about where they'd been fired on the second floor. He'd not seen or heard any sign of Olivia, but the two bodies in the hall made it safe for Jacobi to assume she was dead too.

He was the only one left, and he aimed to bring this to a close quickly. Jacobi crouched angling himself toward the foot of the staircase. He heard the voices come through the bullet holes again, and he sprung forward, ran up the stairs, turned left, and brought his sword back as he rushed the door at the end of the hall.

---◆---

Olivia's eyes were open, but it took a few minutes for her to become fully aware. She stared up into the black starless night, and a slight breeze brought with it the smell of campfire and country air. It reminded her of being a child back at her family home in Georgia. On nights after summer had made its exit and fall was quietly creeping in they would have family gatherings with a large bonfire out in one of the fields on their property.

It was also an excuse for the groundskeepers to burn off all the branches, leaves, and other overgrown foliage they were made to purge at her mother's request. The grass around Olivia's body felt cool and was thicker and softer than she was used to it being. She spread her arms out and moved them up and down like she was making a snow angel while her fingers enjoyed the unique tactile sensation.

Suddenly, Olivia noticed a wall about six feet from where she lay. The wall was attached to a house, and the house was not familiar. Then, she realized the air in fact did not smell like a family bonfire on a slowly cooling Georgia night but was instead acrid and reeked of fuel.

Olivia pushed herself up into a sitting position and struggled to turn her stiff neck so she could get a look around. The sudden shock of pain was what brought her the rest of the way out of her haze, and now she knew exactly where she was, and what she was supposed to be doing. Her head, neck, and back screamed in protest as she attempted to sit up straighter.

She remembered falling off the roof, but couldn't remember what caused it to happen? Olivia couldn't imagine it was carelessness on her part, and was now beginning to wonder if she'd been attacked from behind? If so, they would've surely finished her off, wouldn't they? It had to have been something else altogether, although she couldn't imagine what?

She recalled an explosion in the backyard, and fire in the sky before the final bit she'd been wracking her brain to remember shook loose. There was a second explosion, but from the front side of the house this time, and much closer. Close enough to shake the entire structure and send Olivia head over heels off the roof.

Her purse still hung from its strap diagonally across her torso, and she could feel the gun and compact still inside through the material of the bag. She remembered the dagger was stuck somewhere near the top of the wall but didn't even try to look up and find it. She had no idea how log she'd been out, but when she heard shots come inside the house Olivia knew she didn't have time to attempt another climb to the roof.

If she were going to be able to contribute at all to the fight, she was going to have to break the rules this time. She rolled over onto her stomach and pushed herself up to her feet while various points of pain ignited throughout her body in rebellion against her movements.

It wasn't hard for Olivia to compartmentalize pain to the point of mentally blocking it out for extended periods of time, and though she'd yet to take a step she could already tell she wasn't injured as bad as she'd been in past situations. She'd once fractured her ankle and dislocated her shoulder on a job, and still killed the three well-dressed gentlemen she'd been sent into the luxury penthouse suite to dispatch without being compromised by her injuries. Afterward, the Cadillac Man picked her up in front of the building and let her out in front of the emergency room.

No bones were broken, which was always a plus, and while a few ribs may have been cracked it was equivalent to a skinned knee as far as she was concerned. Otherwise, the entire inside of her body felt like one giant deep bruise, and she saw many hours of soaking in her hot tub with a cocktail of painkillers in her future, but first she had a job to do.

Olivia rolled her neck from shoulder to shoulder to work out the stiffness much to her muscles' chagrin. She had a slight limp as she headed to the front of the house, but it was gone completely by the time she rounded the corner. The porch was in ruins, and pieces of charred planks were scattered across the massive front yard all the way out to the street.

Now she knew exactly what caused her to fall from the roof and judging from the damage it was a wonder she hadn't been injured worse or even killed. It was like a wrecking ball had been used when a sledgehammer would've done the job just fine, but she was no stranger to the Cadillac Man's penchant for overkill. Olivia guessed the object Anton had been holding in his palm back at the street was responsible for the excessive destruction.

At the center of the still smoldering rubble was a small ingress which she guessed Anton used to enter. It stood in ridiculous contrast against the ring of destruction encircling it, but Olivia had to admit it was impressive how the structure held up against such tremendous force. Unless of course it was incompetence on Anton's part somehow in the way the explosives were deployed, which was a possibility as well. Either way it didn't appear as if he had an easy time getting into the house. Olivia remembered the shots she heard and wondered if Anton had perhaps walked into a trap?

She couldn't see anything but light through the opening from where she stood, and Olivia removed the small pistol from her purse as she approached what was left of the steps leading up to the demolished porch. The planks were split clean through and would no longer support any weight, so she stepped lightly along the far edge of the busted lumber.

Olivia kept to the side of the opening not wanting to just walk right up in case someone was inside waiting for her to step into their field of vision. She crouched against the partially collapsed wall next to the makeshift door holding her pistol at the ready and leaned slowly over to look inside. Olivia quickly pulled back when she saw the blood, then moved slowly toward the opening again this time leading with the barrel of her gun.

Inside there was no motion, no sound, and no one watching. Olivia had a clear view of Anton's body and the crimson circle surrounding like someone was shining a macabre spotlight down on it to highlight the details of his death. From the corner of her eye, she saw someone crouched in the darkness at the far end of the hallway, and instantly trained her gun in their direction.

It didn't take her long to realize they weren't moving, but shadows hid any other details. Olivia stepped through the opening silently and with caution still not entirely sure she wasn't walking into a trap. As her right foot came down on the inside of the house the floor buckled and creaked prompting her to pull it back out for fear she would fall through. She tried again this time putting her foot down farther to the right where the floorboards appeared much sturdier.

Olivia's head and pistol swiveled in sync as she scanned all around the hallway while stepping the rest of the way into the house. She slowly made her way over toward Anton's body, and her eyes adjusted to partial light of the hall the closer she got. She stopped at the edge of the pooled blood and saw swollen pink and red tissue pushing out from around the crossbow bolt stuck in his eye. It was dimpled and folded in on itself like melted candle wax.

Olivia was impressed with the accuracy of the shot, the obvious precision in the execution. She looked up and squinted through the darkness at the motionless figure awkwardly crouched at the end of the hall expecting to see a crossbow dangling from their lifeless fingers, but quickly realized that was not the case.

She'd hoped for a scenario in which this was the person who'd shot Anton, and now they too were dead either by way of one of the others, or perhaps even Anton himself was able to get off a final lucky shot as he fell to the floor. He didn't have a gun though, and there was no crossbow clutched in the cold dead fingers of a fallen family member.

Instead, there were twin sliver pistols on the floor at the feet of the other woman who'd come with them to the house. Olivia couldn't remember her name, but recognized the dark, shoulder-length, curly hair, and the knockoff designer dress. It was too dark for her to see beyond the end of the hall into the kitchen, and from where she stood, she had a decent view into an opening she guessed led to a living room area. It too was dark, but from what she could see it appeared to be empty. Olivia cautiously peeked up the stairs and saw no sign of movement there as well.

While deciding which way to go she stood still, held her breath and listened. Across the hall came a creaking sound from the darkened living room, but it stopped abruptly, and Olivia attributed it to the debris still settling from the explosion. Still, she wanted to check it out to be sure. She easily leapt over Anton and his puddle and crept silently in the direction of the living room.

The creaking started up again but was accompanied this time by what sounded like moaning. Olivia stopped and strained her ears hoping to hear the telltale sign of a person, but the noise had stopped as suddenly as it came on. She took another step, and a tremendous crash came from the same direction followed by the cry of someone in pain, or angry, or perhaps both.

A fresh could of dust billowed into the hall from the opening to the room, and Olivia sprinted the rest of the way down the hall for cover. She passed the dead woman whose name she still couldn't remember and continued into the kitchen where she didn't notice the pile of a person on the floor until her bare foot found a dislodged kidney.

Olivia slid a foot or two before falling back on her ass where her body's momentum carried her across the floor through a mess of blood and guts. She lost her grip on the small six-shot Derringer as she fell backward. She grabbed uselessly at the air trying to will it back to her hand, but the gun clattered across the floor through a deluge of human slop before sliding beneath the stove. The family home had claimed a second weapon from Olivia, and she seethed with anger over the loss.

Tremendous pain wracked her body when she hit the floor, and the uncomfortable tingle in her ribs turned searingly hot. She didn't scream or cry out, but instead gritted her teeth against the pain refusing to allow any sound to escape her lips. Olivia knew better than to give up her position, and before making another move, she listened again. After several seconds of silence elapsed, she carefully maneuvered to her feet, and carefully stepped out of the red slop.

Her entire outfit was ruined, and blood and bodily fluid now drenched the backside of her head and hair, but these were things she'd address when her mission was complete. Another crash came from down the hall but was accompanied by grunts rather than moans as if someone was exerting themselves. Olivia moved to side of the entrance to the kitchen, and peeked slowly around the doorframe.

Standing just inside the opening to the living room nearly filling the entire frame was the mammoth silhouette of the person responsible for noises she'd been hearing.

————— ◆ —————

Pap and Angie leapt back from the door as Jacobi's sword cleaved through sending splintered chunks flying off in all directions. They retreated to the back of the room for the partial cover the makeshift barricade provided, and Pap was already cursing himself for leaving his rifle behind when Brie called them over. He could already be unloading into the door with the high caliber weapon turning the sword slinger on the other side into Swiss cheese, but he'd blown yet another opportunity to protect the family, *his* family.

He ducked around the side of the overturned bed while Angie, ever agile, flipped backward over the dresser landing on her feet with her crossbow at the ready. The girl's ability never ceased to amaze him, but he wished they could say the same for him. As far as he was concerned the only 'ability' he'd displayed lately was that of buffoonery.

"Brie!"

Angie cried out for her cousin, and Pap suddenly realized she wasn't behind the barrier with them. Before he had a chance to react Angie had already released a flurry of crossbow bolts at the door and was back on the other side of the barricade. Pap stood to look over and almost dropped the rifle.

Brie was still crouched on the floor close to the door, but now the sword was buried three inches deep into her left shoulder blade. Through the hole in the door Pap saw red-rimmed yellow eyes and a dingy pointed smile attached to a stark white face, as the attacker pushed his way into the room.

His skin was pale as ivory except in places where blood and soot marred the smooth alabaster presentation. The man-like creature wore tattered pants but no shirt revealing the taut musculature of his body responsible for the brute force he was currently exerting. He pulled his sword back and a gush of blood spurted from the wound in Brie's shoulder like it was chasing after the blade.

Two of the bolts Angie fired struck from the man's left forearm where he'd used it to block his face, which meant he could move incredibly fast. Worse than that were the three bolts buried in what was left of the door behind him. Angie had missed. Angie never missed.

Brie dropped the rest of the way to the floor, rolled onto her back, but was only able to raise one of her pistols, as her left arm hung limp, and useless, and wracked with a pain that registered like fire. In another display of his dangerous speed the attacker kicked Brie's wrist snapping the bone and sending the Glock across the room where it hit the wall and dropped to the floor like a bird flying into a window.

With an agile spin on the ball of his foot in the opposite direction the beast-like man caught Angie with a powerful kick to the gut as she ran up on him firing bolts the whole way. Every one of them missed, and Angie was thrown back across the room where she crashed against the overturned dresser.

She lay there unable to pull in breath as her muscles seized around her midsection. Her mouth opened and closed soundlessly as she crumpled into the fetal position trying to pull herself together.

The sound of the bone breaking was what ignited the fuse in Pap, and seeing Angie get kicked across the room was what launched him. He pushed over the toppled bed and charged, as the sword was already coming down on Brie.

———◆———

Olivia ducked back behind the kitchen's doorframe as soon as she saw the man's form begin to emerge from the darkened living room. She hoped she hadn't been seen, but there was a chance he'd glimpsed her from the angle he had. If she had to engage him now so be it, but she would prefer the element of surprise. Plus, with her gun underneath the stove on the other side of the kitchen she was going to have to get creative, and she could use a few extra seconds to quickly brainstorm possible tactics.

She heard the thud of the man's first steps into the hall fall slow and heavy, but couldn't immediately tell if they were moving toward the kitchen or away? Suddenly, from somewhere nearly directly above Olivia came a loud crash directly followed by another announcing the action was happening on the second floor.

A moment later the hollow thump of the man's footfalls turned wet and squishy, as he stomped through Anton's blood on his way to no doubt aid the family in the ensuing battle. She still didn't dare move so as to not accidentally give him a reason to change course.

His foot came down on the first step hard, and the resounding thud returned followed by a loud creak as the stairs moaned with age beneath the man's lead-footed ascent. When it was clear the footsteps had reached the second floor Olivia peeked slowly into the hallway to confirm another family member hadn't emerged behind the lopping giant to lie in wait.

Olivia stepped out into the hallway, paused by the folded corpse of the woman, and looked down at the silver pistols on the floor beside her. She kicked them over against the wall and continued toward the stairs, and the commotion grew louder the closer she got.

Guns just weren't her style, and she'd been less than thrilled about having to tote around the Derringer now lost to the bottom of the stove. Weapons like that were too clunky for Olivia's taste; there were too many moving parts. They possessed a lack of refinement she found brutish and boring. Using guns worked to deaden feelings of appreciation for the moments leading up to, and immediately following death.

Olivia preferred much more of a hands-on approach, although she did enjoy getting creative every once in a while, and right now she was feeling especially inspired.

———————◆———————

Jacobi was surprised how easy his sword went through the door, and as hoped he caught the family members completely off guard. He could see them scramble to the back of the room for cover through the opening he'd created as he brought his sword down through the door a second time.

He felt the catch of flesh immediately when the blade sank into the girl's shoulder meat. He pushed through the hole in the middle of the door drawing his sword back and brought his forearm up to block two of the crossbow bolts another girl fired at him.

Jacobi flaunted his preternatural speed by breaking the girl on the floor's wrist while nearly simultaneously putting the crossbow girl out of commission with a well-timed roundhouse to the solar plexus, as the rest of the shots she'd fired missed their mark. He was starting to think

Carla had been right about this being too easy, although he still didn't believe in luck.

He thought he might have spoken too soon when the bedframe crashed over, and the old man rushed forward lunging for Jacobi with his bare hands. The rifle had been left behind the barricade when the sight of the girls being injured triggered an animalistic rage in Pap. All sense of human logic was abandoned for the single raw instinct, 'protect the young'. Jacobi was already sweeping the sword down to the girl on the floor's neck, and this distraction did not affect or alter his stroke as the blade found its mark slicing her neck open all the way to the spine.

Two hands, Pap's hands, hit the floor beside the girl's nearly severed head like a pair of birds that'd been shot out of the sky. It seemed his rage induced a misguided attempt to block the sword with his own arms. A second later Jacobi was hit in the chest with the warm blood spray from Pap's severed wrists as the dazed man fell into him.

———◆———

Angie could only watch. This wasn't right though; this wasn't the way it was supposed to happen. She'd been told for as long as she could remember that *she* was special, *she* was supposed to be the one who restored the family to their former glory. And, when the chips were down it was Angie who would drag them back from the brink of defeat and propel them on to victory.

Instead, she was lying on her side, curled up into a ball, unable to move or breathe as she watched Brie and Pap get chopped up not twenty feet away, and she couldn't do a thing about it. Everything she'd learned, the countless hours of practice, and all the preparation were rendered useless in the one moment they were needed most. It was all a waste, and as her diaphragm loosened just enough to let half of a gasp into her lungs Angie knew she wasn't special.

She never had been.

Pap barreled into the monstrous swordsman taking him in an awkward bear hug, while jets of blood exploded from his handless stumps marring the attacker's paper-white bare chest. Angie drew another small amount of breath, and then a tiny bit more as she watched the tip of the sword poke through Pap's back quickly followed by the remainder of its length.

The sword continued in a downward motion splitting the man completely through from sternum to groin. It seemed like Pap's insides all fell out at once with a solitary wet smack like someone suddenly dumped a bucket of pig-slop on the floor. The sound and smell together were sickening stimuli to those two senses, and if there was a comparison to be made, Angie did not want to know what it would be.

Pap teetered on his feet for a few moments gently swaying as bodily fluid and dislodged organs continued to trickle from his gaping cavity. One of his kidneys dangled stubbornly from a thin sliver of tissue refusing to drop to the ground and join its mate.

Pap's handless arms dangled limply at his sides, and the blood drained out in thin rivulets now like it had been diverted through a colander. Without his heart pumping to create pressure the rest of Pap's blood would have to be coaxed out by gravity.

His gurgled death rattle choked its way up through the blood in his throat a moment later, and Pap finally, mercifully, collapsed giving Angie an unobstructed view of the creature responsible for his death. The albino man with the face of a monster leered at her, and a flat black tongue slithered from his mouth as he licked his lips.

Angie choked down another partial breath and the tension in her muscles was beginning to relax. She found she was able to clench and unclench her fingers finally, as the ability to control her own movements was slowly being handed back over to her. Angie forced more air into her lungs, and the swordsman took a step toward her.

Out of the corner of her eye she could see the butt of her crossbow just a foot or so away from her feet. She struggled to move her legs, but all she could muster was a twitch in one of her ankles, and the man with the sword advanced another step. Angie expanded her lung capacity another increment and tried to shake her limbs into action by attempting to roll over onto her back.

If she could kick the weapon hard enough to slide it across the floor and into her hands she might, *might* be able to get a shot off. Maybe two. The man took another step, and his open-mouthed smile showed off an obscene amount of thin, pointy, yellow teeth.

He raised his sword and Angie saw blood, Pap's blood, smeared across the oddly shaped blade. She watched drops crash against the wood floor in miniature, soundless, crimson explosions. Suddenly, she could move her knees and elbows. Angie took her eye off the approaching attacker and looked to her feet where she watched her legs move back a few inches before coming forward against the crossbow with enough force to create the desired result.

The blade came down hard enough to split the weapon in two, and one of the useless halves continued across the floor before coming to a stop after smacking into Angie's forehead.

"Well, that was a close one," the man with the sword said as if patronizing a child. "Wasn't it?"

He drew both words of the question out hit each 't' extra-hard adding another layer of condescension. Angie stared up at him but said nothing. The muscles in her midsection continued to relax, but she didn't dare move.

"I have to say," he continued, "of all my trips out to *visit* the family in the past, this has by far been my favorite one."

Angie hadn't encountered Jacobi during her short tenure with the family until now, but if what he said was true it meant Pap and Uncle Dwayne must have known him. Uncle Rory must have known him. The thought

390

pushed away the passive acceptance of death and replaced it with an intensely urgent need for vengeance. She wasn't ready to give up yet.

"Becaus-s-s-s-s-e," he stood over her now practically hissing, "it's about to become the *last* one."

The man looked up suddenly and cocked his head like a dog when it hears a whistle. His smile stretched even wider across his face stopping just below his ears further accentuating the attacker's non-human features.

"And it looks like not a moment too soon," he continued bringing his attention back to Angie at his feet. "My ride just got here."

———————— ◆ ————————

The sudden change was jarring, but mostly confusing. Angie was looking up at the pale man-like creature with the sword, as her mind raced furiously to come up with one last cunning plan of escape when it happened. She felt it first, the warm and wet chunky spray, which only made things more confusing until she realized the man's head was gone.

Angie didn't see the detached noggin fall to the floor in front of her, so she knew it hadn't been severed. It just was not there anymore. There was something else now, something different in its place. It was square-ish though, and large, and appeared to be made of stone. It was coated in blood, and glistening bits of brain clung randomly in chunks obscuring the object's true form.

The sword fell from the attacker's twitching fingers and clattered loudly against the hardwood floor. A moment later the headless body crumpled awkwardly to the ground like a paper doll being slowly crushed by a child. The bloody stone rectangle pulled away as the body collapsed, and Angie lit up instantly.

It was Uncle Rory, and he'd obliterated the sword-wielding creature's head with his massive hammer, the hammer he'd been given by the family. Angie's excitement leveled off when he stepped forward, and she got a better look at his face.

Rory's soft, round, cherubic features were now stretched and distorted by the bruised and swollen tissue beneath. His nose was flattened down to the left, and both nostrils had swelled shut turning the center of his face into a misshapen lump. In place of Rory's trademark smile were torn and jagged lips puffed out cartoonishly with pus seeping from every crack, and a mouthful of busted teeth attached to a broken jaw.

His eyes were nearly completely swollen shut and ringed in purple so dark it was almost black. Perhaps most horrifying was the lump in the middle of his forehead. The gash running down the center of it was so deep Angie could see traces of her uncle's skull peeking from between the bulbous mangled flesh surrounding the wound. The lump had grown startlingly larger since the accident and gave the impression of a smaller head trying to push its way out of Rory's.

"Uncle . . . " Angie gasped and choked on a sob. "Uncle Rory, they—"

Angie was overcome by emotion and tears flowed freely, as she pushed herself up into a seated position. Rory set his hammer on the floor next to him balancing it upside down on the heavy, gore-drenched, stone head. He made a moaning sound and shuffled forward extending his hand to pull Angie to her feet.

————◆————

Olivia brought her foot down gently on the first step wary of causing any noise that might alert another hidden family member to her location. She had no idea how many were in the house to start with, but at least one of them was dead in the kitchen. Of course, *two* of the Cadillac Man's team were lying dead in the hall, and Olivia had no intention on joining them.

She wasn't scared though, despite the grim condition

of Anton and 'what's her name', and was more annoyed than anything, put out even. Olivia liked to get in and get out. Efficiency was the name of the game for her, and after years of working with the Cadillac Man she had it down to a science. The mess in the hallway smacked of sloppiness to her, arrogance.

Olivia was also annoyed at having been instructed to go in through the roof and was getting sick of the added difficulty level the Cadillac Man tacked on to every job assigned to her. She knew he was looking to get a rise out of her, cause her to lose the composure she so effortlessly maintained always. Most recently she was annoyed with having been unconscious for an undetermined amount of time, because she fell off said roof. To be more precise, she was 'blown' off the roof by an explosive set by someone who was supposed to be on her team.

She had no doubt the first explosion behind the house was a product of further incompetence facilitated by that idiot albino henchmen, or the woman attached to his hip, or both. When Olivia had come to, she could see from the side of the house the raging bonfire in the backyard was no more. It was nothing but a smoldering pile of char dotted with small pockets of orange and yellow peeking through the rubble like demon eyes.

Now, the woman was dead, and if Jacobi was still alive, she'd yet to see him, but based on what she'd seen so far, she wasn't holding out any hope. Olivia didn't know what purpose, if any, there was for the explosion, but to her it was just another example of working sloppy, and she did *not* work sloppy.

By the time Olivia was halfway up the staircase the feelings of frustration melted away, and when she reached the top, they were like a dream she couldn't quite remember. It had always been like that for her though. If she thought she might be experiencing an actual emotion the concept would quickly slip just beyond the reach of her understanding.

It was why she was so good at what she did, why she was so efficient.

Olivia paused on the top step and shifted up against the wall so she could surreptitiously peek around the corner. The commotion she heard earlier had mostly quieted when she'd reached the steps, and now it was silent again. A quick look down the second-floor hallway gave her a snapshot of the layout. The big man's back was still to her, so Olivia took another look around the corner.

The door at the end of the hall had been broken down, or through, as evidenced by the splintered remains still clinging to the frame. She guessed this to be where all the noise had been coming from, but the giant lumbering oaf shambling his way down the hall blocked her view into the room. His right hand clutched the long, thick, wooden handle of the massive hammer he was dragging along with him. Its exaggerated proportions added a frightful implication of what the weapon was capable of.

Olivia hadn't seen it when they were downstairs, and figured he'd been holding it against his chest with both hands while she'd only glimpsed his back. Olivia might describe the size of the hammer as cartoonishly large if it were being wielded by anyone else, but next to the man's hulking frame it didn't look at all out of place.

He lifted the hammer when he reached the broken door and rested it over his shoulder, as he stepped into the room like a slugger on his way to the batter's box. Olivia slipped around the corner into the hall with her back to the wall, and from her new vantage point could see inside the room. Jacobi was there with his back to the door looking down at something or someone at his feet, but she couldn't tell who or what? He was completely oblivious to the man with the hammer coming up behind him.

Olivia started down the hall but stopped before she reached the door to linger in the shadows. The man was now only a few feet from Jacobi, and he held the enormous hammer in the air like a child with a toy. She could easily save him by simply calling out a warning. Jacobi would easily be able to whirl around and cut the man's guts out in a fraction of a second, but instead she said nothing. Instead, she waited.

Olivia pulled the strap of her purse over her head, removed the silver compact, and let the bag fall quietly to the floor. A moment later she watched the hammer turn Jacobi's bald white pate into moist red slush with one swing. Olivia was genuinely impressed.

The hammer was huge, but to be able to bring it down with enough controlled force to annihilate Jacobi's entire head was a true demonstration of the man's strength. A pink mist hung in the air over the headless body shimmering the way clouds against a sunset do but dissipated quickly into nothing as Jacobi's headless body folded to the floor.

She could now see the young woman he'd been standing over. As the giant man reached out to help the girl to her feet, Olivia slipped silently into the room.

————— ♦ —————

Angie's body trembled when she reached out to accept her uncle's large calloused hand, and the muscles in her torso shrieked with pain to let her know she hadn't fully recovered. She faltered some, but Rory bent down lower so she wouldn't have to reach. A second later she was up on her feet, arms wrapped around her uncle, and head pressed into his abundant chest soaking it with tears.

Angie knew this moment was fleeting and dwelling in it didn't change anything about what happened, or what was going to come next. She knew the road ahead would be a hard and lonely one filled with grieving. Rory had saved her, but he was in bad shape and his recovery would be lengthy and painful, *if* he recovered. Angie knew she was destined for a heartbreaking stretch of time and was prepared for what her role in it would be, but right now she wanted to hug her uncle just a little longer.

This was the moment she would look back on in the darkest times of the coming months to renew her drive, to bolster her spirits. Angie would remember the moment she knew it was finally over, *this* moment, and it would remind her the bad times, no matter how bad, do eventually come to an end. She would learn and grow from each experience, then move on applying her newly acquired knowledge to conquering the next obstacle life presented.

Angie finally pulled back from her uncle, but Rory kept hold of her shoulders until she was sure she could stand on her own. When he let go, she looked up at him through bleary eyes, tears further distorting the mask of swollen flesh his face had become. She blinked them away, and then vigorously rubbed her eyes with the back of her hands.

Angie wasn't aware her uncle felt someone tapping his shoulder from behind, but noticed he was turning around when she opened her eyes again. A woman stepped back and out from behind Rory's hulking frame as he turned to face her. A scream stuck somewhere in Angie's clenched throat as she stepped forward stumbling, but Uncle Rory was already raising his hammer having yanked it up to the ready with ease like it was a croquet mallet.

Angie didn't take her eyes off the woman, but there wasn't time to look away either. She was holding up something shiny in the palm her left hand, and the shape clicked in Angie's mind registering immediately as an open makeup compact. The woman lifted the compact and blew across the powder inside sending a cloud directly into Uncle Rory's face. The hammer hit the floor behind him creating a large splintered divot in the hardwood, and he now used both hands to scratch and tear at his own face.

His hands came away with chunks of flesh, as the cloud settled completely around Rory's head and started eating him. He made muffled chokes and moans that came feverishly as he tore into his face like he was trying to beat the strange substance from the compact to his own chewy center.

It was a race he'd clearly lost as indicated by the liquid dripping thick and slow from his ears. Rory's hands refused to quit digging though, his fingertips scraping indecipherable handfuls of wet red face-meat from where it had been attached to his skull.

His hands started to slow down when the lump on his forehead collapsed in on itself like a deflated balloon, and then stopped completely when his entire face did the same. Rory fell backwards and his body began to seize as soon as he hit the floor. That was when the scream finally loosed itself from Angie's bruised and swollen insides with an intensity propelled by all the death she'd just witnessed.

———————◆———————

"Sorry about the mess."

Olivia's arm was already locked around the screaming girl's throat. She brought her free hand around to grab the girl's face beneath her chin before continuing.

"It was sloppy, I know, and that's not really my style."

Olivia tightened her grip and violently yanked the girl's head up and to the side cleanly snapping her neck. The crack was loud and satisfying, and silence rushed up to fill in the space as the sound decayed. The girl's life departed instantly, and her body sagged limply from Olivia's awkward headlock until she slipped her arms free letting it fall to the floor.

"I'm typically much more efficient."

Olivia stood there for a moment, her guard still up, and waited for any surprises the family might still have up their collective sleeves, but there were no more surprises to come. The scene in the room around her was like something from a spectacularly grisly nightmare, but Olivia had long since been desensitized to such butcherous carnage.

A soft sizzling sound came from the giant man's still melting head, although it was mostly a yellow and pink puddle now that had already begun to eat through the floor as well. The closed compact was still clutched in Olivia's palm, and she dropped it onto the barrel chest of the headless man on her way to the door. There were two bodies she'd glimpsed when sneaking up on the man, but now she could saw the totality of violence enacted in their deaths.

A handless man lay open and gutted in a heap while another young girl was next to him with her head nearly severed. Her arm was stuck reaching up while her hand dangled limply from broken bones piercing the skin around her wrist, as if she'd been reaching for help but received something else instead. Olivia looked from the tangled evisceration on the floor to the other headless corpse across the room, Jacobi. He was an idiot, but up until his head was smashed like a melon it looked like he had been the only one of the Cadillac Man's team having any success until Olivia showed up, of course.

The sharp tangy scent of mixed death was overtaking the room, and it was time for her to go. She took one more look at the tableau of death that appeared to have spared no portion of the room having laid its touch upon every inch. Only Olivia escaped the impossibly sharp barbed snares, but it came as no surprise to her.

She stepped through the broken remnants of the door and headed down the hall to the stairs. Olivia felt the same thing she did every time she finished a job. Nothing.

———————— ◆ ————————

The night had gone silent as Olivia walked across the expansive front yard on her way back to the road. The fire in the backyard was all but out now, the pops and hisses having stopped shortly before she exited the house. A long slow creak came from the house behind her followed by a jarring crash as part of the front porch collapsed.

The sound stood out like cannon blasts against the stillness of the night, but Olivia didn't flinch or even turn around. She kept her eyes straight ahead where a big black

Cadillac was parked on the side of the road. As she approached the slight incline the Cadillac Man stepped from the car and walked around to greet her. He was smiling.

"So much for helping out back there, huh?" she spouted sarcastically as she walked up the rise in the yard to the asphalt of the road.

The Cadillac Man cocked his head slightly and gave it a gentle shake.

"Come on, Olivia," he said through the side of his grin. "You of all people should've known I wasn't *really* coming back to help. I will say though, this was over a lot faster than even I'd anticipated. You're the only one, I presume?"

"No," Olivia said opening the front passenger side door. "Everyone else is *right* behind me."

She got in the car, shut the door, and as if on cue a sound like the long and exaggerated yawn of a very old man came from deep inside the house just before it collapsed, a physical punctuation of her cynicism. The Cadillac Man offered no comment as he entered the vehicle on the driver's side.

The Cadillac started moving away from the family's house back in the direction they had come, and Olivia closed her eyes. Her body ached and she could feel every bit of the pain from her broken ribs now that the adrenaline was gone. She was anxious to get home and put her head back to try and relax. Olivia wanted to take off her clothes, wrap her ribs, and soak in the tub for the next two days at least.

Afterward she wanted to go shopping to replace her shoes and purse, as well as anything else that caught her fancy in the moment. Olivia found shopping helped distract her from feeling numb for a while, and having unlimited disposable income made it a distraction she indulged in often.

They drove in silence for a while, and Olivia found herself able to actually start to relax. Her mind began to wander beyond bath bombs and shopping sprees to shapeless swirls of color morphing in and out of different faces. Some were familiar, but most were too distorted by evil to be human or anything else she would recognize.

Olivia didn't know how long they'd been driving having lost herself in the gentle lull of the rolling road. She almost opened her eyes to check but decided to keep them closed a bit longer to ensure she wouldn't be disappointed by their location. It felt good to keep them closed anyway, and while she was sure she wouldn't doze off it was nice to be disengaged.

"Olivia."

The Cadillac Man's voice sounded softer and farther away than usual, and she paddled against the slowing flow of her mind struggling to hear him.

"I need to talk to you about the roof."

Olivia was overpowered by exhaustion though and was sound asleep before she heard anything the Cadillac Man said.

———————◆———————

Olivia knew something was wrong the moment she was conscious again. In the fraction of a second before her eyes opened, she could tell she was outside, and was lying on her back against something flat and hard. It was morning but early, and the sun was still no more than a pink haze on the horizon.

The cool air was perfumed with the scent of deep-fried food, and Olivia quickly sat up unable to believe what she was seeing. Directly in front of her was the small, square, shack of the Dairy Queen they'd visited on their way into town. She was on top of one of the picnic tables facing the walk-up order window. The steel security shutters were closed over the outside of the glass, and Olivia couldn't remember if they had been closed when they left the prior night? After what she'd done to the unfortunate, two-person, closing staff on the other side of the window, she doubted the shutters would ever be open again.

Olivia scooted off the table and cursed when her bare feet hit the gravel. The sharp edges stuck her already tender soles, and she quickly made her way to the narrow concrete sidewalk that circled the small shack. She brushed the away the pieces of gravel stuck to the bottom of her feet and walked around to the front side of the Dairy Queen.

The small parking lot was empty, as she'd expected it to be, and she went back around to side with the order window. Olivia looked across to the picnic table she woke up on to see if something had been left there for her, but there was nothing. She made a slow lap around the building looking for any sign of the Cadillac Man, and she could find none.

If this was another one of his attempts at provoking a reaction out of her then mission accomplished. Olivia was officially pissed. She was sick of the Cadillac Man injecting added difficulties into nearly every aspect of her life, and for what to try to break her? To prove she could be broken?

Olivia stomped toward the road through the gravel lot unconcerned with the pain in her feet any longer. She was going to flag down the first car that drove by, break the driver's neck, and head straight home without stopping. If he wanted to witness her 'reaction' for himself, he would have to come get her. She'd only made it a few steps away from the sidewalk when she heard something behind her. Olivia stopped and turned around half expecting to see the Cadillac Man standing by the window smiling, and eating a macabre confection, but there was no one there.

She heard it again and stepped back onto the sidewalk to try and pinpoint where it was coming from. When she heard it a third time there was more of a rattling to it, which helped her quickly pinpoint its location. It was coming from behind the order window. The outside security shade was still down over the glass, but there was something moving behind it causing it to shake.

Olivia slowly approached the window keeping her head on a swivel in case this was meant to distract her from something, but all that had changed was the smell. She thought she'd stepped downwind of the dumpster, but it was on the opposite side of the building. The security shade began to rattle harder, as the smell of dead fish and fetid meat slow cooking in a bucket of shit filled her nostrils.

The steel shutters shot up suddenly having been pried open from the inside and crumpled into itself from the force. Olivia stood slack-jawed in utter disbelief. Standing on the other side of the open window was Jacobi. His yellow smile was wild reflecting madness, and he was wearing a Dairy Queen uniform complete with hat and apron.

"Better hurry and get changed," Jacobi said chuckling. "It looks like you and I are working the opening shift . . . partner!"

Jacobi flung another uniform through the window, and it hit her in the chest before landing in a pile on the sidewalk at her feet. Olivia turned to face the sun just as it broke fully clear of the horizon, and the sound of Jacobi's idiotic laughter filled the air around her.

About the Author

John Wayne Comunale lives in Houston Texas to prepare himself for the heat in Hell. He is the author of *Death Pacts and Left-Hand Paths, Scummer, As Seen On T.V., Sinkhole, The Cycle* and more. He hosts the weekly storytelling podcast John Wayne Lied to You, co-hosts the podcast Vital Social Issues 'N Stuff with Kris and John Wayne with horror author Kristopher Triana, and fronts the punk rock disaster johnwayneisdead. He currently travels around the country giving truly unique and most excellent performances of the written word.